The Nicholas Feast

Also by Pat McIntosh

The Harper's Quine

THE NICHOLAS FEAST

Pat McIntosh

CARROLL & GRAF PUBLISHERS
New York

Carroll & Graf Publishers
An imprint of Avalon Publishing Group, Inc.
245 W. 17th Street
New York
NY 10011-5300
www.carrollandgraf.com

AVALON
publishing group incorporated

First published in the UK by Constable,
an imprint of Constable & Robinson Ltd 2005

First Carroll & Graf edition 2005

ISBN 0-7867-1570-7

Printed and bound in the EU

For Gil's godmother,
who recognized William's real crime immediately,
with gratitude.

The University of Glasgow

Nobody could write about the early days of the University of Glasgow without consulting the magisterial *The University of Glasgow 1451–1577*, by John Durkan and James Kirk (University of Glasgow Press, 1977). I have made copious use of it; everything I have got right is from Durkan & Kirk, and everything I have invented or got wrong is of course my own.

A list of people around the University might be useful. Those marked with an asterisk are known to history.

Regents (lecturers) and other members of the staff
*Maister John Doby, the Principal Regent (head of the Faculty of Arts and of the University)
*Maister Patrick Elphinstone, Dean of the Faculty of Arts
*Maister Patrick (Patey) Coventry, the Second Regent
*Maister Thomas Forsyth, a senior regent
Maister Nicholas Kennedy, a junior regent
*Maister David Gray, the Faculty Scribe (a lawyer)
*Maister Archibald Crawford, Faculty and University Promotor (a lawyer)
*John Gray, the University Scribe and Beadle (a lawyer)
*John Shaw, the Faculty Steward
Fr Bernard Stewart, a Dominican friar with responsibility for the University
Andro and Tammas, two of the servitors
Agnes Dickson, the cook
Tam, Adam, Aikie, kitchen grooms
Eppie, a kitchen maid
Jaikie, the University porter

Students
Alan Liddell, a Theology student (postgraduate)
Magistrand (fourth-year student)
John Hucheson, who makes a speech
Senior bachelors (third-year students)
Ninian Boyd (playing Diligence)
Michael Douglas (playing a daughter of Collegia)
Lowrie Livingstone
Nicholas Gray (helping in the kitchen)
Junior bachelors (second-year students)
Ralph Gibson (playing Collegia)
William Irvine
Robert Montgomery
Richie (playing the Scholar)
Henry (playing Frivolity)
Walter and Andrew (playing two of Collegia's daughters)
Bejants (first-year students)
David Ross
Billy Ross

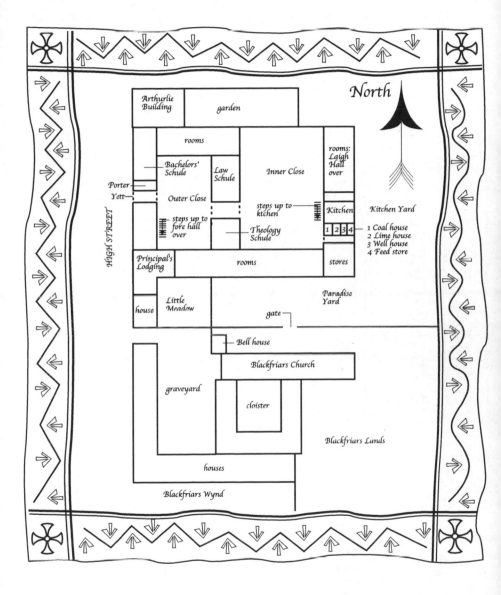

North

Arthurlie Building

garden

rooms

Bachelors' Schule

Law Schule

Inner Close

rooms: Laigh Hall over

Porter

Yett

Outer Close

steps up to kitchen

Kitchen

Kitchen Yard

1 2 3 4

1 Coal house
2 Lime house
3 Well house
4 Feed store

steps up to fore hall over

Theology Schule

HIGH STREET

Principal's Lodging

rooms

stores

house

Little Meadow

Paradise Yard

gate

Bell house

Blackfriars Church

graveyard

cloister

Blackfriars Lands

houses

Blackfriars Wynd

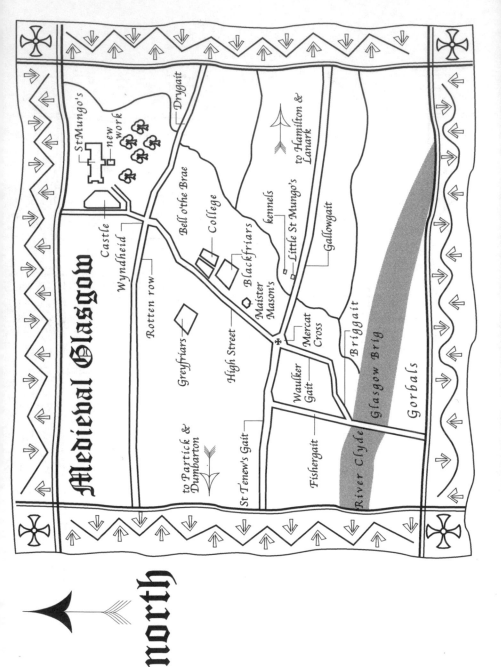

north

Chapter One

Gil Cunningham said later that if he had known he would find a corpse in the coalhouse of Glasgow University, he would never have gone to the Arts Faculty feast.

'But then,' said Alys his betrothed, considering this seriously, 'you would never have met Socrates.'

The day began well enough. In the bright sunshine after early rain Gil, his academic robes in a bundle under his arm, had strolled down the High Street past the University, where several people in gowns and furred hoods were already exchanging formal bows with a lanky red-haired student before the great wooden door. Further down the street, in the rambling stone-built house called the White Castle, he found Alys and her father the French master mason, just breaking their fast with the rest of their household after hearing the first Mass at Greyfriars.

'Gil!' said Alys in delight, and sprang up to kiss him in greeting.

'*Bonjour*, Gilbert,' said Maistre Pierre cheerfully, his teeth white in his neat black beard. He rose broad-shouldered and imposing from his great chair and waved at an empty stool. 'Have you eaten? What do you this early on a Sunday morning?'

'The Nicholas Feast,' Gil reminded him. He smiled at Alys, still standing slender and elegant beside him in the brown linen dress that matched her eyes. Like most unmarried girls in Scotland she went bare-headed, and her honey-coloured hair fell over her shoulders. He savoured the sight for a moment, thinking again how fortunate he was, that this clever, competent, beautiful girl was to be his wife, then tipped her face up with a gentle finger and kissed the high narrow bridge of her nose. 'I hoped Alys would help me robe,' he continued. 'The procession will start from the college, and if I must walk there alone in these ridiculous garments I had rather do it from here, four doors away, than from Rottenrow. At least when we ride up to St Thomas's I'll be in company with the whole of the Arts Faculty.'

'They are not ridiculous garments!' Alys said indignantly. 'They are the insignia of your learning! Come and sit down, Gil.'

'Why is it called the Nicholas Feast?' asked Maistre Pierre, ladling more porridge into his wooden porringer. 'St Nicholas' day is in December. This is May.'

'The Feast of the Translation of St Nicholas was last Tuesday,' Gil said. He bowed to Alys's aged, aristocratic nurse, and nodded to the rest of the household, who were ignoring the French talk at the head of the table. Setting the bundle of his robes on the floor he sat down and accepted a bannock from the platter Alys passed him. 'When he was translated to Bari, I suppose, though where from I don't recall. And this is the first Sunday after. The man who founded our feast left exact directions. We're to ride in procession to hear Mass at eight of the clock in St Thomas Martyr's, out beyond the Stablegreen Port, and come back down through the town with green branches, and then we have a meeting, and then we have the feast.'

'He left money for the feast, too, I hope?' said Maistre Pierre.

Gil nodded, spreading honey on his bannock.

'There is some, but we are all expected to pay up as well. Eighteen pence it has cost me.' The mason pulled a face. 'It would be double that if I had a benefice.'

'I had hoped,' said Alys with diffidence, 'we could write to your mother today. Her letter needs an answer, you must agree.'

12

'Oh, aye, I agree,' Gil said ruefully. 'But not today. I am committed to the feast. Perhaps tomorrow.'

When grace had been said, the dishes had been carried out and the great board lifted from its trestles, Alys's nurse Catherine rose stiffly and said to the mason, 'I leave your daughter in your charge, *maistre*.'

'Yes, yes,' said Maistre Pierre. 'And the baby is with Nancy. Go and see to the boy, if you will, *madame*.'

She curtsied with arthritic elegance, said, '*Bonjour, maistre le notaire*,' to Gil as she passed him, and stumped out of the hall among the hurrying maidservants. Alys unfolded Gil's robes.

'Your mother's letter,' she said again, shaking out the cassock. 'Is it – is that really what she thinks?'

'She'll come round to it,' Gil said. 'Remember, my uncle is in favour.'

'But if your nearest kin can't agree about your marriage –'

'Perhaps when my uncle can spare me, I should go out to Carluke,' he suggested.

'Yes!' She smiled up at him. 'If you can discuss it with her, I'm sure you will coax her round.'

'Tell her how Alys will be dowered,' said Alys's father robustly. 'That will persuade her.'

'It's possible,' said Gil, concealing his doubts. He pulled off his short gown and began to unlace his doublet. 'Meantime I need help with these ridiculous garments.'

'They are not ridiculous!' she said again. 'Which way round does this go?'

Maistre Pierre watched in mounting astonishment as Gil was arrayed in the black cassock and cope ('At least this one has two slits for my hands. Some only have one.'), the furred shoulder-cape, the blue fur-lined hood, proper to a Master of Arts of the University of Glasgow.

'All of these garments are wool,' he observed. 'You will be warm. And what is that scarf thing? At least that is silk, though it is furred as well.'

'Oh, father,' said Alys. 'You remember the men of law wearing those in Paris, surely? It goes on his shoulder. It's

13

a pity it's red when your hood is blue,' she added. 'Does it need a pin, perhaps?'

'This is the first time I have worn it all complete,' said Gil, craning over his shoulder at the hood. 'I must look like a Yule papingo,' he added in Scots.

'A parrot?' said Maistre Pierre, grinning.

'No, no, it looks magnificent,' Alys declared.

'At least I won't be alone. The entire procession will be in formal dress.'

'And you are to ride in those long skirts?' continued the mason, as Alys shook the moth-herbs out of the white rabbit-skin lining and stood on tiptoe to pin the red *chaperon* on to the layer of fur already on Gil's shoulder. 'Where is your horse?'

'My uncle sent down to the college earlier with half a dozen beasts loaned from the Chanonry. I'll have the use of one of those.' Gil settled his felt hat on his head, then took Alys's hands in his and kissed them. 'I must go. Tomorrow we'll write to my mother, sweetheart,' he promised her.

'Which reminds me indirectly,' said Maistre Pierre. He got to his feet. 'I see you to the street. Our neighbour is expected in town.'

'What, Hugh Montgomery?' Gil turned to stare. 'What brings him to Glasgow? The King's at Stirling, by what my uncle says, and the rest of the Court with him.'

'Catherine thought it might be to do with the college,' said Alys.

'How does Catherine learn these things?' Gil wondered. 'She speaks no Scots.'

'Your pardon, maisters, mistress,' said an anxious voice from the kitchen stairway.

They all three turned. In the door at the head of the stairs stood a stout, comely woman dressed in respectable homespun. As they looked she bobbed a nervous curtsy and came forward.

'Your pardon for interrupting,' she said again, 'but they're saying in the kitchen you're for the college the day, maister? Is that right?'

14

'This is Mistress Irvine, Gil,' said Alys. 'A kinswoman of Kittock's –'

'Aye,' agreed Mistress Irvine, nodding and beaming. 'My good-sister's good-sister, that's who Kittock is, and a good friend to me and all.'

'– and Davie's aunt,' continued Alys. 'She has come from Paisley to see him.'

'How is the boy today?' Gil asked, with sympathy.

'He's still sleeping the maist o' the time,' said Mistress Irvine, looking troubled. 'And he minds nothing even when he's awake. I think it was you that found him, maister? Blessings on ye for that, sir, and his mother's and all.'

'He improves slowly,' said the mason.

'It's only two weeks, father,' said Alys. 'It takes longer than that for a broken skull to mend. Mistress Irvine was very distressed to see her nephew in such a state, Gil, the more so as her foster-son at the college is strong and healthy.'

'The contrast must be painful,' Gil commented wryly. The mason's injured mortar-laddie was a reminder of an episode which he would have wished to forget, had it not resulted in his betrothal to Alys. 'Has the other boy visited Davie? The company would be good for him.'

'Och, no. William's ower busy at his studies,' explained Mistress Irvine, and bobbed another curtsy. 'I wonder if I might trouble ye, sir? It's just to leave this paper for him with the man at the yett. It's for William Irvine.' She produced a folded and sealed package.

'That's no trouble.' Gil put his hand out. A line of verse popped into his head: *Little Sir William, are you within?* Which of the ballads was that?

'Only he said he'd be busy today, he can't come to see me, and I don't like to go back, the porter was as awkward yesterday about sending to fetch him to the yett, and if they're all taigled with this feast I'd only be in the way. It's a shame I never took it with me when I went out to Vespers.'

So the guardian of the college's great wooden door must

15

be the same fellow Gil remembered from his own time. 'It's no trouble,' he said again.

She put the little package into his hand and curtsied again. 'Blessings on ye, sir. Oh, here, you've lost your wee scarf.' She stooped to lift the swatch of silk and fur. 'You'll not need that round your neck the day, maister, it'll be warm enough when it's no raining. And I'll away back down to the kitchen, mistress, and see to that remedy I promised Nancy for the bairn. We'll see if we can't get him taking more than milk with honey and usquebae, won't we no?'

'We will be aye grateful if you do, mistress,' said Alys. 'I believe he has eaten only by accident since his mother died.' She watched Mistress Irvine puffing her way down the kitchen stair, then turned to fasten the scarf back on Gil's shoulder. 'There, I have used two pins this time. Take care,' she said earnestly. 'Of the Montgomerys, I mean.'

'Yes indeed.' The mason made for the door. 'Maybe you do not go about alone for a while. Bah! It is raining again.'

'The Montgomerys have killed no Cunninghams for at least six months,' Gil said. 'That I know of,' he added.

He hugged Alys, and bent to kiss her. For a long moment she returned his embrace, with the eager innocence which he found so enchanting; then she drew away, suddenly shy, and he dropped another quick kiss on the bridge of her nose, and followed Maistre Pierre down the fore-stair and across the courtyard in the rain.

Pacing up the High Street with the dignity imposed by the heavy garments, Gil glanced at the tall stone house belonging to Hugh, Lord Montgomery and wondered again what that turbulent baron wanted in Glasgow. Montgomery had no Lanarkshire holdings and no need to keep on the good side of the Archbishop, unlike Gil's own kindred, and the holdings and privileges in Ayrshire which were the cause of Montgomery's bloody dispute with the Cunninghams were all administered from Irvine. Perhaps, Gil speculated, Alys's governess was right and the family wished to make its mark on the college in some way.

The High Street was now completely blocked outside the college gateway by the mounts waiting for the procession. John Shaw the Steward was welcoming another arrival. Gil avoided the heels of a restless mule and picked his way to the door. Here he was met by the same student he had seen earlier, a gangling youth with a faded gown and a fashionable haircut, who bowed deeply, flourishing his hat so that raindrops flew from it.

'*Salve, Magister*. The college greets you. May I know your name?'

'Maister Gilbert Cunningham,' said Gil, 'determined in '84.'

The student straightened abruptly, clapping the hat back on his head.

'Gang within, maister, if ye will,' he said, cutting across Gil's greeting to the college. 'The Faculty's in the Fore Hall.' He waved a long arm towards the great wooden yett and the vaulted passage beyond it, and turned away.

A little startled by this incivility, Gil made his way into the passage, pausing at the porter's door. As he had surmised, the occupant of the rancid, cluttered little room was the same man he remembered from his own days at the college, a surly individual with a bald head and a flabby paunch.

'Good morning, Jaikie,' he said politely. 'I see you're still in charge here.'

'Oh, it's you, Gil Cunningham,' said Jaikie, looking him up and down. 'I thought ye'd be here earlier, but maybe since ye're to be married, ye're done with early rising.' He produced an unpleasantly suggestive leer. 'And I hear there's a bairn already?'

'There is,' agreed Gil, ever more politely. 'A motherless bairn being fostered by the household.'

'Aye, right. And what do you want?' demanded Jaikie. 'I've enough to see to, dealing with this feast, without idle conversation round my door.'

'I have a package here for William Irvine.'

The man's expression flickered.

'Ye have, have ye? Let's see. From Billy Dog, is it?'

17

Gil handed over the folded paper. Jaikie turned it in his hands, flicked at the seal with a dirty thumbnail, and grunted.

'It's no from Billy Dog. Well, ye can deliver it yirsel. That's William Irvine out there at the yett, capering like a May hobby, welcoming the maisters.'

'The boy with the red hair?'

'Aye, the same.' Jaikie cast a glance out of his window at the crowd in the street. 'Ye'll need to be quick. They'll mount up soon.'

Gil went back out to the doorway and waited while the rain stopped, the sun came out, and the red-haired boy greeted another pair of graduates with flowery compliments about the college's sons. One of them produced a stock phrase in reply, about the fountain of wisdom; the other grunted, 'Aye, thanks,' and pushed past Gil into the tunnel.

'William,' said Gil. The boy turned, and recognizing Gil raised his hat briefly and attempted to look down his nose at him. Tall though he was, Gil topped him by several inches, so he was unsuccessful in this, but he assumed an expression of vague contempt.

'I have a package for you from Mistress Irvine, William,' said Gil politely, holding it out. *Little Sir William, are you within?* he thought again.

'From –? Oh,' said William, taking it. He turned the little bundle over, reading the clumsy writing on the cover. 'Thank you,' he added, as if the words tasted unpleasant, and then, almost warily, 'Did she say anything about it?'

'Not a thing,' said Gil. 'You'll need to open it to find out.'

'Well, it's what one usually does with a letter,' said William, with casual impertinence. Gil raised one eyebrow, and the boy looked down and turned away. 'Thank you, maister,' he said again, ostentatiously studying the writing on the package.

Gil made his way through the tunnel into the Outer Close where he paused, savouring the scene. The place had scarcely changed in the eight years since he had left; the thatch was sagging, the shutters were crooked, even the weeds between the flagstones seemed the same. Now, where had that ill-schooled boy said? Yes, in the Fore Hall.

One or two Faculty members were about in the court, but judging by the noise most were above in the hall. As Gil turned towards the foot of the stair, William hurried across the court, in too much haste even to lift his hat to a passing Doctor of Laws. He appeared to be making for a tower doorway in the south range, but before he reached it a man in the robes of a Dominican friar emerged from the tunnel which led to the Inner Close. William, catching sight of him, checked and turned to intercept him.

'Father Bernard,' he said clearly. 'I have something here that will interest you.'

As Gil reached the top of the stair he settled on a word for William's expression: gleeful.

In the outermost hall of the college building a roar of polite Latin conversation rose from the assembled Faculty of Arts of the University of Glasgow, thirty or forty men in woollen copes like Gil's or the silk gowns of the Masters of foreign universities circulating in an aroma of cedar-wood and moth-herbs. Gil paused in the doorway to look over the crowded heads and decided against making his way to his proper station, among the other non-regent Masters, the graduates of the University who did not hold teaching positions. If he waited here, he could slip into his place as the procession left.

He could recognize many of the company. Yonder was John Doby, small, gentle and balding. He was the Principal Regent in Arts, in charge of teaching and all matters of the curriculum, and had taught Gil Aristotle thoroughly and exactly. Beside him, tall and silver-tonsured, Patrick Elphinstone the Dean, whom Gil remembered as a conscientious and alarming teacher. There was David Gray the Scribe, a poor teacher and an ineffectual man, with the red furred hood of a man of law rolled down on his shoulders and straggling grey hair showing round his felt cap.

The procession was forming up. Gil stood aside from the

19

door, and the Dean and the Principal passed him in their high-collared black silk gowns and long-tailed black hoods, each with the red *chaperon* of a Cologne doctor trailing from his left shoulder. As they reached the doorway the light changed, and the May sunshine gave way to another vicious May shower.

'Confound it!' said Dean Elphinstone, stopping abruptly. 'The hoods will be ruined! Principal, why did you insist on the silk hoods? Fur at least would dry out.'

'It's summer, Dean.' Maister Doby peered past his taller colleague. 'A wee bittie rain'll not hurt you.'

Gil looked over their heads at the large drops bouncing off the paving stones of the Outer Close and remarked, 'Now if only we were allowed to wear plaids with our gowns . . .'

Both men turned to look at him. Behind him the cry of 'It's raining!' had run round the hall, in Scots and Latin, and some jostling began as people dragged silk-lined hoods and rich gowns over their heads in the crowd.

'Ah, Gilbert,' said the Principal, switching to the scholarly tongue. 'It is good to see you. Do you remember David Cunningham's nephew, Dean, who was one of our better determinants in – let me see – '84, wasn't it? And then –'

'Paris, sir,' Gil supplied. 'Law. Licentiate in Canon Law.'

'Oh, aye. And now trained as a notary with your uncle, I believe?' Gil nodded, and bent a knee briefly in response to the Dean's inclined biretta. Someone complained as his elbow met a ribcage, and he threw a word of apology over his shoulder. The Dean was speaking to him.

'Are you the man about to be married?'

'I am,' agreed Gil, bracing himself for the usual congratulatory remarks. At least this is an educated man, he thought. Not like Jaikie.

'Hmf. It seems a pity to waste your education,' the Dean pronounced. 'Why marry her? Why not take a mistress, if you must, and pursue the church career?'

Gil swallowed his astonishment.

20

'My uncle thought otherwise,' he said, taking refuge in politeness again.

'Hmf,' repeated the Dean, and surveyed him with an ice-blue stare. 'You have never undertaken the required course of lectures, Gilbert?'

'What, since I left here? No, sir. The opportunity has not presented itself.'

'Would you come to see me about that? We cannot get regents from outwith the college, and if you were to carry out your duty in delivering such a course it would benefit both the bachelors and yourself, since the bachelors could add another book to their list, and by it your degree would be completed and you would be properly entitled to the master's bonnet you are wearing.'

'Yes, sir,' said Gil, torn between annoyance, embarrassment and admiration. Patrick Elphinstone nodded, and turned to look out at the weather.

'Aha! I think it's easing a bit. *Amici, scholastici*,' he said, pitching his voice without difficulty to reach all ears above the buzz of conversation. 'We can set out now. Full academic dress, I remind you. The rain is no excuse. Shall we go, Principal?'

Bowing politely to one another, the two men stepped into the drizzle to descend the stair to the courtyard.

'All right for him,' muttered a voice behind Gil as the Masters of Arts followed on. 'The number of benefices he's got, he can afford a new gown every week if he wants.'

'He'll hear you,' said Gil, turning to look into the black-browed, long-jawed face at his shoulder. 'Is that you, Nick? I thought I knew the voice.'

'Aye, Gil.' Nicholas Kennedy, Master of Arts, grinned briefly at him. They slipped into place behind the last of the graduates, and Maister Kennedy continued, 'You're not too grand to speak to me, then, having been to Paris and all that?'

'I would be,' Gil responded, 'but you heard the Dean. I'm not entitled to this bonnet, and I take it you are.'

'Christ aid, yes.' His friend grimaced, his shaggy brows twitching. 'Course of twenty lectures to the junior bachelors on Peter of Spain. This makes the fourth year I've delivered it. What an experience. I tell you, Gil,' he said, making for the horses ahead of his place in the order of precedence, 'the man who invented the regenting system was probably a torturer in his spare time.' He hitched gown and cassock round his waist and swung himself into the wet saddle. 'Did one of the songmen tell me you're betrothed? Is that what the Dean was on about? I thought you were for the priesthood and the Law, like the Dean said.'

'That's right,' said Gil, standing in his stirrups so that he could bundle the skirt of his own cassock to protect his hose. 'It's all changed. Married life awaits me. My uncle and Peter Mason are working out the terms, and we hope to sign the contract this week or next.'

'And that's you set up for life. Congratulations, man. You always did have all the luck,' said his friend enviously. 'God, what I'd give to get out of this place, chaplain to some quiet old lady somewhere, never see another student in my life.' He stared round, and nodded at a knot of students in their belted gowns of red or blue or grey. 'That lot, for instance. They'll sing Mass for us like angels, Bernard Stewart'll make sure of that, but they're a bunch of fiends, I tell you. If we get through the entertainment without someone deliberately fouling things I'll buy the candles for St Thomas's for the year. Oh, God, there's William.'

'The entertainment,' repeated Gil. 'I'd forgotten the entertainment. Don't tell me you're in charge, Nick?'

'Very well, I won't,' said Nick, 'but I am. For my sins.'

'What are you giving us?'

'Oh, it's a play, as prescribed. I won't tell you any more,' said Nick rather sourly. 'I don't want to raise your expectations. What does your minnie say about your marriage? I mind she had other plans for you.'

'She'll come round to it,' said Gil, uncomfortably reminded of Alys's remark about his mother's letter.

With much shuffling and jostling, and delays caused by people struggling back into gown and hood and retrieving felt caps dislodged in the process, the Faculty got itself on horseback and arranged in order. The University Beadle, peering back along the line, nodded, raised his hat to the Dean, and gave the signal to move off as the sun came out again.

Clattering up the High Street, Gil hitched at the layers of worsted he had wadded to sit on, and looked around at the other Faculty members present. At the head of the procession the Beadle was attended by a handful of senior students, presumably all those who could muster a horse and gown for the occasion. Demure behind them, decked in the Faculty's collection of blue academic hoods, rode a favoured five of the non-regent Masters, followed closely by those other Masters of Arts who, like Gil, were living in the burgh and had been unable to avoid the requirement to attend, and Maister Kennedy, quite out of his proper position. The Faculty's Man of Law and Scribe, side by side in their red legal robes, were succeeded by someone Gil did not know, who must be the Second Regent, and beside him baby-faced old Thomas Forsyth, his tonsure hidden by a round felt hat with a stalk like an apple's. Behind them rode the Dean and the Principal, with four college servants in blue velvet, and bringing up the rear, wearing the expression of a man who knows disasters are happening in his absence, was John Shaw the Faculty Steward on a fat pony. Some way behind him rattled a donkey-cart laden with the green branches which would be handed out at St Thomas Martyr's.

'Why do we have the Beadle with us?' Gil asked Nick Kennedy. 'He's a University servant and this is an Arts Faculty affair.'

'Ah, but John Doby is Rector this year,' Nick pointed out, 'and John Gray as Beadle is the Rector's servant. So we invited him along to make the procession look good, and quite incidentally to lend us the tapestries and cushions he keeps for graduations. Half our costumes for the play are out of his store,' he added.

The procession clopped and jingled up through the town. Dogs barked, and several small boys ran alongside

23

shouting rude remarks, until Dean Elphinstone himself identified one by name and promised to call on his father.

'That man is an asset to the college,' Gil observed to Nick Kennedy.

'Oh, he is. You should see him in Faculty meeting. He has all those old men following him like an ox-team, and Tommy Forsyth and John Goldsmith agreeing with one another. He's some kind of cousin of William Elphinstone in Aberdeen, and you can see the resemblance.'

'And who is that riding beside Maister Forsyth?'

Nick twisted round in time to see the man in question put out a hand to Maister Forsyth's bridle as the horses lurched up the steep portion of the High Street called the Bell o' the Brae.

'That's Patey Coventry the Second Regent. He's from Perthshire somewhere. A madman. He's all right.'

'Mad? How so?'

'He's Master of Arts from some obscure foreign place, he's already collected a Bachelor of Decreets from St Andrews, and now he's working on a Bachelor of Sacred Theology here as well as delivering a full set of lectures and disputations. Says he just likes learning.' Nick hauled on his reins as his horse attempted to go down the vennel that led to its stable. 'Get on, you stupid brute, we've a way to go yet!'

Past the Girth Cross, past the almshouses of St Nicholas' Hospital, past the Archbishop's castle, the procession continued. Residents of the upper town, cathedral staff, clergy and their dependants, paused about their business to watch. Outside the crumbling chapel of St Thomas Martyr beyond the Stablegreen Port, the leaders halted. More servants appeared to hold the horses while elderly academics dismounted. The students behind the Beadle leapt down and hastened into the chapel.

Gil, watching, saw the red-haired William pause by David Gray the Faculty Scribe as he straightened the creases from his gown. Whatever the boy said, it carried only to the lawyer's ears, where it was unwelcome; Gil thought Gray's narrow disappointed face paled, and he shook his head without speaking. The student vanished after his fellows, his red hair still visible in the shadows within.

Curious, thought Gil, and finding himself beside Maister Forsyth, lent a hand as he tried to straighten his fur-lined cope.

'Thank you, Gilbert,' said the old man. 'That was a very elegant answer you gave on your last disputation. What was the question again . . .?'

'I don't recall, sir,' said Gil, holding the slit at the front of the cope open.

'Ah, I have it. It was in the *Metaphysics*, I believe.' Maister Forsyth's gloved hands popped out of the single opening. He sketched a benediction, and hurried into the chapel after the other senior members. Gil cast his mind back over the years, discovered that his last disputation had indeed been the one on Aristotle's *Metaphysics*, and marvelled. That would have been in '84. Since then, he had spent better than five years abroad; Scotland had been convulsed by a rising which had killed King James, third of the name, and replaced him by another James, fourth of the name and the same age as some of these students; Gil's own father and elder brothers had died in support of James Third, and he himself had spent another couple of years almost imprisoned in the Cathedral Court learning to be a notary. Maister Forsyth appeared to have noticed none of this.

'It's the Mirror of Wisdom effect. Should we go in?'

Gil looked round, and found the Second Regent at his elbow. He was a small man in his thirties, in a blue cloth cope and hood which appeared to have been made for somebody taller; his tonsure was surrounded by a mop of black curls, and he peered up at Gil from one bright blue eye, the other being directed firmly at the bridge of his nose in the worst squint Gil had ever seen.

'I'm sorry?' he said blankly, following him into the little chapel. In the chancel, beyond the heavy semicircular arch, a choir of students was arranging itself round the huge music-book on its stand, and behind them in the dimness movement suggested the presence of the priest.

'Senior University men,' said the small man in graceful Latin, 'see the world entirely through the mirror of wisdom, like poor James Ireland. This mirror does not reflect matters of politics, public life, private life, or money. Maister Forsyth is probably quite unaware of how long it is since he heard your elegant answer. How long is it, in fact?'

'Eight years.' Gil grinned. 'I see your point.'

'Forgive me – I know your name, Nick Kennedy pointed you out, but I should introduce myself –'

'I could say the same.'

The unseen priest's voice issued the invitation to prayer, and as the six students round the music-stand tossed the words of the *Kyrie* higher and higher Gil suddenly realized that this was the first full Mass he had heard since his life turned upside-down. A week ago these words had formed part of his own destiny; this morning, although he did not know where he would find a living, he knew it would be on this side of the chancel arch, with Alys as his wife. The idea seemed to reshape the Mass; he found himself stumbling over the responses, which he should not have been making, like a half-taught clerk. The velvet-gowned Faculty servants beside him looked askance, and moved away a little. Pulling himself together, he tried to concentrate on the singing, over the murmured prayers and other conversations of the members of the procession.

Whatever setting they were using, it was being dominated by the first alto line, sung in a confident, rich head-voice slightly ahead of the other singers, and Gil was not surprised to find as his eyes adjusted to the dimness that the singer was the same red-haired William.

'Listen to the little toad,' muttered Maister Kennedy at his shoulder. 'What did I say? He sings like an angel. That cousin of his would be quite good if William wasny there.'

'Hush,' said the Second Regent. 'Later.'

Maister Kennedy snorted, but held his peace. The Mass

wore on, and the light at the chapel's tiny round-headed windows faded, brightened, faded again. When the door was finally dragged open and the Faculty stood back for the senior members to leave, the same group of students was revealed waiting to hand out dripping branches of hawthorn improbably decked with bunches of daisies.

'Christ aid!' said Maister Kennedy. 'We'll be soaked. The University will be wiped out, for we'll all be dead of lung-rot.'

Gil, looking over the heads of the congregation, was watching William. The boy seemed exalted, his bony face flushed, his eyes glittering as if he had stepped into a new life. He handed a branch of wet leaves to the Principal, with a murmured comment which brought Maister Doby's head round sharply. William smiled broadly, and moved on to present another bough to John Shaw the Steward. Maister Shaw, attempting to oversee the green boughs as well as the horse-holders, waved him aside impatiently, and got another murmured remark. He shook his head angrily, and William moved away, looking down his nose. The Steward paused almost fearfully to look at his retreating back.

'The more people are present,' said Patrick Coventry behind him, 'the longer it takes, in a kind of geometric progression.'

'You mean two people take more than twice as long?' Gil prompted absently. William had moved out of sight now.

'Two people take four times as long, and three people take nine times.'

'This means there must be a limit to the numbers for an event like this,' said Gil, thinking about it, 'or we would reach a point where it took so long to get everyone mounted that the older members would have succumbed to their years before the procession moved off.'

'We may have reached that already,' Maister Coventry observed.

'What are you two talking about?' asked Maister Kennedy. 'Are we to be here all day?'

Achieving the door, Gil stepped out into the sunshine, received a dripping branch from the very young treble, and got back on his horse, remarking to the Second Regent, 'I feel we will get wet if we are here much longer.'

Patrick Coventry, eyeing the black clouds piling up above the houses of the Chanonry, nodded agreement.

'It looks like thunder, indeed. I think we will move off soon. And when we get back we make one more procession on foot, right round the outer court and into the Lang Schule –'

One of the students attending the Beadle worked his way through the throng under the hawthorn branches, looking harassed and saying, in alternate Latin and Scots, 'Places, please, maisters! Order of precedence, maisters! Places, *please!*'

'– for the Faculty meeting, *to ensure that we are at peace with one another and with the other faculties,*' quoted Patrick Coventry resolutely. 'And then we have the feast and then, Heaven help us, we have the entertainment. I still think it should have been before the meeting.'

'What, now?' said Gil, startled. 'I thought it was in the statutes – it's supposed to be after the feast.'

'Well,' said Maister Coventry, 'there was the year two of the Muses were sick, whether from excitement or over-eating, and ruined their costumes. There was the year the bejants got hold of a skin of wine by mistake, and the audience was full of drunken fourteen-year-olds. But I think what settled the matter in my mind was the year everyone who ate the aigre-douce of pork was out the back lined up for the privy and the play had to be abandoned. I've been arguing in favour of the Lang Schule before the feast for a year or two now. Perhaps we should take our places.'

The other graduates did likewise, the elderly members were helped back into the saddle, and straggling somewhat, the Faculty made its way down the length of the High Street to the Mercat Cross, rounded it, accompanied by occasional comments, ironic cheers and whistles from the burgesses of Glasgow whose Sunday business was

28

being interrupted, and returned, past the Tolbooth, past the mason's house, past Blackfriars, to the college gateway.

Here they dismounted, and after some more milling about the procession formed up again on foot. Led by the Beadle, the Faculty made its stately way through the arched tunnel into the outer court of the college, once round the courtyard to the accompaniment of singing, and into the largest of the three lecture-rooms, where academic order of precedence broke into some rather unseemly jostling for seats on the long benches. Gil, finding himself an unobtrusive corner, was surprised to be joined by both Maister Kennedy and Maister Coventry.

'Should you not be near the front?' he asked. 'Do you not intend to speak?'

'I intend to sleep,' said Maister Kennedy, 'and anyway once the Dean gets going nobody else can get a word in.'

'I remember,' said Gil. '*Full of fruyte and rethorikly pykit.*'

'You and your quotations,' grumbled his friend. 'Move up, will you, and let me in against the wall.'

When the Dean began to speak, Gil perceived the wisdom of this. It was a long speech, expounding the duties of a scholar, ornamented with illustrations, parables and epigrams. The masters listened with polite attention, except for Maister Kennedy. The students developed the glazed look of young men listening to speeches. Finally the Dean sat down, to polite applause, and Maister Forsyth spoke at rather less length, dwelling on only two of the scholarly duties which the Dean had enumerated. He should, he declared in elegant concise periods, treat all fellow scholars as his brothers, and love them accordingly; and he should regard the college where he was educated as his mother, and treat it with the respect due from a loving son.

'He's never met my minnie,' said someone quietly near Gil, and someone else sniggered.

Maister Forsyth achieved his peroration and seated himself, to more enthusiastic applause. The Principal, in the lecturer's pulpit, invited the rest of the Faculty to join in the discussion.

'Not that you can call it a discussion,' commented Maister Coventry, 'since all the speakers are on the same side.'

In descending order of rank, Masters of Arts rose and delivered laboriously constructed speeches agreeing with the propositions already put forward. The youngest students, the bejants, became restless. Gil was aware of his stomach rumbling. Two rows in front of him, the red-haired alto appeared to be writing in his wax tablets, to judge by the cupped left hand just visible round his faded blue shoulder. Taking notes? Gil wondered.

'I want my dinner,' said Nick Kennedy, waking. 'Where have we got to? Oh, it's the magistrand. Not long now.' He paused to listen to the raw-boned fourth-year student who was drawing a somewhat repetitive parallel between the care of a mother for her sons and that of the Faculty for its students, and turned to Gil. 'Is that what it's been about?' he asked in sudden dismay. 'The college as mother?' Gil nodded. 'Oh, fient hae it!'

'What ails you, Nick?' asked Maister Coventry across Gil.

'The Dean has probably stolen all our best lines,' said Maister Kennedy gloomily. 'You'll see. It's too close by far to the theme of our play.'

'Sh!' said Maister Coventry. 'I want to hear Lowrie Livingstone. He will speak next.'

The fourth-year student sat down, to applause from his peers and teachers. The younger students were fidgeting audibly now. A fair boy two rows from the front began to gather himself together to rise to his feet, but before he could do so the red-haired alto stood up and said in clear and fluent Latin, 'Teachers, masters, brothers, I have a question to ask.'

Heads turned. The fair boy dropped back on to his bench, mouth open. Gil, looking at the senior members of Faculty seated in the stall-seats on either side of the pulpit, saw David Gray freeze like a hare that hears a dog.

'Then ask, William,' said the Dean. William bowed gracefully.

'This is my question,' he said. 'We are taught to regard the college as our mother.' The Dean inclined his head. 'But what if one discovers that another of her sons is ill-using her?'

'Make yourself clearer,' directed the Dean after a moment.

'What if another of the college's sons has misused her money,' said William in that clearly enunciated Latin, 'or has inculcated heretical beliefs in her students?'

There was a sudden murmur of scandalized exclamation. The Dean, lifting his voice over it, said, 'If one were to suspect such terrible and painful things of another member of the college, he should go quietly and reveal his suspicions to the Principal of the college, who would set due enquiry in motion.' He fixed William with his eye. 'Does that answer your question?'

'But what if,' persisted William, 'the Principal is not impartial in the matter? To whom should one go then?'

'What is the little toad up to now?' asked Nick Kennedy.

'He should go to the Rector,' said the Dean, his manner cooling with every word, 'when those are separate persons. If they are the same person, as for instance just now, then he should go to the Chancellor of the University, that is to Robert our Archbishop. However I must point out that one who brought such serious allegations against a fellow scholar without a firm foundation of truth would be guilty of perjury, being in clear breach of his oath of allegiance to the Rector and to the college.' There was a crackle of ice in his voice. 'Does that answer your question?'

'It answers it,' said William, allowing a shred of doubt to creep in.

'Then let us continue,' said the Dean.

Chapter Two

'But what was he playing at?' Gil asked, as the procession entered the Fore Hall for the feast.

'Who knows?' Nick Kennedy, drawing Gil firmly to the table for the non-regent Masters, claimed two places and gestured at one. 'Sit down. Indeed, who cares, except those who have to sit next to him?'

'He is not popular?' said Gil. He dipped his fingers in the faintly rose-scented bowl which a blue-gowned student was holding for him, and wiped them on the linen towel, nodding his thanks. He got an abbreviated bow in return, and looked again at the boy, reminded of William's discourtesy at the yett. This was a different fellow, with darker hair springing from a wide brow, but the way he looked down his nose at Gil's scrutiny was similar.

'Depends who you speak to,' said Maister Kennedy. He dabbled his fingers in his turn and wiped them on his cope. 'I think he's a clever arrogant little toad, but Bernard Stewart thinks the sun shines out of his – his ears, and the Dean says he's one of our most promising students, though I think he wasn't best pleased with him today. Aye, Robert,' he added to the boy, who moved off, a gleam of amusement in his expression. Nick said roundly, 'I don't want to think about William. Tell me about Paris.'

Gil's description of Paris drew in the Master of Arts opposite, who had been there shortly before Gil himself, and the Master on the end of the table, who had lectured there for a year. Nick listened in discontent until the college chaplain rose to deliver a very long grace in a strong, musical voice. Gil looked at him with some interest, recognizing the man whom William had accosted in the Outer Close. He was, as usual, a Dominican, wearing the robes of his order rather than an academic hood, but instead of the fair chubby man who had held the post in Gil's time this was a dark, intense creature in his forties with sunken eyes and a mouthful of large teeth.

When the grace was over Nick said, 'St Peter's bones, how I wish I'd gone abroad when I had the chance. I wouldn't be stuck here at the hinder end of nowhere teaching ungrateful brats to dissect syllogisms. What's the library like at Paris?'

'Do you mean the library of the Scots College?' asked the man at the end of the table, whose name Gil had not caught. 'Or the library of the Faculty of Arts? Or those of the Faculties of Theology, Canon Law, Civil Law?'

Maister Kennedy groaned, and hid his shaggy eyebrows with one hand as the first course of the feast was borne in. To some rather muffled music supplied by a group of students with recorders and lute, a pheasant in train was carried round to be admired, and a succession of mis-matched plate and pewter went to the high table, where the Dean ceremoniously broke a loaf and placed it on the alms dish to be given to the poor. The student musicians, hastily tucking their instruments under a bench, armed themselves with long towels and wooden platters and waited to bear portions of freshly carved roast meats away from the impromptu servery midway down the long wall. Harassed servants carried in more dishes to set on the lower tables, one between four.

'What have we got?' said Maister Kennedy, sniffing. 'Oh, God, rabbit and ground almonds. It's the Almayne pottage again. Pass me the red comfits, Gil.'

Spooning indifferent stew, Gil studied the other guests at the feast. Behind him across the hall another table sur-rounded by non-regent Masters buzzed happily. At the far end, two tables of students produced an astonishing level of noise and, as the ale-jug went round, a continuous flight of bread pellets like finches in a hedgerow. By the servery the ubiquitous William was in close colloquy with the fingerbowl boy. As Gil's eye fell on them, Maister Shaw the Steward bustled up. William sauntered off to join the singers, and the other student, accepting an obvious rebuke with gritted teeth, seized a dish and ladle and plunged across the hall towards the high table.

Not a pleasant young man, little Sir William, Gil thought.

On the dais, in front of painted hangings from the Beadle's supply, the Faculty office-bearers and regents were ranged along one side of the elaborately draped board as if they were people in a prayer-book miniature, conversing politely or glaring at the students, as prompted by temperament. The Dean and Maister Doby were instructing the Steward; David Gray the Scribe was staring into a flan dish as if he could see the flames of Hell among the points of pastry which decorated it. Next to him was old Tommy Forsyth, and then Patrick Coventry, putting out a steadying hand as a ladleful of bright yellow stew slopped alarmingly near to Maister Forsyth's fur-lined cope.

'Where will the play be?' he asked Maister Kennedy, who took another handful of the cinnamon comfits and said gloomily,

'Below in the Lang Schule. There'll be yet another procession, round the yard and in at the door. I hope they're setting up the hangings for us now. I'll need to go and see to that before the second course is done.'

'Did you write it?'

Nick nodded. 'I and two of the older boys. There's been some friction,' he added grimly. 'William has improvements to suggest every time he opens his mouth, but since they all enlarge his part, which is already large, at the expense of others I didn't take many. Had it not been made clear to me that it was expected he would take part,' he added, the passive verb forms falling neatly in the Latin, 'the little toad would have been booted out the second time he criticized someone else's acting.'

'The same William? The lanky redhead who hinted

34

about peculation and heresy? The one with the striking alto voice?'

'The Dean,' remarked the man on the end of the table, 'asked us to put these painful ideas from our minds for the sake of the feast.'

'The same,' agreed Nick, ignoring this.

'He greeted me when I arrived,' Gil said thoughtfully. 'He was very civil until he found I was a Cunningham.'

'Oh, very likely. St Peter be praised, Bernard has a better ear than I for a tune. We've split the entertainment between us – I did the play, he did the music – and it meant neither of us had to deal with William the whole time.' He turned his head. 'Oh, God, talk of the devil. They're going to sing for us. That's Bernard giving out the beat. His mother's a cousin of the Lennox Stewarts and his father was one of the French branch of the family. Been here two years, I think, or maybe it's three. You know how they move around, all the friars, from one house to another.'

'A learned man,' said the man at the end of the table. 'He does most of the teaching in Theology.'

Gil twisted round to look. The gangling William was at the centre of the hall, flanked by the fair-haired boy whose speech he had interrupted, and the boy for whom he had just earned a scolding by distracting him. Two more students joined the group, and under the intense direction of the Dominican chaplain the five young voices rose in praise of music.

'That's David Ross,' said Nick in Gil's ear, 'the treble. He and his brother lodge with the Principal. They're far too young really, but we have to keep the Rosses sweet after what happened to whatsisname. You know he's teaching in the Sentences here? There he is at the other table.'

Gil nodded. The story of Robert Ross, blinded in one eye by a flung cabbage stalk, and the resulting parental wrath, was known to most graduates of the college.

'And the second alto is a Montgomery,' continued Nick, 'in case you were thinking of being civil to him.'

'Oh, is that his trouble? We're supposed to be at peace,'

35

Gil rejoined. 'It must be six months at least since there was any difficulty. William isn't an ensemble singer, is he?'

Nick winced as the mellifluous tones floated high in the climax of the piece, twining round the treble, making it sound slightly flat.

'You wouldn't expect him to be,' he pointed out. William, ignoring the spatter of applause, strolled away from the group and out of the hall. Gil glanced at the high table and found that David Gray was staring with dislike after the narrow departing back in its blue gown. *The subcharge of the service is bot sair*, he thought. There was a man who was not enjoying the feast.

The remaining singers rearranged themselves, and the Dominican gave out a new beat.

'When's the harper?' asked the man who had taught in Paris. 'I missed a good Scots harper in France. The style is quite different.'

'What harper is it?' Gil asked.

'The man that stays in the Fishergait will come in after the play,' Nick said. 'Now what? Oh, bloody Machaut. I really would as soon not eat my dinner to Machaut. I'm going to see if the players are dressed yet. Bernard lectures in the Theology Schule two hours after noon, so if we overrun we'll have to finish the music without him. Will you risk the second course, Gil, or will you give me a hand? We're dressing in the Bachelors' Schule.'

The smaller lecture-room was occupied by a panicky, half-dressed group, jostling for a sight of the mirror and shouting in bad Latin about costumes and properties. Nick was promptly besieged by several people at once. Gil waited quietly, looking about him. A heap of canvas painted with scales lay on a bench, and beside it a bundle of brocade and gauze suggested women's costumes. Across the room the westward windows showed the near houses on the High Street, with the roof of the Greyfriars church beyond, and dark clouds still piling up above them. It seemed likely that the May sunshine would shortly give way to yet another vicious May shower.

Over by the lecturer's pulpit, William was apparently hearing the lines of a younger boy whose shaggy hair had probably last been cut by his mother when she saw him in September. As Gil watched, William shook his own well-barbered head and with a superior smile clouted the other boy round the ear, wadded up his script and reached up to put it on top of the soundboard of the pulpit. Ignoring his victim's despairing pleas, he walked away across the room, taking something from his purse as he went. Maister Kennedy, looking about him, caught sight of the younger boy standing by the pulpit.

'Gil! You were in the entertainment in our time. Can you take Richie through his part for me? And see him costumed?'

'What, now?' said Gil in astonishment.

'Aye, now! He needs a last run-through. William was just hearing him, but he has to go and sing again. Richie, come here, you imbecile. Why I cast you as a Scholar I'll never know. Get along with Maister Cunningham. Where's your script? And your book?'

'William put them up yonder, Maister Kennedy,' said Richie, almost weeping with anxiety. 'I canny reach them!'

'Speak Latin, fool! Maister Cunningham can reach them, I've no doubt.'

Gil crossed to the pulpit, and put a hand up on to the soundboard to bring down a bundle of papers.

'Is it all here?' he asked Richie, brushing clumps of dust off the creased margins.

The boy nodded, gulping with relief. 'That's my script, maister. But there's still the brown book. It's what I tak to show I'm a student.'

He pushed dark hair out of his eyes in a nervous gesture, and peered hopefully up at the soundboard. Gil put a toe on the seat of the lecturer's bench and swung himself up to look. There were not one but two books up there, bright on top of decades of dust. He reached for them and jumped down, handing them to Richie.

'This one's mine, maister. I dinna ken that wee red one, it's maybe someone else's.'

'Nick? Is this yours?' Gil held the book out.

'I don't know whose it is.' Maister Kennedy gave the book a brief glance, tucked it in the breast of his cassock and turned away. 'Michael, how can you be a daughter of anybody with a face like that? Scrub it off and try again.'

Gil took his pupil into a corner, sorted out the bundle of papers and gave the boy his first prompt. It soon became apparent why Richie was worried; he was nowhere near word-perfect in the badly rhymed Latin couplets and had only the vaguest of ideas about his cues. Gil stared at him in bafflement.

'Why haven't you learned it?' he asked. 'In my day it was an honour to be in the play, and earned favours from the Dean. I was let off two disputations for my last part, it had so many lines.'

'Don't know,' said Richie, reddening. 'I thought it would be easy. I mean . . .' He fell silent.

Gil, in some sympathy, said, 'Well, there's nothing to be done about it now. Why don't you carry the script in your book and read it, as if you're reading Aristotle or Euclid?'

Richie gaped at him as if experiencing an epiphany.

'D'you think Maister Kennedy would let me?'

'I should think he'd let you do anything that saved the play,' Gil assured him.

'Richie! Are you costumed yet!' shouted Nick across the room. 'The singing's finished, we're on next. Now have you all got that clear? We're cutting the scene with Frivolity and going straight to where Idleness enters. Yes, I know, Henry, but you've only yourself to blame, you know even less of your lines than Richie here. Walter and Andrew, you will get that padding out or I will personally remove it and stuff it up –'

'I know Henry's lines.' William was by the door, supercilious under a gold brocade turban. ·

'You can't take three parts, William. And we're doing the first version of your fight, is that clear?' Nick pursued, ignoring the red-haired boy's expression. 'The first version, not the one with the long speeches.'

'It's a paltry little play anyway,' William objected in his fluent Latin, the disdainful expression ever more marked. 'It would be an act of destruction to omit the best speeches.'

'I will not argue,' Nick said in the same language. 'I am in charge of the play. You heard my instructions, William. Right, are we ready? Let's go, before the bejants start a riot.'

Gil paused to snuff the candles by the mirror, and followed the company out into the courtyard and along the west range, past the tunnel that led to the yett and into the Lang Schule. The lecture-room had been transformed since the Faculty meeting, and was now hung with painted cloths. Cushioned settles had been placed for the older members and long benches arranged round a stage set off by a suit of worn verdure tapestries which Gil recollected from the Principal's house in his day. The Masters and senior students were all deep in conversation, as befitted their dignity, but on the side benches the younger bachelors and the bejants, the first-year students, were becoming restless. Slipping in at the side, Gil found himself a seat beside Maister Coventry, who nodded at him.

'I see you survived the feast.'

'I avoided most of it,' Gil confessed. 'I've been helping at the play.'

'Probably safer. And what is Nick giving us? Some kind of allegory, as usual?'

Nick Kennedy, in a grey wig and gold cloak, stepped on to the stage from among the tapestries, bowed to the Dean and Principal and the rest of the audience, and in the usual deprecatory Latin announced that this rough play and its limping metre would depict an allegory of the student's life. The regents and Masters applauded, the students groaned, Nick bowed again and left the stage, and there was a long pause, and some hissing whispers behind the tapestry. Then Richie emerged, stumbling slightly as if pushed, and launched abruptly into a halting account of how as a Scholar he had been nurtured at a grammar school on the milk of Latin and rhetoric but was now of an age to wish for stronger food. He followed the words with his finger in his bundle of papers, and spoke in the curious accent affected by Lanarkshire youth on a stage.

To him entered the gangling William, wearing the gold cloak and turban and introducing himself as Fortune, and in a long speech invited the Scholar to accompany him through the world, promising to lead him to a banquet of the richest food an enquiring mind could wish for. Their journey round the stage was marred by a tendency for the students on the side benches to tramp with their feet in time with the scholarly steps, until the Dean's chilly stare took effect.

'There are only eight bejants,' said Patrick Coventry, 'and two are in the play. How can six boys of fourteen be so wild to handle?'

'Because they're boys of fourteen?' Gil suggested.

Maister Coventry's reply was drowned by whistling and stamping. The Scholar and Fortune had encountered a bevy of veiled ladies, at least one of whom had not obeyed Maister Kennedy's directions about the padding. The Dean deployed his stare again, and in the relative silence Fortune declared that these were Dame Collegia and her daughters, among whom were Learning, Wisdom and Knowledge. Learning and Wisdom looked under their eyebrows at their friends, but Knowledge struck a provocative pose and grinned, displaying several missing teeth, as Fortune informed the Scholar that if he were wedded to one of these damsels he would become one of the Dame's children himself, and would never lack for the finest fare.

The Dame and her daughters sang a motet in praise of the scholarly life, the beat given by Bernard Stewart from the edge of the stage. Gil recognized the music; he hoped that nobody else was familiar with the original words, but Patrick Coventry beside him muttered, 'Dear me.'

The Scholar appeared about to succumb to one or all of these beauties, but William, who had left the stage, re-entered in a linen headdress, dragging two startled boys with him and declaring himself to be Dame Frivolity with her servants Gambling and Drunkenness. Collegia and her daughters, with shocked gestures, left.

'They were going to cut this,' Gil said, as startled as Frivolity's henchmen.

'A last-minute change?'

'The cut was a last-minute change itself.'

Overcoming the Scholar's reluctance, Frivolity enticed him into a game of dice while the goblet went round, then departed. The side benches, who appeared to know what was coming, began whistling again. The Scholar, pushing his hair out of his eyes, read out that he had lost all his money, and just as he seemed about to fall into a drunken stupor, a fearsome dragon rushed onstage. The bejants cheered.

'When did we get the costume?' Gil asked, as the monster rampaged about, threatening the front rows of the audience and making an attempt on the Dean's silk gown.

'In '89, I think,' said Maister Coventry. 'It was a gift from a student's family. We have to make use of it, of course. It barely fits William, as tall as he is. Have you noticed the weather?'

Gil looked up at the tall window. The dark clouds were much closer, and a shutter was banging on an upper floor of the house immediately opposite.

'Any of the bejants admit to being afraid of thunder?' he asked. The regent shook his head.

The dragon was now making a lengthy speech in which it identified itself as Idleness and threatened to consume the Scholar utterly. The Scholar made futile efforts to escape, clutching his script, while Gambling and Drunken-ness refused to help, but nothing availed until a sturdy knight with a wooden sword and well-polished shield

41

tramped on. Pausing only to announce himself as Diligence, the enemy of Idleness and the support and defence of scholars everywhere, he attacked the dragon, which fought back furiously. Dame Collegia and her daughters returned to cheer the knight on. From time to time one or the other combatant broke off to address the audience at length, until the noise from the side benches became too much and the dragon attacked them instead.

'That was a mistake,' said Maister Coventry. Leaning forward he laid firm hands on the two students nearest him, but those beyond had already leapt to their feet and begun baiting the dragon with enthusiasm. The boys from the other side bench rushed across the room and joined in, tugging at the dragon's tail, and as the canvas tore Dean Elphinstone rose to his feet.

'*Tacete!*' he said, in a voice like the crack of a whip.

All movement was suspended. The Dean held the moment; that icy stare swept the room, and returned to Diligence, who swallowed hard and brought sword to shield in a salute. Finally the Dean bowed.

'Pray continue, Sir Diligence,' he said politely, and seated himself again.

The students slunk back to their seats; the dragon gathered up its damaged tail and regained the stage. Diligence, overcoming it with a perfunctory sweep of his sword, turned to raise the Scholar to his feet. As Dame Collegia and her daughters came forward to discuss the Scholar's marriage, William removed the dragon's head and stalked off behind the tapestries, and Gil heard the first rumble of thunder.

The Scholar's marriage arrangements were much more quickly dealt with than Gil felt to be realistic. All present attempted a motet, praising diligence and condemning idleness, and as soon as it was finished the chaplain slipped out of the hall with an anxious expression, presumably to prepare for his lecture to the theologians. Nick reappeared to say that the play was over and the players hoped it had given pleasure. The place where he had cut the line hoping it had not given offence was barely noticeable. Gil, eyeing his friend, felt that this was a man who needed to be plied with strong drink.

As the side benches began drumming their feet by way of applause and the senior members of the audience clapped politely, a few drops of rain rattled on the little greenish panes of the upper window. The students sitting below jumped up to close the shuttered lower portions. They were just in time; as the first turnbutton twirled home, a colossal peal of thunder crashed, and the skies opened.

'Michty me, it's the Deluge!' said someone.

'My Aristotle!' said someone else, and dived for the door. A number of students followed him, including most of the cast of the play. The Dean and Principal watched in disapproval.

'The roofs are no sounder than they ever were?' Gil said to his neighbour.

'Well, no,' said Maister Coventry frankly. 'I've spent a bishop's ransom on thatching the Arthurlie building next door, so it's weathertight for now, but neither Law nor Theology can spare money for the roof of the main building, and Dean Elphinstone won't lay out Arts Faculty money without at least the promise that they'll match it. So the boys in the Inner Close run about with buckets when it rains, and their books and their bedding get spoiled, and then their parents complain to the Principal. It's quite an inconvenience, Maister Cunningham.'

'The building is old,' Gil observed. 'It was not new when Lord Hamilton gave it to the college, and that was before I was born. Maybe another rich benefactor will appear from the sky and solve all your problems.'

'All that appears from the sky is water.' Maister Coventry stared at the rain running down the window. 'The end of the feast is in the Fore Hall, we only have to go outside and up the stair, save those of us who wish to find the privy, but I imagine the Dean will wish to stay seated until this stops. His bladder must be cast iron.' He looked up. 'Ah, Nick. Well done.'

Maister Kennedy, without the grey wig, sat down at Gil's other side, snarling.

'I will strangle that little toad,' he said emphatically. 'You saw him, Patey. He actually took Henry's kurtch off him and went on as Frivolity, after what I said. And he deliberately did the second version of the fight, and he –'

'Perhaps he was nervous,' Gil suggested, 'and simply forgot your directions.'

'Nervous? That? Don't make me laugh. I'll strangle him, I will, as soon as I set eyes on him.'

'Is he not backstage?' asked Patrick Coventry.

'No, he is not. You saw him go – he should have been onstage for the motet, they needed his top line, but no, William was offended, William left.' His fingers worked. 'By God, the little –'

'Nick.' Maister Coventry reached across to touch his arm. 'This is not the place.'

'In fact I'd better not strangle him yet,' Maister Kennedy admitted. 'The Dean has to grant favours to the cast, including William, I suppose. Oh, God, how I wish this day was over!'

'Amen to that,' agreed the Second Regent. 'See, I think the rain has eased a little, and the Dean is signalling to the Beadle. Perhaps we can leave these hard benches and go back up to finish the feast and listen to the harper.'

'They'll all go and stand in line out the back,' said Maister Kennedy sourly. 'I vote we make for the Arthurlie garden. You too, Gil?'

By the time the Faculty reassembled in the Fore Hall the tables had been taken down and the benches disposed in less formal ranks, and the students who had been at the feast had seized the opportunity to absent themselves. One or two junior bachelors remained, their white towels of office by now somewhat spattered, to hand platters of sweetmeats and the two silver quaichs full of spiced wine. In a corner the cast of the play, restored to their belted gowns, greasepaint smudged round eyes and mouths, were gathering round one of the dishes of sweetmeats. Maister Kennedy annexed another, and sat down against the wall as the Faculty members continued to straggle into the hall.

'Here comes the harper,' he said in some satisfaction. 'Mind you, he only has one of his singers with him.'

'This one is his sister. The other one died,' said Gil, watching the Steward conduct two tall Highlanders into the hall. The woman paced like a queen in her loose checked gown; her dark hair tumbled down her back, the threads of silver in it invisible in this light. In one arm she cradled a wire-strung harp. The man who held her other arm was nearly as tall as Gil. He wore a gown of blue velvet, with a gold chain disposed on his shoulders, beard and hair combed over it as white as new milk. 'Less than a fortnight ago,' he added. 'This may be the first time they have performed in public since.'

Although the hall was full of conversation, the harper's head tilted. He spoke to his sister, who looked round, and met Gil's eye. She nodded briefly to him, unsmiling, and continued in the wake of the Steward to the place set for them near the senior members of the Faculty. The Dean began a formal welcome to Angus McIan, harper, and Elizabeth McIan, singer, and Gil reflected that he scarcely recognized Ealasaidh by the Scots form of her name.

'Oh, was that the business I was hearing about?' Nick passed the sweetmeats across Gil to Maister Coventry, ignoring the Dean's stately comments.'Picked up dead in the Fergus Aisle, wasn't she? And the mason's boy did it? Who was she, anyway?'

'The mason's boy did not,' said Gil. 'She was John Sempill's wife. You remember John at the Grammar School?'

'Aye.' Nick chewed on a wedge of candied apricot. 'Ill-tempered brute. Did he do it, then?'

'Hush and listen,' said Maister Coventry. 'How can I silence the students if you talk so much?'

Nick grinned, and leaned back against the wall. The harper had begun a tuning-prelude, the sweeping ripples of sound ringing round the hall while he listened critically to the pitch of the notes. He worked his way from the lowest notes to the highest and back, then stilled the strings with the flat of his hand, threw a remark in Gaelic to his sister, and began to play. To Gil's surprise the singer remained silent, while the harp spun a skein of heavy, solemn melody and counter-melody, almost painful to listen to. Though the harper's long hands moved smoothly over the shining wires, across the width of the hall Gil saw the tremor in arm and jaw. What ails McIan? he wondered.

'That's not music for a feast,' Nick muttered beside him. 'What's he playing?'

'A lament,' said Maister Coventry. 'Did you catch what he said to the woman?'

'I don't speak Ersche,' said Gil, and Nick shook his head.

'He said, *There is death in the hall.*'

'It's the thunder,' said Nick decidedly, but Gil felt a shiver run down his back. The slow, weighty tune wound to its end, and after urgent representations by the Steward the woman rose to her feet and began to recite one of the gloomier portions of the history of Wallace. The Steward, shaking his head, approached Nick.

'Maister Kennedy,' he said, bowing, 'the Dean wishes to offer some reward to the players after the harper is finished. I am to direct you to assemble them at that time.'

Nick pulled a face, but replied politely enough. John Shaw went off to harass the students with the spiced wine, and Maister Coventry said, 'Do you need a collie-dog? Are they all here?'

'Mostly.' Nick got to his feet. 'Richie, Henry, Michael, there's Walter – who's missing?'

'William,' said Gil, who had been watching the cast drifting in.

'You're right,' said Nick after a moment. 'He'll be sulking in the privy after his costume got torn. Well, I'm not going to look for him. He'll turn up at the last moment like

46

a clipped plack, he always does when there's something in it for him.'

'I'll send John Hucheson,' offered Maister Coventry.

'I wouldn't offend John by asking him.' Nick looked around, catching the eye of several of the cast. 'William can look out for himself.'

Wallace eventually reached the end of a chapter, and the harper's sister sat down, to some applause. The Dean raised his hand, and the Steward, standing to one side, summoned the players in ringing tones. As Maister Kennedy and his group progressed formally up the length of the hall, Gil found Ealasaidh McIan at his side.

'Himself wishes me to warn you,' she said without preamble. 'There is death in this place, and more than death. He felt it as soon as we came here.'

'More than death?' Gil questioned involuntarily.

'Strangling and secrecy,' she said. 'Many secrets.'

'Is it someone in this hall?' asked Patrick Coventry at her other side.

She turned to look down at him, shaking her head. 'I am not the one with the sight. You must be asking himself that.'

'Where is William?' said the Dean loudly. 'He must be sought for.'

With the words the harper rose, blank eyes wide, his instrument clasped in one arm, and flung the other hand high with an exclamation in Gaelic that set the brass strings ringing. The Steward and the Dean, arrested in movement, stared at him, as did nearly everyone else in the hall, but his sister hurried to his side. Maister Coventry stepped forward and together they shepherded the tall figure to the side of the hall, answering him in Gaelic as they went. Gil dragged a bench forward and the harper was thrust on to it, his sister scolding him in a hissing whisper.

'Where is Maister Cunningham?' he asked, putting out his free hand in its furred velvet sleeve.

'I am here,' said Gil, alarmed, and grasped the hand. This man was a professional musician and habitually more

47

dignified than the Archbishop. What had shaken him to this extent? He was speaking in Gaelic again, urgent jerky sentences.

'The one the Dean asks for,' Patrick Coventry translated softly, 'is in the dark, behind an iron lock, and he is no longer living.'

Chapter Three

'What does he say?' demanded Dean Elphinstone from the dais. There was a sudden buzz of sound as those nearest, who had heard, informed those who had not.

'Haivers!' said the boy who had played Knowledge. 'Not our William!'

'Speak Latin, Walter,' said the Principal automatically.

'*Quid est Latinus pro* haivers?' muttered Walter.

'How can he ken that?' the Dean pursued in Scots. 'Maister Harper, what gars ye –'

'I am a harper,' said Angus McIan. 'It is given to me.'

'Aye, well, so was old Rory MacDuff a harper when I was a bairn,' said the Dean, 'and he didny take these strunts.'

'Best you look for the one who is missing,' said Ealasaidh urgently to Gil. 'Himself will not be right till the daylight reaches the dead man.'

'It came to him,' said Gil to a nodding Maister Coventry, 'when the Dean asked where was William. Moreover the Dean has already said –'

'Maister Kennedy,' said the Dean, cutting across the rising noise in the hall. 'Rehearse to us the names of those who took part in this play, edifying and entertaining us with well-turned verse and golden precept.' He looked, Gil thought, as if the balanced phrases tasted sour.

Nick, stumbling slightly over the Latin forms of the surnames, listed his cast and the roles they had performed, deprecating the play and commending the players who had learned their parts, identifying William last as Fortune and the dragon Idleness. From time to time he glanced at

49

the door, as if he expected the missing boy to appear round it at any moment. The Dean replied in another elaborate speech, promising each of the cast by name some academic exemption or dispensation as a reward for hard work. At the end of the dais, David Gray scribbled notes, prodding at the wax in his tablet with jerky movements. Gil, watching him, thought he looked dazed, and wondered how accurate the final list would be.

The boy who had played Collegia was pushed forward, and in bleating Latin produced a short but formal acknowledgement of the favours granted in return for this poor entertainment, so ably supervised by their well-loved teacher Maister Kennedy.

'And now William Irvine is to be sought for. His reward will be granted when he is present.'

'Now, Dean?' said Nick.

'Now. I wish to speak to him.'

The well-loved teacher clapped his hands at the cast.

'Find William, then!' he said. 'Hurry! You know the kind of places to look.'

Gil disengaged his hand from the harper's with a quiet word, and went forward to join Nick as the students made for the door. On the dais, the senior members of the Faculty were watching in varying degrees of disapproval; around the hall, now that the harper had stopped providing entertainment, the sweetmeats and spiced wine were circulating again.

'If he is not in his chamber,' said Patrick Coventry at Nick's other elbow, 'nor in the library, then are there likely spots to search or do we comb the entire college?'

'Yes,' said Maister Kennedy, following the group of students. 'It's one of the things I dislike about him,' he added, pausing on the steps outside. 'He crops up everywhere, like columbine-weed, whether he has any business to be there or not. Henry, Walter!' he called. 'Go and check William's chamber. Andrew and Ralph, see if the library is unlocked and if so whether he is there. Ninian, Lowrie, Michael –'

'I thought we'd search the Inner Close, Maister Kennedy,' said the yellow-haired tenor, a lanky youth just beginning to broaden at the shoulders, 'and see if he's troubling the kitchens as well.'

'Very good, Lowrie. You do that. Robert Montgomery, Richie Shaw, you search the Inner Close as well.'

'Please, Maister Kennedy.' The treble from the singing group put his hand up, snapping his fingers like a school-boy. 'What will David and me do?'

'You and your brother may run to the Arthurlie build-ing,' said Maister Coventry promptly, 'and ask anyone you meet there whether William Irvine has been seen.'

'And come back and report to me here,' said Nick as the boys scattered across the wet flagstones.

Gil made his way down the steps. Patrick Coventry followed him, saying thoughtfully, 'Why the kitchens?'

'I wondered that,' said Gil. 'I noticed those three come back together after the rain started, and one of them is lacking his belt.'

He headed for the vaulted tunnel which led between the silent Law lecture-rooms and into the inner courtyard, Maister Coventry behind him. As they emerged into the daylight, shouting erupted in the kitchens at the far side of the courtyard. Gil, hitching up cope and cassock, quick-ened his pace, and sprang up the kitchen stair in time to meet the tenor and his two friends, retreating backwards from a gaunt woman enveloped in a sacking apron.

'And stay out of my kitchen!' she ordered shrilly, with a threatening sweep of her ladle.

'I'm sorry, Agnes,' said one of the boys, the fine-boned mousy-haired one. 'We didny mean to annoy you –'

'Annoy me, he says! Three great louts under my feet asking daft questions – get out of my way, and don't let me set eyes on you this week!'

'Agnes Dickson,' said Gil from behind the students. One of them turned to look at him, and the cook paused open-mouthed. 'I knew you were still cook here as soon as I saw the Almayne pottage,' Gil pursued, with perfect truth. 'I've tasted nothing like it since I left the college.'

'Oh, it's you,' said Mistress Dickson, less shrill but still

51

hostile. 'Is this lot anything to do with you? Getting in my way when I'm short-handed, with the rest of the college still to feed, and half the dishes up in the Fore Hall. They should know better by their age.'

'Senior bachelors are always a trial,' said Gil sympathetically. 'We've lost one –'

'He's a junior,' said the mousy-haired boy quickly.

'Have you seen William Irvine, Agnes?'

'I have not, the saints be praised. I can't be doing with that laddie, aye on my back about the cost of this and that and who's getting extra food at the buttery door. Away and look for him elsewhere. And you, Gil Cunningham, come back when I'm less taigled and tell me if your minnie likes your marriage.'

She brandished the ladle again, and the three senior bachelors slid past Gil and thudded down the stairs. Gil took off his bonnet and bowed, but Mistress Dickson was already retreating into her kitchen where someone demanded to know if he had pounded these roots enough. Gil descended to the courtyard, where the tenor and the mousy-haired boy were making exaggerated gestures of relief.

'Thank you, maister,' said the third student, a stocky fellow with a round red face. 'Agnes can be a bit –'

'She can indeed,' Gil said. Beyond Maister Coventry, Richie the Scholar and the Montgomery boy appeared from one stair and disappeared into another, like rabbits in a warren.

'Did the harper no say William was behind a lock?' asked Lowrie the tenor. 'Why don't we check the cellars while we're here?'

Gil met Patrick Coventry's blue glance.

'But have we a key?'

'I have one,' said Maister Coventry. The three students had already plunged into the vaulted passage behind the kitchen stair, and were trying doors.

'Not in the wellhouse. Look in the feed store, Michael.'

'William? You there? No, not a sign.'

'Not in the feed store. What about the limehouse?'

'The door's open. Didn't we – shouldn't it be barred?'

'St Eloi's hammer, it's dark in here. He's no here.'

'He's no here?' repeated the tenor, on a rising note of incredulity.

'Don't think so. Fiend hae these sacks –'

'Don't lick your fingers, you fool! Try that corner.'

'No, he's no here.'

'Should we look in the coalhouse?'

'Aye, try the coalhouse.'

'But we left him –'

'Wheesht, you gormless –'

'The coalhouse is locked.'

'Isn't it always locked?'

'No in the daytime. The kitchen needs in to get coals for the dinner.'

'It's locked now. William? You there?'

'Stand back, please.'

Maister Coventry, after some ferreting under his brocade cope, had produced a large key. As two more students came running across the courtyard he fitted it into the coalhouse lock and turned it. The door swung outwards, boxing the three senior bachelors into the dark passage beyond it.

'He's no in the library,' said someone behind Gil, 'and John Hucheson says he's no been there, and Walter says his chamber door's locked.'

'Speak Latin, Ralph,' said Maister Coventry, 'and stand back out of the light. William?' He peered into the coalhouse. 'William?'

'What is it? Have we found him?' said someone else from the courtyard.

Gil, looking over Maister Coventry's head, shaded his eyes against the light from the courtyard, and suddenly turned to the students at the mouth of the passage.

'Go and tell Maister Kennedy to come here,' he ordered, 'and bring a good lantern.'

'You gentlemen too,' said Maister Coventry, closing the door over so that the group beyond it could emerge. 'Go and send Maister Kennedy, and then wait in the Outer Close.'

'Why?' said Lowrie. 'Is William there? But how did he get in there?'

'Is he – is he hurt?' asked the mousy-haired one. The stocky boy said nothing, but stared at the door as he edged past it into the courtyard, then suddenly broke into a run. His friends galloped after him, and they went into the tunnel to the outer courtyard in a tight knot. Gil watched them out of sight, then reached over Patrick Coventry's head and opened the door again.

'Is it William?' asked the Second Regent.

'I think it must be.' Gil stepped forward, cautious in the dim light. 'Ah, there is a window.' He unbarred the shutters and turned to look at what lay at the foot of the heap of coal, nearest the window, furthest from the door.

'Lord have mercy on us,' said Maister Coventry. 'Are you certain? It doesn't look like –'

Gil swallowed hard, suddenly regretting the Almayne pottage.

'The clothes are William's,' he said, 'and the build and the hair are William's. He has been strangled, which is why he is unrecognizable. And look at this. Look what was used to strangle him.'

He bent to close the bulging eyes so far as was possible. The effect, if anything, was worse. Averting his gaze, he lifted the end of the leather strap which lay across the shoulder of the blue gown.

'This is someone's belt,' he said.

'The poor boy,' said Maister Coventry.

'There's worse,' said Gil, still peering at the body. 'Look – his hands are bound.'

Producing a set of beads from his sleeve, Patrick Coventry bent his head and began the quick, familiar muttering of the prayers for the dead. Gil stepped past him and out of the coalhouse as the sound of hasty feet in the courtyard heralded Maister Kennedy.

'Nick,' he said.

'Where is the boy? What's come to him? Andrew and Ralph said –'

'Nick, are you wearing any sort of belt?'

His friend stared at him, his mobile brows twitching.

'My belt? No, as a matter of fact, I'm not. No room for a purse under this, and no need for one over it, in these robes.'

'Do you have one? Where is it?'

'In my chamber. Do you need it? What's happened, Gil?'

'William's dead,' said Gil bluntly. 'He's been strangled, with someone's belt, and his hands are tied with another one. Whoever makes enquiry into this will be very interested in belts.'

Nick Kennedy looked from Gil, to Patrick Coventry still murmuring prayers, to the shadows in the coalhouse.

'Christ aid,' he said. 'He will, won't he. Let's have a look.'

Gil slipped past the Second Regent and into the dim space again, positioning himself carefully away from the window. Nick, following him, checked visibly at the sight of the distorted face and lolling tongue.

'Christ aid,' he said again. 'You wereny mistaken about the strangling. Well,' he said to the indifferent corpse, 'I've threatened to throttle you myself often enough, but I suppose I'm sorry now someone's done it. Poor laddie. Should we no move him, Gil?'

'William is certainly beyond aid,' Gil pointed out. 'There is little point in moving him, and I think we should notify the Dean and the Principal first. Moreover, this is clearly secret murder, and I know last time I viewed a body I could have done with seeing her where she died.'

Nick looked from the corpse to the shadowy heaps of coal and stacked wood.

'If you say so,' he said. 'Well, I'd better tell them. Will you bide here or come with me?'

Gil, who had been giving some thought to exactly this question, said, 'Would you say, Nick, we three have been within sight of one another the whole time, since the end of the play?'

Both men stared at him. Maister Coventry's lips still moved, but Maister Kennedy's mouth had fallen open. After a moment he recovered it.

'St Peter's bones,' he said, without inflection. 'Someone did this, didn't they? And I threatened to throttle him. I swear by the Rood, Gil, I've never been so glad in my life to have taken a driddle in company. We were maybe not all three in sight of one another, but none of us could have got here from the Arthurlie garden with time to do this and be back before the other two noticed he'd gone.'

Gil nodded.

'Maister Coventry,' he said. The Second Regent raised his head. 'I suggest you lock the door and let none past until the Dean and Maister Doby are here.'

The small man nodded, without interrupting his prayers, and followed them out of the coalhouse. Locking the door carefully, he stationed himself in front of it and took up his beads again as Gil and Nick set off across the courtyard.

The students who had formed the search party were at the foot of the stairs to the Fore Hall. The three senior bachelors were standing aside in a row, the stocky boy in the middle; two more were wrestling, some others kicking a stone about. As their seniors approached the games ceased.

'Is it William, Maister Kennedy?' said someone. 'Is he hurt?'

'Why was he in the coalhouse?' asked someone else.

'It is William,' said Nick. 'Yes, he is hurt. He is hurt bad.'

'Will he die, maister?' asked one of the two Ross boys, seated wide-eyed by his brother on the bottom step.

'He is dead,' said Nick.

'Ninian!' said Lowrie the tenor. 'Catch him, Michael!'

Nick was already there as the stocky boy's knees buckled. With Gil's assistance he got the dead weight over to the stair and folded it up on to the bottom step beside

56

the younger Ross, who scrambled out of the way, looking alarmed.

'Loose his collar,' recommended someone.

'A key down his back.'

'That's for nosebleeds. Cold water on his neck.'

'Be the first time in months,' someone else muttered.

Maister Kennedy, ably thrusting Ninian's head down, said, 'I heard that, Walter. Maister Cunningham, can you go up and speak to the Dean and Principal? Michael, give a hand here. Lowrie, you know the prayers we should be saying for William. Will you begin, please?'

When Gil came down the stairs again, with the Dean and the Principal following him, the students were not visible, but the door to the Bachelors' Schule was ajar, and a low hum of prayers floated out. Gil, reflecting on his uncle's dictum that teachers are born, not made, led the way to the inner courtyard. Behind him, Maister Doby was still exclaiming distressfully.

'I cannot believe it to be murder. Are you not mistaken, Gilbert, and it is merely some accident? And why should the boy be here, in the coalhouse? Oh, it is all deplorable.'

'John,' said the Dean in Scots, peering into the shadows at the body. 'Haud yer wheesht.' He stepped cautiously closer, holding his fine silk gown away from the gritty floor. 'Aye, poor laddie. John, this is certainly murder.'

'No a mischance?'

'It canny be any kind of mischance,' said Gil, understanding the anxious tone. 'See, the buckle of the belt lies at the back of his neck. Somebody else did that to him, and did it deliberately.'

'Aye. I see.' Maister Doby bent his head, briefly.

Behind him in the vaulted passage, Patrick Coventry said suddenly, 'Should we close the yett? Whoever did this may still be in the college.'

'I asked the Steward to order it closed,' Gil said. 'But there is the Blackfriars gate, and the Arthurlie yett. The college is hardly secure.'

'Well,' said the Dean. He emerged from the coalhouse,

and turned the key in the lock. 'That puts paid to the Montgomery gift, I fear, John.'

'I doubt you're right, Patrick.'

'We must inform the Faculty,' continued the Dean, setting off across the courtyard with his black silk sleeves streaming behind him, 'and our colleagues in Law and Theology. We must also inform the Chancellor.'

'What, now?' said Maister Doby, hurrying after him. The Dean glanced at him and paused thoughtfully.

'You mean, I take it,' he said, 'that we should hesitate to disturb the Archbishop more often than strictly necessary.'

'Aye. Forbye I think he's at Stirling the now, with the King,' added the Principal. 'The messenger might as well wait till we've something better to send.'

'Aye,' said Dean Elphinstone in his turn. He looked at the key in his hand. 'Whose is this?'

'It is mine,' said Maister Coventry.

In the Fore Hall, most of the Masters who had been present at the feast still sat talking. The harper was playing quietly, cups of spiced wine were still circulating, but the sweetmeats appeared to be finished. As the Dean appeared, conversation faltered, and those who followed him walked into a spreading silence. Behind Gil, Maister Kennedy and the cast of the play entered and clustered in a knot by the door. The young man Ninian looked ill but seemed in control of himself, his friends on either side of him. Another boy had certainly been weeping; even the gap-toothed Walter seemed subdued.

The Dean stepped on to the dais and nodded significantly to John Shaw the Steward, who took up position in front of him and thumped his great staff three times on the floor to attract attention.

'Silence for the Dean,' he commanded unnecessarily, bowed and stepped aside. The Dean's blue gaze swept the hall. Gil moved back against the wall and watched the faces. Old Tommy Forsyth, anxious beneath his felt cap. David Gray still in his dazed state, with a faint dawning of – was it relief? Archie Crawford, the Faculty's blue-jowled man of law, frowning critically. The harper and his sister, intent and concerned, the harper's strange mood dissipated as his sister had predicted now that the body had been found.

'*Horribile dictu*,' began the Dean, and Gil, despite himself, felt a twinge of amusement. The phrase was used as an example in grammar schools all over the educated world, and he had never thought to hear it spoken in earnest. But what the Dean was recounting in his measured Latin was indeed horrible to relate.

In the buzz of shocked conversation which greeted the announcement, Maister Forsyth rose from his seat and bowed formally.

'Dean,' he said. 'This is a dreadful thing which has happened.' Many people nodded agreement. 'Nevertheless, it is a deed committed by human hand. It is incumbent upon us to find the perpetrator and render justice to our dead fellow. The Faculty must act, and soon, to name one or more people to be responsible for this solemn duty.'

Maister Crawford rose in his turn, to stand small and neat staring across the width of the dais at the Dean.

'Is it not rather,' he began, 'the duty of the Faculty to report this deplorable deed to the Chancellor, Robert our Archbishop? This having been done, he may consider the facts and name some one of our number to be *quaestor*.'

'He's feart the Faculty would pick him,' said Patrick Coventry in Scots at Gil's side.

'You can tell,' agreed Gil, grinning.

Maister Doby was explaining that the Chancellor was in Stirling with the King when he was interrupted.

'*Magistri, scholastici*.' McIan had risen to his feet. 'I ask leave to speak. There is one here,' he continued without waiting for permission, his Highland accent very strong, 'has won justice already for the woman dear to me, murdered in secret in St Mungo's yard.' The outflung hand indicated Gil's direction. *He heard me answer Patrick Coventry just now*, thought Gil. 'He is careful and discreet and a member of your community. I commend him to you.'

*   *   *

'There was some debate,' said Gil to Maister Peter Mason. 'But eventually it was agreed. Then I asked permission to send for you, and my clothes.'

He bundled cope and cassock together, put them down on the bench of Maister Kennedy's reading-desk, and began to lace himself into his doublet.

'I appreciate your wish for my support,' said his prospective father-in-law. 'I think,' he added. He inspected the bench, appeared to decide it would take his weight, and sat down cautiously, his short black beard jutting against the light from the open window. 'The more so, indeed, as the baby has refused the infallible remedy and is still crying. Alys was a good child,' he added reflectively. 'I had forgotten how fatiguing a crying baby is to listen to. What must we do, then? What have you set in motion?'

'I have someone making a list of all those who were present at the feast,' said Gil, 'and what each of them claims he did after the end of the play. That is urgent, I thought. We can hardly imprison the entire Faculty of Arts until we find justice for William.'

'You are certain it was someone at the feast?'

'No,' Gil admitted. 'There are the members of other faculties, there are the students who couldn't afford the necessary contribution for the feast, there are the college servants. The Blackfriars have access to the college without going past the porter at the yett.'

'I remember the porter,' said the mason, pulling a face. 'And I have done some repairs to the Blackfriars gate. It leads into the kitchen-yard, not so? Do you suspect them?'

'We must suspect everybody.' Gil shrugged on his short gown and lifted the master's bonnet to which the Dean had taken exception. 'Come and view the corpse. I have a lantern now.'

Maistre Pierre, confronted by the gruesome scene in the coalhouse, contemplated it in silence for a short time, swinging his Sunday beads in one big hand, then remarked, 'There have been too many people across this floor. I suppose the kitchen must want coals several times a day, but I see more than one pair of feet here.'

Gil nodded. 'So I thought. At least I prevented them moving the body.' He peered round. 'If he was killed in here I would expect more sign, nevertheless. There are all these tracks from the door to where he lies, and those are my prints from when I opened the window. Someone bound his hands and then strangled him, but his feet were free, and all students play football, he could have kicked hard, or run away, or put up some sort of struggle, and I see no sign.'

'Was he perhaps attacked by more than one person?'

'It's possible, but I would expect to see sign of that too. I wonder if he was killed elsewhere and then put here.'

'I agree,' said the mason after a moment. 'These are the prints of whoever carried him in here. Look, there is one as he stepped round to this side of the heap of coals. A pity they are so scuffed. But why? Why move him here?'

'For secrecy?'

'It was not secret for long.'

'Long enough, perhaps.'

'He was last seen alive at the end of the play, you say?' said Maistre Pierre thoughtfully. 'How long ago was that?'

'More than two hours since.' Gil was feeling the swollen face. 'He's cold, and beginning to set. It is cold in here under the vault, and the shutters were closed. He would cool quite fast.'

'Should we unbind his hands?'

'I want to move him into the light first.' Gil reached for the lantern. 'Take note of how he lies, Pierre.'

William was sprawled on his left side, his bound hands awkwardly in the pit of his belly, his head tipped back and the dreadful distorted face turned towards the light from the window. The right arm was cocked up so that a darn in the elbow of the blue gown showed. His legs, half-flexed under the skirt of the gown, ended in a pair of expensive-looking boots.

'How do we move him? And to where?'

Two college servants and a hurdle saw the corpse removed from the coalhouse and set down in the court-yard, the dreadful face covered by a cloth begged from the kitchen. A small crowd gathered immediately, commenting with interest on the spectacle. It included some of the kitchen hands and also Maister Forsyth, who stepped forward at the same moment as the Dominican chaplain emerged from the pend that led to the kitchen-yard.

'Will you be long, Gilbert?' he asked. 'It is urgent that Father Bernard and I begin the Act of Conditional Absolution, you understand.'

'Not long, sir,' said Gil. 'Could you perhaps . . .?' He waved at the crowd, and Maister Forsyth nodded and turned to make shooing motions which were largely ignored. Gil bent over the corpse, considering the white dust caked on the blue wool of the gown, and sniffed.

'Pierre, do you smell cumin?'

'Cumin?' Maistre Pierre stepped closer. 'I do. Not strong, but – was there a dish with cumin at the feast?'

'Not at our table, we had rabbit and ground almonds and a couple of flans. Perhaps one of the other tables. That might be it.'

'Now we loose his hands?' prompted the mason.

They rolled the limp body over on the hurdle to get access to the buckle, and eased it free. The boy's bony wrists were marked where the coils of leather had dug in. Gil turned them carefully, looked at the small neat hands, pushed up the sleeves to look at the forearms.

The mason, working on the unpleasant task of unfastening the other belt, remarked, 'His gown is dry on the shoulders. He has not, I think, been out in the rain lately.'

'Interesting,' said Gil. 'The hem is damp, at the back only, here where the scorch marks are, and there is coal-dust on one elbow and something white on the other.'

'And on the skirt of his gown,' said Maistre Pierre, looking along the length of the garment.

'And these boots are scuffed on the toes.'

'Many people scuff their toes.'

'The boots are quite new and otherwise well cared for.' Gil took the belt from the corpse's wrists, a well-worn strap of ordinary cowhide with a cheap buckle, tried it round the waist of the gown, then rolled it up and put it in the breast of his doublet.

The other belt had sunk deeply into the swollen flesh of throat and neck and required to be coaxed, but finally came free. To judge by the mark on the leather it belonged to someone of heavier build than the first one, but it was otherwise just as unremarkable. Gil measured it likewise against the corpse's waist, then examined the length of it closely, to muttered comments from the group of onlookers.

'Why's he doing that?'

'College canny afford a bloodhound.'

'Pierre, will you take this?' Gil said, handing it over. 'We need to keep the two belts separate, I think. I wonder where his purse is?' He patted the breast of the faded blue gown, but found nothing. 'That is odd,' he added, searching more carefully. 'I'll swear he had a purse earlier.'

'Is there anything else to learn from him?' asked the mason, sitting back on his heels.

'I don't think so.' Gil turned the empurpled face to look at it. 'Perhaps I spoke too soon. Look at this.'

'What is it?'

Gil touched the mark carefully. 'Aye, the skin's split. The flesh is much swollen but I think the jaw must be about there.'

' Someone has fetched him a blow.' The mason made an involuntary movement with one fist.

'I think so. You know, that's a relief. It's possible he was dazed or unconscious when he was throttled. I must ask someone that he shouldn't be stripped until we can be present.' Gil got to his feet, looking round for Maister Forsyth, who hurried forward followed by a student with a censer and another with holy water and an asperger. 'Now we have to report to the Principal.'

*   *   *

The Dean, the Principal and the two men of law were in the Principal's house, where the great chamber was hung with painted cloths depicting various learned men as bearded worthies in academic robes. In front of a long-nosed Socrates receiving a scroll from Philosophia herself, Maister Doby waved them to padded stools and said anxiously, 'Well, Gilbert, what can ye tell us?'

'Little more yet,' said Gil. 'We are both certain it is murder rather than any sort of accident, but beyond that –'

'The belt about his neck must belong to someone,' said the Dean in incisive Latin. 'Find the owner and we have found the culprit.'

'The belt about his neck may be his own,' said Gil. 'However I agree that the other may very probably lead us to the malefactor.'

'But can we offer a better scent to the hounds?' asked Maistre Pierre in French. 'Did the young man have enemies?'

'At least one, clearly.' Archie Crawford still wore the critical frown. 'What do you mean, very probably? I should have said it was a certainty.'

'He means, Archibald, that the malefactor might have used the property of another,' said Maister Doby kindly. 'What must you do next, Gilbert? How should the Faculty help you?'

'Tell me about the dead boy,' Gil invited.

There was a brief stillness, in which he was aware of powerful minds working; then the Dean said firmly, 'An able student, an ornament to the college. Learning has lost one of her dearest sons.'

'That will sound well in the letter to his family.' Gil looked from face to face. 'Was he really that able? The impression I had, seeing him today, was of someone a little too clever for his own good.'

A flicker of something like agreement crossed Maister Doby's expression, but the Dean said, 'How can one be too clever?'

'What are the facts, then?' said Gil. 'Who was he? Was he an Ayrshire man, as the surname suggests?'

'He was a bastard,' said David Gray suddenly and ambiguously.

'His mother, it seems, is an Ayrshire lady now married to another,' said the Dean, 'and his father is a kinsman of Lord Montgomery.'

'Supported by the Montgomerys? In their favour?'

'Yes,' said the Dean, as if the word tasted bad. 'And well supported.'

'A rich bastard,' qualified Maister Gray. He still seemed dazed, like a man who can hardly believe what fortune has brought to him. Good fortune or bad? Gil wondered.

'Certainly there has been no shortage of drinksilver,' agreed the Principal.

'What, actual silver?' said Gil in surprise. 'Not meal or salt fish like the rest of us?'

'Oh, that as well,' said the Dean. 'But he has always seemed to have coin.'

'And more of it lately,' said Maister Doby in thoughtful tones.

'Was he liked? Who were his friends?'

There was another of those pauses.

'He had no particular friends, I thought,' said the Principal with reluctance. 'When he was a bejant he roomed with his kinsman Robert, and Ralph Gibson, and they were mentored by Lawrence Livingstone and his friends, but I do not think he has –'

'What friends are those?' Gil asked. 'Of the boy Livingstone, I mean.'

'Ninian Boyd and Michael Douglas,' said the Principal. 'Ninian played Diligence very well, I thought. I wish he knew the meaning of the word in his studies.'

'Ah,' said Gil. 'Michael must be my godfather's youngest. I thought I knew that jaw. A Livingstone, a Boyd, a Douglas – what a conspiracy!'

'Indeed, I do not think that can be right, Gilbert,' said the Principal seriously.

'William spends – spent time with Robert Montgomery,'

the Dean interposed, 'and with Ralph Gibson, poor creature. Either of these may tell you more than his teachers.'

'Did he still share a chamber with them?' Gil asked.

'He did not,' said Maister Doby, shaking his head. 'Sooner than share his good fortune with them, whatever its source, he has withdrawn from his friends this year. He has a room here in the Outer Close. John Shaw assures me all is paid for.'

'And yet his legitimate kinsman has a shared chamber in the older part of the building,' said Gil.

'I told you he was a bastard,' said David Gray. Gil looked at him, and wondered if he was sober. Certainly his narrow face was flushed, the colour contrasting unbecomingly with the red hood still rolled down about his neck.

'Where did the money come from?' asked Maistre Pierre.

'From his home, I suppose,' said the Principal. 'He had no benefice or prebend as yet. Where else would he get money?'

'Was there money on him?' asked Maister Crawford. 'Maybe he was robbed.'

'By a fellow student?' said the Principal, shocked. 'Surely not!'

'Don't be daft, John. One of the servants, maybe, or some passing –'

'It was hardly a passing robber,' said the Dean, 'that left him locked in the coalhouse. And I hope our servants are more conscious of the good of the college than –' He stopped, apparently unwilling to finish the sentence.

'Do you wish to ask us anything else,' demanded Maister Crawford, 'or can we get on with our own business?'

'I have two further questions,' Gil admitted. 'In the first place, when William rose at the Faculty meeting –'

'I have no idea,' said the Dean firmly. 'I know neither what prompted him to speak nor what the matters were of which he spoke.'

'Ask his friends,' said Maister Crawford.

'He hinted at heresy and peculation,' Gil said. 'These are both matters of some importance. Could he have mis-interpreted something?'

'I have no idea,' said the Dean again. 'And the other question?'

'I must ask this of everybody, you understand,' Gil said. They watched him with varying expressions: Maister Gray wary, Maister Crawford still critical, the Principal with the intent look of a teacher with a good student, the Dean clearly formulating his answer already. 'After the end of the play, where were you all before returning to the Fore Hall? And who was with you?'

'Most of the senior members came here to the Principal's house,' said the Dean promptly. 'The four of us now present, Maister Forsyth, Maister Coventry –'

'Not Patrick Coventry,' said the Principal. 'He and Nicholas went over to the Arthurlie building. You were with them, Gilbert, were you not?'

'We were here perhaps a quarter-hour,' the Dean continued, 'in this room or near it, standing or walking about, until Maister Shaw came to inform us that the procession was re-forming. Is that what you wish to know?'

'Were you all within sight of one another for most of that time?'

The four men exchanged glances, and nodded.

'I should say we were,' pronounced the Dean.

'Would you swear to it if necessary?'

There was another of those pauses.

'I should swear to it,' agreed the Dean.

Chapter Four

'They were lying,' said Maistre Pierre positively. 'Oh, not about where they were, I think we can accept that, but they know more about the dead than they would tell us.'

'I agree.' Gil stopped in the inner courtyard, looking about him. 'Maybe if I speak to them separately I'll learn more. But before that we need to look at William's chamber, which seems to be locked from what one of the boys said, and I think I want a look at the limehouse. We must also talk to those three senior bachelors, and to the two boys named as William's friends, even if one of them is a Montgomery.'

'Did you say you had ordered the yett shut?' asked the mason.

'Aye, and we'll need to let it open soon. Once Maister Coventry has finished that list I asked him for, we can let folk go.'

'Then do you go and inspect the limehouse and I will find out the young man's chamber.' Maistre Pierre looked about, and caught the eye of one of the numerous students who somehow happened to be crossing the courtyard. 'You, my friend, may guide me! Where did your lamented fellow pursue his studies?'

'Eh?' said the boy.

'William's chamber, you clown!' said the next student. 'It's in the Outer Close, maister. I'll show you, will I?'

Gil, retrieving the lantern from the coalhouse, lit the candle in it with the flint in his purse and unbarred the next door. Behind it was a similar vaulted chamber, unwindowed and smelling sharply and cleanly of limewash.

Neatly ordered sacks were ranged against the walls, several wooden buckets and paintbrushes sat on a board near the door, and a fine sifting of white powder lay on everything. In it were displayed a great confusion of footprints, particularly immediately in front of the door. As Gil peered into the shadows, the light from the courtyard was cut off behind him.

'The chamber is locked indeed,' said the mason.

'We'll find someone with a key.' Gil stood aside so that the other man could see past him. 'Look at this.'

'But he was not here, was he?'

'I don't know about that. I thought one group of searchers expected to find him here.' Gil stepped carefully in over the dusty floor. 'These prints are theirs. No, look, Pierre, this is quite clear. Some large object has been put down here, in the centre of the floor, and then moved.'

'I see,' agreed Maistre Pierre, following him in. 'But I can make no sense of the footprints. There are quite simply too many. This is a good dry store,' he added approvingly. 'The walls are excellent work. What have you seen?'

Gil bent, directing the light from the lantern at the floor near one pile of sacks.

'I don't know,' he said after a moment. 'Can you see something? It isn't a footprint, I would say.'

'A smudge,' said the mason. 'Someone put his hand or his knee to the floor.'

'I wonder.' Gil hunkered down, staring at the shapeless print in the dust. 'William's purse is missing. I know it was on his belt earlier, for I saw it –'

'The belt which was used to strangle him,' said the mason intelligently.

'Precisely. Was there anything valuable in the purse? Why should it be thrown on the floor?'

'Whoever removed the belt in order to strangle the boy must have drawn it out of the purse-latches,' offered the mason, with a gesture to demonstrate, 'and discarded the purse.'

'Why is it no longer here?'

69

'All good questions,' said Maistre Pierre. 'You think that is the mark of the purse?'

'It could be.' Gil stood up and looked around him. 'I must speak to the Principal, or perhaps the Steward. This store must be searched. The purse may be here, behind one of these sacks.'

'I can do that.' The mason stepped carefully towards the door. 'I have worked with John Shaw, we are good friends. He will send two or three of the college servants if I ask him. What will you do? Seek a key to the boy's chamber, or –?'

'No, we should both see that.' Gil was still studying their surroundings. 'I think I will question those senior bachelors.'

Another of the many passing students directed Gil up the wheel stair just beyond the kitchen. It led past one of the doors of the Laigh Hall, where four tonsured Theology students were debating a fine point of exegesis over bread and stewed kale. As Gil climbed on up, someone said, 'But Wycliff –' and was instantly hushed.

At the top of the stair he came to a narrow landing with two doors. Voices murmured behind one. He knocked, and after a moment footsteps approached. The door opened a crack, and one alarmed eye examined him.

'I think you need to talk to me,' he said. The eye vanished, as its owner turned his head to look at the other occupants of the room. 'I'm alone,' he added reassuringly.

'Let him in,' said a strained voice.

'Ninian –' expostulated the boy at the door.

'I better tell someone,' said Ninian. 'Come in, maister.'

The room was large, stretching the full width of the attic, but four small study-spaces had been partitioned off with lath-and-plaster panels, and the remnant was a very awkward shape and had only two windows. By one of them the mousy-haired boy sat on a stool hugging his knees; he did not rise as Gil entered. Lowrie the fair-haired tenor closed the door, saying, 'We don't have a chair for a visitor, maister, but this is the best stool.'

'I'll sit on the bench,' said Gil, moving to the other window. Three pairs of eyes watched apprehensively as he settled himself. 'Good day to you, Michael. And how is your father?'

'He's well,' said Michael, startled back into civility. 'Is madam your mother well, maister?'

'She is, and like to be in Glasgow soon.'

'Will you have some ale, maister? I think we've got some ale,' offered Lowrie, apparently accepting the social nature of the visit.

'It's finished,' said Ninian hoarsely.

Gil looked from Michael, now twirling the turnbutton on the shutter, to Lowrie, still standing by the door, and then at Ninian huddled in blankets in the bed.

'Three of the enemies of the Crown,' he said, straight-faced. 'It must be a conspiracy.'

They stared at him.

'I think that was before we were born, maister,' said Michael eventually. 'In James Second's time, maybe. This is just us.'

'And our wee bittie problem,' said Lowrie.

'Tell me about it,' Gil invited.

'How much do you ken, maister?' asked Lowrie.

'Quite a bit,' countered Gil. 'Which of you hit him? Where was he then?'

'It was me that hit him,' said Ninian, shivering. 'He was there.' He nodded at one of the little study-spaces. 'I was angry at him already, the way he clarted up the fight scene in the play, and then I came up to move my Aristotle when the rain started, and there he was, in Michael's carrel, where he'd no right to be, speiring at things that don't concern him. I shouted at him, and he did that trick of looking down his nose and strolling off, like a cat on a wall. So I hit him, and he fell down, and hit his head on the stool. Then the other two came in.'

'That's right,' said Lowrie, and Michael nodded.

'And then you put him in the limehouse,' prompted Gil,

as the conversation died. They looked at each other in what seemed like relief.

'That was my idea,' said Lowrie.

'Didn't he argue?' Gil asked.

'He wasn't stirring,' said Lowrie. 'So we tied his wrists with Miggel's belt and got him down the stairs, between the three of us, and round to the limehouse.'

'With Michael's belt? Why did you not use his own?'

'We'd have had enough snash from him as it was,' said Lowrie frankly. 'If we'd damaged his property he'd certainly have complained to Dobbin. Much better to use one of ours.'

'We'd never have got it back,' said Michael, as if continuing an argument. 'I suppose we canny have it back now, maister? No, I thought not.'

'How did you carry him?' Gil asked. 'Did nobody else see you?'

'They had a leg each and I had his shoulders,' said Ninian, in surprised tones. 'That's why we tied his wrists. And everyone else in the Inner Close was all gone back to the feast, and the Elect were in the Law Schule waiting for Father Bernard, so there was none to see us. Maister, he wasny deid when we left him!' he burst out. 'He was stirring and gruntling like he was drunk, so we left him lying on his side. He wasny deid then!'

'Which side was he lying on?'

They exchanged glances, and Michael mimed the position.

'His right side,' he said. 'Aye, the right side. He wasny deid then,' he echoed.

'And where did you put him?' Gil asked carefully.

'Just lying in the middle of the limehouse,' said Ninian.

'No hidden or anything,' elaborated Lowrie. 'Anyone that opened the door would see him there. Likely they'd hear him too,' he added.

'And what did you do with his purse?'

'His purse?' repeated Ninian.

'Damn,' said Michael. 'We should have checked that.

72

He'd aye paper, or his bonny wee set of tablets to make notes on. Tod, did you –?'

'Not I,' said Lowrie, and added politely to Gil, 'I don't think we touched his purse.'

'So you left him in the limehouse.' All three nodded. 'And you're sure nobody else saw you?'

'We took good care nobody saw us,' Michael pointed out.

'I wondered,' said Ninian, 'how much Bendy Stewart saw, or maybe heard. You mind, he followed us across the close, and we were talking about it?'

'I never saw him,' said Lowrie. 'You told us to curb the bummle, I mind that.'

'I saw him,' said Michael. 'But we were nearly at the pend before he came into the Inner Close from the kitchen-yard. He wouldny see where we'd been. How much he heard I don't know either.'

'And why did you shut William in the limehouse? Why there? Why not the coalhouse?'

'The kitchen's aye after more coal,' said Michael. 'He'd have been found in no time.'

'But why shut him in at all?'

'So we could bar him in,' said Lowrie after a moment. 'I don't know why the limehouse has that bar on the door, but I thought we could –' He stopped, reddening. 'It seems a daft idea now. I thought we'd get at the sweetmeats in the Fore Hall before he did, and I thought and all that we'd get him into trouble for once. If he never turned up to get his reward for the play the Dean would be displeased, and he wasn't best pleased wi him already after the meeting. I never meant –'

'But surely,' said Gil, 'he had only to tell the Dean why he was not present?'

'But then we would tell the Dean why we locked him up,' Lowrie explained.

'It would never have worked,' said Michael suddenly. He had a surprisingly deep voice. 'He could wammle out of anything, kale-worm that he was.'

'He was not popular?' Gil asked innocently.

'He had friends,' Lowrie said. 'Robert Montgomery, Ralph Gibson.'

'Not friends I would choose,' said Ninian, sucking his knuckles.

'But you didn't like him,' Gil prompted. They eyed him carefully, and said nothing. 'Did he often look at things that did not concern him?'

'No,' said Ninian.

'Yes,' said Lowrie at the same moment.

'He was aye poking at my books,' said Michael. 'Him and Robert and that Ralph were on the same landing as us, see, last year when they were bejants. We were mentoring them,' he added, pulling a face. 'Ralph and Robert was all right, but William thought he should have free run of everything we owned. I've not seen my Aristotle since last summer.'

'What was he looking for?'

'He looked,' said Lowrie, 'for secrets. Things you would rather weren't known. Everyone has things he'd rather weren't known.'

'I haveny,' said Michael, raising his pointed chin.

'Except for Michael, everyone has things they'd rather weren't known,' amended Lowrie. 'And the dear departed went round ferreting them out. He wrote them down. *With pen and ink to report all readie.*'

'He did, too,' said Michael rather sharply.

'And then he'd come privately and ask you what it was worth not to tell Dobbin.'

'I see,' said Gil evenly. 'And did he make any profit from this scaffery?'

'That's the word!' said Ninian.

'No from me, he never,' said Lowrie firmly.

'Was that why Dobbin wanted you last week?' said Michael.

Lowrie grinned. 'Aye. Dear William found my uncle's notes and when I wouldny pay up he went and told Dobbin my ideas weren't my own. He hadn't read the notes properly. They were from old Tommy's lectures on Aristotle, in about 1472, and I'll swear Tommy gave the identical lectures last winter. I showed them to Dobbin, and he agreed with me. Not that he said so, but you could tell. And of course Dobbin taught my uncles at the grammar school at Peebles before he came here. Before they all came here,' he amended. 'Separately.'

'We get the idea,' said Michael.

'Do you know if William made a habit of this?' Gil asked.

'He made a good living from it,' said Lowrie roundly, 'for I saw him.'

'*Of wikkit and evil lyf, of tyranny and crimynous lyfing*. Good enough to pay for a chamber to himself in the Outer Close?' suggested Gil. 'Or do you suppose he had some kind of hold over Maister Shaw?'

'I've no idea how much he won,' said Lowrie, 'though I'd guess it was silver rather than copper, but if you want to know who else he was putting the black on, you'll have to ask around yourself. Maister,' he added with belated civility, and straightened his shoulders so that his faded blue gown creaked.

'Fair enough,' said Gil. 'Ninian?'

'He saw me in the town,' said Ninian, reddening. 'One night I hadn't leave to be out.'

'Ning!' said Lowrie sharply. 'You never gied him money?'

'No, I never!' returned Ninian. 'I gied him my notes on Auld Nick's Peter of Spain lectures.'

'Was that all?' Gil asked.

Ninian looked uncomfortable. 'He was wanting more,' he admitted. 'He'd asked me for a sack of meal.'

'Ambitious,' said Gil. 'Would you have given it to him?'

'Maybe,' said Ninian. 'But maybe I'd just take my chance. Dobbin's fair, if you plead guilty. It would have been a beating, maybe, or a week's loss of privilege. A sack of meal was too much. I hadn't answered him yet.'

'Michael?'

'I've no secrets,' said Michael flatly.

Gil waited, but Ninian burst out again with, 'Maister,

what came to him? Was it the bang on the heid? Why was he in the coalhouse?'

'It was not the bang on the head,' Gil said firmly, 'or the blow to the jaw. That was not what killed him, Ninian.'

Ninian stared at him, sucking his knuckles again. Then he relaxed, sighing.

'So it wasn't me that killed him,' he said, and scrubbed at his eyes. 'But how did he get in the coalhouse?'

'That is what I would like to know,' Gil said. 'Show me your feet,' he said suddenly to Lowrie, who gaped at him, then closed his mouth and turned up the soles of his boots one at a time to the light.

'No coal, I hope,' he said lightly.

'No coal,' Gil agreed. 'There's lime on the hem of your gown –' He stopped, recalling the hem of William's gown. Quicklime and damp wool – that would account for the scorch marks.

'Mine too,' said Michael gruffly.

'Mine are on the kist yonder, maister.' Ninian nodded across the room. Gil stooped to inspect Michael's boots, then made his way round the great box of the bed. As he lifted Ninian's downtrodden footwear heavy steps pounded on the stair, and there was a hammering at the door.

'Lowrie! Lowrie Livingstone! Is Maister Cunningham there? He's wanted!'

Lowrie opened the door. Two students were on the landing, and eager footsteps suggested more on the stair. The nearest, the irrepressible Walter, said urgently, 'Maister, can you come quick?'

'There's something in William's chamber,' said the boy behind Walter.

'It's a ghaist,' said Walter. 'We heard it!'

'If it's no the deil himself,' said someone on the stairs.

'That's nonsense,' said Gil firmly.

'We heard it!' said Walter again. 'It's wailing and girning like the Green Lady. Come and hear for yirsel, maister!'

'I do not believe William's ghost can be in his chamber,'

76

said Gil, 'much less the deil himself. Why should the devil be in William's chamber?'

'I could tell you that,' muttered Michael.

'But we heard it, maister! Please will you come and listen?'

'Why were you at his chamber door anyway?' asked Lowrie. 'You lodge here in the Inner Close, no out-by.'

'Billy Ross went with a message from Maister Doby,' said Walter virtuously, 'and heard the noise on the way past, so he cam and tellt us and we all went and we heard it an' all. Will you come, maister? There's certainly something there, for I heard it.'

'We all did,' said someone on the stairs. 'It goes Ooo-oo.'

'That's foolishness!' said Gil. 'How can a ghost make a noise like a screech-owl? Walter, what is a ghost, tell me that?'

'A ghost is the spirit of a dead man,' said Walter nervously, clearly quoting something.

'It has no body, has it?' Walter shook his head. 'So how can it make a noise? Whatever is making a noise, it must be something in possession of a body.'

'Aye, the deil,' said a voice on the stairs.

'All of you,' said Gil. 'Go and ask Maister Coventry and Maister Kennedy, if they have finished the list I asked them for, to meet me in a quarter-hour at William's chamber door. Can you mind that?'

Walter repeated the message in a rush, nodded, and thudded off down the stairs. The boy behind him reiterated, 'There's something in William's chamber, maister, for we heard it!'

'All of you,' said Gil again. 'In a quarter-hour, by William's chamber.'

He shut the door on the departing crowd and turned to the three senior bachelors.

'Ninian, are you wearing your belt?' he asked.

'Aye,' said Ninian, pushing back the blankets to display the item.

'May I see it?'

The belt was old, and had clearly been worn by Ninian as he filled out, for a succession of holes had been stretched by the buckle. The most recent was easy to identify, but the older ones were beginning to close up as the leather itself stretched. Gil, concluding that the belt was Ninian's and nobody else's, handed it back.

'Have you any other belt?' he asked.

'We have a spare,' Lowrie said. 'Where is it, Miggel?'

'In your carrel,' said Michael. A brief search uncovered the spare belt in Ninian's kist. Gil inspected it for the sake of the thing, though his aim had been only to locate the object, and handed it to Michael, who put it on.

'Two more questions,' he said.

'Don't you want to see my belt?' asked Lowrie.

'I can see it from here. What did you eat at the feast?'

'I never ate,' said Michael. 'I wasn't hungry. Besides, I had to get painted up for the play.'

'I had a mouthful of flan,' said Lowrie indignantly, 'and then Bendy Stewart came along fussing about me spoiling my voice. I got some wine, though,' he added.

'Snoddy Tod,' said Ninian tolerantly. 'I had rabbit stew, and foul it was, too. She'd put ground almonds to it.'

'And the other question?' prompted Lowrie.

'You mentioned the meeting. When William rose –'

'God, that was funny,' said Ninian, whose spirits were improving by the moment. 'Did you see all their faces? And old Tod Lowrie here waiting to speak.'

'It was not funny,' said Lowrie. 'I spent hours getting that speech by heart. It might have gone right out of my head, with William interrupting me like that.'

'What did he say again?' said Gil, who remembered perfectly well.

'*What if another of the college's sons has misused her money,*' quoted Michael, in excellent imitation of William's clearly enunciated Latin, '*or has inculcated heretical beliefs in her students?*'

'What did he mean?' wondered Ninian.

'Exactly,' said Gil. 'Who was it intended for?'

'Hanged if I know,' said Lowrie. 'I thought by his

expression it was a shot at someone, not just random unpleasantness, if you see what I mean, but I don't know who.'

'One of the Elect?' said Michael.

'I doubt it,' said Lowrie. 'Bendy Stewart would root out heresy in his students if they even sniffed it, I'd have thought.'

'I don't think we know, maister,' Ninian said to Gil.

'Are you going to see after this ghost?' Lowrie asked.

'I am,' Gil agreed. 'But you three are not coming with me.'

'How not?' said Ninian.

'We have to go and confess,' said Lowrie heavily. 'Who should we tell, maister?'

'Either Maister Doby or Maister Coventry,' advised Gil. 'And if I were you I should offer it as sacramental confession. They are both priested, either of them can hear you.'

'Yes,' said Lowrie, scuffing thoughtfully at the floor-boards with his toe. 'Yes, it's perjury, isn't it? We've broken the oath about brotherhood and amity.'

'He started it,' said Ninian.

'No defence,' said Michael. He got to his feet, and braced himself. 'Come out of your burrow, Ning. Better get it over with.'

'I offer my sympathy in advance,' said Gil. 'I'll speak to you again.'

As Gil reached the courtyard, the bulky form of the mason emerged round the kitchen stair, followed by three of the college servants dusting at their clothes. Sighting Gil, he made his way to meet him, grinning.

'Success!' he proclaimed. 'Thank you, all of you, that is all!' Coins changed hands and the men went off, looking less gloomy. 'Here it is. It was hidden behind the sacks, as you thought.'

He held out a plain leather purse, somewhat greasy. Gil took it, and weighed it.

'It is not empty,' agreed Maistre Pierre. 'I have not looked, I kept it to show to you.'

'It doesn't feel like a key,' said Gil, loosening the strings. He tipped the contents jingling into his palm.

'Well, well,' said Maistre Pierre. Gil sorted the coins.

'Two, two and a half – three merks in silver, and several groats. A total of two pounds and eighteen pence Scots,' he said, 'simply carried about in his purse. And this.' He pushed the little set of tablets along his fingers.

'I use tablets when I am working,' observed the mason, 'but I should have thought these too small to be much use for taking notes.'

'He had a small hand,' said Gil, 'and there are several leaves.' He shook the purse. 'Is there anything – ah!'

White flakes fell to the flagstones. The mason pounced, and came up with two pieces of paper, one folded into a long curling spill, one wadded square.

'What have we here?' he said, and unfolded the long piece.

Tiny writing, in ink, covered one side and half of the other.

'It is notes of some sort,' said the mason after a moment. 'What does it say?'

'*M will be in G,*' Gil read, taking the much-creased sheet. 'He believed in making full use of the paper, didn't he? *H passed through for Irvine.* I wonder who H and M might be?'

'Friends of the boy's? And why ever fold it like this?'

'Who knows? What of the other piece?'

Maistre Pierre unfolded the thick square.

'It makes no sense,' he complained.

Gil peered over his shoulder, tucking the coins back in the purse.

'You're right,' he said. 'It's in some kind of code.'

'Certainly no language that I know.'

'A game of some sort?'

'He has sustained it well,' said the mason thoughtfully. 'It is a long passage to put into code, merely for a game.'

'Well, we can try to decode it, though I suspect it will take time. And the tablets.' Gil slipped the leather case off and turned the little block to admire it. 'Very pretty, with this chip-carving on the outside. What has he written down? *M will be in G* – it seems to be the original notes for the long piece of paper.'

'Why did he simply transcribe them?' Maistre Pierre wondered. 'More usual, surely, to expand – to say who he meant by M.'

Gil grunted absently, turning the little wooden leaves.

'What's this?' he said, tilting the last opening to read the tiny writing incised on the green wax. 'It looks like a will.'

'I thought you said he was a bastard,' said the mason.

'I did,' said Gil in puzzlement. 'He couldn't make a will. What does it say? *I, William Montgomery, sometime called William Irvine, being in my right mind and now able to make a will, commend my soul to Almighty God and direct that . . .* Whatever is he about?'

'It is not signed,' observed Maistre Pierre. 'Nor witnessed.'

'He would hardly get it witnessed still in the wax like this, even if it had any standing. His kin may take it as an instruction if they please, but if I know the Montgomery . . . He wishes his property divided equally between Ann Irvine, whoever she is, and Ralph Gibson. Poor boy,' he said thoughtfully. 'Was this fantasy? Or folly?'

'Should it be either?'

Gil tapped the frame of the tablet with a long forefinger.

'He is pretending, here, to be legitimate. Either it was a private game, committed to writing, or he was deluding himself into believing it.'

'Do not we all delude ourselves, at his age?' Maistre Pierre took the long spill of paper back and folded it carefully with the larger sheet. 'I myself was convinced from the ages of nine to twelve that I was of noble blood, snatched away at birth. I still remember the disappointment when I realized that I had no birthmark by which my true exalted parent could recognize me when I rescued him from drowning.' He laughed, the white teeth flashing in his neat beard. 'We lived, you understand, two hundred leagues from the sea.'

'I see where Alys gets her love of romance,' Gil commented. 'Come and see if Patrick Coventry's key will open the boy's chamber. There is something strange there.'

William's stair was easily identified by the huddle of students at its foot. As Gil and Maistre Pierre approached, first one boy and then another put his head in at the doorway and ducked out again grinning with bravado.

'What are you doing?' Gil asked, making his way through the group.

'Listening for the ghost, maister,' said Richie the Scholar.

'A ghost?' said the mason. 'In broad day?'

'There is no ghost,' Gil said. 'How can a spirit with no body make a noise?'

'Like the wind does?' said somebody else smartly.

'I heard it, maister,' said one of the Ross boys with pride. 'It went Ooo-oo.'

'You dreamed it,' said Gil. 'Stay down here, all of you.'

William's door was halfway up the stair, and therefore had only a narrow wedge of landing. Maister Coventry and Maister Kennedy were waiting there, still in formal academic dress, both with the appearance of men who would rather be elsewhere.

'Gil!' said Maister Kennedy. 'Thank God you're here. Listen to this – there is something in there.'

They listened.

'I hear nothing –' said the mason, but Patrick Coventry's upraised hand cut him off. Then they all heard it, through the heavy oak door: a high-pitched sobbing, unearthly, dying off in a wail. Gil felt the hairs stand up on the back of his neck.

'No mortal throat made that sound,' said Maistre Pierre through dry lips, and clutched at the crucifix on the end of his set of beads.

'Does that open this door?' Gil asked, looking at the key in the Second Regent's hand. For answer, the small man fitted it into the lock and turned it. The tumblers clicked round. Gil lifted the latch and pushed, and the door swung ponderously open.

'Christ aid!' said Maister Kennedy.

The room was in complete disarray. Books and clothing were strewn about, the bed-frame yawned emptily and mattress and blankets were tumbled in a heap, a lute lay under the table.

'Faugh!' exclaimed Maistre Pierre. 'What a stench!'

'Yes,' said Gil, relaxing. 'What a stench, indeed.'

He stepped into the room, placing his feet with care, and halted. The mason moved watchfully to stand at his back, saying, 'But what has happened here? Is this the work of devils? Is that why the stink –?'

Gil, surveying the wrecked room, said absently, 'No, I think not. Watch where you step, Pierre.' He moved forward as the two regents followed them, staring round. 'I think we can conclude,' he continued, 'that someone has found William's key and made good use of it.' He bent to lift the rustling mattress back into the bed-frame, and piled the blankets on top of it.

'He had many possessions, for such a young man,' said the mason, still watchful at Gil's back.

'And what in the name of all the saints was making that noise?' said Maister Coventry.

'That?' said Maister Kennedy in alarm.

They all looked where he was pointing. A heap of clothing lay under the window, a tawny satin doublet, a red cloth jerkin, several pairs of tangled hose. As they watched, the jerkin moved, apparently by itself. The high wailing began again, and something appeared from the cuff of the sleeve and became a grey hairy arm.

'Ah, the poor mite!' said Gil. Under the mason's horrified gaze he strode forward and lifted the clothing. The jerkin came up, swinging heavily, with a grey shaggy body squirming in its folds.

'*Mon Dieu*, what is it?' said the mason as a long-nosed face appeared through the unlaced armhole.

'A dog,' said Gil. 'At least, a puppy. Wolfhound, deerhound – one or the other. Some kind of hunting dog, certainly.'

He disengaged the animal from the garment and set it on its feet, a gangling knee-high creature consisting principally of shaggy legs and a long nose. It promptly abased itself, pawing appealingly at his boots. He bent to feel at its collar. 'Perhaps three or four months old, far too young to be wearing a good leather collar like this. That's the source of the stink,' he added. 'Watch where you put your feet. Bad dog,' he said to the pup, which flattened its ears and wagged its stringy tail, trying to excuse its lapse of manners.

'William should certainly not have been keeping a dog in his chamber,' said Maister Coventry.

'That's William for you,' said Nick Kennedy.

'Who do you suppose searched the place?' said Maistre Pierre, watching Gil soothing the dog. 'Was it the same person who killed the young man?'

'Quite possibly,' said Gil. 'But it was certainly the same person who hit this fellow over the head.' He lifted the pup again, its long legs dangling, and turned its head so that they could all see the blood clotted in the rough hair behind one ear. 'I'll wager he tried to defend his master's property, eh, poor boy? – and was struck or kicked. When he recovered he began to howl, and the boys took him for a ghost.'

'Poor brute,' said Maister Coventry. 'What a way to treat a young animal!'

'What about this chamber?' said Maister Kennedy, cutting across the mason's comment. 'Do we search it, or lock it, or send for John Shaw to get it redded up?'

'I'm afraid,' said Gil, 'that we must search it ourselves. It should not take the four of us long.'

'What are we looking for?' said Maister Kennedy in resigned tones.

'Anything the boy should not have had. Possibly papers, or money, or jewels.' Gil settled the pup in a nest in the blankets and turned away. It promptly staggered out and pawed at his boots again.

'Papers, you say?' Maistre Pierre stared round again. 'Gil, I see very little paper here. Surprisingly little, for a student's chamber.'

'What about the students?' said Patrick Coventry. 'There are a great many boys below in the yard working themselves into a terror about the ghost.'

'Let them,' said Maister Kennedy callously, stooping to lift a book. 'Peter of Spain. This is the library's copy, with Duncan Bunch's own notes in it. Plague take the boy, I've been wanting this for months. As well they never saw the brute,' he added, 'or they'd have kent it for Auld Mahoun himself.'

'And what do we do with it?' worried Maister Coventry, shaking out the satin doublet. 'We canny keep a wolf-hound when we've forbidden the students to keep dogs.'

'Properly he belongs to William's next kin,' said Gil doubtfully, 'but he must be fed and physicked before they can be here to claim him.'

'That's true. It seems to like you, Maister Cunningham. Would you take it? As regent with a duty for the late keeper,' said the Second Regent formally, 'I ask you to have a care to this animal until its right owner can be identified. Will that do?'

'Admirably,' said Gil, and grinned. The pup licked his hand with a long wet tongue. 'Do you suppose Alys would give me some bread and milk for him, Pierre?'

'And this,' announced Maister Kennedy, practically gnashing his teeth, 'is the library's second copy, bound up with Laurence of Lindores' commentary on the *Book of Suppositions*. I have been hunting for this for over a year!'

'It was not the only treasure in his chamber,' said Gil, setting several bundles on Maister Doby's reading-desk.

'So I perceive,' said the Principal, eyeing them askance. 'What are all these?'

'Four books belonging to the library.' Gil indicated the

85

little volumes. 'Who is librarian just now, maister? Perhaps some change to the rules?'

'I will recommend it. And these?'

'Two more books, apparently William's own. One belonging to the senior bachelor, Michael Douglas, which I will return to him. A green silk purse with a surprising amount of money, and some jewels.' Gil unrolled the red cloth jerkin, to reveal the three elaborate brooches which he had pinned to the cloth.

'He should certainly not have kept these in his chamber,' said the Principal after a moment, 'setting temptation in the way of his fellow students.'

'Quite so. There are also two rings, which I stowed in the purse with the money, and these.' He unrolled the jerkin further. 'We can ask at the armourer where he got a pair of daggers like that, but I suspect it wasn't in Glasgow.'

There was a high wailing sound from the antechamber.

'What is that noise?' asked the Principal, distracted.

Gil, aware he was going red, said, 'It's William's dog. It's taken a liking to me. Maister Mason was going to take it to his house to wait, but it's reluctant to go with him.'

'A dog? How could the laddie keep a dog in secret?' asked Maister Doby, perplexed.

'It may not have lived in his chamber,' Gil speculated. 'Maister, may I ask some questions?' The older man inclined his head. 'Can you suggest who might have been William's enemy?'

'Oh, no. Not to such an extent. Although he was clever he was not admired,' admitted Maister Doby, 'and he was not as popular as one might expect, but surely he had no enemies?'

'Clearly he had one at least, as Maister Crawford said,' said Gil. 'Can you offer me any interpretation of his question at the Faculty meeting? That might lead us to his enemy.'

'But it might also lead us to suspect unjustly someone who was in fact innocent.'

'Maister,' said Gil patiently, 'the boy deserves justice. Moreover, the person who killed him needs the succour of

Holy Kirk, to bring him to repentance and confession of his sin.'

'That is true,' agreed the Principal. He thought deeply for a short while, then sighed and said heavily, 'I can shed no light on the suggestion of heresy, and I suspect you will not find anyone who will.'

'Probably not,' agreed Gil.

'But I wondered if the charge of peculation might be a garbled recollection of something that happened when John Goldsmith was Principal.' Maister Doby paused, and counted carefully, tapping his fingers on the edge of the desk. 'Aye, in '85. The college had borrowed money from old John Smyth, you remember him?'

'My uncle has mentioned him. He was senior songman at the cathedral, was he no?'

'Quite so.' The Principal glanced at his door. 'That dog sounds to be in pain.'

'It'll stop greeting when it sees me,' said Gil, embarrassed.

'Then in God's name have it in and silence it.'

Gil fetched the pup from the anteroom, where the mason gave it up with some relief, and returned to his seat with the creature, trying to repress its ecstatic embraces.

'That's a dog of breeding,' Maister Doby remarked acutely, watching as it sat down at Gil's feet and laid its head on his knee. 'Someone will ken where he got it from. Where was I? Oh, aye, old John Smyth. Well, he wanted his money back, and Maister Goldsmith couldn't just put his hand on it, and David Gray was Bursar at the time and catched in the midst of the ding-dong. I mind he was ill with the worry of it at the time. You follow me?'

'I think so,' said Gil with caution. 'You are saying that there was a little trouble about money, and Maister David Gray was caught up in it.'

'But without fault,' said the Principal firmly. 'I mind the whole thing. John Smyth got his money in the end, we had to borrow from the archdeacon to pay him, and one or two said David had mismanaged it, but they didny see the books, and I did, for I was Wardroper that year. In any case, Gilbert, David was at the high table with the Dean and me, he canny have throttled the boy.'

'He was, wasn't he,' agreed Gil, recalling the way Maister Gray had sat staring into the flan-dish before him. 'What were you eating up there, maister? Was it any better than what we got?'

'I think Dean Elphinstone commended the spiced pork,' said Maister Doby, 'but to tell truth, Gilbert, I have no sense of taste these days. One stew is much like another. There was raisins in it, I can tell you that.' He got to his feet. 'I will lock these things away. Have you the inventory? Good. And signed by Nicholas and Patrick. Excellent. You were aye one to think of everything, Gilbert.' He bent and held out a hand to the pup, which inspected it solemnly and administered a minuscule lick. 'But we willny lock you away, treasure or no, eh? Take care of the brute, Gilbert. They eat like a student, at this age.'

The Principal turned to the door, as there came a tapping on the planks from the other side. He opened it, and a fond smile crossed his face.

'Well, Billy? This is William Ross, Gilbert. He and his brother lodge at my house. What is it, Billy?'

'If you please, maister,' said William Ross, stepping confidently into the room and bobbing his head in a schoolboy's bow, 'Jaikie at the yett sent me to say there's a bonnie young lady asking for Maister Cunningham.'

Chapter Five

Jaikie the porter was blocking the vaulted tunnel to the yett, hands on hips, glaring red-faced and indignant at Gil and the mason as they approached. The wolfhound at Gil's knee began to growl quietly, and he hushed it as the porter launched into aggressive speech.

'Now, you ken the rules as well as me, Maister Cunningham! Even William Irvine never had a leman calling at the yett for him –'

Gil glanced over the man's shoulder. At the far end of the tunnel Alys stood patiently in the street, her plaid drawn over her head against yet another pattering shower.

'The lady,' he said coldly, 'is Maister Mason's daughter, and it would have been common courtesy to ask her in out of the rain.'

The porter snorted in disbelief, but Maistre Pierre said, 'It is indeed my daughter, and I am here to protect her from your lecherous students.'

Jaikie opened his mouth to comment, assessed the mason's size and breadth of shoulder, and closed it again. As Maistre Pierre stepped past him into the tunnel he recovered somewhat and expostulated, with a puff of spirituous breath, 'Ye canny bring a lassie in here just the same! It's as much as my job's worth if the heid yins catches ye here with her. And another thing – is that no William Irvine's dog?'

Gil suppressed anger.

'Let the lady past, if you please,' he said, emphasizing the word. 'She is here about the business I am conducting for the Principal and Dean Elphinstone.' Whether it's true or no, that ought to silence him, he thought.

Jaikie glowered at him, and finally stepped aside as Alys emerged from the tunnel on her father's arm, bringing with her the feeling that the sun had come out again. Catching Gil's eye she curtsied and said formally, 'May I speak to you, Maister Cunningham? I have information which may be of value.'

Her father's eyebrows went up and Jaikie gaped at her, but Gil, forewarned by her expression, replied in the same language, 'Indeed yes, for I am sure your news will be worth hearing.'

'That's Latin!' said Jaikie suspiciously. 'How can a lassie ken Latin?'

'Same way a student kens it,' said Gil crisply. 'Now stand aside, man.'

Biting his thumb and glowering, the porter stood aside and watched them. His mutter followed them across the courtyard.

'I don't know. Even William never had a leman at the yett, and he'd the half of Glasgow leaving messages for him.' As they reached the door of the Bachelors' Schule the mutter rose to a shout. 'And is that dog to go back to Billy Dog now or no? He's been asking for it.'

'Gil, you must come to our house,' said Alys, her hand on his arm. 'Mistress Irvine is in great distress.'

'Irvine,' Gil said. He disengaged his arm and put it round her shoulders. The pup lay down firmly on his feet. 'I should have thought. *How can I answer you, mother, When my schoolmates have me slain?* I take it she gave him her own name?'

'Or her husband's,' said the mason, sitting down opposite them on another of the long hard benches. 'That must be why the boy named her when he wrote his will.'

'It has been more than a little trying,' said Alys. 'When Mistress Irvine found it was her foster-son who was dead –'

'Did the McIans tell her?' her father interrupted.

'No, they had left by then. Kittock mentioned it, and then she ran out in the street –'

'Tell us from the beginning,' Gil said. He tightened his clasp on her shoulders, and she leaned a little against him.

'The McIans came by the house,' she said patiently. 'The harper was a little upset, and wanted to ask after the baby. Mistress McIan told me about what happened – about the dead student, and how her brother knew where he was –'

'Not exactly,' Gil said. 'He knew he was behind a locked door.'

'Oh. They spoke to Mistress Irvine, too, to thank her for trying to get the bairn to eat, and then they left. It was only a little while ago that Kittock said something about the dead man in Mistress Irvine's hearing, and repeated enough to make her sure it was her boy. She became very distressed.'

'Poor woman,' said her father sympathetically.

Alys threw him a glance, and nodded. 'She ran out in the street, and found some people coming from the feast, still in their gowns and hoods, and asked them who was dead, and what happened. They told her his name, and that he had been throttled – is that right?' Gil nodded. 'It took several of us to get her back into the house. I sent to Greyfriars, and Father Francis is with her now. But the thing is, Gil, that I think she may have information for you. She has mentioned knowing the young man's mother, and that money comes from the Montgomery estates for his keep.'

'This could be valuable,' Gil agreed, 'but there are matters I must see to here before I can leave. Alys, what you could do for me if you will –' She looked up hopefully. '– is take this animal home and feed him for me.'

'If he will go with you,' said the mason. 'And I have a task for you also.'

'Can't I do anything else?'

91

'Not yet.' Gil smiled at her. 'And the dog must be fed.'

'Very well.' She bent to offer the pup her hand to sniff. 'He is a handsome dog – not like Didine at all, is he, father?' As the mason grunted in agreement, she explained to Gil: 'Catherine had a little dog when we came to Glasgow, a pop-eyed yappy creature. She died last year. This fellow is much more to my taste. What is his name?'

'I have no idea. Probably Bran or Gelert or some such thing,' said Gil disparagingly. 'Everyone and his granny calls his wolfhound Bran. His head needs looked at, too.'

'I see that.' She stroked the rough flank, and the hairy tail beat twice on the floor. 'Poor beast. And your task, father?'

The mason felt in his sleeve, and drew out the much-folded papers they had found in William's purse.

'See what you can make of that,' he said, handing them to her. 'The square one is in code.'

'In code?' She unfolded it carefully, and tilted it to the light. 'Simple substitution,' she said after a moment. 'Look, here is the same group of letters, and here, and again here. I can decipher that,' she finished confidently. 'What about the other?'

'Notes of some sort, transcribing the tablets.' Gil held the little set out on his palm, and she glanced at it, and looked closer.

'I saw those in Maister Webster's shop,' she said. 'Yes, I am certain it's the same set. I thought them too dear for something so small.'

'William obviously thought otherwise.' Gil slipped the leather cover off to look at the carved outer faces again. 'This is fiddly work. It would have taken time.'

'As for these notes.' Alys looked down at the second sheet of paper. '*M will be in G.* I suppose G might be for Glasgow?'

'Then M might mean Montgomery,' said her father. 'Who else!'

'It's possible,' agreed Gil. 'Very possible.'

Alys refolded the papers and tucked them behind her busk. 'If I have time, I will work on that this evening.'

'*Is nane so witty and so wyce.* I think you can do everything,' said Gil in admiration.

She threw him a glinting look, and got to her feet. 'I must go and see to the kitchen. Will you be in to supper?'

'Who knows?' said her father. 'There is an entire college to question, I think. You see her out, Gilbert. I go to find John Shaw.'

Gil roused the pup and they walked down the shadowy tunnel to the yett, Alys's pattens clopping on the paving-stones. There was movement in the porter's small chamber, but the man did not appear. At the yett Gil paused, and pushed the animal towards her.

'I have not forgotten my promise,' he assured her. 'If you wish to take part in the hunt, you shall do so, outside the college. I wish you could help inside as well.'

She put up her face for his kiss.

'Some day there will be a college for women in Glasgow,' she said composedly, and bending to take the dog's collar led it out into the street. The effect of her parting speech was completely spoiled by the wolfhound, which, realizing it was being separated from its new hero, dug its paws into the mud, squirmed from her grasp and flung itself yammering back at Gil, with Alys in pursuit. Gil, laughing in exasperation, bent to gather the animal into his arms.

'Leave the beast with me,' he said, avoiding its passionate and muddy demonstrations of relief.

'I think I must,' she agreed, laughing with him. Her laughter faded as a mounted party went up the High Street, spurs jingling, and Gil paused in the gateway to watch them go, looking past her in dismay at the pack-mules laden with mud-splattered bales and boxes. 'What is it? What have you seen? Is it the Montgomerys?'

'No, not the Montgomerys,' he said, in slightly hollow tones. 'We have less time than I thought to get this sorted out. I know those riders, and I'd know the bay with the two socks if I met him in Jerusalem. Those are my mother's outriders. She'll be in Glasgow by tomorrow night.'

The college kitchen, having long since served up dinner in the Laigh Hall for the remaining scholars and regents, was resting from its labours. The charcoal fires out of the long brick cooking-range had been tipped into the hearth and lay in smouldering heaps, the blue smoke curling up past the long iron spits. Two sturdy lasses and a pair of grooms were scouring crocks in a corner, and another groom and a boy in a student's belted gown were carrying them away. Some older women were seated round the table and Mistress Dickson, in a great chair in the corner, her feet in their large cracked shoes propped on a stool, was just sending another groom for some of the college's wine.

'Well, Maister Cunningham!' she greeted him. 'Sit you down and tell me about your marriage, then. What like's your bride? Can she bake and brew?'

'With the best,' Gil assured her. He drew up the stool she indicated and the pup settled beside him on the flagged floor. 'Agnes, is there any chance of some scraps for this beast? He must be yawpin with hunger, poor creature, for he can't have been fed since before Terce.'

'There's some of the rabbit pottage left that it could have,' said one of the women at the table, 'and a wee take of the spiced pork. The plain roastit meat's all ate up.'

'There were just the two made dishes, is that right?'

'Aye, and that was enough,' said Mistress Dickson briskly. 'For the money they allowed me, I did them proud, anyone'll tell you that. Two made dishes, one of them kept for the high table, three sorts of plain roastit meat, an onion tart with flampoints to each table, all the breid they could eat.' She checked the items off on long bony fingers. 'And for the second course, a pike, kale pottage with roots in, a big dish of fruminty to each table. Raisin-cakes and cheese to clear it with.'

'And the pheasant,' said someone.

94

'Aye, I forgot the pheasant. Sic a trouble it was to get it back in its skin.'

Gil, uncertain of how such a young animal's belly would react to spiced pork, negotiated tactfully for a portion of the Almayne pottage, and began to remove the meat from the splintery bones with his knife. The dog accepted each morsel delicately, making no attempt to snatch or snap at his fingers, its hunger apparent only in the speed with which it swallowed. Mistress Dickson watched approvingly, over a cup of wine.

'So that William turned up,' she said at length.

'He did,' agreed Gil, picking another fragment of bone out of the bowl. 'In the coalhouse.'

'Tam, there, was in the coalhouse not an hour before he was found,' said Mistress Dickson. Gil looked round, and found one of the grooms grinning importantly. 'Weren't you no, Tam?'

'I was, and all,' agreed Tam. 'He wisny there, but,' he added in tones of disappointment.

'Saints preserve us, what a thocht!' said one of the sturdy girls in the corner. The other one giggled.

'Well, he wouldny be,' said the student helping Tam. 'Seeing it was the limehouse he was in anyway.'

'What time was that?' Gil asked. 'Was it raining?'

'What time? It was when I sent him for coals,' Mistress Dickson interpolated.

'And when would that be?'

After some discussion, with help from the three women at the table, it was agreed that Tam had gone for coals after one shower but before another.

'What were the coals for? Whose dinner were you cooking by then, Agnes?' Gil asked.

'Aye, now you're asking.' Mistress Dickson scowled at the pup for a moment, chewing her lip. 'I think it was the college dinner. I think I got the feast cooked on one carry of coals, and Isa there put the water on for the kale for the college dinner, and then we needed more. And lucky we did, for if Tam'd been later he'd have found the coalhouse door locked, by what I hear, and the dinner still to cook.'

'And was that about the time the thunder started?' Gil asked.

'By here, you're right, maister!' said Tam. 'For I mind now, I heard thunder when I was in the coalhouse. I thought it was the coals falling down on me!' He laughed hugely at his own joke.

'It was after that he went in the limehouse,' observed the student.

'It was the coalhouse, Nicholas,' said Mistress Dickson crossly, 'as Adam there'll tell you.'

'They said they'd put him in the limehouse.'

'Who said that?' asked Gil, feeding the dog another morsel.

The young man Nicholas, finding everyone looking at him, went red, but persisted. 'When Maister Shaw sent me back to help with the crocks. I saw Lowrie Livingstone and the other two carry him into the passage that goes by the limehouse. They didny see me,' he added.

'They put him in the coalhouse, Nicholas,' repeated Mistress Dickson. 'I don't know why you're aye on about the limehouse.'

'They said the limehouse,' repeated Nicholas sulkily.

'When did they say that?' Gil asked.

'When they came out of the passage. I was at the top of the kitchen stair,' said Nicholas, pointing at the door, 'and they came out just under my feet laughing about it. One of them said he'd be heard when he shouted, and Lowrie said *In the limehouse? The walls are three feet thick.* Then they went away across to the Outer Close.'

'So was it them that killed him?' asked one of the women at the table.

'Why did they lie about him being in the limehouse?' wondered Tam.

'Well, it's certain he was found in the coalhouse,' said one of the men scouring crocks, 'for I helped to bear him out of there.'

'Aye, you did, Adam,' agreed Mistress Dickson. 'Just

when I was needing you to fetch me another sack of meal.'

'Did you see Father Bernard?' Gil asked.

Nicholas looked blank. 'Him? No. Was he about?'

'One or two people were about,' said Gil vaguely. 'Who else was here in the kitchen?'

'I was,' admitted Adam, pausing again in his work, 'and I mind now, Nicholas, you came in and said something about William in the limehouse. I wonder how he got into the coalhouse,' he speculated, 'for he couldny open the door, with his hands tied like that. Strange we never heard him shouting or anything.'

'Was his hands tied?' said another of the women at the table avidly.

'You heard nothing?' asked Gil. 'Where were you all?'

'We were all here,' said Mistress Dickson, 'for Adam and Aikie yonder had shifted the most of the crocks already, while they were all at their play, and there was no more for us to do in the Fore Hall.'

'Everyone who's here now?' Gil persisted. They looked round at one another, and several people nodded.

'And Robert,' said Tam.

'I'd sent Robert to make sure all the crocks was shifted,' said Mistress Dickson. In the corner, the two scullery-lasses looked quickly at one another and away again. 'Rightly that's John Shaw's business, but he'd enough to see to, he asked me to oversee the crocks.'

'I saw that William before that,' said the third woman at the table.

'Did you so? Where was he?' Gil asked.

'He crossed the Inner Close, here, and went up the next stair. He seemed as if he was in a hurry.'

'Maybe you were the last to see him alive, Eppie,' said the woman beside her with a pleasurable shudder.

'Except for who killed him,' Eppie pointed out. 'I wondered at the time,' she added, 'for they were all still at their daft play, and I ken fine his chamber's in the Outer Close where the siller dwells, but we've been ower thrang here, maister, to worry about one ill-natured laddie getting somewhere he shouldny.'

'You found him ill-natured?' said Gil innocently. A courteous paw was placed on his arm, and he handed over the last piece of meat. 'The Dean and the Principal spoke very highly of him.'

'Oh, aye,' said Mistress Dickson. 'They'd find him sweet-natured enough. He'd keep on their right sides, would William.' She tilted her cup of wine to get the last mouthful, so that the steam-whitened underside of her tight red sleeve showed, and looked into its empty depths. There was a brooding silence. 'He was aye on at me about the cost of food,' she added. 'If Maister Shaw was satisfied, what business was it of his, I said to him, but back he'd come with a note of who got a spare bite at the buttery door and who got wheaten breid when he should have had masloch. As if I'd turn away hungry laddies,' she added.

'If he could get a man into trouble, he would,' said Tam. 'I'm no sorry he's away. Well, I'm no,' he added on a defiant note.

'He got your lass turned out,' observed one of the other men. 'What was it for?'

'He said she took food home to her minnie,' said Tam resentfully. 'And what if she did?'

'Aye, well,' said Mistress Dickson, swinging her feet down off the stool. The pup, taken by surprise, backed against Gil's knee and produced a rather squeaky growl. He hushed it, and it flattened its ears in apology. 'This isny getting tomorrow's breid kneddit. There's water there, Maister Cunningham, if you wish to clean your hands before you leave my kitchen.'

'Who do you think killed him, maister?' asked the woman opposite Eppie, as the kitchen work began again. 'Was it Lowrie Livingstone and them?'

Gil, drying his hands on his doublet, shook his head. 'I don't know yet. Who do you think?' he countered.

*　　*　　*

'They had no useful suggestion,' he said to Maistre Pierre. They were standing at the gate between the college orchard and the Blackfriars grounds, watching the dog, which was casting about in the grass.

'I think nobody has one,' said the mason. 'What was the useless suggestion?'

'That one of his friends had throttled him. I asked who his friends were, but they were not willing to answer. He seems to have had few enough friends.'

'Perhaps we should speak to those few next.'

'After we have looked at the body again. Did John Shaw tell you anything?'

'I have a list,' said Maistre Pierre, drawing his own tablets from his purse, 'of those who were waiting at the feast, and of what dishes were served. He became quite eloquent about serving the pike.'

'It's not everyone can splat a pike,' Gil agreed. 'Did you ask him if William had tried his extortion on him?'

'I did not. I have to work with this man, remember, and whether he answered me honestly or not, I do not think he would forget that I asked. Besides, I think you are better than I at such questions.'

'I hope that is a compliment.' Gil nodded at the tablets in his friend's large hand. 'Who was serving?'

'These three are college servants – Aikie Soutar, Tam Millar, Adam Anderson. Then these four are students, hired for the occasion – Nicholas Gray, Robert Montgomery, William Muirhead, George Maxwell. I asked,' said Maistre Pierre slowly, 'who went to the play and who would be clearing the crocks from the hall where the feast was. It seems the students were permitted to watch the play, since their fellows were acting in it.'

'So the college servants were clearing the crocks,' said Gil, 'and crossing back and forth through the Inner Close and the Outer. Did all these four go back to their task after the play?'

'It seems so. These two – the young men Muirhead and Maxwell – were handing sweetmeats and wine, and the other two were helping to shift the last of the crocks. That dog has done his duty. Should we go and pay our respects to the dead?'

In the bellhouse, which also served as mortuary chapel, there were candles and nose-tickling incense, and a rapid mutter of prayers. A pair of the Dominicans knelt, one on either side of the convent's bier, where the corpse lay shrouded already. Their fingers flickered over their plain wooden rosaries.

'I asked that he be left clothed till we could be there,' said Gil, in some annoyance.

'He was beginning to set,' said Maister Forsyth, coming forward from the stone bench at the wall. 'Aye, Maister Mason. Are ye well? His clothes are here, Gilbert, I kept them back, but the laddie himself is washed and made decent. And what have you deduced this far?'

'Precious little,' admitted Gil. 'Can you tell me about William, maister?'

'Not a lot, you know.' The old man made his way back to the bench, and Gil and the mason settled on either side of him. 'Let me see. He must be fifteen or so. A very able scholar, very good in the Latin, a few scraps of Greek, a little French. A good grasp of logic, a very clever disputant. A liking for secrets, and a powerful memory for oddments of knowledge. He had the occasional moment of generosity – I have seen him give coin to a beggar – but for the most part very close with his property or his learning.'

'You did not like him,' Gil suggested.

Maister Forsyth turned to look at him, the candlelight glittering in his eyes. 'Have I said so?'

'Was he likeable?'

'No,' said the old voice after a moment. 'God has not given it to all of us to be lovable.'

'God himself loves us all, even so,' said the mason.

'Amen,' agreed Maister Forsyth. 'William was admirable, but no lovable. One of the clever ones, for whom it is never enough.'

'*Erth upon erth wald fain be a king*,' Gil offered.

100

'Indeed. And it goes on, does it not, *And how that erth goes to erth thinks he no thing*. Poor laddie. He made me think of a flawed diamond. Brilliant and glittering, ye ken, but if we tried to cut or polish him more he would fly in pieces. Now you, Gilbert, are like ivory or maybe jet.'

'Jet?' Gil repeated, startled.

'Aye. Plain and serviceable, no show about ye, but taking a fine polish. A fine polish,' he repeated approvingly.

'Do diamonds have flaws?' asked Maistre Pierre.

'Who knows? But the figure is instructive.'

Gil, recovering his poise, said after a moment, 'What do you suppose William meant by his questions at this morning's meeting?'

'I have no idea,' said Maister Forsyth promptly in Latin. 'It was a quite regrettable display of malice, but whether it was founded in any fact I do not care to speculate.'

'Malice,' repeated Maistre Pierre in French. 'Was it only that?'

'Maister Doby thought the remark about money might be a misunderstanding of the problem the college had about John Smyth's loan,' Gil said.

His teacher stared at the candles, while the prayers drummed on like rain.

'It might be,' he said at length. 'It might be. John would remember that tale better than me, he was Wardroper at the time.'

'Or it might be a dig at the Steward,' Gil continued. 'I gather William was exercised about the cost of food going through the kitchen.'

'You canny starve growing laddies.' Maister Forsyth was still watching the candles. 'No, Gilbert, I dinna ken. Nor have I the smallest idea of what prompted the hints about heresy,' he added in Latin.

'It is an unpleasant thing to suggest,' said Maistre Pierre in French.

The old man shook his head. 'Ask another question, Gilbert.'

'It seems,' said Gil with some delicacy, 'that William was

given to extortion. Do you have any knowledge of this, maister?'

'It grieves me to say it,' admitted Maister Forsyth, 'but I do.' He heaved a sigh. 'The poor laddie. I feared as much.' He looked round at Gil. 'He came to me privately one day last autumn, with a list of things I had said, taken out of context, hinting that it might be worth his while repeating them to Robert our Archbishop.' He shook his head again. 'I showed him the error of what he was doing. I also assured him,' he added, with a gleam of humour, 'that I had made most of these remarks to Robert Blacader in the first place. He went away, and I have prayed for him since. I feared that if he approached me in such a way he might approach others, to the danger of himself or of his . . .' He paused, considering the next word. 'Victim,' he finished.

'That is valuable information, maister,' said Gil.

'Well, well. Do you have more to ask me?'

'What did you have to eat at the feast, sir?'

'At the feast?' Maister Forsyth smacked his lips reminiscently. 'Agnes did well, on the money we gave her. Spiced pork with raisins. Fruminty. There was a pike, but I canny take pike. Tastes of mud. A great onion tart with cloves. Agnes canny cook Almayne pottage, but she's a good hand with pastry. It was a good feast, and the spiced pork hasny repeated on me the way it often does. And then we had the play, and William's costume was torn. A pity, that. The dragon is always popular with the younger students.'

'And what did you do at the end of the play?'

The round felt hat bobbed as Maister Forsyth turned to look at Gil again.

'The senior members of the Faculty retired to the Principal's residence to ease themselves. We remained there for perhaps the quarter of an hour, and then went in procession back to the Fore Hall.'

'Who are the senior members?' asked Maistre Pierre.

Maister Forsyth, finally accepting the mason's understanding of Latin, enumerated the Dean, the Principal, the two lawyers and himself.

'And Maister Coventry was not there,' said Gil.

'No,' agreed Maister Forsyth, 'though he ought to ha been. I thought I saw him and Nick Kennedy gang the other way, to the Arthurlie building.' He looked down at the pup, which after nosing the bundle of William's clothes carefully had gone to sleep on Gil's knee. 'And what is this, Gilbert?'

'We found him in William's chamber. It's against the statutes to keep a dog, isn't it?'

The old man tut-tutted. 'There ought to be a statute about keeping statutes. They mostly gets ignored. It's fair taken on wi ye, Gilbert.'

'Do we wish to look at the dead?' asked Maistre Pierre. Gil nodded, and gathering up the pup under his arm rose to his feet. The two friars by the bier ignored him as he loosened the tape holding the shroud in place and folded the linen back. The dog stretched its neck and extended a long nose to sniff the red hair, bright even by candlelight, and Gil turned in haste to hand the animal to the mason.

'Poor beast, I never thought – hold him for me, Pierre.'

'I do not think him distressed,' the mason said, watching as Gil felt carefully over the dead boy's skull. 'He may not recognize the scent. All I can smell is incense and soap. What have you found?'

'Confirmation.' Gil parted the springy hair, and moved one of the candles closer. 'Aye, he's hit his head on something. There's a lump, and a bruise. That's all I need, I think.' He straightened up. 'Bring the pup here.'

The pup, held up to see the corpse, sniffed briefly at the ghastly face, paid a little more attention to the grooved and swollen neck, then laid its head on Gil's arm in a manner which spoke volumes. The nearer of the two bedesmen reached up without missing a syllable to scratch the rough jaw and was rewarded, as Maister Doby had been, with an infinitesimal lick.

'One final thing,' said Gil, gathering up the ill-smelling

103

bundle of William's clothes with his free hand. 'Who would have a reason to kill him?'

'Many people might have a reason,' said Maister Forsyth, 'but that doesny say they did it.'

'Agreed,' said Gil, but the old man would say no more.

'Now what do we do, my plain and serviceable son-in-law?' said the mason, closing the Blackfriars gate behind them.

'But well-polished,' Gil reminded him, setting the dog on its own paws. 'We must look at these garments and then send them to be washed. We must speak to William's friends. I must talk to Nick Kennedy about that list he made for me. Then, I hope, we can go back to supper and I must speak to Mistress Irvine.'

'Ah, good, a short day.' Maistre Pierre looked about him. 'This is good land the college owns. They could rent it out.'

'They use it.' Gil was heading downhill under the apple-trees, towards the kitchen garden which lay at the back of the sprawling college buildings and sloped down to the Molendinar burn and its watermills. 'The students gather here on fine evenings to dispute or to hear half-solemn disputes between two of their teachers. They play football here too,' he added, 'though they should really go out to the Muir Butts for that.'

'Half-solemn? You mean only one disputant may make jokes?'

Gil grinned, but before he could answer Maister Kennedy appeared round the corner of the buildings, exclaiming, 'Gil! There you are! You're wanted, man. Montgomery's here, and he wants blood. Come and defend us.'

'Not my blood, I hope,' said Gil.

'Possibly not,' said Nick. 'It seems he'd just ridden into the burgh, and when the Dean sent word concerning William he came round breathing fire. There's been a bit of a ding-dong already.'

'What help am I likely to be?' asked Gil, following Maister Kennedy through the pend into the inner courtyard. 'He'll no be comforted to learn that a Cunningham's trying to track down whoever it was killed his kinsman.'

'Have you nothing to tell him? At least you can assure him you're doing something.'

Hugh Lord Montgomery was standing before the empty fireplace in the Principal's lodging, radiating rage like a hot brick. When Gil entered the room, with the mason watchful at his back, the Dean was explaining why no word had yet been sent to Archbishop Blacader.

'You tellt me all that already,' said Montgomery, glaring at Gil. 'Is this what's trying to sort it out? This – this Cunningham?'

'Gil Cunningham, of the Cathedral Consistory,' said Gil, bowing with a flourish of the illegal master's bonnet. 'And this is Maister Peter Mason, of this burgh.'

The man who had been head of his house since he turned fourteen, who had personally killed two Cunninghams and a Boyd, was big, though not so big as the mason, and his dark hair sprang thickly above a square-jawed face. Dark angry eyes glittered under thick brows as he stared down his nose at Gil.

'And what, if anything, have you done to the point?' he asked. 'Why have ye no hangit the ill-doer already?'

'Gilbert is an able –' began the Principal injudiciously.

'I dinna want *able*,' said Montgomery quietly. 'I want *quick*.'

'The trouble with *quick*,' said Gil, 'is that it might also be *wrong*, and then where would we be? Supposing we hangit a Drummond or an Oliphant, or worse, a Murray or a Ross, and then found out he wasny guilty, my lord, who do you think his kin would attack? The college or the Montgomerys?'

'I'll take my chance on that,' said Montgomery.

'I think the college would prefer not to,' said Gil. There was a pause, which seemed very long. Then Montgomery

105

produced a sound like a snarl and flung himself down in the Principal's great chair.

'Well, tell me what you have found, then,' he said savagely.

'The young man called William Irvine was strangled with his own belt,' said Gil, picking his words with care, 'and hidden in the college coalhouse. This makes it secret murder, not murder *chaud-mellé*. We are working from two directions, trying to establish who had a reason for killing him and also who had the opportunity.'

'And who had a reason?'

'I have found no good reason so far,' said Gil.

'Folk gets killed for bad reasons,' said Montgomery. 'Look for the bad reasons, Cunningham law man. What about opportunity? Who had the chance to kill him?'

'Most of the college, at the moment,' said Gil. 'We will get closer than that once we speak to everyone.'

'Pick a likely culprit and put him to the thumbscrews,' said Montgomery. 'I've a set I can lend ye, if the college has none. That'll get ye a confession, quick as winkin.'

'That will not be necessary,' said the Principal.

'Listen, Maister Doby,' said Lord Montgomery, getting to his feet. 'This is Sunday, right? We'll have the funeral Tuesday or Wednesday, and if this long drink of water hasny named our William's killer to me by the time William's in the ground, I'll come in here myself with the thumbscrews and –'

'Not,' said the Dean in glacial tones, 'on University premises.'

There was another of those pauses.

'No?' said Lord Montgomery softly. 'Then how about outside? Ye canny hide in yir two closes *in saecula saeculorum*, clerk. I'll be waiting. I'll pick them off as they go into the town, and put them to the question. Ye've got till after the funeral,' he said again to Gil, and strode past him.

The mason stepped out of his way, and closed the door carefully behind him.

'He must think a great deal of William,' he observed,

moving to the window which looked out into the court-yard.

'I confess, Patrick,' said Maister Doby in wavering tones, 'that I feel the college could do without that man's money now.'

'I too, John,' agreed the Dean. 'Is that all you have learned so far, Gilbert?'

'Not quite,' said Gil. The Dean waited. So did Gil.

'We speak to William's friends next, no?' said the mason after a short time. 'Where do we find them?'

'I will have them sent for,' said the Dean, giving in.

'You may use this chamber. But you must make haste, Gilbert,' said Maister Doby anxiously, 'for Vespers will be early and solemn tonight and the college will go in procession to the Blackfriars kirk from the Fore Hall.'

Ralph Gibson proved to be the lanky boy who had played Collegia, now revealing a remarkable crop of spots. Traces of paint still showed in front of his ears and at his hairline, and there was blue on his puffy eyelids. He sat down when bidden, and stared at Gil anxiously, his bony hands clasped between his knees.

'You know what has happened, Ralph?' said Gil. The boy nodded. 'William Irvine is dead, and somebody killed him.' Ralph nodded again.

'It wisny me, maister!' he bleated earnestly. 'William was my friend. Him and Robert and me.'

'That's why I hope you can help me,' Gil said. 'Tell me about William.'

'He was just William,' said Ralph, taken aback.

'Was he good company?' Gil asked. Ralph nodded again.

'Oh, aye, he was. He knew all sort of things,' he added.

'William told you things?' said the mason. The boy glanced sideways at him under the blue eyelids. 'What sort of things?'

'All sort.'

'Such as what?'

'Well, where Maister Forsyth got his lecture notes from.

107

Who tellt Maister Stewart that you canny believe all the doctors of the Kirk have wrote.'

'He told you these things?' Gil said, with no particular intonation.

'Well, maybe no.' Ralph wriggled a little. 'But he kent them himsel. He said so. And I tellt him things.'

'That hint about Father Bernard – was that what William meant by his question at the meeting?'

'Maybe,' said Ralph, floundering slightly. 'I think quite likely, maister.'

'William was a good friend?' asked the mason.

Ralph, understanding the phrase in the Scots sense, nodded again.

'He got me out of trouble with Maister Gray,' he disclosed, 'and he lent me money to pay my fees when my faither's rick-yard burnt out. Maister, will I hae to pay that back?' he burst out. 'For I haveny got it. William's heir might want it, mightn't he no?'

The pup, curled up on Gil's gown by his chair, raised its head to study him, then tucked its nose under a hairy paw and went back to sleep.

'William was a bastard,' Gil said. 'His nearest kin will get his goods and money. If there is nothing written down, Ralph, there is no proof of the loan at law –'

'Oh, but he wrote it down,' Ralph said. 'In his wee red book.'

'A red book?' Gil asked, memory stirring faintly. 'What book was that?'

'He wrote everything down,' said Ralph, with vicarious pride. 'He was aye making notes.' He mimed a careful scribe, writing small into his cupped left hand. That was it, Gil thought, recalling the sight of William writing in his tablets while the Dean's golden oratory rolled over their heads. Writing that draft testament we found? 'He said, you never kent when a thing would come in handy, and there it would be in his bookie.'

William's kin would not be bound by what the boy set out in his fictive will, but they might be prepared to be guided by it, Gil considered, looking at the tearstained face in front of him. And half of William's goods, or even a quarter of the worth of what they had found in the wrecked chamber, would be a considerable sum to this mourner.

'Whoever is the nearest kin,' he said, 'I will speak for you in the matter of the loan. Now, tell us, Ralph, what did you do at the end of the play? Was anyone with you?'

'At the end of the play?' Ralph stared uncertainly for a moment. 'Oh, aye. We all ran out when the rain begun. Robert and me went to our chamber, for he'd left some notes of William's at his window and I'd left my other hose to air. Wringing wet they were, too,' he added.

'Where is your chamber?' the mason asked. Ralph produced some tangled directions to one of the stairs in the inner courtyard.

'And then you both went back to the Fore Hall?' said Gil. 'Did you go anywhere else first? How about the privy? Did you see anyone else?'

'Well, everyone else was running about too,' said Ralph reasonably. 'There was Henry and Walter, up our stair, for I heard them shouting about Walter's boots. And when I was back down in the close I mind there was Andrew, and Nick Gray. And then I just gaed back and took off my costume and cleaned my face, and then I gaed up to the Fore Hall, for there was some of the comfits for the players.'

'And Robert went with you, did he?' asked Gil. 'This is Robert Montgomery?'

'No, no, he'd to go back to the kitchen. He'd been serving at table, see,' Ralph explained. 'He had to go back and clear. Walter and Henry and Andrew and me,' he counted off on his fingers, 'all gaed back to the Bachelors' Schule thegither. Robert and Nick were wantit in the kitchen. Maister Shaw was there and sent them back.'

'Did they go to the kitchen together?' Gil asked. Ralph shook his head. 'I didny see. Likely they did.'

'What did you eat at the feast?' Gil asked.

Ralph, startled by the change of subject, blinked at him, but answered readily enough, 'Rabbit stew and some of the onion tart. I didny get much. We had to go and get changed for the play.'

The mason turned from the window where he had been looking out into the outer courtyard.

'Tell us this, boy,' he said. 'Who do you think might have killed William?'

'I don't know, maister!' There were tears in the young voice. 'But I wish he hadny done it!'

'Poor boy,' said Maistre Pierre, when Ralph had gone.

'A poor creature,' Gil agreed. 'I suppose William saw that too.'

'And what of this red book?'

'I have seen such a thing.' Gil frowned. 'I can't remember where.'

'It will come to you,' said the mason with certainty. 'Shall we have in the other boy now? Maister Doby said we should make haste.'

Having seen the head of the family, Gil felt there was no doubt that Robert Montgomery was entitled to his surname. The dark hair sprang from the wide forehead in the same way, and there was the same effect of radiant rage, no less powerful for being subjugated to the good manners of a well-taught student.

'The Dean said you wished to question me, maisters.'

'That is true,' said Gil. 'Please be seated.'

The boy sat down, staring intently at Gil.

'Well? What d'you wish to ask me? We're singing solemn vespers for him, I have to go and robe,' he said. 'And I need time to con the line, since I'll be singing his part and no my own.'

'William was your friend?' said Gil.

'I suppose you could say that.' A shrug of one shoulder. 'He's – he was one of ours, even if he was a bastard. We spent time together.'

'Did you like him?'

'I don't have to like all my kin, thank God.'

'Amen to that,' said Gil ambiguously. 'Tell me about William. Do you know who his parents were?'

Again that intent stare.

110

'If I did I wouldny say so,' the boy declared roundly. 'If you want the dirty linen, you can ask at my uncle Hugh. And good luck to it.'

'Then what can you tell me about him?'

Another shrug. 'Clever bastard. Liked to know things. Kept himself separate.'

'Would you say, nosy?' asked the mason. Robert turned to stare at him.

'You could say that,' he said after a moment. 'Some folk collects money, or relics, or plate armour. William collected information.'

'What kind of information?'

'All kinds. Who wedded who, what estates the King's giving away, how the harvest was in Avondale – he'd write it all down.'

'And sell it?' said the mason. Robert froze for a moment, then turned to face Gil again.

'I dinna ken,' he said, with another shrug. 'He wouldny tell me if he did, would he?'

'Was his question at the Faculty Meeting about that kind of thing, do you think?' Gil asked.

'I tell you I dinna ken. I've no idea what he was on about.'

'Ralph thought it might be about something the chaplain had said,' said Gil, in deliberate misrepresentation.

'Ralph's a fool,' said Robert dismissively.

'Do you recognize this creature?' Gil stirred the pup gently with one foot. It produced a muffled yip and its paws paddled briefly.

Robert's angry gaze softened. 'That's a good wolfhound. Looks like one of Billy Dog's.'

'Billy Dog?'

'His right name's William Doig. He stays out the Gallowgait, beyond the East Port. Breeds dogs.'

'I have heard of him,' said the mason.

'You've never seen this one before? This is the dog we found in William's chamber.'

'In his chamber? I didny –' began Robert, and checked.

111

'I didny ken he had a dog in his chamber. I thought it was against the statutes.'

'It is,' said Gil.

'It wasny in his chamber last time I was there.' Robert considered the pup, which was now sitting up yawning, and snapped his fingers at it. 'It's a bonnie beast, right enough. Maybe he was keeping it down at Billy Dog's,' he suggested. The pup went forward, stretching out its long nose to sniff at his hand. He patted it, feeling gently at the shape of the skull.

'Good bone on him,' he said, and then, indignantly, 'Who's cut his skull for him, then?'

'We found him like that.'

'That should ha been seen to before now,' said Robert, turning the pup's head to the light.

'I'll get him physicked when I go home.'

'Billy Dog would gie you something for it. They say he'll cure anything on four legs.'

They all watched as the pup turned and wobbled drowsily back to its makeshift bed, circled once and lay down with a sigh.

'You were serving at table, I think,' said Gil after a moment.

Robert blinked slightly. 'Aye, I was.'

'When did you eat? What did you have?'

'Anything I could get a mouthful of,' he said frankly, 'every time I went back to the servery. They never tellt us we'd have to eat after the rest, and handing out all that food on an empty wame was more than I could do.'

'What did you think of the Almayne pottage?' Gil asked, and smiled slightly at the grimace the boy pulled. 'Agnes is famous for it.'

'I've no doubt.'

'Did you get a taste of the spiced pork?'

'I did not. I canny take fennygreek. Gives me hives. We never get it at home. I'd some of the onion tart, and a lump of the pike after John Shaw had mangled it. Never saw anyone make such a mess of splatting a pike.'

Gil glanced at the mason, and went on, 'And after the play, what did you do?'

'Went to close my window and move some of my notes out of the rain.'

'Your notes. Not William's?'

'Mine.' The square chin went up. 'Then I went back to the kitchen, to see if there was any food, and found myself shifting crocks from the Fore Hall.'

'Who else did you see when you went to your chamber?'

Robert paused, considering this question.

'Ralph cam with me. He's my chamber-fellow, poor fool. I heard Walter and Henry. I heard Andrew, and Nick Gray cam into the kitchen just after me. I think I heard Lowrie Livingston and that, arguing on their stair. They're aye arguing, those three, though if you look sideways at one of them the whole three of them gets on to you.'

'Any more?'

'If I think of any more I'll tell you.' Robert looked past the mason at the sky. 'I need to go, maisters. Is that all your questions?'

'Just the one more,' said Gil. 'Who would have a reason to kill William?'

There was a pause, in which the anger built up behind Robert's intent stare again.

'How the deil would I know who he'd done an ill turn to?' he said softly, and rose. 'Good e'en to ye, maisters.'

The door closed behind him with a gentle firmness which was somehow more offensive than if it had slammed. The mason whistled.

'*Veuillez votr' université,*' quoted Gil ironically, '*prier pour l'âme.*'

'Even his friends do not regret him,' Maistre Pierre agreed. 'Except for that poor Ralph. Now what must we do? I confess, every time you ask about the feast I am more aware of being hungry.'

'We should clearly speak to this Nicholas Gray, but he will shortly go to Vespers like the rest of the college.' Gil bent to lift the pup and reclaim his short gown. 'I want one

113

word with Nick Kennedy, and then I think we can go home to supper, provided Alys has not fed it to the pig.'

'I think you may be too late for Maister Kennedy also.' The mason closed the shutters as the sound of the *Te Deum* floated in from the courtyard. 'The procession is leaving already.'

Chapter Six

'Let me see, what do we know?' said Gil.

They were seated in the mason's panelled closet, with a jug of ale circulating. The household had long since eaten its supper, but Alys had greeted them with pleasure and produced a substantial meal for all three of them. The wolfhound was still licking hopefully at its empty plate, holding it down with a large hairy paw.

'We have been told, and we may believe, I think,' said the mason, picking crumbs off a platter which had earlier held half a raised pie, 'that the young man was knocked unconscious and put in the limehouse as a joke of sorts.' He pulled a disapproving face. 'Prentice stuff. One expects better of scholars, surely.'

'No,' said Gil, recalling his own student days.

'No, father,' said Alys.

Maistre Pierre grunted. 'And we have deduced that quite shortly after he was put there he was throttled, still in the limehouse, and transferred to the coalhouse after he was dead.'

'How can you know that?' asked Alys, her brown eyes intent on his face.

'No sign of a struggle, in either place,' Gil said. 'He was killed before he recovered his senses, and it seems he was already beginning to stir when he was shut in the limehouse.'

She nodded. 'Are you looking for one person, or two?'

'One person at the moment,' said Gil. 'It is simpler. But I agree, it could almost be two, or even three. However I am reasonably confident,' he added, 'that we have not yet spoken to the person who searched William's chamber and struck this fellow over the head.'

'I must see to that.' Alys drew the animal to her by its collar, and studied the injury. 'It's a clean cut – if we wash off the blood, it should heal well enough.' She patted the pup, which was wagging its stringy tail at her, and lifted the tray of empty dishes. 'It all hinges on the order in which things happened after the play,' she continued thoughtfully, her gaze on Gil again.

'You see that too?'

'I do not,' said the mason. 'Surely it is enough to find out who searched the chamber?'

'If the regent's key opened both the coalhouse and the boy's chamber, other keys may do likewise,' Alys pointed out. 'How many such keys are there? Who has them?'

'We need to ask,' said her father.

Alys put the tray down again, and looked from one to the other. 'Could the Dean be right? Could it be a passing malefactor, or a discontented servant?'

'Easily,' said Gil, a little grimly. 'And two of the servants at least had a reason to dislike the boy.'

'No, but wait. If I understand you, this limehouse is in a closed pend by itself, or at least with the coalhouse, so only people with business there would pass the door. If William was not killed by the boys who put him in the limehouse –'

'I'm reasonably sure of that,' Gil said. 'They were shocked and frightened by news of his death, and greatly relieved when I told them how he had died. Having seen their acting,' he added, 'I am certain they were sincere in this.'

'Then how did the person who killed him know he was there?'

'A good question,' said Gil.

Her elusive smile flickered. 'That always means there is either a very good answer, or no immediate one.' She collected more scraps off the dishes on the tray and put them absently into the wolfhound's plate, where they were immediately swept up by its long pink tongue. 'Which is

116

it?' Gil shook his head in reply. 'Who had the chance? When was he killed?'

'Just after the play ended,' said Gil, 'there was a great clap of thunder and the rain began.'

'I heard it,' she said, nodding.

'All of the cast and many of the other students scattered to shut windows or put books out of danger. Ninian Boyd found William poking round their chamber, and knocked him down. By the time they had tied him up and carried him downstairs most of the others had gone back to the hall where the feast was, to get at the sweetmeats, so they thought they were unseen, but one of the scholars helping at the feast overheard them and told the kitchen hands. I think this all happened before the Dean rose to retire from the place where we saw the play, so none of the masters knew at this point.'

'What of the other students?' asked Maistre Pierre. 'Theology, the Laws?'

'We must ask, or get someone to do it for us.'

'But suppose someone found out where William was,' Alys persisted, 'never mind how for the moment, would it have been possible for him to get to the limehouse, do away with the boy, and move him, unperceived by anyone else? In broad day? Who had the chance to do that?'

'Conspiracy,' said her father.

'You must question all of the kitchen people,' Alys said. She rose and lifted the tray. 'Someone may know something, or have told someone else, or been overheard. Nobody pays attention to servants.'

She backed out of the door with her tray, and they heard her feet on the stairs.

'There is still no reason to throttle the boy,' said Maistre Pierre, sitting back in his great chair. 'Or none better than another.'

'And there is this question of the smell of cumin on the belt he was throttled with.' Gil poured more ale for them both. 'None of the people who ate the spiced pork had the opportunity, and none of the others ate the spiced pork.

117

I think,' he added. 'Perhaps I should also ask the kitchen if any of them tasted it.'

'Very likely they did.' The mason sighed. 'I had misgivings when I saw the messenger from the college, and I was right. At least there are no Campbells this time, but only that supremely unpleasant Lord Montgomery.'

'Who is son-in-law to the Great Campbell himself,' said Gil. Maistre Pierre looked enquiringly. 'His wife is a daughter of Chancellor Argyll,' Gil confirmed. 'He is uncle-by-marriage to John Sempill's late mistress.'

'I should have guessed,' said the mason in disgust.

'What is more, he seems determined to cleanse Ayrshire of Cunninghams.'

'I know he has killed more than one –'

'With his own blade he has killed my kinsman Alexander Lord Kilmaurs, the head of the house, on Sauchie Muir in '88,' said Gil with restraint, 'and Alexander's son Robert in '89, in an armed encounter outside the court at Irvine. He has burned and harried and confiscated Cunningham property the length and breadth of north Ayrshire, the district called Cunningham, and in Lanarkshire as well.' The baby wailed, elsewhere in the house. 'And it is this man's kinsman for whom we are charged to win justice. I would feel better about that if I knew what degree of kinship there was.'

'A very unpleasant man.' The baby wailed again, closer, and Maistre Pierre sat up. 'That infant has still not eaten, I would judge. Why is Alys bringing him upstairs?'

'Because Nancy wishes to hear Vespers at Greyfriars.' Alys, returning with the tray, was followed into the little room by the silent girl who was the baby's nurse. 'There, Nancy, give him to me now and go with the others.'

'Poor little one,' said the mason as the swaddled bundle changed hands. 'He is still hungry?'

'Mistress Irvine's remedy, that we tried this morning, came straight back up.' Alys bounced the baby hopefully. *'The cattie rade to Paisley, to Paisley, to Paisley.* No, the milk with honey and a little usquebae is still the best, and he

118

won't grow big and strong like his daddy on that, will he? *The cattie rade to Paisley, upon a harrow tine.'*

The baby grizzled at her.

'Which daddy?' said Gil.

'Well, the harper calls daily,' Maistre Pierre pointed out, 'whereas Maister Sempill has not been here once since we fostered the bairn. Let me hold him, Alys, and you may see to the dog.'

'The difference lies between knowing it is your bairn, as McIan does,' suggested Gil, 'and simply needing it as a legal heir, like Sempill. No,' he said firmly to the pup, which was goggling at the baby.

'Let John see the dog,' said Alys, sitting down. She lifted the rag and the bowl from the tray, and captured the pup between her ankles. 'See, baby. What's this?'

Child and dog stared at one another, and the baby stopped wailing. Alys, taking advantage of the pup's distraction, washed the dried blood out of the rough hair and inspected the injury. Gil watched the deft movements of her slender hands, and suddenly found himself imagining her tending to him like that. Would she wear the same look of intent concern? he wondered, and then thought, This is foolish. But the image lingered.

By the time Alys was finished the baby was reaching out towards the dog.

'As I thought,' she said, smearing the wound with something green from a small pot. 'A clean cut. It should heal well. There, little one,' she said to the pup, releasing it. 'Is that a doggie, John?'

John made a remark, waving his arms. The doggie moved closer. The mason took a firmer grasp of the baby, ready to move quickly if necessary, but Gil shook his head.

'He is not hunting,' he said, 'he's curious. Look – his hackles are still down.'

The wolfhound reared up with one paw on Maistre Pierre's knee, bringing its muzzle within reach of the baby, who reached out with both arms. One small hand grasped a soft grey ear, the other reached for the shiny black nose.

The pup's tail swung, and there was an unfamiliar sound.

John McIan or Sempill was laughing.

'Well!' said Alys.

'Well!' said the mason, and freed one hand to wipe his eyes. All three adults exchanged idiotic smiles, while the pup scrambled awkwardly on to the mason's knee beside the baby.

'The question is,' said Gil, watching critically as it tried to hitch up a dangling back leg, 'whether the dog will stay with John or follow me when I leave the room.'

'Where are you going?' said Alys, looking up quickly.

'To speak to Mistress Irvine. What can you tell me about her?'

'That she is a Paisley body, married to one of Montgomery's tenants, not lacking for money in any way,' said Alys, on an apologetic note, 'and that she has gone to hear Vespers with the rest of the household. They will be back in good time. What else do you need to see to this evening?'

'The boy's clothes,' said the mason. 'Where did you leave them, Gil?'

The pup looked anxious, but did not attempt to follow Gil, and wagged its tail in relief when he returned with the unsavoury bundle.

'*Of all vanegloir the lamp and the mirour.* William certainly had his vanities. His hair was newly barbered, and these are excellent boots,' he said, unrolling them from the folds of worn blue-grey stuff. 'They do not match with the gown at all.'

'Nor with the remainder of the garments,' agreed Alys, prodding fastidiously at the hose. 'These are past washing, they must be burnt. Have they nobody to mend their heels and toes? I will put the linen to soak and it can be washed tomorrow.'

'Are there not statutes concerning dress?' asked the mason.

'There are,' said Gil. He set down the boots and lifted the gown. 'Most folk ignore them if they can afford better. This was not new when William got it, I would say. It has seen much use.' He turned the garment, looking at the frayed lining. 'No – I hoped there might be somewhere to conceal secrets, but it appears not.'

'Perhaps the doublet?' suggested the mason, easing the sleeping baby into a more convenient position. 'What sort of secrets do we search for?'

'Just secrets.' Gil put the gown aside, and Alys picked it up and began to fold it neatly. 'William was a magpie for stray facts, as far as I can make out, and there is this red book the boy Gibson mentioned, which was certainly not concealed in his room.'

'Or if it was,' observed Maistre Pierre, 'the searcher found it before us, with the other papers. There were no papers in the chamber at all.'

Gil looked up from William's doublet. 'Yes, I suppose so. He – the searcher – would be at pains to destroy any evidence against himself.'

'Surely,' said Alys, lifting the other side of the doublet where it trailed on the floor, 'the best evidence is what you deduce from sign, like a huntsman? The book can only suggest names to us.'

'I think I will teach you philosophy,' said Gil. 'You think more logically than most men I know already.'

She coloured, and looked down at the doublet. Gil put out a hand to caress the side of her face, and found his fingers caught in her hair as she bent her head, suddenly intent.

'What's this? There's something in the lining. It feels too big to be a coin.'

'A medallion?' suggested the mason. Alys turned the inside of the garment to the light.

'He has slit the lining and made a pocket for this,' she reported, easing at the cloth. 'I think he did it himself, because it's a very tight fit. Ah, here it comes!'

Something with the dull gleam of bronze slid on to her lap.

'*Mon Dieu!* Look at that!' she said. She lifted the object,

121

and handed it to Gil. Their fingers caught and clung for a moment as he took it.

'Whatever is it?' he wondered, and turned the object over. It was a disc about as large as the palm of his hand, with a flat outer ring which could turn about the inner portion. The centre was engraved with the portrait of a saint whose attributes Gil could not make out, and around the saint and on the outer ring were two sequences of letters in order. 'Some kind of bronze hornbook?'

'Have you never seen one of these?' Alys took it back, and turned the outer ring carefully. 'It's a cipher disc. See – if I set the A on the outer ring against the D on the inner one, then all the other letters are set against the letter four along, and all I have to do to cipher a message is to read off the letters I want to make the word, instead of having to count on my fingers. This will be very useful. Which reminds me, father,' she added, 'I deciphered the letter from John of Castile. He writes that the mad Italian has got money for his voyage. He may have sailed by now, who knows?'

'What, that man who wants to find the western passage to the Indies?' Gil asked.

'Sooner him than me,' said the mason. 'Can you imagine? How long will it take him, do you suppose? And shut up on a boat with a crew of madmen, for he will certainly not find sane men to sail with him.'

'The inner ring is rearranged,' said Alys, still studying the cipher disc. 'It doesn't generate a simple substitution. It must be one of a pair, then. I wonder who has the other disc? It means, you realize,' she went on, looking up at Gil, 'that I can decipher that paper from the boy's purse as soon as I get the time.'

'Ah, yes, the paper,' said the mason. 'What of the other, the one which is not in code?'

'This one?' Alys turned and reached on to her father's tall writing-desk. From under a green-glazed pottery frog she drew a sheet of paper. 'Yes, this is the one. It refers to many people, but only by an initial.'

Gil took the paper, tilting it as the mason craned to see without disturbing his sleeping burden of child and dog.

'*M will be in G*,' he read again. '*H passed through for Irvine.* I wonder–'

'Montgomery is in Glasgow,' Alys said. 'I think that must be right. And Catherine tells me Lord Hepburn went to Irvine last week to take ship for France.'

'Oh, yes, about the King's French marriage.' Gil looked down at the paper again. 'It's a list of small facts like that.'

'Did he collect them for his own interest, do you suppose,' speculated Maistre Pierre, 'or for someone else's?'

'He bought these boots recently,' said Alys. She turned one up and showed them the sole, still flat and even.

'Yes,' said Gil thoughtfully. 'And he had that device for writing in cipher in his possession.' His eye ran down the creased paper, and he grinned. 'Alys, we are observed. See this line? *C marriage to dau of burgess.* And yet I had to tell him my name. He's had this by hearsay.'

'He has collected all the gossip of Glasgow,' said Alys. 'I wonder who he was selling it to?'

'Espionage, in effect,' said the mason.

'Yes,' said Gil. 'And the question, as Alys says, is who he was spying for.'

'But I know where he was getting the gossip,' said Alys. Gil looked up and met her eye.

'The barber's,' they said together.

When the household returned from Vespers Gil and Alys were in the courtyard, seated on the stone bench at the foot of the stairs while the wolfhound ranged about inspecting the flower-pots.

'When will your mother reach Glasgow?' she asked, drawing away from his arm as the voices echoed in the pend.

'God knows.' Gil rose reluctantly to his feet, checking the pup, which was growling at the approaching group. 'If she lies tonight at Bothwell with my sister Margaret she'll be here before Nones, but if she makes the entire journey in one day tomorrow, it might be this hour. The men may have brought my uncle word of her plans. No doubt I'll find out when I go up the hill.' He took her hand, to draw her into the house. 'I must speak to Mistress Irvine. Will you find out if she is able to talk to me now? And that reminds me, Alys. I have a task for you.'

She looked up at him, brown eyes smiling, her mouth most deliciously curved with kissing. He dropped a final kiss on her forehead and went on, 'The two lassies in the kitchen at the college know something, I'm certain of it. Could you get a word with them, maybe, or get one of this household to speak to them?'

'The college kitchen,' she repeated thoughtfully. 'One of our girls will know who they are. It may take a little time.'

'Time we do not have,' said Gil. 'Hugh Montgomery is waiting for us to fail.'

Mistress Irvine, although supported across the courtyard by two of the maidservants and still very puffy in the face, professed herself willing to speak to Gil.

'Vespers was bonny,' she said, 'the singin an that. And Faither Francis is that kind, he was a great comfort to me the day. I must send an offering. And for prayers for William. Oh, my poor laddie!' she exclaimed, turning her face away.

'Come and sit down and tell me about him,' suggested Gil. 'How old was he?'

'Just sixteen. He was born on May Day. Oh, he was the bonniest bairn,' she exclaimed, following him into the hall. 'Never sick, never greetin, and he walked and spoke sooner than any I've nursed. Exceptin his sainted mother, maybe.'

'You knew his mother?' Gil asked.

'I nursed her and all. So who should she turn to but me to foster her bairn? Though she never tellt me whose it was,' she added, in some dissatisfaction.

'Who was she?' Gil asked innocently.

'Oh, maister, I canny tell ye that. Lord Montgomery would ha my hide for it.'

'But if she's deid,' Gil suggested, 'no harm in it, surely?'

'No, maister. Dinna ask it, for I canny tell ye.'

'Tell me about William, then.'

She sat down on the stool he indicated, and launched into an extensive eulogy which bore little resemblance to the portrait of William painted by his friends at the college. Gil let her talk, picking the occasional nugget out of the torrent. William was cleverer than any, his manners were more polished than all the Montgomerys, his voice was sweeter than the lady Isobel's had been. When he was eight he had defeated a juvenile Douglas in scholarly dispute. Hugh Montgomery had intended to make a churchman of him, and legitimation proceedings had begun.

'Did the lady Isobel marry someone else?' Gil asked casually.

'She did indeed, before her bairn was a twelvemonth old, Lord Montgomery found her a husband and he was good to her. Poor soul, she fell sick afore Pace, there, and was shriven and in her shroud afore May Day. Five bairns she's left greetin for their mammy, and the oldest but thirteen year old. Nae doubt their daddy'll take another afore the year's end.'

'Did William know her?'

'He kent her name, but he never met her, no since he was, oh, the age of the bairn here. She'd send him gifts now and then, but she was far too far to visit, even if Gowdie'd kent about him. Poor soul,' sighed Mistress Irvine. 'She was a bonnie bairn and all. So when the letter cam, with the paper for William in it, I brocht it to Glasgow, seeing I was coming to see how our Davie did.'

'A letter? You can read, Mistress Irvine?'

'Oh, aye,' she agreed. 'Well, my name, and a wee bit more. I can write my name and all. I learned when the holy faither learned her, when she was a wee thing. She would have him teach me at her side. That was like her,' she confided, her face softening. 'Bonnie and loving and generous, she was, but she was obstinate as they come. Once she decided I'd to learn my letters and all, there was no shifting her. That's how I kenned Lord Montgomery would never learn whose bairn it was, no matter the beatings he threatened her. Not that he'd have done any of those things. So,' she continued, unexpectedly recovering the thread of her answer, 'she'd put my name, and she'd writ clear so I could read it that the other bit paper was for William. The messenger said it was in her jewel-box when she dee'd.'

'Was that the letter I delivered for you? Do you know what it was?'

'I don't,' she said regretfully. 'It never said in her letter, and it was sealed that close – well, you saw it yourself. Did he get it, maister? I wouldny like to think he went to his death without a word from his minnie.'

'I gave it into his hands. But we never found it in his room,' said Gil thoughtfully. 'Was he expecting it?'

'He was expecting it today, since I tellt him yesterday I had it, but I know he'd no more idea what it was than I did, for I asked him. I journeyed here yesterday with Sandy Wag the carrier who was fetching sacks of meal up for Lord Montgomery,' she elucidated, 'and I went to ask for him as soon as I'd heard Vespers, but I never had the paper wi me then, for I didny recall how close the college lies to the Greyfriars kirk. And the man was that disobliging about sending for him. Oh, and if I'd kenned that was my last speech with him –'

'Lord Montgomery took an interest in William,' Gil prompted.

'Aye, that he did. Paid me well to foster him. I think he'd a fondness for her – for the laddie's mother,' she confided, 'they all did, come to that, but it would never ha done. Too close, they were. Holy Kirk would never consentit.' She turned her head as Alys approached from the other end of the hall. 'I understand there's to be a wedding in this house,' she said, with tear-stained archness. 'I wish ye very happy, maister, and you, my lassie. I was never in such a well-run house. Such kindness as I've been shown under this roof, maister.'

'Thank you for your good wishes,' said Alys, taking Mistress Irvine's large red hand in hers. 'You are most generous. Gil, have you any more questions? Kittock has brewed a posset to help her friend to sleep.'

'Then she must drink it while it's hot. Thank you for talking to me, mistress.' Gil helped the woman to her feet, and watched as she was led off to the kitchen.

The mason found him deep in thought, staring out at the garden which sloped in the evening sunlight down towards the mills on the Molendinar. The pup was seated on his feet.

'By what Alys tells me, that was not hunting,' he said. 'That was poaching.'

'Like tickling trout,' Gil agreed. 'Poor woman, her grief at least is genuine. *She wept the starns doun frae the lift, she wept the fish out o the sea.* My uncle might know who this Isobel was. He might know about the legitimation procedure as well, since it would have to go through the Archdiocese. I must go home, Pierre.'

'Alys is seeing to the bairn. She will be down in a little. Shall we keep that dog tonight? The baby has taken a liking for him.'

'Aye, and Maggie will have enough to do seeing to my mother's men, without finding scraps for a growing dog. I'd be grateful. That is, if he'll stay.'

'If we put food in front of him, he will stay. What must we do tomorrow?'

'I need to speak to Nick Kennedy. I could do that on my way home. Tomorrow I must see the young man Nicholas Gray, and I think the chaplain, and we must talk to the dog man, and to William's barber. There is the list Nick made for us, of who was present at the feast.'

'Alys must decipher those papers for us. Is that all?'

'We need to look for William's notebook.'

'Indeed. None of this seems likely to lead us to the killer,' complained the mason.

'It could have been nearly anybody,' Gil agreed, 'or almost nobody.'

'If you sleep on it,' said Alys, emerging from the stair that led to the upper floors, 'it may become clearer. I am taking this bairn to Nancy. Gil, I set milk to warm for the dog. If you bring him down to the kitchen we can feed him.'

In the kitchen, the household was beginning to settle itself for the night. Two of the maidservants were clearing crocks, cooking pots which had been scoured earlier and set to dry by the fire were waiting to be carried out to the scullery, straw mattresses spilled out of an opened press. Kittock and her guest had their heads together in a corner, drinking something pungently herbal out of wooden beakers. A pottery jar with a face on it, of the sort that contained usquebae, stood on the floor at their feet.

Alys led the way to the fire, handed the infant John to Nancy and drew the little crock of milk from the ashes.

'Bread and milk,' she said, pouring the warm milk over the crumbs in another bowl. 'That will fill his belly. Ah, I have heated too much milk.'

She prodded the soaking crumbs with a carved spoon, while the pup's nose twitched.

'I think he is used to bread and milk,' said Gil. He set the animal down, and John immediately exclaimed something and waved his hands. Alys put the dish of bread and milk on the floor, and the pup plunged into it, tail swinging.

'Oh, mem!' said Nancy. 'Oh, mem, look!'

She held the baby up. He was gazing intently at the pup, and smacking his lips.

'He's hungry!' said Nancy.

Leaving Alys spooning bread and milk into the willing baby while the wolfhound watched with interest, and her father exclaimed his intention of walking up to Greyfriars later to hear Compline, Gil went out into the High Street and strolled the short distance to the college gate. It was shut, and he had to bang on it with the hilt of his dagger before Jaikie came to open the postern.

'Oh, it's you, Maister Cunningham,' he said, standing aside grudgingly as Gil stepped over the wooden sill. 'What are you after at this hour? I'd a thocht you'd be in a warm bed by this,' he added, descending into an unpleasant camaraderie. 'And better than a hot stone to warm it, eh?'

He nudged Gil, and grinned at him, releasing fumes of usquebae and spiced pork.

'My day's darg isny done,' said Gil with intense politeness, 'unlike yours. We haven't found who killed William yet.'

'Oh, him. Small loss, he is. I dinna ken why you bother.'

'What did you know of the boy, Jaikie? What like was he?'

Jaikie looked cautiously up the tunnel towards the courtyard, and beckoned Gil into his little room, where a rush-light competed with the small illumination from the narrow window. Closing the door behind them both he leaned close to Gil and hissed, 'He was a nasty, boldin wee bystart.'

'He'd a good opinion of himself, had he?'

'Oh aye. He had that. Well, you seen him yourself, Maister Cunningham, out in the street to greet the company as if he'd been the Dean his self. And he wouldny be tellt. None o' the rules was to touch him, but he'd run about looking to see who broke the by-laws and report them to Maister Doby. Even those that did him favours,' he added bitterly.

'I'm sure he found nothing to report about you,' lied Gil.

'Oh, no,' agreed Jaikie. He turned to poke at the brazier, and belched, adding his own contribution to the smells which already choked the room. 'Though I did him favours enough,' he added, leering sideways above the reluctant flame, 'and small return for them.'

'What kind of favours?'

129

'Oh, just things.'

'He collected information,' said Gil thoughtfully. 'Someone like you, here at the yett where everyone comes and goes, must have plenty information.'

'Oh, you'd be dumfounert, maister. They come through here, down the pend, past my door, aye talking, and no always in the Latin tongue. I hear a thing or two, I can tell you.'

'And William paid you for it?'

'Paid! That lang-nebbit rimpin pay for a thing? No, it was *Jaikie, I seen such-and-such of your doing that the Dean would like to ken. Tell me what you've got, or I'll pass him the word.* And then he'd leave papers for me to give to this or that man chapping at the yett, and aye sealed.'

'Small gain if they hadn't been sealed,' said Gil deliberately, 'for they were in code. We've found a page all in code, that was in his purse.'

'His purse? I thought that was stolen.'

'Who told you that?'

'Oh, one of them.' Jaikie jerked his head towards the courtyard. He left the brazier finally alone and flung himself down in his great chair, reaching for the stone bottle beside it. 'Usquebae, maister? No? Ye'll no mind if I take a wee drop. Ye'd be surprised at the secrets I get out of a jar of usquebae.' Removing the rag which did duty as a stopper, he tipped the bottle, swallowed and wiped his mouth. 'Aye, well, code, was it? Doesny surprise me.'

'Who collected these papers?' Gil asked.

'Just folks. They'd ask for them. No anybody I'd seen before.'

'You were just telling me how much you learn, here by the street door,' Gil observed. 'Is there anybody in Glasgow you don't know by sight?'

'Oh, aye,' said Jaikie sourly. 'The reason being, I'm tied here by this door, so if they don't come up the High Street, I canny see them. Anyway, it wasny Glasgow folk. You could tell by the way they spoke. Ayrshire, maybe, or over that way somewhere. I got a sight of a badge one time, same as on that house along the way. Montgomery's place.'

'What, the men had Montgomery's badge?' said Gil, startled. 'You mean he was simply writing letters to his kinsman?'

'Aye, maybe,' said Jaikie after a moment. He took another pull at the usquebae, and grunted irritably. 'That's another one finished. Well, it can join the others.' He rose, to add the bottle to a row standing under the shut-bed which occupied one end of the room, and took another from the press under the narrow window. 'Will ye have some of this one, maister?'

Gil shook his head, and the man sat down again and took out his eating-knife to break the seal on the new bottle. 'Aye, maybe he was just writing home. But he made a rare parade of it. And near every week. None of them writes letters every week, even the ones that misses their mammies.'

'And the dog?' Gil asked, recalling something. 'Was that another of the favours he asked you?'

'Oh, aye. He'd leave it here for Billy Dog to fetch away, or Billy 'ud bring it to wait here for him. He was training it, it seems. So he said. Billy's been here looking for it three times the day, starting when they were all at that feast.'

'You mean it wasn't William's dog?'

'Ask at Billy Dog. I wouldny ken. It answered to him well enough.'

'Thank you, I will.' Gil turned to open the door, and turned back. 'These letters. Was it only Montgomery's men that collected them? Were there any for anybody else?'

Jaikie, taking another draw at the usquebae, lowered the bottle and wiped his mouth before shaking his head.

'They wereny all from Ayrshire, if that's what ye mean, maister, but as to where they were from – I could make a guess, maybe. If it was worth my while.'

'You saw no other badges?'

'No on the messengers.' Jaikie eyed the stone bottle broodingly. 'No on the messengers. But I'll tell you one I did see,' he added.

131

'What one was that? Where was it?'

'Aye, ye'd like to know, wouldn't ye no? I'll tell ye what it was, though.' Jaikie took another mouthful of spirits, and belched resoundingly. 'The fish-tailed cross, it was.'

'What, the cross of St John?' said Gil, startled. 'Who was carrying that?'

'Secrets, secrets,' said Jaikie, leering at him. 'No Christian soul, I'll tell ye.'

Feet sounded in the tunnel, and someone knocked on the twisted planks of the door. Gil drew it open and Jaikie said aggressively, 'And what are you after, Robert Montgomery?'

'Maister Kennedy wants his friend sent for,' said Robert, looking down his nose in a manner very like his dead kinsman's.

'What friend? Is it this one here?'

Robert transferred his gaze to Gil, now looking at him round the door, bent the knee briefly and said with more civility, 'Maister Cunningham, aye, it is. Maister Kennedy wants you.'

'Thank you,' said Gil. 'Is he in his own chamber?'

'Aye,' said Robert, 'and he's got his troubles the now.'

The truth of this became evident as they stepped into the courtyard. A number of students loitered about the door of Maister Kennedy's stair, sniggering from time to time, and the well-loved teacher's voice floated out, raised in what Gil at first took to be fervent prayer and then recognized for equally fervent cursing.

'What in the world –?' he said.

'Ye should go on up, maybe,' said Robert. 'Maister Kennedy's a wee thing overset.'

'I can hear that.' Gil picked his way through the group and into the stair tower. The words became clearer as he ascended, a startling mixture of several languages, presumably gleaned from colleagues who had studied abroad. He reached the chamber door as its occupant paused for breath.

'What ails you, Nick?' he began, and stopped, open-mouthed on the threshold as the question answered itself.

The room was wrecked. Like most scholars, Maister Kennedy had few enough possessions, other than his books, but what he possessed was strewn across the floor and trampled. A shoe with the sole ripped off lay on an ink-dabbled shirt, more ink daubed the fur of a shoulder-cape on the bench, paper in single sheets was everywhere, and the straw mattress had been slashed open and emptied. The bookshelf gaped unoccupied.

'Christ and his saints preserve us,' said Gil. Maister Kennedy turned to look at him.

'Come in, Gil,' he said savagely. 'Come and see the reward for three years' work. I think they got everything.'

'When did this happen?' Gil asked.

'While we were at Vespers. The Dean did William proud – Christ aid, you'd think he'd been the next Pope but two, the way he went on – must have been near an hour for that alone, let alone the singing. I got back here not long since and found this.'

'Has anyone else been searched?' Gil began lifting handfuls of straw and stuffing them back into the mattress.

'How would I know? I've been here.'

'Have you told the Principal? The Steward?'

'I tell you I've been here. The students ken – maybe they've tellt someone.' Maister Kennedy picked his way to the bench and sat down. 'I canny think. Maybe I should tell the Principal.'

'I'll send someone.' Gil left the mattress and went down to the courtyard. The group of students was beginning to disperse now that Maister Kennedy was no longer performing, but a few remained.

'You two,' he said to the nearest, 'will you carry a word to Maister Doby for me?' They nodded, looking apprehensive. 'Say to him with my compliments that I'd be grateful to see him in Maister Kennedy's chamber as soon as convenient. Can you mind that?'

One of them repeated the message accurately enough, and they hurried off. Gil looked at the remaining boys.

'And you can find out for me, if you will, whether anyone else found anything wrong when they came back from Vespers, and if so, send them to me here.'

'Aye, maister,' said one of them. 'How bad is it, maister? It looked a fair old fankle.'

'Well, I hope nobody intended a joke,' said Gil, 'for it's far beyond that.'

He went back up to the fair old fankle. His friend was now lifting odd sheets of paper and throwing them down again, staring round helplessly.

'I canny see what's missing,' he confessed. 'St Nicholas' balls, Gil, they've wrecked my only shoes, I'll ha to wear these boots till I get them seen to.'

'Who was it?' Gil wondered. 'And what were they after?'

'None of the college. We were all at Vespers.'

'All?'

'I think so. We can find out. Besides, who in the college –?' Nick looked round. 'Maybe someone hates me.'

Slow footsteps on the stair proclaimed the arrival of Maister Doby. He halted in the doorway as Gil had done, staring, until Patrick Coventry appeared at his back and eased him into the room.

'My faith,' said the Principal at length. 'Who has done this?' He groped his way to the other end of the bench and sat down. 'What a day! What a day, with two such evil-doers in our midst. All your papers, Nicholas, and your ink-horns. And your books!' he exclaimed in horror as Maister Coventry lifted an abused volume from under the bed-frame.

'Principal, if I might make a suggestion,' said Maister Coventry in the brisk tones of one actually giving an order, 'I think our brother Nicholas would be better out of this. Might you take him back to your lodging the now? Then Maister Cunningham and I can sort matters here, till the Steward can spare a couple of servitors to redd up.'

Gil, admiring the way the Second Regent did not say

that the servitors could not be trusted to deal with the books and papers, added, 'Perhaps you would have a drop of aqua-vita or usquebae for him, maister? I think he could do with a restorative.'

'Aqua-vita,' said the Principal, brightening. 'A good thought, Gilbert. Come, Nicholas. Come to my lodging and we will think about where you are to lie tonight. Certainly you canny sleep here.'

Nick, with the prospect of strong drink, was persuaded to accompany the Principal. As Maister Doby's shocked exclamations dwindled down the stairs Maister Coventry said, 'Is the Principal right? The same as searched William's room, or not?'

'What do you think?' countered Gil, lifting the neighbour of the savaged shoe.

'William's property was not damaged. This is vicious.'

'Or unlearned. An unlettered man or men, unused to handling an ink-horn, searching for something particular.' Gil extracted a book from the fireplace and smoothed the pages. 'Something small, flat, easily hidden. A bundle of paper, perhaps, of a different size or quality from this stuff Nick uses.'

'William's writing was very distinctive,' observed Maister Coventry. 'I have seen it often when he took notes. He wrote very small, with the hooks and tails cut off short. Nick's writing is not the same at all. Even an unlettered man could tell the difference.'

'True,' agreed Gil, recalling the tiny script he had been studying earlier. 'So, an unlearned man or men searching for paper with William's writing on.'

'Or a book?' Maister Coventry lifted another ill-treated volume and shook straw from the leather binding. 'Or both?'

They had lifted and stacked the pages of Maister Kennedy's vigorous, looping fist which were flung around the room, and were restoring his six books to their place on the bookshelf when Maister Shaw appeared with two of the college servants, exclaiming in shock and annoyance at such a thing happening in the college.

'And during the Office, too! What a day, what a day! Tammas, you lift that straw. Andro, see to the clothes. That sark'll take a year's bleaching.'

'Was everyone at Vespers?' Gil asked, standing aside to let the men start work.

'Nearly everyone,' admitted the Steward. 'The kitchen would be busy. With Vespers being early, the scholars' supper was put back to after it. But they'd all be under Agnes Dickson's eye.'

'This cape's all ower ink,' said Andro, lifting it cautiously. 'And the hood an all.'

'Maister Kennedy will be vexed,' said the Steward.

'It isn't Maister Kennedy's,' said Gil in dismay. 'It's mine. So's the gown.'

'So was the gown,' corrected Maister Coventry, holding it up. The heavy woollen stuff was slashed and ripped, the lining hanging out here and there. 'I think this is past repair.'

Nick, when he learned of the damage, was more than vexed.

'I wouldny have had that happen for all sorts, Gil,' he exclaimed on a blast of the college aqua-vita. 'Oh, will you look at the cape!' He produced a slightly tipsy chuckle. 'If it was only splashed here and there you could have said it was ermine, but that's past praying for.'

'I'll say one of the skins is in mourning,' said Gil. 'John Shaw has all in hand, says your chamber will be habitable by the morn, and I must be away up the town. What happened to that list you and Maister Coventry made for me?'

'Patey's got it.' Nick looked into his glass, but it remained empty. 'We made the fair copy up in his chamber in the Arthurlie close. I think I left my cope there and all. Fortunately. Likely it'd be covered in ink like your fur if it'd been over this side. God, I loathe Peter of Spain. Three years' work, and all to do again.'

'I think when you have put the pages in order you will find there is less damage than appeared at first,' said Maister Coventry in his graceful Latin. He drew a bundle of papers from the breast of his gown. Something stirred in Gil's memory, but the Second Regent went on, 'Here's your list, Maister Cunningham. I hope you may be able to read it. We wrote down who was present, where they were after the play, and who was with them. Nobody seems to have been alone, so it may not be of much assistance.'

'If I can eliminate names from the hunt,' Gil said, 'it will be of great assistance. And I have another task for you, Maister Coventry, if you are willing.'

The Second Regent's eyebrows went up.

'It seems Nick Gray heard the three senior bachelors talking, after they had put William into the limehouse. He told the kitchen, but I'd like to know who else knew of it.'

Patrick Coventry opened his mouth to reply, closed it again, and gazed thoughtfully at Gil with his good eye.

'Not easy,' he said at length.

'No,' agreed Gil, 'but better done by an insider.' He held up the sheaf of papers. 'I thank you both for this piece of work. And now I must be off. If any of the students comes complaining of another chamber being searched, keep him for me till the morning.'

'Patey can see to that too,' said Nick. 'I'm for my bed. Maister Doby's put me in a corner here, for which I'll say a Mass in his name the morn, I swear it. Come and find me in the morning, Gil. If I haveny dee'd of an apoplexy from all the excitement,' he added sourly. 'Tell your minnie I was asking for her.'

Gil bade goodnight to Maister Doby, who had taken refuge in a soothing volume of St Jerome, bundled his damaged finery over his arm, and made his way out of the Principal's lodging. In the evening light a few students were still standing about in the courtyard, but although some nodded or said good evening none accosted him. At the yett he stopped and glanced into Jaikie's fetid den. The man was sprawled in his chair, with the bottle of usquebae in his grasp. He looked up, but did not speak.

'Who was past the yett while they were all at Vespers?' Gil asked.

'I never saw a thing,' pronounced Jaikie with slow emphasis. 'No a feckin thing.'

'If you think of any more badges,' Gil said, 'send and let me know.'

Jaikie leered at him.

'Maybe I will,' he agreed indistinctly, 'and maybe I'll no. Secrets, secrets,' he said again, and held up the bottle. 'The secrets I've learned from you, my wee friend.' He waved the bottle at Gil. 'Pull the yett ahint ye, maister. I'll bar it later.'

There seemed to be no point in continuing the conversation. Gil unbarred the yett and stepped out into the quiet street, realizing as he did so that he was still holding the folded list of names in his free hand. He tucked it into his doublet and strode on up the High Street.

It all happened with great suddenness. It was the rush of feet behind him which alerted him. He sprang sideways and whirled, weight on one foot, and as the three men reached him placed a kick with the other where it would do most damage. Its recipient went down in the muddy street, crowing and retching. Gil leapt backwards, groping for his whinger, and realized belatedly that he was not wearing it. His remaining attackers, circling warily now they had lost the advantage of surprise, recognized this in the same moment and moved in. One had a short sword, the other a cudgel. Gil drew his dagger right-handed and raised the other arm, embroiled in heavy folds of fabric, in time to balk the sword.

His opponents were hooded and cloaked in black, the free weapon arms black-garbed. He could see no faces, but a glitter of eyes betrayed another sudden movement, and he was barely in time to duck the cudgel. He whirled, lunging with the dagger, but the man twisted like a salmon and the weapon slashed harmlessly through cloth. The sword whirred, and he jerked his left arm up to parry again, meeting the hilt of the weapon with the bundle of heavy cloth. His other hand came round with the dagger, and he felt the blade connect and heard the grunt of pain.

As he tugged the knife free, the cudgel made vicious contact with his forearm, and the dagger dropped from suddenly useless fingers. He danced sideways to deliver another kick, bringing his protected left arm round as a shield, and his boot made contact with the swordsman's arm. The sword fell to join his dagger, but as he stepped back there was a stunning blow to his head. The gasping fight, the peaceful street, spun away from him.

Just before they vanished he thought he heard shouting. It sounded like the mason. It can't be, he thought. He's at Compline. Then darkness took him.

Chapter Seven

'Did you know them?' asked Maistre Pierre. 'They made off when I shouted, and I was more concerned to see to you than to pursue them. If Alys had not insisted that we left Compline early . . .'

'I never got a sight of their faces.' Gil leaned back against the lavender-scented pillow-beres of the mason's best bed, and eased his feet out from under the wolfhound, which had been fed already and had returned to its self-appointed guard duty. It appeared to have grown over-night. 'I am very grateful that you came by. This is damnably inconvenient, but it could be a lot worse.'

'It isn't broken, Brother Andrew said.' Alys set down the tray with the porridge-bowl to reach across and test the temperature of the compress on Gil's wrist, but would not meet his eye. 'And nor is your head. I think a night's sleep has made a lot of difference.'

'If I'd been wearing my other hat it might be a different story.' Gil pushed his hair cautiously out of his eyes. Beware of what you wish for, he thought. You might get it. 'I wish I knew what they wanted, that they attacked me in the High Street in broad day.'

'It wasn't your purse,' said Alys, lifting the tray again. 'That was untouched. I thought one of them snatched something from your doublet before he ran.'

'From my doublet?' repeated Gil. A memory surfaced, and he went on in dismay, 'Maister Coventry had just given me the list of names. I think I put it in the breast of my doublet.'

'I found nothing like that. It would have crackled when

140

we stripped you.' Still avoiding his eye, she put the tray on a stool and turned to reach for the muddy bundle of his clothes. 'These must be brushed,' she said critically. 'I should have seen to it last night. And I know of a furrier who can rescue the cope, but the gown will take several days' work. There are no papers here, Gil. Do you suppose your friends made a copy?'

'But why steal a package of papers?' said Maistre Pierre.

'Presumably because the right paper was not to be found in William's chamber or in Nick's,' Gil said slowly. 'Ah, no, you haven't heard about that. When I got to the college last night I found that Maister Kennedy's room had been searched while they were all at Vespers. It looked as if a whirlwind had been through it. That was when my gown and cope were damaged.'

'But they didn't find whatever they were looking for,' said Alys, 'and thought it might be in the papers in your doublet.'

'There was no loose paper in the boy's chamber,' said Maistre Pierre. 'I still think that curious, in a student's lodging.'

'But though William's property was in disorder, nothing was damaged,' said Gil. 'I think someone different searched Nick's chamber, someone unlettered perhaps. Alys is right. It might have been one of the three who attacked me.'

'One of them won't be walking straight this morning,' the mason observed with satisfaction. 'That was a handy kick you fetched him, Gil. Almost one would have thought you were in Paris.'

'That's where I learned the trick.' Gil tried to move his fingers, and winced. 'I wonder if Nick still has the notes.'

'Send word to ask.'

'It's too long a word for Luke to remember, and I canny write. We'll have to postpone the betrothal,' he added, 'if I canny sign my name.'

141

'You must just make your mark left-handed, and we will witness it,' suggested the mason.

'What, like a tinker in the heather? I think not.'

'I shall write to the college for you,' said Alys firmly, 'and we can send Luke, as soon as he is back from taking word to your uncle.'

'And then he may go and do a little work, if it is not too much trouble.'

Gil looked up at his prospective father-in-law. 'Do you intend to work too?'

'What do you want done?'

'Someone should speak to the dog-breeder, and I thought of another thing that should be done, but it's left my head.'

'I must go up to the *chantier*. Wattie knows what must be done this week, but best if I let him tell me first it is impossible. If Robert Blacader is ever to see his new chapel finished, let us hope I am right and not Wattie.' The mason looked about him. 'Then I will come back, and we will think about this matter. Alys, where is my scrip?'

'It is down in the hall, father.' She smiled at Gil at last, and he felt the sun had come into the room. 'I will fetch pen and ink, and see the baby fed, and return to you.'

She lifted the tray and left, slender in her blue dress. The wolfhound raised its head to watch her go, then curled up again. Gil threw back blankets and verdure tapestry counterpane, and swung his legs out from under the sheet.

'Pierre, help me with my points before Alys comes back,' he requested, peeling the compress off his wrist.

'No, no, keep that on!' exclaimed the mason. 'Oil of violets to draw out the black humour in the bruising, and sage leaves for the numbness and loss of movement in the fingers –'

'I am not going about Glasgow smelling of oil of violets,' said Gil decidedly, trying to pull on his hose one-handed. 'Give me a hand here, or Alys will get a sight of my drawers.'

'She has seen them. She and I stripped you last night,'

said Maistre Pierre, obliging. 'How tight do you wish to be trussed? I do not think you are fit to go about Glasgow anyway. That was an unpleasant crack on the head.'

'Fit or not,' Gil began, and was interrupted by a knocking at the great door of the house.

'*Que diable?*' The mason went to the window and leaned out in the sunshine. 'Ah, good day, Maister Cunningham! Enter, pray enter! I will descend to you.'

'My uncle?' said Gil, battling with his doublet. 'Sweet St Giles, what did Luke say to him? He hasn't been down the town since Yule.'

'I bade him say you had a blow to the head and we had kept you here.' Maistre Pierre was hastily lacing the doublet. 'No saying what he told them in the kitchen, of course, and Maggie would relay it with embellishments. Stand still or this will be crooked. There – now you are fit to serve the King. Wait here, I bring your uncle.'

He drew the bed-curtains shut and bustled down the stair to greet his guest. His voice floated up, loud, affable and reassuring, through the floorboards. Gil set out two of the mason's tapestry backstools and sat down on the window-seat with the sun on his back, wishing his head did not ache so much.

Canon David Cunningham, senior judge of the diocesan court, Official of Glasgow, who rarely left the cathedral precinct at the top of the High Street, ducked under the lintel behind Maistre Pierre and surveyed his nephew with a chilly grey eye. After a moment he relaxed, and nodded.

'Your mother will be in Glasgow by Nones,' he said, 'and I've no wish to greet her with the news that you're at death's door.'

'She would likely take exception to the idea,' Gil agreed.

His uncle's mouth twitched, but all he said was, 'Well, well, I can see you are not much damaged. What have you been about? What is this about the college coalhouse? No, let us sit down, Gilbert, Peter Mason here tells me you'd quite a bang on the head.'

Alys brought elderflower wine and small biscuits and slipped away again while Gil and Maistre Pierre between them recounted the events of the feast and what followed. The Official sipped the wine from his little glass, holding it up to the light appreciatively, and said at length, 'Patrick Elphinstone's no fool.'

'He never was,' Gil said, and got a sharp look.

'What he'll want is first to find a culprit he can show Hugh Montgomery, and then to deal with a trial and sentence himself, behind the college yett. He'll realize soon enough that Montgomery won't be satisfied with that.'

'I think Maister Doby has seen it already,' Gil said.

'Aye, very likely.' David Cunningham set his wineglass down. 'John has had experience of men like Hugh Montgomery.'

'When was that?' asked the mason. 'Maister Doby seems a quiet man.'

'He wasn't at fault. When he was maister at the grammar school at Peebles . . .' Canon Cunningham paused to count on his long fingers, but shook his head. 'I canny mind when. A good few years ago now. There was a boy killed when the lads were playing at football. A broken neck, I think. The family were very threatening.'

'Football is a dangerous game,' agreed the mason.

'That's interesting,' said Gil thoughtfully. 'Is it widely known, sir?'

'Anyone that's in the diocese would know. The kirk at Peebles is a prebend of St Mungo's,' the Official explained to Maistre Pierre. 'The grammar school there's in our gift as well.'

'William was given to extortion,' said Gil. 'I saw him speak to Maister Doby before the Mass.'

'Aye, this William.' David Cunningham sat back. 'Who did you say his parents were again?'

'The Dean described him as *the son of an Ayrshire lady now married to another*,' Gil quoted, '*and a kinsman of Lord Montgomery*. His foster-mother, who was nurse to his mother, called her Isobel and said she was close kin to Montgomery and married a Gowdie.'

144

'If both parents are close to Montgomery,' said the Official, 'they may have been too close to marry. Gowdie. Gowdie.' He stared thoughtfully over Gil's head at the thatched roof of the mason's drawing-loft opposite.

'Mistress Irvine said something of the sort,' Gil agreed.

'Legitimation procedures,' prompted Maistre Pierre.

'I wonder if his mother was Isobel Montgomery?' said Canon Cunningham, lowering his gaze to meet Gil's. 'Her father would be a first cousin of Hugh Montgomery's. There were three sons and the one daughter, and Montgomery had the disposal of the marriages.' He paused again, considering. 'He was provident in that, for all he was no more than eighteen or so himself. If I mind correctly, all in one winter, he married one of Argyll's daughters, he got a Lennox lady for his brother Alexander and a Maxwell for one of the cousins, and betrothed this Isobel to a Maxwell adherent. Pretty good, for one season's work. I heard she died recently,' he added.

'That would fit,' Gil said.

'I hadn't heard of a bairn. I wonder who its father might have been?'

'It was fostered secretly, perhaps,' said Maistre Pierre.

'Mistress Irvine didn't know who the father was,' Gil said, 'and she said Gowdie didn't know of the boy's existence.'

'And you mentioned legitimation procedures.' Canon Cunningham stretched his long legs and began to gather himself together. 'Aye, well. I haven't time for idle gossip. If you'll call my groom, Maister Mason, I'll away up the hill to my desk and see what I can find out.'

'Thank you, sir.' Gil rose as his uncle did.

'I wonder who the father might be,' the Official said again, frowning. 'Montgomery's kin is not so wide.'

'A groom?' speculated the mason robustly. 'The steward? The chaplain? What men does a girl of such a family get to meet?'

'Who would the chaplain have been?'

'From the Benedictine house at Irvine, maybe. Or a

kinsman, indeed?' The Official gazed absently at the flowers in the sunny courtyard, then shook his head. 'Aye, well. What will I send to your mother, Gilbert?'

'What should you send?' said Gil uncomfortably. 'I must see to this matter. Hugh Montgomery is waiting for us to fail, and we have less than two days to it. I will be home tonight.'

'Aye, well. I think she might take exception to that idea and all.' Canon Cunningham clapped his legal bonnet over the black felt coif, and shook out the skirts of his cassock. 'See to your duty, Gilbert. I'll send something.'

He raised a hand in his customary blessing, and turned to go, then stopped so suddenly that the mason collided with him.

'Christ and his saints preserve us, what's that?' he demanded, staring at the great best bed.

Gil, following his gaze, began to laugh.

'It's the young man's dog,' he explained.

The wolfhound did not move from its position, long nose poking between the tapestry bed-curtains, one bright eye just visible, but they heard its tail beat on the mattress. Gil moved forward, and the tail beat faster. 'It's taken a notion to me,' Gil went on, drawing the curtain back, 'and the harper's bairn's taken a notion to the dog.' He urged the animal down on to the floor, where it inspected Canon Cunningham more closely and allowed him to scratch its jaw. 'He should go outside, Pierre.'

'He should,' agreed the mason resignedly. 'Come, dog. Outside and do your duty.'

Alys slipped back into the room as soon as Maistre Pierre and his guest reached the courtyard.

'I didn't stay,' she said, lifting the tray of little glasses, 'because I wanted to tell you what I thought of you getting up, and I couldn't very well do so in front of your uncle.'

'Why? Do you think he might repudiate the contract when he finds how I'm going to be henpecked?'

Gil stretched his good hand to her. She moved closer, but

146

said earnestly, 'You should have stayed in bed. Brother Andrew –'

'When we are married I'll stay in bed as long as you like,' he promised, smiling. She looked away, and the colour rose in her face. 'For now, sweetheart, I've a matter to investigate for the college, and too little time to do it in. We must write a word for Nick –'

'I've done that,' she interrupted. 'I told him you were attacked, not much injured, and the papers stolen, and asked if he took a copy. Luke carried it there a while ago.'

'You can do everything,' he said admiringly, drawing her down to kiss her. 'Even rescue me from robbers. What made you leave Compline early? It was well timed.'

'I don't know,' she said. 'I was uneasy. The Office was no comfort to me, I felt I should be elsewhere. And then we came out of Greyfriars' Wynd and saw the fighting, and realized it was you.'

'I'm glad you did,' he said again. 'I really think you can do everything.'

'Except make you stay in bed when you should,' she complained. He would have answered, but her gaze sharpened, and she stared beyond him at the yard. 'What is my father doing?'

Gil turned to look out of the window. Down in the courtyard the mason was peering into one of the tubs of flowers, assisted by the wolfhound, which had stood up with its front paws on the rim of the tub. As they looked, Maistre Pierre drew something out of the earth under the marigolds. The pup offered to take it, but he held it up out of the animal's reach, and seeing their watching faces waved the item at them.

'Papers!' he called.

'It was the dog,' he said, when he had brought papers and wolfhound up to the best chamber. 'He examined all the tubs, as they do, but he paid extra attention to that one, and then sat down by it and looked at me.'

'He is an exceptional dog,' Gil said, patting the creature. 'I wish I could keep him.' He unfolded the bundle one-handed, shaking the earth from it. The wolfhound sniffed at the paper and lay down with its head on Gil's feet. Alys eyed the scatter of soil on the waxed floorboards, but said nothing. 'Our Lady be praised, they have numbered the pages. Four, five, six – and what's this? This doesn't belong –'

'It's different writing,' said Alys.

'It's Nick's writing. I looked at enough of it when Maister Coventry and I picked up the mess in his chamber. *And this most discriminating Peter . . .* Aye, it's a page of his book.'

'He has written a book?' said Alys. 'I should like to see that.'

'How did this get here?' asked her father. 'How did the papers find their way into your flower-pot, *ma mie*, and how did a page of the book get into the list of names? Whose is the other writing? Who wrote down the names?'

'I assume Maister Coventry wrote them down,' said Gil, leafing clumsily through the pages, 'and thank God for that. His writing is far clearer than Nick's. As to how they got there – they were in the tub nearest the pend, weren't they?'

'They were,' agreed the mason. 'You are thinking that anyone could have come that far, in from the street, hidden them under the marigolds and run off, without being noticed.'

'I am.'

'Luke has been in and out,' said Alys thoughtfully, 'and Annis is sitting with Davie this morning, and Kittock has swept the front steps and the yard, but otherwise there has been nobody at the front of the house since Prime except for ourselves up here. Your uncle came through the court-yard. Oh, yes, and a messenger from Lord Montgomery.'

'A what?' exclaimed Gil.

'A messenger from Lord Montgomery.' She coloured up again. 'I'm sorry, I should have told you sooner, but it was only a piece of impertinence. I was to ask you if you were ready to give up the search yet. It was while your uncle was here.'

'What did you say to him?' asked Maistre Pierre.

She glanced shyly at Gil. 'I was annoyed by the way he spoke. And his expression was – anyway, I said, *A Cunningham never gives up*, and shut the door on him. I hope that was the right thing to say.'

'You couldn't have bettered it,' said Gil, looking at her in amazement. 'Alys, you are a wonderful woman. How soon can we be married?'

'You must be handfasted first,' said Maistre Pierre.

'What puzzles me,' she persisted, 'is how Lord Montgomery should know you were here, and why he should think you would give up now.'

'That's true, you know,' said her father. 'How would he know you were here?'

'Could he have seen you carrying me home?' Gil asked. 'How dark was it by then?'

'Plenty of light.' The mason scratched his jaw, his thumb rasping in his neat black beard. 'I suppose he could, although we were close under the wall when we passed his yett.'

'But father,' objected Alys, 'I was carrying the hat and cloak, and you had Gil head down over your shoulders. Even his mother would not have known him if she had looked out and caught sight of us.'

'Unless,' said Gil, 'Montgomery knew already that I was injured. What was the messenger like, Alys? Had you seen him before? Would you know him again?'

'He had the Montgomery badge on his shoulder,' Alys said. 'Otherwise he was quite ordinary, like anybody's groom. Middling height, brownish hair, not past forty. Oh, and a limp.'

The mason looked at Gil.

'As if he had been kicked recently?' he suggested. Alys burst out laughing.

'Yes, of course! If I'd realized I'd have offered him a poultice!' She saw Gil's expression, and sobered, adding, 'I'm sure he could have applied it himself.'

'And he could have tucked these papers under the marigolds as he came into the yard,' said the mason.

It was, Gil reminded himself, the effect of running a large household; but he knew he had shown yet again how startled he was by Alys's particular combination of genuine maidenly modesty and breadth of worldly knowledge.

'What do we know from this?' he asked rhetorically, recovering his countenance. 'We know the papers were taken from me by violence last night and returned by stealth this morning.'

'They were taken by someone looking for something in writing,' said Alys.

'But not this writing,' agreed Gil.

'And it could have been Montgomery who took them, who returned them, who is searching,' contributed the mason.

'And has still not found what he seeks,' said Alys.

'And it is likely that the same person –'

'Or persons,' put in Alys.

'Or persons,' Gil agreed, 'searched Maister Kennedy's chamber and carried off at least one sheet of his writing. But most likely it was someone else who searched William's chamber.'

'But what are they all looking for? Not the young man's red book, I take it, since they snatched a heap of loose papers.' Maistre Pierre gestured at the list of names. 'Gil, there is the ciphered writing we found in the purse. Remember?'

'I remember.' Gil looked at Alys. 'It could be important. Have you had time to look at it?'

'I have not,' she said firmly, sounding very like her father. 'What with nursing the sick and injured, the grieving and the fasting, and keeping my hand on this household, my time has been full. I hope to sit down with it this morning,' she added. 'Then we may know if it's important enough to be a prime mover in the matter.'

'And I must get up the hill to St Mungo's,' said her

150

father, 'to make sure Wattie has not decided to put in a chimney where I have marked a window.'

'What, for when they elect the next Archbishop?' said Gil. The mason grinned, then looked beyond Gil into the courtyard. The grin faded.

'Who is it now?' he said resignedly. 'One of the friars, and a student. Who can it be?'

'It's Father Bernard from the college,' said Gil, twisting to look. 'The chaplain.'

Sighing, Maistre Pierre rose and went away down the stairs. Alys knelt to whisk the scattered earth on the floor into her apron, lifted the tray with the little wineglasses and followed him, eluding Gil's attempt to make her sit down beside him.

Below, in the hall, the mason could be heard clearly, greeting his guests. The chaplain answered him with the friars' customary Latin blessing, spoken in his deep musical voice. At Gil's feet the wolfhound stirred, and raised its head.

'But certainly,' said Maister Mason. 'He is above stairs. Come up, come up. Some refreshment, surely? My daughter will –'

'Not for me, I thank you.' Father Bernard's Scots was accented like the mason's. 'But I'm sure Michael here would be glad of something.'

Michael's voice, muffled, assented to this. The wolfhound rose slowly to its feet. Gil stroked it and was startled to find its rangy frame rigid and trembling, with the coarse grey fur standing erect. Feet sounded on the stair, and a faint growl began deep in the dog's throat, becoming gradually louder as the feet approached.

'Quiet,' said Gil firmly. The animal's tail swung against his knees, but the growl continued. Gil grasped the long muzzle, then flung his injured arm round the dog's chest just in time, as Maistre Pierre led Father Bernard into the room, the friar paused in the doorway to pronounce his blessing and the wolfhound, with a scrabble of claws on the floorboards, tried to launch itself snarling at the intruder.

151

'What ails the beast?' asked the mason, startled into French.

'I don't know. Quiet!' said Gil again. 'Down! I'm sorry about this.'

'Think nothing of it,' said Father Bernard, eyeing the pup's display of white teeth warily. 'Dogs often dislike me. Possibly they find the robes alarming.'

'Shall I remove him?' offered the mason.

'He won't go with you in this state,' Gil pointed out, hanging on to the sturdy collar. 'Down! Oh, Alys! Will he go with you?'

'Whatever is the matter?' Alys, grasping the collar in both hands, dragged the snarling animal across the floor. 'What has angered him?'

'Take care,' said Father Bernard anxiously. 'He may bite you.'

'I'll feed him,' said Alys. 'Come, dog! Come with me! Gil, you must name him. How can we give him orders if he has no name?' She hauled the dog bodily out on to the stairs, and the mason shut the door quickly behind her.

'No name? Is it not your animal, then?' asked Father Bernard.

'It seems to have belonged to William Irvine,' said Gil precisely. 'Good morning to you, sir.'

'Oh, that dog! Aye, good morning, Maister Cunning-ham,' said Father Bernard in his melodious voice. He sat down on one of the tapestry backstools indicated by the mason, and put back the hood of his habit. The dark hair round his tonsure was cut short, and curled crisply; the sunken eyes in the cadaverous face regarded Gil intently. 'I bring you greetings from Dean Elphinstone and the Principal,' he continued. 'Your man brought word that you were attacked in the open street. What a dreadful thing to happen in this peaceful place. But I find you on your feet and clothed. Did you take any scathe?'

'Very little, thanks to Maister Mason.' Gil eased his position on the window-seat. He was finding other aches and pains, and his head was throbbing.

'God in his mercy be praised,' said the friar, and raised his hand to make the cross.

'Amen to that. This is very kind of you, father, to visit like this.'

'The college was most distressed to hear of your mis-adventure,' said Father Bernard largely. 'And was it rob-bery? Did they make off with anything valuable?'

'Some papers only,' said Gil.

'Nothing important, I hope?'

'Nothing that cannot be replaced.'

'Did you know them? Were they common blackguards of the burgh, or someone's dagger-men? What could their motive have been?'

'I never got a sight of their faces,' said Gil.

'They seemed expert fighters,' remarked Maistre Pierre. 'And used to working together, I thought, Gilbert.'

'Aha!' said the chaplain. 'Maister Doby will hear that with relief, and I admit to the same.'

Maistre Pierre looked startled, but Gil said, 'No, it was none of your flock, father. These were all older than I am, by their movements, and seasoned fighters as Maister Mason says. As to motive, I have no clear idea, but since the papers they took were connected to the matter I am investigating for the college, I assume it was related to that.'

'Ah, yes. Poor William. *Requiescat in pace.*' Father Bernard made the sign of the cross, and Gil and the mason both murmured *Amen*. After a moment he continued, 'His burial will be tomorrow, after Sext, and we have arranged a quodlibet disputation in Theology after dinner, to give the boys' minds a better direction and prevent them falling into melancholy.'

So we have until noon tomorrow, Gil thought, to bring this to a conclusion.

'Did you know the dead boy well, father?'

'Why, no, hardly more than his fellows.'

'There are only forty students just now,' Gil pursued, 'few enough to spend the whole year with. Did nothing distinguish William Irvine from the others?'

153

'I could not say so. I had little contact with him, except for the music. I know the students of Theology well, of course,' expanded Father Bernard, 'mature individuals with well-formed minds, but the young men of the Faculty of Arts come less in my way, other than those who confess to me.'

Gil thought of some Theology students he had known, but did not comment. Instead he said, 'Who was William's confessor?'

'I think perhaps Dean Elphinstone.'

'Do you know who his parents were?' asked the mason.

The dark eyes turned to him. 'I can tell you nothing about his parentage.'

'Or about his habits of extortion?' Gil asked.

'Extortion? Did he – It seems hard that he should be dead in such a way, poor boy, and slandered as well. I am sure he did not practise extortion. Have you discovered nothing that might tell us who killed him?'

'So he never approached you with threats of any kind?' Gil asked.

'Certainly not! What could he threaten me with?'

'None of us is blameless,' pronounced the mason.

'That is very true,' agreed Father Bernard, attempting to regain control of the conversation, 'but I hope my faults are not such that a boy of sixteen could frighten me with threats of exposure.'

'What did he have to show you, father, yesterday in the Outer Close before the procession?' Gil asked.

'Yesterday? He showed me nothing,' began Father Bernard.

'I brought him a package from his foster-mother,' Gil said. 'I gave it to him before the college yett, and went into the close. William passed me, and spoke to you in the courtyard. I thought he said *This might interest you*, or some such thing. I wondered if it had anything to do with the package.'

'Oh, now I recall.' Father Bernard's sunken eyes turned piously to the ceiling. 'The poor boy. He wished to show

154

me something, and I had not time to hear him, for I still had to arrange for the music to be carried to St Thomas's. I promised to give him time later, perhaps after I had given the ordinary Theology lecture, but of course by then he was dead. The poor boy,' he said again. 'I suppose we may never know what troubled him.'

'He is salved of all troubles now,' Maistre Pierre pointed out. He and Father Bernard crossed themselves simultaneously.

'And he had never threatened, for instance,' said Gil almost at a venture, 'to report you to the Vicar-General of your Order for heresy?'

'For heresy?' repeated Father Bernard harshly. 'Why should he do that?'

'For quoting Wycliff, perhaps,' Gil suggested, 'or discussing Lollardy in your ordinary lectures?'

'One must encourage students to dispute these points, so that one may expose the fallacies on which they are grounded,' retorted Father Bernard in Latin.

'That alone might create trouble if one were in Paris,' Gil observed.

The theologian snorted. 'Paris! They're still licking at Louis' heels on the nominalist question. They can't have it both ways.'

'While Glasgow follows *Albert, the subtil clerk and wys.* The path of orthodoxy is narrow,' said Gil, watching the friar carefully, 'and William was industrious in detecting those who stepped from it in other segments of the University sphere. I speculated, merely, on whether he had approached you in the same way.'

'No,' said Father Bernard. Gil waited, while the mason looked from one to the other. 'But I had wondered,' said Father Bernard after a moment, reverting to French.

Gil, still waiting, was aware in the corner of his eye of movement in the courtyard. There was a knocking at the house door. Father Bernard's expression grew troubled and portentous.

'I thought the boy might have been gathering information,' he admitted.

'We know he was doing that,' Gil agreed. Down in the courtyard Alys in her blue gown hurried out to the pend beside a groom in well-worn riding-gear. 'Any sort of information in particular?'

'Information to sell,' pronounced Father Bernard. The musical voice took on a note of grief. 'Information of value to one faction or another, the selling of which could only increase the discord with which this poor country is riven.'

'Espionage?' said Maistre Pierre. 'It seems very possible. But who would he sell to, here in Glasgow?'

Gil turned his gaze away, in time to see Alys crossing the courtyard again, leading a guest in to the door in the most formal way. The hand laid on her arm belonged to a slender, graceful woman in muddy travelling-garments, her hair bound up in a coarse black cloth under a battered felt hat like a sugar-loaf with a brim.

Has she not given that hat to the poor yet? he thought in resignation, and looked back at the Dominican, who had closed his mouth over his yellow teeth with the air of one having summed up a situation.

'Are you saying, father,' he said, 'that William was in truth selling information to someone? Which faction did you have in mind?'

'I have no way of knowing,' stated the chaplain. 'He was kin to Lord Montgomery, which would give him an entry to Argyll and his followers.' Gil nodded, and wished he had not. 'And he messed with Michael Douglas, who is below in your kitchen, and his friends last year. He would have contact with the Hamiltons and Douglases through that boy.'

'I think Michael dislikes him,' Gil observed.

'A false face, surely, designed to conceal the truth.' Father Bernard looked over his shoulder as footsteps sounded in the other room. 'You have another guest,' he said, rising.

Alys entered the room first.

'See who is here, father,' she said. 'It is Gil's mother.' She

156

stepped aside to allow the woman in the sugar-loaf hat to follow her.

Most landholders, when they travelled, took time near their destination to find a sheltered spot, groom the horses and change their clothing, in order to make a good appearance by riding into burgh or castle in velvet and satin and jewels rather than stained travelling gear. This woman's heavy woollen skirts were bedraggled and spattered, there was mud on her hat and her long-chinned, narrow face, and the gloves she drew from her hands as she stood in the doorway were dark with her horse's sweat.

Getting to his feet, Gil was aware of a single quick, penetrating, maternal glance before her attention was turned to the mason stepping hastily forward to greet this guest. Watching her dealing expertly with Maistre Pierre's words of welcome and of apology for not having been at the door to meet her, Gil recalled that Egidia Muirhead, Lady Cunningham, had for years occupied a senior place in the household of Margaret of Denmark, James Third's devious and melancholy Queen, encountering the many foreign visitors who made their way through the court.

'*Et tecum*, Bernard,' she was saying now in response to Father Bernard's blessing. 'How long have you been back in Scotland? You're not teaching at the college, are you?'

'I am indeed,' said Father Bernard in his deep musical voice.

'And here is your son,' said Maistre Pierre.

Gil went down on one knee to kiss the offered hand so like his own. Her long fingers gripped his, hard and briefly, and she said in Scots, 'I'll have David Cunningham's hide for cushions. He sent Tam out to meet me, to bid me have no ill-ease for you, so of course I brattled on into Glasgow with all possible haste, and here I find you at the clack with half the burgh. Get up, son, and we can all sit down.'

'Hardly the half of Glasgow,' Gil protested, obeying.

Her grasp on his hand tightened again as he straightened up, but all she said was, 'Don't argue, my dear. It's unseemly.' She seated herself on one of the tapestry chairs, and asked kindly, 'So when did you return to Glasgow, Bernard?'

'Some years since,' admitted Father Bernard. 'And you, madam? I believe you are alone now? Is all well with you?'

'As well as a poor widow can expect,' said the lady of Belstane. 'I have my dower lands. We win a living. Is your mother still alive?'

'She died two years since at the feast of St Remy, and is buried at Irvine,' said Father Bernard with precision. Lady Egidia raised her eyebrows, and he added, 'She died as the widow of Lord Montgomery's kinsman Robert. His grand-sire's brother, I believe.'

'God rest her soul,' said Lady Egidia. 'And what are you doing at the college, Bernard?'

'I have the honour to be chaplain there, and to deliver a course of ordinary lectures. Which reminds me . . .' He cast a glance at the sky through the glazed upper portion of the window. 'I must not tarry longer. I have a disputation to prepare for this afternoon. My colleagues in the Faculty of Arts will rejoice to hear that you took little scathe, Maister Cunningham.'

In a flurry of mingled bows and benedictions he got himself out of the room, followed by Maistre Pierre. Gil's mother, hardly waiting for their footsteps to disappear down the stair, sat down again saying with satisfaction, 'He never could stand being questioned. Wretched man. And his mother was a good woman,' she added. 'Well, Gil, what is this you've got yourself into?'

'Mother,' said Gil, 'this is the demoiselle Alys Mason.'

'We've met,' said Lady Egidia, smiling at Alys, who still stood by the door. 'I was met most graciously and hospit-ably at the yett, and welcomed into the house. It is truly kind of you, my dear, to take my abominable boy in when he was hurt.'

Alys, who had opened her mouth to speak, closed it again, and looked uncertainly at Gil. Suddenly she was wearing the pinched look of distress he had seen before, her high-bridged nose very prominent.

'Mother, we are –' he began.

'You are embroiled in something at the college, Tam tells me,' his mother persisted.

'Mother, what are you –?'

'Forgive me,' said Alys. 'There are things I must see to in the kitchen.'

She slipped out, and Gil began again.

'Why don't you –?'

'A most accomplished lassie,' said his mother, 'and certainly not the kind to take as your mistress. This is a well-ordered house, and Maister Mason seems a cultured man. I can see they are people who –'

'I had your letter.'

'Oh, you did? I assumed it had gone astray.' She tipped her head back to look at him. 'I see you can still blush, dear. Then you know my feelings.'

'My uncle thinks differently,' said Gil. 'He favours the marriage.'

'Your uncle! He's a sentimental old man,' said Lady Cunningham crisply. 'We educated you for the Church, Gilbert, and '

'I ken that, mother, and I value my learning next to my hope of salvation, but –'

'– and I don't want to see you throw it all away for the sake of a pretty face,' she continued as if he had not spoken.

'I have no intention of throwing it away. My uncle is certain I will still get a living in the Law.'

'What does he know about it?' demanded his mother, dismissing the senior judge of the Archdiocese with a snap of her fingers. 'We were determined one of our sons was for the Church, Gil. Your share of the money went to pay for your learning, and I've no more to give you. You must have a benefice to live on, so you must be a priest, it's that simple. Besides, who will say Masses for your father and Hugh and Edward?'

'Masses?' repeated Gil. His head was beginning to throb again. 'What's wrong with the Masses being said for them already in Carluke? I thought you paid Robert Meikle for that!'

'Aye, but it's better if it's said by blood kin.'

'Mother, if I had died at Stirling instead of Edward, who would say the Masses then?'

'Yes, but you didn't,' she said unanswerably.

Footsteps, and a rattle of claws, sounded in the room nearest the stairs. Alys appeared in the doorway as the wolfhound scurried in past her, slithered on the waxed boards, and flung itself, yammering ecstatically, into Gil's arms.

'Your pardon, madame,' she said, 'but Michael wishes to speak to Maister Cunningham, and he must be back at the college soon.'

Michael, following her, made a brief general bow in the doorway. Gil, fending off the pup one-handed, acknowledged the boy's presence with a sort of relief, but his mother said, 'Come in, godson. Should you not be at a lecture?'

'I've missed that,' admitted Michael. 'We're supposed to be gated till after St John's day, but Lowrie said we should tell you, Maister Cunningham, and I drew the straw and Maister Doby said I could get out for this because we're sort of kin. Just. If you'll forgive it, madam.'

'What should you tell me?'

'Our chamber's been searched.'

Chapter Eight

The wolfhound, having made certain that its idol was safe, thrust its long muzzle under Gil's arm and rolled its eyes at him.

'Was anything taken?' Gil asked. 'Or anything damaged?'

'Not that we can see.' Michael grinned. 'You would hardly tell it's been done, except for Lowrie's idea.'

'And what was that?' asked Lady Egidia.

'Hairs,' said Michael. 'We knotted one of each of our hairs together in threes, Tod – er, Lowrie and Ninian and me, and put them among our papers where they would fall out if someone else meddled, but they wouldny blow away by accident. That was after William's chamber was searched,' he explained. 'And they were still there after Vespers but no after dinner.'

'What might they have been looking for?' asked Alys. She was still wearing the pinched look of distress, but she sounded perfectly composed. Michael glanced at her and went red, to his own obvious embarrassment.

'I don't know,' he said. 'We've no secrets. None like that, any wise.'

'Surely this is some kind of student joke,' said Lady Egidia. 'I can mind a tale or two from your time at the college, Gil.'

'Well, but this was serious,' said Michael. 'I mean, there wasn't any foolery with it. They'd not left any humorous drawings, or stuffed a shirt to look like a lassie at the window, or – or anything.' He threw another glance at Alys, and went red again.

'Hm,' said Lady Egidia.

'Has anyone else been searched?' Gil asked.

Michael shook his head. 'We asked, but nobody's saying. Oh, and I was to give you this. It's from Auld – from Maister Kennedy. He said it was in his cassock in Maister Coventry's chamber and could that be what they sought when his room was wrecked.'

He held out a small red book. Gil took it and turned the pages clumsily, one-handed.

'It's William's writing,' added Michael helpfully, 'but it doesny make sense.'

'Code again?' said Alys, moving to look over Gil's shoulder.

'Not code,' said Gil. 'Initials, parts of words, a kind of private shorthand. It's the boy's red book with all his notes in it. Some of this will be harder to decipher. I mind now, it was on top of the pulpit in the Bachelors' Schule where you were all dressing for the play. I asked Maister Kennedy if he knew about it and he took it for safe keeping. Michael, tell him I don't know if it's what they sought, but it will certainly be useful. Anything of William's is likely to tell us something.'

'Oh, and Jaikie at the yett bade me say he had a word for you,' added Michael. 'He said it was about something you spoke about yesternight.'

Feet sounded again in the outer room, the softer scuffle of one of the maidservants in her worn shoes. Jennet bobbed in the doorway.

'If you please, mem,' she said to Alys, 'there's water hot and set in your own chamber, and a comb and towels and all.'

'Thank you, Jennet,' said Alys, and turned to Gil's mother, the pinched look submerged in the procedures of a civil welcome. 'Would it please you to wash, madame?'

'That sounds good,' said Egidia Muirhead, rising. 'You will come and see me while I'm in Glasgow, godson. I have messages from your home for you, and a great cake with plums in it.'

Michael agreed with enthusiasm that he would certainly

162

wait on her, and bowed as she followed Alys to the stair.

'Tell me what had been searched,' said Gil. The boy's expression changed.

'Everything we'd marked, maister,' he said warily. 'Ninian's carrel, my carrel, Lowrie's. All our kists. My books had been moved about, for they wereny in the order I keep them, but the other two wereny sure.'

'Papers?' Gil asked.

'I think so. They'd been careful,' he said, 'you couldny have tellt, except for Lowrie's idea, and we got tired of knotting hairs after a bit, so if they went through all our papers one by one we'd no way of knowing.'

'And what could they have been looking for?' Gil asked. 'We think William was involved in more than simply some scaffery round the college.' Michael eyed him from under the thatch of mousy hair. 'He may have been selling information to one faction or another. Could one of you have had something he might find valuable? A letter from home, perhaps, or a paper of some sort?'

'William's dead, maister,' Michael pointed out. 'He canny be searching the college. He's in the bell-tower next door with two friars praying for him. They'd notice if he got up to go and search our chamber.'

'I know,' agreed Gil, 'but someone is looking for something, possibly for more than one thing,' he added, recalling a comment the mason had made, 'which must be connected with William's murder. A book like this, or some papers. Can you think of nothing one of you might have had that would fit that description?'

'We've seven books between us,' Michael said, 'and papers in plenty. But nothing's been taken, that we can see, maister.'

'Could William have hidden something in your room,' asked Gil desperately, 'for someone else to collect later?'

'That's just –' began Michael, before civility stopped him. 'No, for we were all through our papers before Vespers, and we'd have seen his writing then. You couldny mistake it.'

Gil eased the wolfhound's head on his knee. It hardly stirred.

'In this notebook,' he said, 'which I suspect is a list of secrets which William was using as a basis for his extortion, there is a page headed with a heart, which might be held to stand for the Douglases, and the letter M beside it.' Michael, descendant of the Douglas who carried the heart of Robert Bruce to the Holy Land, said nothing, staring at him. 'Here it says *A scripsit Eng.* Could the Great Douglas – the Earl of Angus – be writing letters to England? And this line has an M and another heart, and the little sign they use in pedigrees to signify marriage, and *L Kilmaurs.* I assume you aren't marrying into the Cunninghams,' he said lightly, but Michael's expression did not change. 'So this probably refers to the rumour which is going round my family too, that Angus is hoping to marry his daughter Marion to my kinsman Lord Kilmaurs.'

'It's old news now,' Michael said.

'William has drawn a line through it,' Gil agreed, 'which probably means he has either sold the information, or found it unsaleable.'

'Is there more?' asked Michael after a moment.

'A little,' said Gil, 'but I need more time to interpret it. Can you cast any light on what should be here?'

There was another pause. Then, the ready colour rising again, Michael burst out with, 'Maister, you willny tell my faither?'

'What is there to tell him?' Gil asked. 'That you talked to a fellow student? Where did the word come from? Does it come from home?'

Michael nodded, biting his lip. 'You ken the way the old man gossips. Forbye, I think he hopes I've a future as one of the King's officers. Chancellor, or treasurer, or some such. So he writes all this news to me, how Angus is writing to England, and negotiating with Kilmaurs for his daughter's marriage, and trying to get the Douglas earldom revived. I don't know where he gets the half of it himself.'

'And William found one of these letters?'

'Aye.' Michael scowled. 'I kept them shut away, but last year when we were mentoring him and his fellows, he poked about in my carrel, and sold what he found to the Montgomery, who likely passed it all to Argyll. Then when the King set siege to Angus at Tantallon, you remember? William told me what he'd done and threatened to tell my father I'd sold it on if I didny tell him more. I tried not to,' he said desperately, 'but he'd some way of knowing when I got word from home, and he'd come and make more threats.'

'Are all the letters still there? Was that why your chamber was searched?'

'No, no, I looked for those the first thing after my books and my notes. They've no been touched.'

'Why did you not tell your friends about this?' Gil asked. 'I'd have thought the three of you together were equal to anything.'

'That's what they said last night,' Michael admitted, shamefaced. 'But the more he demanded, the harder it got to tell anyone. I feel a right fool now.'

'You're not alone in giving in to his demands,' Gil said, leafing one-handed through the little book. 'There are a lot of entries here I can make little of. Near every page has a different heading. What a busy young man William must have been.'

'Aye, he was,' said Michael grimly, then added with a sudden show of maturity, 'but I'm free of his threats now, and he's deid, and never shriven of his misdeeds.' He grinned mirthlessly. 'It's like that poem my father's aye on about. How does it go, about riches? *Winning of them is covatice*, and *Keeping of them is curious.*'

'*Quhat blessitnes has than richess?*' Gil capped the lines, aware of a quite ridiculous level of pleasure in the boy's implicit compliment. 'Indeed. So William has found, I suppose.'

'I'm no one for poetry,' Michael confided, 'no like Lowrie, or my kinsman Gavin at St Andrews, but whiles ye can see the point of it.' He looked at the sky. 'Maister, I must be gone. I've missed two lectures now and it'll soon be dinner time.'

'Very well,' said Gil. 'Give Maister Kennedy my message. And will you also tell Nicholas Gray I need a word with him? I hope to be at the college later today and I can speak to him then.'

'Yes, Bernard was the Montgomery's chaplain,' said Egidia Muirhead. She sat back as Alys began to clear the small table at which they had eaten. 'That was quite delicious, Mistress Mason. For, I suppose, ten years. Certainly from the time Hugh and his brother were still in tutelage. Bernard's mother used to boast about how well Montgomery trusted him, until the scandal.'

'Scandal?' said Gil.

She looked affectionately at him. 'You sound like your uncle David. Yes, a scandal. I forget the details, which I suppose is an object lesson. One thinks at the time one will never live it down, but the world forgets. Let me see – was it land or a leman?'

'This was in Ayrshire?' Gil prompted. She nodded, accepting a glass of Alys's cowslip wine. 'How did you hear of it?'

'Gil, it was fifteen years ago, the year your sisters had the measles. I heard about it when I went back to Stirling after Elsbeth died. Or am I thinking of that business of Meg Douglas's? Your good health, Mistress Mason.'

'It must have been difficult for Father Bernard, being chaplain to Lord Montgomery,' said Alys, when they had drunk a toast each. Gil and his mother both looked at her. 'These great houses are usually full of dogs,' she pointed out.

'That would be no trouble for Bernard,' said Lady Egidia blankly. 'He used to hunt with the household, his mother told me. I recall her boasting about some occasion when he saved Montgomery himself from being slashed by a boar. They'd be hip deep in dogs.'

'Curious,' said Gil, looking down at the wolfhound,

166

which was lying at his feet watching him with an alert eye. 'This fellow tried to attack him as soon as he saw him, and his explanation was that dogs often dislike him because of his robes.'

'What a strange thing to say,' said his mother. 'Of course, he wouldny hunt in his habit. Does the beast attack other friars?'

'He's a very well-mannered dog,' said Alys, before Gil could speak. 'Whoever schooled him has done well by him.'

'He had no objection to the Dominicans at prayer beside William's bier.' Gil looked down at the animal again, and it raised its head hopefully. 'Later,' he said, and it sighed and put its nose on its paws.

'Bernard always was inclined to say what seemed right at the moment,' said Lady Egidia. 'I should make little of it, Gil. Now, are you coming up the hill with me?'

'I can't,' he said. 'I must go back to the college and speak to the young man's friends.'

'You should be staying quiet,' said Alys, 'with that compress on your wrist again.'

'My fingers are less painful.' Gil tried to move them, and stopped. 'I have until noon tomorrow to find out who killed William Irvine, or Hugh Montgomery will take the law into his own hands. I should have been out questioning half the college this morning.'

'Then I shall see you at supper tonight,' said his mother.

'It depends,' he said cautiously. 'If Maister Mason returns from seeing to his men he will help me, and things may go faster, but I may be late home.'

'Very well, dear. I'll wait up for you.' Lady Cunningham rose, and turned to Alys. Gil thrust his feet into the pair of the mason's slip-slop shoes Alys had procured for him and rose likewise as his mother continued, 'Mistress Mason, I must thank you again for your hospitality, and for your charity in taking in my son. And now I must trespass on your time no longer. Is my groom still in your kitchen?'

'He is,' said Alys, 'and your horse is easily fetched, but

will you not stay longer? I am sure my father would like to talk to you. He only went out because his journeyman sent to ask his advice.'

'I am expected in Rottenrow.' Lady Cunningham smiled sweetly at Alys and shook out her muddy skirts. 'I am quite sure we'll meet again, my dear. Your father and my son appear to be good friends.'

'Mother,' began Gil in exasperation, but Alys returned the smile with equal sweetness and bent her knee in a formal curtsy.

'I'm sure we will,' she agreed. 'I look forward to it.'

Gil stared rather grimly at Lady Cunningham and her groom vanishing round the curve of the High Street.

'I don't know what to say,' he said. Alys put a hand on his arm.

'Don't say anything you'll regret,' she counselled. He looked down at her with a reluctant smile, and she drew him back through the pend into the courtyard of her father's house.

'She's being very difficult,' he said. 'And I haven't time to coax her round now.'

'Does coaxing her round work?' Alys asked, watching the wolfhound which was stalking a bee.

'No,' he admitted. 'She makes up her own mind. My sister Dorothea's the same.'

'That's your oldest sister? The one who is a nun?' He nodded, and flinched. 'Gil, does your head still ache?'

'No.' He sighed. 'I need to look at that list of names your father got out of the flower-pot. I need to speak to people at the college. I hope you can get to the kitchen-girls, and there's William's notebook and William's coded writing to decipher. I can't think what to do first. And more important than all of these, more important to me than the future of the college, I want my mother to like our marriage.'

'Come into the house,' said Alys. 'We can do nothing about courting your mother's good opinion at this moment, but the other matters can be dealt with. I haven't had time to tell you yet – Annis brought the two college servants by our kitchen this morning, and I got a word with them.'

'Alys!' He stared down at her. 'What did they have to say?'

She pulled a face. 'Not girls I would have in my household. Good enough workers, I've no doubt, but silly. I wouldn't leave them in charge of a bowl of milk. So it took me a while to get them to the point. Is it always like that, questioning witnesses?'

'It can be,' he agreed. 'Did they recall what you were asking them about?'

'Eventually. It was difficult, for I had to speak to them out here where Mistress Irvine wouldn't hear, and they were alarmed by being taken aside by Annis's dame. Eventually I had to resort to flattery.'

'I've always found it a useful weapon.'

She smiled quickly, and nodded. 'It worked in this case. In the end, all it came down to was – I hope I have the names right – that they heard Nick Gray say that William was in the limehouse, poor boy, and that Robert Montgomery also heard it and – so they said – laughed a vengeful laugh.'

'A vengeful laugh,' he repeated.

She nodded again. 'They seem addicted to ballads. I took it to be the perception of hindsight.'

'*And a vengeful laugh laughed he.*' Gil scuffed thoughtfully at the cobbles with the toe of his borrowed slipper. 'So they felt Robert disliked William.'

'I asked them that, and they said nobody liked William. What a dreadful thing, to be disliked by everybody.'

'He had one admirer among his fellows,' said Gil, 'and Robert his kinsman tolerated him, but I should say he was one who liked himself well enough for nobody else's opinion to matter.' He sighed. 'Well, we can set that aside now. I had hoped it would be of more value.'

'I have also –' She tugged at his arm. 'Come into the house and I'll see the dog and the baby fed. I have also begun work on the coded notes.'

169

'When did you find the time?' he marvelled. 'And . . .?'

'I have discovered the correct setting of the cipher disc, and deciphered the superscription.'

'The superscription? You mean it is a letter?' Gil followed her up the stair to the door, the dog at his heels.

'To his kinsman, Lord Montgomery.' Alys paused to look back at him. 'Why would he write to his kinsman in code?'

'Ah,' said Gil. 'That fits with something Michael said. William sold some information to the Montgomery last year – obviously he was still collecting for him. What else does it say?'

'That I have yet to find out.'

'It could,' said Gil slowly, 'this letter, be what they were searching for when I was attacked. I'm reasonably sure those were Montgomery's men, possibly even the man himself, in which case I'm lucky to be alive. And they didn't find what they wanted, since they returned what they took. Alys, we need to know what it says.'

'Well, I got no further – Annis arrived with the two girls – but now I have the disc set it should take little time. Shall I go on with that, or do you want to look at the list out of the flower-pot, or the notebook?'

When Alys returned to the mason's panelled, comfortable closet, carrying a little beaker and a jug of something which gave off a herbal-scented steam, Gil had the pages of Maister Coventry's neat writing spread out on the desk.

'I think we must deal with this first,' he said. 'From this I can decide who to question next, and then you can decipher the coded letter. If you have the time,' he added, raising his head to look at her.

'The dinner is in hand. What does this tell us?'

Gil bent to the orderly sheets again.

'He said they asked where each was after the play,' he recalled, 'and who was with them. If we can put them all

170

into groups who confirm one another's lists, we should be able to eliminate most of them.'

'We may need a slate,' said Alys. 'Or several. Drink this.'

'What is it?' he said suspiciously.

'Mostly willow-bark tea. It should help your head.'

'My head is –' he began, but she held the beaker out insistently. 'Oh, very well.' He tossed back the dose and made a face. 'I've tasted worse. You'll never make an apothecary if your potions are palatable.'

'I won't bother putting honey in it next time. Now what must we do with this list?' She bent over one of the pages. '*Maister William Anderson, crossed Outer Close and Inner Close, stood in kitchen-yard, with Maister John Scoular, Maister Robert Kerr, Maister James Murray, saw many students in the close.*' She looked thoughtfully from one sheet to another. 'Your friends have done half the work in the way it is set out. I will fetch a slate, or perhaps two, and we can divide up the groups as you said.'

'You will have to write,' he said ruefully, looking at his damaged hand.

'Yes, and you may soak that in this hot water. I put mallow in it, and violet leaves.'

'I don't need anything for it,' he said.

That once settled, they started rearranging the list. Gil was surprised by how rapidly it went. He sat by the window, his bruised arm immersed to the elbow, and read each entry aloud to Alys. She stood at the tall desk, and copied the names down in a grid which she had drawn up on one of the large slates from the heap in the courtyard, nodding and muttering to herself as each of the blocks filled up.

'This is strange,' she said as they reached the final page.

'What is?' Gil asked, finger on the next name on the list.

'There seem to be two different sets of people who can say they saw Father Bernard.'

'Perhaps there were.'

171

'No, but –' She looked from one box to another. 'They didn't see one another. These four were crossing the Inner Close when they saw him, and this pair stayed in the Outer Close.'

'Perhaps he crossed one and then the other,' said Gil, 'on the way to or from Blackfriars.'

'Mm,' she said, still scowling at her grid. 'What does he say himself?'

'He doesn't seem to have been asked,' Gil reported, turning pages one-handed.

'Well, you must ask him. Give me the other names.'

Gil read the names for her, and she wrote them carefully in the appropriate boxes, and finally sat back and shook her head.

'No, it still doesn't fit. People contradict themselves, and nobody remembers everybody they saw, but everyone else was seen by someone from more than one group. See, you and your friends are here, where this group saw you going to the Arthurlie building, wherever that is, and here, where this group bears them out, and here again where two of this larger group noticed you returning. But only these people here noticed Father Bernard in the Inner Close, very soon after the play, and only these two saw him crossing the Outer Close.'

Gil peered over her shoulder, holding his wet arm out to one side, and finally shook his head.

'I can't see it. I accept what you say,' he said hastily as she drew breath to explain again, 'but I can't make it out. Maybe when my head's clearer. What interests me is what he was doing in the Outer Close. The door to the Theology Schule is in the Inner Close.'

'Was he giving a lecture?'

'So Nick Kennedy said.'

'Gil, you're dripping everywhere. Let me dry that.' She lifted the towel she had laid ready and mopped carefully at his wrist. 'Is it any easier now?'

'Maybe.' He tried his fingers again. 'Maybe a little.' He put his arm over her shoulders, drawing her close, and turned back to the spidery lines on the slate. 'What you are saying is that everyone else is vouched for, but Father Bernard, who was not interviewed, seems to be in two places at once.'

'I don't know what I'm saying about Father Bernard. Something is strange, and I need to look at it more closely. But, yes, everyone else is spoken for.'

'That's a relief.'

'It is.' She turned to look up at him, and her flickering smile lit her eyes. 'You could hardly have kept them till this morning, just the same. Your friends have asked the right questions.'

'I told them what I needed to know. They have done it well.' Gil stared down at the slate. 'I wonder . . . Alys, I need to go round to the college. It is past Nones, and I must speak to so many people. Including Father Bernard, as you say.'

'You had much better –' she began, and was interrupted.

'Mistress? Are ye there, mem?' One of the maidservants was puffing up the stairs.

'What is it, Annis?'

'Here's Wattie, mistress, wondering where the maister might be, and there's two more laddies at the door for Maister Cunningham. Where'll I put them all?'

'Where my father is?' repeated Alys. 'But he went up to the site!'

'I'll come down,' said Gil, rolling down his shirt sleeve. 'Are they in the hall?'

Alys on his heels, he descended the spiral stair, stepping with care in the borrowed shoes, and found the mason's grizzled journeyman admiring the fit of the stones behind the tapestry hangings. Beyond him, beside the display of plate at the far end of the shadowy, beeswax-scented hall, the two Ross boys stood shoulder to shoulder in their belted gowns. They turned as he stepped off the stair, and bowed hastily, saying across Wattie's greeting,

'Can ye come, maister?'

'Maister Doby sent us –'

'It's important.'

'What has happened?' he asked, nodding to Wattie, and crossed the room to them. 'Has Maister Doby learned something new?'

They moved closer together, and the older boy put out his hand to touch one of the silver cups gleaming on the cupboard in the dim light, the kind of thing to be seen in the hall of any well-to-do home, as if he found it reassuring.

'It's Jaikie,' he said after a moment.

'He's deid, maister,' said the younger one, on a rising note. 'Like William.'

'What, throttled?' said Gil involuntarily.

'It was a knife,' said the older boy. 'Someone's killed him in his chamber.'

'There's blood,' said his brother, and sniffled. 'And he's all sharny.'

'Let me put my boots on,' said Gil.

'Gil,' said Alys in a small voice. He turned to her, nearly falling over the wolfhound, and found that Catherine had come up from the kitchen and was standing behind her nurseling, staring inscrutably at Wattie from under her black linen veil. 'Gil, Wattie says my father has not been to the site today.'

'Perhaps he went somewhere else?' Gil suggested, taken aback. 'It must have been a pressing matter, to take him out of the house when he had a guest.'

'I understand,' said Catherine in her gruff French, 'that there is a little difficulty with *madame* your mother? Perhaps our master absented himself as a matter of diplomacy.'

'He went out because Wattie sent for him,' said Alys in Scots.

'Oh, aye, I sent for him,' agreed Wattie, 'but he never came.'

'Could he have met someone else he wanted a word with?' said Gil, wondering privately if Catherine was not right.

'But who else? And for so long?'

'My uncle?' Gil suggested. 'Perhaps he thought of some-

174

thing they needed to discuss. You know what they're like when they get together.'

'That's likely,' said Wattie.

'*Vraiment*,' agreed Catherine.

'Perhaps,' said Alys doubtfully, 'but he has not been home to eat, either.'

'Maggie would feed him if he's talking to my uncle. Perhaps,' Gil added hopefully, 'he and my mother are coming to some harmony by now.'

'*Maistre le notaire a raison, ma mie*,' said Catherine.

'Now, who would do him harm, mistress?' said Wattie, in the tone of one regretting that he had raised the subject. 'He's no enemies, and the size he is nobody'd trouble him.'

'I'm sure you are right,' she said in unconvincing tones, and became aware of the maidservant still standing openmouthed by the stair. 'Annis, take these laddies down to the kitchen and find them a bite to eat while Maister Cunningham gets his boots on. Bide here, Wattie, while I think what to do.'

She drew Gil back up the spiral stair to where his boots, newly waxed, stood neatly at the corner of the best bed. As he eased the first one on, pulling awkwardly one-handed at the heel, she said in anxious French, 'I do not like it. He never vanishes like this.'

'He is a grown man,' Gil observed. 'He may not be pleased if you set up a search for him without reason.'

'I know that.'

'How long since he left the house?'

'When Father Bernard did. Gil, that is what worries me.'

Gil straightened up to look at her.

'I don't trust Father Bernard,' she said earnestly. 'I think he isn't being truthful, and he knows more about William than he says. What if he has –'

'I agree,' said Gil slowly, 'that Father Bernard doesn't appear completely truthful. I have already caught him out in something. But that doesn't make him capable of harming your father, who must be twice his size. It's Jaikie who has come to grief, not your father.'

'No, but –'

He trod down on the heel of the second boot, wriggled his toes into position, and said, 'Alys, I must go to the college. I want to see the porter before they move him. I will ask for Father Bernard when I am there – after all, he left here to go and prepare a disputation, he should be about the place. If I learn anything that causes me worry I will send to you immediately.' He cupped his hand round her jaw. 'Your father has done something unexpected and it has taken longer than he intended. I'm sure that's all, sweetheart. Send Wattie back up to St Mungo's, and stop worrying.'

She bit her lip and nodded.

'There has been only the two of us and Catherine for so long,' she said after a moment. 'And in Paris –'

'This is Glasgow, not Paris, and there are three of us and Catherine now.' Gil shrugged on his short gown and kissed her. 'Go and find those boys, and try not to be foolish.'

The college yett was shut again.

'Maister Doby shut it behind us,' said the younger Ross.

'They're all in the pend,' said his brother. Gil looked at them. They had followed him, slightly sticky and a little more cheerful, from the mason's house, but were becoming round-eyed and quiet again.

'I'll knock at the yett,' he said. 'You two go round by the Blackfriars gate, in case Maister Doby's in his house, and tell him I'm here.'

'We could go in at his door,' said the younger boy. 'We're allowed.'

'On you go, then.' Gil watched them run back to the street door of the Principal's house, then turned and hammered on the yett with the hilt of his dagger, as he had done the previous evening. The postern swung open immediately, and he found himself face to face with the missing Maistre Pierre.

'At last!' said the mason, at the same time as Gil said, 'So this is where you are!'

'I sent for you a good half-hour since,' said Maistre Pierre reproachfully.

'Wattie sent for you,' Gil countered, 'and has just come down to the house looking for you.'

His friend's face changed.

'Alys will be worried. I must send –' He stood back, so that Gil could enter. The pend was crowded and noisy with conversation and a buzzing of flies, and there was a foul smell in which Gil identified a top-note of burning paper. Yet another group of marvelling students was taking turns to stare in at the door of the porter's small room, past the barricade provided by a resolute Lowrie Livingstone. The mason laid a big hand on the shoulder of the nearest blue gown, which jumped convulsively as its owner twisted to look at his assailant.

'You, my friend. Run down to my house, which is the one with the sign of the White Castle,' he instructed, 'and tell them there that Maister Mason is at the college. Ah, Maister Doby,' he continued seamlessly. 'My son-in-law is arrived.'

'Oh, Gilbert,' said Maister Doby, pushing through the dissolving crowd of onlookers as the messenger, recovering his poise, slipped past Gil and away in a cloud of flies. 'We are finding out who last saw him alive. Is not this a dreadful thing? Who could have done such a deed? Is it connected to William's death, do you think? I would have moved him long since, but Maister Mason said –'

'Tell me what has happened,' said Gil. The last of the goggling students drifted out of the pend into the courtyard, and Lowrie, with obvious relief, lowered his arm and stepped to one side.

'He's in there,' he said unnecessarily. 'Someone's knifed him.'

Just inside the doorway, Jaikie lay on his back beside his overturned chair, his head tipped back and away from them, one leg drawn up and his codpiece and the legs of his hose dark and stinking. His mouth was wide open, showing his blackened teeth. He could have been drunk, except for a dribble of blood running from his mouth down towards his ear, and the flies crawling on that, on his wide-open eyes, and on the bloody rent in the breast of his greasy blue livery gown.

On the floor beside the brazier a bundle of blackened papers explained the smell of burning.

'Well,' said Gil.

'Well, indeed,' said the mason.

Maister Doby, clutching his beads to his nose as if they would ward off the smell, said, 'Poor man. Poor man. He had his faults, but he hardly deserved this.'

'Nobody deserves this,' said Gil absently, gazing round the room. 'Is this how he was found? Who found him?'

'We did,' said Lowrie from the pend.

'Go on,' said Gil. 'Who is *we*?'

'Us. Michael and Ninian and me,' said Lowrie reluctantly. 'We came down to ask who came into the college yesterday while we were all at Vespers, and there he was. So I stayed here and the others went to tell Maister Kennedy and he tellt Maister Doby and here we all are.'

'Where are the others now?'

'Out in the yard,' said Lowrie. 'It was a bit much for Ning.'

'The boy Ninian was a little overcome,' elaborated the mason, 'so I sent him away.'

'Very wise,' muttered Maister Doby, still staring at the corpse. 'Gilbert, can we do nothing about these flies? It is not seemly.'

'Is this how you found him? You touched nothing?'

'I'll say we touched nothing,' agreed Lowrie vehemently. 'We could see – with the flies and that – and the blood. You could tell he was dead. He looks like a day-old fox kill.'

'Not as much as a day.' Gil was still looking about the room. 'So you moved nothing.'

'That's what I'm saying. Except to take the papers out the brazier.'

'Pierre?'

'Nothing more has been touched,' agreed Maistre Pierre. 'What do you miss?'

'Last night he had a stone bottle of usquebae, and I'll swear there were several empty ones in yon corner.'

'The alehouses will give you money for the empties,' said Lowrie. 'So I've heard,' he added hastily, one eye on Maister Doby. 'There they are, yonder under the bed.'

'Perhaps he knocked them over when he fell?' suggested Maistre Pierre.

'No, for they were right under the bed, I recall now.' Gil stepped into the room, and bent to touch the corpse, waving the flies away without effect. 'How long is it since you found him?'

'An hour?'

'Longer than that, surely, Lawrence,' said Maister Doby. 'It must be more than an hour since you sent to me.'

'He's beginning to stiffen.' Gil was feeling the jaw and neck. He tested the arms, and straightened the bent leg. 'It's been a while since. Two-three hours, maybe.'

'Less,' said the mason decidedly. 'He is lying by the brazier. It happens faster in heat.'

'Who do you think has done this?' asked Maister Doby again.

'If he was drunk as he usually was, almost anybody,' said Gil. 'Someone about his own height, who can use a dagger, which must include half the grown men in Glasgow.' He patted at the front of the porter's unsavoury gown, avoiding the bloody rent, but could feel nothing under the cloth except flabby flesh. There was a purse hanging at the straining belt, which proved to hold only a few coppers and a worn lead pilgrim badge of St Mungo. He attempted to tie the purse's strings again, then gave up and got to his feet. 'There is no sign of a fight. Pierre, would you agree?'

'The chair?'

'More likely he knocked that over as he went down,' Gil surmised, looking round the room again. 'The table is untouched, see, and the brazier and the pricket-stand are undisturbed. I need to speak to Ninian and Michael, and anyone else who was past the yett today. Maister Doby, do you wish to get him moved? Then we can search the room properly, and get a look at these papers.'

'Search the room?' repeated Maister Doby.

'The bottle of usquebae?' said the mason.

But when the stiffening corpse had been removed by two of the college servants, there was no sign of any stone bottle still containing usquebae. The four jars rolling about under the shut-bed were empty and dry.

'And a spider in this one,' reported Maistre Pierre, shaking the creature on to the floor.

'Strange,' said Gil.

'There are marks in the dust down here, see,' continued the mason. 'Someone has searched under this bed recently.'

'Not Jaikie.'

'Perhaps whoever stabbed him?' suggested Lowrie Livingstone, watching with interest. 'And he took the full one away with him? St Mungo's bones, what a stink. *Sonar slais ill air na suord.*'

'But why?' wondered Gil. 'Why take it away?' He crossed to the window and opened its shutters wide, then bent to look in the press beneath it.

'I never knew that was there,' said Lowrie.

'You have been in this room?' asked the mason.

'Well,' said Lowrie diffidently. 'Aye. It's a blag, see? A dare,' he elucidated. 'The bejants has to get in here when Jaikie's no here, and borrow something.'

'Borrow?' said Gil, his head still inside the press. Maistre Pierre got to his feet and began poking fastidiously at the blankets in the rancid bed.

'Well. You ken what I mean.'

Gil, who had undertaken the same dare himself, emerged from the press and shut the door carefully.

'Nothing in there except a dog-collar and leash,' he reported, tucking the strips of leather into his doublet.

'A dog-collar?' repeated the mason. 'There is no bottle of

180

usquebae, but look at this. It was under the mattress, on this little shelf.'

'Likely off William's dog,' said Lowrie offhandedly.

'You knew about the dog?' Gil said, crossing the room to join Maistre Pierre.

'Most of us did. He got it a new collar a couple weeks ago. Too good for a beast that age, I thought, but it wasny worth saying so to him. It'd be like Jaikie to keep the old one.'

'Where did William get the new one?' Gil asked. The mason put a heavy purse into his hand, and he weighed it and whistled.

'Anderson the saddler made it to him.' Lowrie eyed the purse. 'Is that where he kept it?'

'Kept what?' Gil took the purse to the window and peered into its mouth. 'It's mostly coppers, but there must be a fair sum here. Where did Jaikie get this much money?'

'In drink-money,' said Lowrie reasonably. 'No off us, for certain, but all the folk that comes to the gate would give him something for sending to say they were here.'

Gil stared at him. It would never have occurred to him to tip a college porter. Which perhaps explains Jaikie's attitude to the members of the college, he thought.

'You ken that's William's writing on the papers?' added Lowrie.

'I wondered when we would get to that.' The mason picked something off his sleeve and crushed it carefully. Gil, setting the purse down on the small table, bent to lift the singed bundle, making a clumsy task of it with his left hand. Lowrie came to help, and rose, shedding flakes of burnt paper as he shuffled the surviving fragments together.

'Gently,' said Gil. 'We may want to read them.'

'Oh, there's nothing interesting here,' reported Lowrie, already peering at the tiny writing. 'This looks like his copy of Ning's notes on Peter of Spain, and that's Aristotle. It's lecture notes, maisters.'

'What, all of it?'

'I think so.' Lowrie tilted more sheets to the light. 'Aye, I remember that point. Do you have to learn your lectures off by heart, maister, so you can give them the same every year?'

'I know where these have come from,' said the mason. 'You recall I commented on how little paper there was in William's chamber?'

'I think you must be right,' said Gil. 'But how the devil did it get into the brazier? Jaikie sent word by Michael he wanted to speak to me – could it have been about this?'

'Jaikie might have found them somewhere,' suggested Lowrie, reaching the last legible page. 'Aye, it's all lecture notes, maister, barring William's own notes for a disputation I mind he won. If there was anything else here, it's burned past reading.'

Behind the student, Maistre Pierre caught Gil's eye, shut his mouth and shook his head significantly. Gil accepted the smoky bundle from Lowrie and said, 'These should go with William's other property. I suppose they belong to his kin, though I hardly think they'll be valued. Now let us try and find out who last saw Jaikie alive.'

Chapter Nine

The courtyard was occupied by several knots of students, standing about discussing this newest happening. Ninian and Michael were seated at the foot of the stairs to the Fore Hall, and as Lowrie followed Gil and Maister Mason into the courtyard they came forward to join their fellow, but were shut out by one of the bigger groups which surrounded them, full of eager questions.

'Was it a robber?'

'He tellt someone to go round by Blackfriars gate and they stabbed him.'

'No, he dee'd of the stink in his chamber. A'body kens bad air can kill ye.'

'What, wi a great knife?'

'Is that right his throat's cut, maister?' demanded the irrepressible Walter.

'Who did it?'

'Auld Nick,' muttered someone at the back. 'He was uncivil to him one time too many.'

There were sniggers, but Ralph Gibson, nearest to Gil, said, 'Maister, did Jaikie kill William? Was it a judgement on him?'

'Don't be a fool, Ralph,' said Maister Kennedy, emerging from the stair which led to his chamber. 'Jaikie was killed by some human agency. How could that be a judgement on him when we don't know yet who killed William?' Ralph stepped back, blushing scarlet, and the well-loved teacher surveyed the group and continued, 'Good day to you, Maister Cunningham. I had a word with most of these earlier, and it seems to me Robert Montgomery was the last in the college to speak to Jaikie. Anyone else that was down at the yett after Nones can wait here too. The rest of you go and wash your hands if you want to be allowed to eat dinner today.'

Ralph, with the air of one undergoing martyrdom, took up position beside his room-mate, and two other boys remained while the rest of the group drifted off, elaborately casual. Gil looked over his shoulder and found Lowrie with Ninian and Michael, conferring quickly in low tones.

'We didn't see anybody, maister,' said Michael in his deep voice. 'Not when we came down to speak to Jaikie, and not earlier. He was fine when I came back into the college.'

'He was alone then?'

'Aye – sitting in his great chair scowling at the door. Mind you –' Michael grinned. 'If I'd not seen William's dog with you, maister, I'd almost have sworn it was in Jaikie's chamber.'

'What made you think that?' asked the mason curiously.

Michael shrugged. 'I thought I smelled a dog-kennel, in among the rest of the reek. Likely he'd stepped into the street, got dog-sharn on his boots or something. I checked mine.' He turned them up, one by one, as Lowrie had done when Gil was looking for coal dust. 'I look where I'm stepping.'

'When did you get back?' Gil asked.

'I was just in time for Maister Coventry's lecture at noon. I'd sooner have missed that, as it happened, for it was Euclid and I hadny prepared my answer.'

Gil nodded. The mason looked at the sky and frowned.

'He must have been dead very soon after that,' he commented. Michael's eyes widened.

'How can you tell that?' Lowrie asked curiously. 'You said something like that already.'

Maistre Pierre stepped aside and began a concise little discourse on the progress of stiffening in a dead body. Gil met Maister Kennedy's eye, and moved towards the other students.

'When did you last see Jaikie, then?' he asked Ralph Gibson.

Ralph, blushing and stammering, eventually admitted that he had not been near the yett all day. 'But I thought Robert . . .' he said inconclusively.

'Thought I what?' asked Robert challengingly.

'Thought you might . . .'

Gil, watching the boy writhe, took pity on him.

'You thought Robert might be glad of your company,' he suggested. Ralph went scarlet with gratitude, and nodded. Robert said nothing, but his face, turned away from Ralph, was eloquent. Gil looked at the two bystanders, recognizing them now as two more of the cast of the play. Frivolity and one of the daughters of Collegia, he thought.

'Well, Henry? Andrew?' prompted Maister Kennedy.

'We saw him just after Michael came in,' said Henry importantly. 'Andrew wanted to know where Maister Shaw the Steward was, and somebody thought he was talking to Jaikie. But he wasny. It was a . . . a big man,' he finished, his voice trailing off as he heard his own words.

'What kind of a man?'

'A big warlike kind of man,' offered Andrew. 'Wi' a whinger. He was at the yett talking to Jaikie, and Jaikie said to us he didny ken nor care where Maister Shaw was and to go and get Robert Montgomery. And that's the last we seen him.'

'I'll tell you what kind of a man,' said Robert Montgomery impatiently. 'It was no more nor less than my uncle Hugh asking for me. Jaikie let him in and sent these two to fetch me, and gave my uncle an earful of incivility the way he always does – did,' he corrected himself, 'when he spoke to him about William. And by the time my uncle Hugh had done with me, I was late for Maister Coventry's lecture in the Bachelors' Schule, so he never asked me my question, and it took me all morning to con the answer.'

'What did your uncle want with you?' Gil asked.

185

'Family business.' The challenging glare was directed at Gil now.

'There was nobody else about at the yett at the time?'

'No that I saw.'

'And that was the last you saw Jaikie?'

'It was.'

'He was alive when you left? Did you or your uncle leave him first?'

'We left together. I went up the pend and my uncle stepped out at the yett. And that was the last I saw Jaikie.'

'Alive?'

'What would I kill him for? Or with, if it comes to that? You ken fine we've no daggers about the college, maister, or has it changed that much since your day?'

'Robert,' said Maister Kennedy in warning tones. The boy looked at him, and reined in his anger. Dropping his gaze to the chipped flagstones under his feet, he muttered something which might have been an apology.

'Did you see anything like papers burning in the brazier?' Gil asked.

'There was just coals in the brazier when I got there,' said Robert indifferently.

'Your uncle had no papers? Or Jaikie?'

'There was just the coals burning when I got there,' Robert repeated.

'And Jaikie was alive when you left him,' Gil persisted.

Maister Kennedy frowned, and Robert said with weary defiance, 'When I saw Jaikie he was alive. I didny kill him, maister, and you may as well stop asking it.'

'Thank you,' said Gil. 'That will be all just now, Robert.'

Robert ducked his head in a kind of bow and set off rapidly for the pend leading to the inner courtyard. Ralph, who had been standing staring, gulped and hurried after him, exclaiming, 'Robert, wait! Wait for me!'

'And you two can go and wash your hands,' prompted Maister Kennedy.

Andrew and Henry left obediently, with sidelong glances at Gil, and Maistre Pierre said, 'You were severe.'

'He was evasive,' Gil said. Maister Kennedy, about to comment, stopped with his mouth open, clearly listening to the conversation again.

'So he was,' he agreed at length. 'He's aye so sneisty it takes your mind off what he has to say. He never answered you straight, save to say he didny kill Jaikie.'

'Which I never thought,' added Gil. 'If anyone, I'd suspect his uncle.'

'I'd put nothing past the Montgomery,' said Maister Kennedy. 'It's a quarter-hour to dinner, I'd best go and wash like the scholars. How are you, Gil? Who was it attacked you? They didny kill you, anyway. Oh, I near forgot,' he added. 'Maister Doby asked would you go by his lodging and tell him what you found.'

Dean Elphinstone glared at Gil and Maister Doby impartially.

'If someone can step in off the street and kill our porter, a man carefully selected by our Steward here to ward the gate,' he added, with a brief bow towards John Shaw who was frowning as he tried to keep up with the incisive Latin, 'how are we to keep forty scholars safe, not to mention their regents and the college servants? We need to know, Gilbert, whether this was a deliberate act of vengeance on this man, or the result of a quarrel, or an attack on the college itself.'

'Or an attempt to reach one of the scholars,' suggested the mason in French.

The Steward looked worried, but the Dean nodded, and continued, 'The man was impertinent and unsatisfactory, but he was a college servant and we are responsible for him. Have you discerned any likely reason for this violent death? Are you able to pursue justice for him?'

'It was not theft,' said Gil, 'since that bag of coin I gave you was hidden in his bed, and probably not an attack on the college. Beyond that, Dean, I can only speculate at present.'

'And what do your speculations tell you? Surely one proposition is more likely than another,' said the Dean.

'I hope not an attempt to reach one of the scholars,' said Maister Doby. 'No, surely not. None of our students would attract such enmity.'

'William did,' said Gil. There was a short silence, in which the bell began to ring for the college dinner.

'Do you hold, then, that the one death is connected to the other?' asked the Dean, in the exasperated tone of a teacher who cannot see where his student's error lies. Gil spread his hands, and flinched as his bruised wrist twinged.

'I think we must assume that they are connected,' he said, 'although it is not obvious how, simply because it defies logic that, in a community as small as the college, two violent deaths in two days should be unconnected.'

The Dean snorted, but made no answer. Through the open window they could hear a buzz of voices as the students who lived in the outer courtyard made their way towards the pend.

'What else must you ask?' said Maister Doby. 'Do you need more from us, Gilbert? I must go and say Grace for the scholars.'

'I need to speak to Father Bernard again,' said Gil, 'but I suppose I must apply to Blackfriars to find him, and I would be grateful for a little of Maister Shaw's time.' He nodded at the Steward, who smiled doubtfully.

'Father Bernard had a lecture,' said the mason.

'He'll have finished that,' said the Dean. 'You're right, he'll be back in Blackfriars by this. Aye, go and say Grace, Principal, and I'll follow you. The Steward can come back here once he's convoyed you into the hall, can't you no, John?'

They all rose and bowed the Principal and Steward from the room, and as the door closed behind them the Dean sat down and said in sharper French, 'Give me your suspicions, Gilbert, Maister Mason. Where are you at with finding William's murderer, first?'

Gil looked at Maistre Pierre.

'We haven't had an opportunity to talk this through,' he admitted, 'for it's been an eventful day already. We have established that William was given to extortion, which should point us to a suspect, but most of the people whom I know he had approached were in plain sight of one another at the time when I believe he was killed.'

'Conspiracy?' said the Dean.

'Is always possible,' Gil agreed.

'It seems clear,' said the mason, 'that the boy got into the limehouse as a matter of mischief rather than malice.'

'But after that we are less certain of the course of events.'

'So all you've done is show who couldn't have killed him?'

'So far, yes.'

The Dean grunted. 'Well, if you go on that way long enough, you'll end up with one man, I suppose. You will have heard that William's burial is tomorrow after Sext?'

'I have,' Gil said. 'We are searching diligently, Dean, and we may well know a lot more by then. If you are willing to invite Lord Montgomery into the college after the burial, then even if I can't name the boy's killer as he demanded I can at least explain what conclusions I have reached by that time.'

'I suppose that might placate the man for the time being.' The Dean glared at them both again. 'And this newest business? The death of our porter? What did you mean about speculation?'

'Just that. We spoke to the scholars, and established the time of death. We searched the man's chamber, and found the bag of coin which is now in Maister Doby's strong-box, which must be Jaikie's savings, all in coppers as it is, and we found a great bundle of William's lecture-notes which someone had put in the brazier. There's nothing else to point our direction, so we must speculate.'

'St Nicholas' bones!' said the Dean. 'Jaikie was burning

William's lecture-notes? How did he get hold of them?' He paused, looking from Gil to the mason and back. 'Are you saying it was Jaikie killed William? How could he leave his post without being seen?'

'No, I think not,' said Gil. 'William was killed and moved into the coalhouse by someone who knew where he was hidden. Jaikie would have no way of learning that and acting on it, in the time available.'

'So was it Ninian and his fellows?'

'No,' said Gil. 'They say they left him in the limehouse, and we found evidence which confirms their story. I am reasonably convinced William was alive when they left him.'

Dean Elphinstone snorted, and got to his feet.

'I must go to the Laigh Hall if I am to get any dinner today. Where do you dine, Gilbert, Maister Mason? Do you have time for dinner?'

'Our dinner awaits us at my house,' said the mason. 'But there was the matter of a word with John Shaw.'

'Oh, aye.' The Dean led the way out into the courtyard. 'I'll send him back to ye, if he's in the hall. Let me know as soon as you've anything to report, Gilbert. We must write to the Archbishop soon, whether or no we've found the answer.'

'I know that, sir.'

The Dean sketched a benediction for which they both bowed, and strode off across the grey flagstones, his every-day woollen cope billowing at his back.

'I am glad he is on our side,' said the mason doubtfully, then, as the Dean stepped aside to allow someone to emerge from the pend, 'Ah, there is John Shaw. Poor man, he has all to do and too many masters telling him how. Good day, John. It is good of you to spare us a moment.'

'And what a day, maisters,' said the Steward in harassed tones. 'How am I to ward the college now, I ask you? Jaikie was a dirty ill-tempered beffan, but he did his duty, and now I've to find a replacement before Vespers, and his chamber like a fox's den to be cleaned out before the new man's in place –'

'Ask Serjeant Anderson,' Gil suggested. 'He might recommend one of the constables to act as porter for a day or two. He'd know if they were trustworthy. Or would the Blackfriars have a lay-brother they could spare?'

'The Serjeant . . .' The Steward tasted this idea. 'One of the constables? Maybe. Maybe you're right, maister. Aye, I'll do that.' He looked suddenly more cheerful. 'And how can I help ye, maisters? Was it something you wanted done?'

'Information, rather, John,' said the mason. 'Come and sit down and tell us about yesterday.'

'Yesterday?' Maister Shaw followed them into the Bachelors' Schule. 'Oh, what a day, what a day. What d'ye need to know, Peter? You were there, and so was Maister Cunningham.'

'Not I,' said Maistre Pierre, 'not until after it all happened. Tell me about it. You had the procession and the feast to order, did you not?'

'I did that. And that William underfoot,' added Maister Shaw bitterly. 'Correcting and criticizing, amending my greetings to the guests and the members, till I went off and left him to get on with that. I thought he might as well make himself useful,' he added. 'I'd to see the garlands on to Willie Sproat's donkey-cart, with the donkey trying to eat them and Willie killing himself laughing at the sight, I'd to make sure there were horses to all the maisters, and the moth out of all the Faculty hoods, and the music to the Mass put on the donkey-cart, and John Gray the Beadle misplaced his robes and I found them in here, where that William had put them down –' He nodded at a cupboard under the lecturer's pulpit. 'Oh, what a day, what a day!'

'But all went smoothly,' said Gil. 'Indeed, I thought the morning went very well, Maister Shaw. It was later, when the thunder started and they were all running about the yards, that things went wrong.'

'I don't know what you mean by wrong,' said Maister

191

Shaw, bridling slightly, 'I thought it was bad enough when the boy Maxwell served half the high table with a dirty towel over his arm, and as for that William distracting Robert Montgomery while the Dean waited for the made dishes, words fail me, maisters, they do.'

'None of these things prevented us enjoying the feast,' said Gil soothingly.

'But you have high standards, John,' interposed the mason. 'And when the thunder started, what happened then?'

'Ha! All the scholars running about, shutting windows that should never have been left open, neglecting their duties. It took some doing to get them back to their tasks, I can tell you, Peter. I had to send a whole lot I found in the Inner Close about their business.'

'Who would that be?' Gil asked. 'Can you remember?'

'Now you're asking,' said Maister Shaw doubtfully. 'Henry and Walter, that's certain. You canny miss Walter,' he added, with disapproval. 'Andrew. Robert Montgomery, I sent him back to the kitchen, and that soft-head Ralph, poor laddie, and I met John Gray's nephew Nicholas in the pend and chased him back to the crocks and all. There might have been more.'

'Nicholas and Robert were not together?' Gil asked.

'I don't think so. Oh, what a day!'

'And then we found William in the coalhouse. Tell me this, Maister Shaw,' said Gil. 'Who would have had a key to that door?'

'Oh, near everyone,' said the Steward, looking startled. 'All the regents, for certain, as well as me and Agnes, even some of the scholars. Anyone that had a chamber with a key to it. Most of the college doors is the same, maister. I've a notion Archie Bell only kens three patterns of lock, and we've got all he ever made of one of them.'

'And the Blackfriars yett?' Gil asked, with a sinking feeling.

'That, too. Not that you'd need a key by daylight, the gate stands open from Prime to Compline. I've tellt Maister Doby many a time,' he confided, 'we ought to get a different lock put on the coalhouse door, for the coals goes down faster than they should. Maybe now he'll listen.'

'So anyone could have put William in the coalhouse,' said the mason, watching the Steward's retreating back.

'Anyone with a key,' agreed Gil. 'So we are no further forward. Anyone who had or could borrow a key could walk into the college by the Blackfriars yett, if they were not inside its walls already, and unlock the coalhouse door and lock it again after.'

'And this other matter.' Maistre Pierre jerked one large thumb over his shoulder at the mouth of the porter's pend.

'Yes, indeed. How do you come to be present?'

'Ah. Well. I had something to attend to at Blackfriars.' He stared across the courtyard, and finally admitted, 'I tell you from the beginning. Come into the middle of the yard here.'

Gil, puzzled, strolled forward to the centre of the flag-stones, where none could overhear them without being seen.

'I walked up to Blackfriars with Father Bernard,' began Maistre Pierre.

'When he left your house before Nones?' Gil interrupted. 'The women thought you had gone up to the site.'

'I intended to,' said the mason impatiently. 'Wattie had sent the boy for me, I intended to go on there afterwards. But I spent longer in Blackfriars kirk than I thought to. First I was alone, and then I spent some time with Father Bernard, if you understand me.'

Confession? Gil wondered. Why now? Of course, Father Bernard speaks French. He nodded, and the mason went on.

'We had to end the matter, for he had a lecture to deliver, and I walked into the college with him and found it buzzing like a bee-skep, those three in the yard here exclaiming what they had found, the Principal becoming

193

flustered, half the college crowding in to look at the dead. So I had them send for you and made Lowrie stand guard with me. I would have shut the door and locked it, though small good that would have done if all the keys in the college fit the lock, but you saw how he lay. We could not close the door without moving him.'

'And you saw nothing that might be useful?' Gil prompted. 'No bloodstained dagger-man running across the courtyard?'

'No,' agreed the mason with regret, 'although he was probably not bloodstained. Most of the bleeding will be internal, I would say. No, but I heard something that might be to the point.'

'Yes?'

'Do you know Blackfriars kirk?'

'I was a student here,' Gil reminded him.

'Ah, of course. Then you recall the altar of St Peter? Tucked away in a corner beyond St Paul?' Gil nodded. 'I was on my knees there, quite unobtrusive, when I overheard a conversation out in another part of the church. It must be one of those echoes you get sometimes,' he added thoughtfully, 'where the vault is of just such a shape as to direct the sound, for they were not within my sight.'

'Go on. Who spoke?'

'Father Bernard was very clear, the other voice less so. The father wished the other to take some document or other. *You recognize the writing,* he said. *There is nothing there of value, it must be disposed of.*'

'Ah!' said Gil. 'So that's how the meat got into the nut.'

Maistre Pierre glanced at him. 'Indeed. The other asked, I think, how he came by it, and was told that he did not need to know. Then he said – the friar said – *Our intentions are the same in this. Have no fear, my son.* Then two of the other friars entered the church, talking about tomorrow's funeral, and our man went to join them.'

'Mm.' Gil considered this. 'You got no sight of the other party?'

'I did not. A young voice, I thought.'

'And having heard this, you still spent time with Father Bernard?'

The mason shrugged. 'I had already asked him, I could not readily withdraw. I took care, in the circumstances, to raise nothing of great import.'

'And you were with him until you both walked across the Paradise Yard? Where the apple-trees are,' he elucidated. Maistre Pierre nodded again. 'So we can leave him out of the reckoning for Jaikie's death.'

'Indeed, we can. Though not for the other, I think?'

'No.' Gil stared unseeing at the door of the Principal's lodging. 'But if the relationship is as I think, I do not see why he would have killed William.'

'This is no place to discuss it. I can hear the scholars in the Inner Close. They are coming from their dinner, and we must go to ours. Alys will be sufficiently displeased with me already.'

'She was very anxious,' Gil said.

'I was thoughtless.'

Gil, whose parents and siblings had come and gone without consultation throughout his youth, made no comment, but said, 'I wish to find Father Bernard. Some points need clarification.'

'Then we shall see you later?' Maistre Pierre turned towards the pend that led to the street, and paused. 'Ah, no, I am forgetting. The yett is barred. I must go out by Blackfriars.'

'Then we can both look at Jaikie's body, if he has been washed by now.'

William still lay in the mortuary chapel, his lanky form shrouded but identifiable, with two Theology students kneeling by his head with their beads. As Gil and Maistre Pierre entered the chapel, two more students stepped forward from the shadows to relieve the watchers. Jaikie, as a college servant, was naturally laid out here too, neatly shrouded on a trestle next to William, with candles about him and a small stout Dominican at his feet working his way stolidly through the prayers for the dead. Gil knelt briefly by the trestle, the mason for rather longer, and the brother finished his petition for mercy and got to his feet, saying,

'Was it you that found him? Do you need to see him?' He drew back the shroud without waiting for an answer. The theologians around William recoiled, and two of them averted their eyes. 'His jaw's well set, or we'd have closed his mouth. There's the wound. Simple stab wound, nothing fancy but it did someone's work for him.'

'I see,' said Maistre Pierre. 'There would be little bleeding, I think.'

'Likely he bled within, poor man,' said the friar. 'And at the mouth, of course.'

The students going off duty left hastily, and the two remaining knelt with great reluctance. Maistre Pierre prodded at the gash in Jaikie's chest and nodded.

'A dagger or the point of a whinger,' he said. 'Perhaps this wide.' He held up finger and thumb an inch or so apart.

'There can't be more than two thousand such in Glasgow,' Gil observed. 'Was it you that washed him, brother? Was there anything in his clothes we should know about?'

'In his clothes,' said the brother, with a sudden lapse in charity, 'there was nothing beyond himself, an entire company of Ru'glen redfriars, and a peck of dirt. We'd to burn them, gown and all. They were past giving to the poor.'

The mason looked blank, but Gil was aware of the nearer student bedesman withdrawing the skirts of his gown. He too stepped back from the trestle and moved towards the offering-box by the door, saying, 'God rest his soul. I think that's all we need to see, brother.' He dropped a couple of coins into the box. 'Can you tell me where Father Bernard might be?'

'I am preparing tomorrow's quodlibet disputation,' said

Father Bernard, staring at Gil over a rampart of books. 'I can spare you a little time, I suppose.'

'Thank you, father,' said Gil. He drew a stool up to the librarian's table and sat down. His head was beginning to ache again, and he felt extremely weary. 'It is merely to clarify a few points.'

Father Bernard ostentatiously closed a volume of St Augustine, with a slip of paper in his place, and folded his hands together on top of the book. Sunshine poured in at the window of the library. In the shadows beyond the chaplain, the ranks of the college theology collection were dimly visible, the shelf-numbers showing black on the pale out-turned fore-edges. Nearer the door, rows of smaller, much-handled volumes showed where the Arts Faculty's Aristotle and Euclid were shelved.

'In fact, now I think of it,' said Father Bernard, 'I would welcome a word with you, Gilbert, about your own future.'

'My –' Gil stared at him. 'What has that to do with it?'

'I am responsible for your spiritual well-being, as a member of the University,' Father Bernard reminded him, 'and it gives me grave cause for concern to see you about to take a step which can only be detrimental to your future career.'

'What step is that?' said Gil. 'Do you mean my marriage?'

'I do indeed. It seems a rash step for a man who is widely spoken of as an able scholar and a promising man of law. If you were to enter the Church, I am very sure you would have entry to positions of power and responsibility –'

'I am training as a notary,' Gil said. 'More notaries are married men than churchmen nowadays. Now may I ask you –'

'But the most successful are churchmen,' said Father Bernard triumphantly. Gil, lacking facts to argue this statement, hesitated, and the chaplain ploughed on. 'You see, if your energies are directed to controlling and disciplining that very headstrong young woman, they cannot be directed to your calling.'

'Headstrong?' said Gil, staring. 'Discipline? I shouldn't dream of trying. She is the most intelligent girl I ever met, and thinks more clearly than many men.'

'Then, Gilbert, I fear you will have a sad marriage. Come,' said Father Bernard, leaning forward over his books, 'admit it. You are led to this union by the desires of the flesh.'

'If I did not know better, I would think you had been talking to my mother,' said Gil. 'I am led to the marriage by the advice of my uncle, who was approached first.'

'Ah,' said Father Bernard, sitting back with a faint air of disappointment. 'I had not realized that. I feared you had allowed yourself to be diverted by a lovely face and figure.'

Gil found himself smiling at the image this conjured up for him, and straightened his expression.

'Father Bernard, we are taking up time you can ill spare. As I have said, there are a few points I wished to clarify about William's death.'

'About his death?' Father Bernard looked down at his folded hands for a moment, then up at Gil. 'I cannot imagine why you should think me able to help you, but I will try. Well?'

Gil gathered his thoughts with an effort. 'At the end of the play, yesterday, what did you do?'

'At the end of the play?' Father Bernard repeated. 'Why, I returned to the House.' He nodded at the view from the library window, across the Principal's garden and into the Blackfriars grounds, cemetery and gatehouse and bell-tower clearly visible.

'To Blackfriars? So you crossed the Inner Close and the kitchen-yard, and went through the gate.'

'That is the way to the convent.'

'Using your key to the gate?'

'Why, no. I have a key,' Father Bernard touched the breast of his habit, 'but I hardly use it. The gate stands open all the hours of daylight. It was certainly open yesterday.'

'May I see it?' Gil asked innocently. 'Is it local work, do you know?'

A wary expression in his deep-set eyes, Father Bernard fished the key out and lifted the cord over his head. Gil took the object from him and turned it curiously. It was as long as his hand, with a substantial shaft and crooked handle, but the rectangular tablet had only two notches in it. Clearly it operated a simple lock. He weighed the warm iron in his hand, and rubbed at the patch of rust near the end of the shaft.

'It's local work, so the Steward tells me,' agreed the chaplain. 'It serves its purpose.'

'Indeed it must,' said Gil ambiguously, handing the key back. 'And when you crossed the close, did you see anyone? William, for instance?'

The chaplain frowned. 'A few of the college servants were about, but surely William was still at the play?'

'He left before it ended.'

'Oh.' Father Bernard closed his mouth over the yellow teeth and frowned. 'Oh.'

'Does that convey anything?' Gil asked.

'No. Why should it?'

'So when did you return to the college?' Gil asked after a moment.

'Almost immediately. I had a lecture to deliver at two o'clock, and I had only gone for some notes which I needed, so I returned to the college to spend some time in prayer in the Theology Schule before my students joined me.'

'In prayer?' said Gil. 'Is that usual?'

'When lecturing in Theology,' said Father Bernard, 'it is my practice. One does not interpret the will or word of God without asking for assistance.'

Gil nodded, and pain stabbed across his temples. 'Did you see anyone on your return? You came back by the road you went – by the kitchen-yard and the close to the Theology Schule door?'

'Why should I do otherwise? I may have seen some of the students, but I was about to take a lecture, Gilbert, my mind was not on my surroundings.'

'I appreciate that,' said Gil. 'It's unfortunate, for it would help me to confirm some of the other stories I have. Someone in your position, who knows all the students in the college, is more likely to be of help than a Master of Arts who left several years ago.'

There was another of those pauses.

'And you then remained in the lecture-room until after the lecture?'

'Unfortunately, no,' said Father Bernard. He looked out of the window, then down at his hands, then at Gil with an assumption of man-to-man heartiness. 'I was, shall we say, compelled to leave briefly, before I began to speak.' Gil waited. 'The Almayne pottage,' said Father Bernard obliquely. 'It disagreed with me, rather suddenly.'

'So you went back out to the kitchen-yard. This could be very helpful,' Gil said. 'Who did you see at that point?'

'I was not paying attention,' said the chaplain primly. He looked at his hands again. 'I may have seen Robert Montgomery. On my return across the Inner Close I certainly saw a number of people.' He thought briefly. 'There was a group of four men, your age or older. I have been chaplain here less than three years, they were certainly before my time.'

'That is valuable,' said Gil, with perfect truth. 'I know who they were. And in the Outer Close?'

'Consider, Gilbert,' said Father Bernard kindly. 'I was now late for my lecture in the Theology Schule. I had no need to enter the Outer Close. Who knows who was at large there? Not I, for sure.'

'What a pity. It could have been valuable. And after the lecture? What did you do then?'

'At three o'clock I returned to the House, from where I was summoned at length to conduct a Provisional Absolution for William, along with Maister Forsyth.'

Gil considered for a moment. 'How well did you know William, father?'

'You have asked me that before. I knew him as one among the students here, no more.'

'So he never came in your way when you were chaplain to Lord Montgomery?'

'I left before he was born.'

'Why was that? Surely such a position could be yours for life?'

'My superiors decreed that I should go to study in Cologne.'

'And you didn't know William was keeping a dog.'

'I did not.'

'Or that he was practising extortion.'

'Nor that either.'

'And what about his papers? There was a bundle of papers with William's writing on them, smouldering in Jaikie's brazier when the man was found dead just now. How could they have got there? They should have been in William's chamber.'

'I've no idea about that.'

'And have you any idea,' said Gil casually, 'why he wanted to speak to you yesterday morning? Did he show you his letter?'

'Our colloquy was brief and uninformative. Now, if you will forgive me, I am a busy man with teaching commitments to fulfil. If all you wish to do is repeat questions I have already answered – truthfully,' he emphasized, looking Gil in the eye, 'I must call an end to this.'

'On the contrary,' said Gil, 'I hope you will forgive me. One more question, which I haven't asked before. If you didn't know William, you wouldn't know Robert Montgomery either, but can you tell me anything about him?'

'I knew his father Alexander well,' said Father Bernard heavily. 'He died at Stirling field, like your father, I believe. God rest their souls.'

'Amen,' said Gil, with an unlikely surge of fellow feeling for a Montgomery.

'Robert is very like him. They're all alike, these Montgomery men. A strong sense of family, a strong sense of property, a hot temper.'

'You could call it that,' said Gil. He rose, and bowed.
'I will leave you, father. So you were not in the Outer Close
after the beginning of the lecture?'

'Not until I left the Theology Schule again.' Father Bernard half-rose also, delivered a remote blessing, and had
seated himself and opened his volume of Augustine before
Gil had left the room.

The way back to the Blackfriars gate led across the Paradise Yard, where a few students were talking in subdued
groups under the apple-trees. On an impulse Gil left the
path and made his way down towards the Molendinar.

Sitting in the dappled sunshine under one of the trees,
he leaned back against its trunk and looked up at the
pattern of pink blossom and young leaves. Somewhere a
blackbird called, and smaller birds chirped and sang in the
bushes. The mills clattered along the burn. The voices of
the scattered groups of students, the burgh and its problems, all seemed very far away.

Small and clear, images danced across his vision. A man
with a sword, who might or might not be Hugh Montgomery. Three armed men, leaping round him in twilight.
The lanky, red-haired William, a *busy ghost aye flickering to
and fro*, darted from victim to victim, gowned scholars who
flinched away from him under the arched branches of the
apple-trees, until he became a victim himself.

'William's victims,' he said aloud, and opened his eyes.
The blackbird was still singing, but most of the students
had gone.

Is that the key? he wondered. The list of those the boy
confronted? The names in the red book? And how was
Jaikie's death connected?

And meantime his own problems loomed large. At
twenty-six he needed nobody's permission to marry,
though since his uncle was his sponsor into the Law it
would be foolish to act without the old man's approval. He
knew he had that, and it had been an unpleasant surprise
to discover that his mother held other views.

But what are her objections? What did she say this morning? That there was no more money – well, I knew that – that he was educated for the Church and the Law – but I will still embrace the Law. And that he must pray for his father and brothers.

I wonder, is that the crux of the matter? he thought, and recalled the last year-mind service in the church in Hamilton. The small altar beside his father's box tomb had been dusty and neglected, and the brocade altar-cloth was so old that mice or moths had eaten it into holes. Beside it the newly painted carving had been bright in the candle-light: the family blazon in the centre of one long side of the tomb, with a kneeling knight on one side, a lady on the other, and their three sons and five daughters ranked neatly behind them.

He could see it now as if he was there. Two of the small male figures were in armour, the third gowned as a scholar. One of the daughters was in her shroud, two had flowing, improbably yellow hair, one wore the same kind of elaborate gold-painted headdress as the kneeling figure of their mother, and the eldest was in the white robes of a Cistercian nun. The image was so vivid that he was quite unsurprised when the nun turned her head and looked directly at him, her long-chinned face narrow and intent within the folds of her veil.

'Gil,' she said clearly. 'Slip the collar, and you will win free.'

'Dorothea?' he said, but she had turned back to her prayers. '*Slip the collar and you will win free,*' he repeated, and woke with a start.

Chapter Ten

As he turned in at the mason's pend, under the swinging sign with its bright image of a white castle, a voice in the shadows said, 'And here is Maister Cunningham. Good day to you, maister.'

He checked, and the harper and his sister emerged into the light. Ealasaidh was clad as usual in her loose checked dress, but McIan was in silk and velvet as if he had been playing for one of the wealthy households of the burgh.

'The bairn has fed,' continued Ealasaidh abruptly.

'Thanks be to God,' said Gil.

She crossed herself with her free hand, but McIan said in his resonant voice, 'Thanks to the dog, it seems. A blessing on the beast, for now I think my son will live.'

'It seems so,' agreed Gil. 'We can all be glad of it. How are you both? Are you well, after yesterday's stushie?'

'Well enough,' said Ealasaidh sourly. 'Maister Cunningham is kind to ask it. At the Provost's lodging they were more anxious to hear about the stushie at the college, as you cry it, than to hear us play.'

'We are both well,' said her brother, 'but you have taken some small hurt, they tell me at the house. Brawling in the street, is it? A fine thing for my son's tutor.'

'I'll try to deport myself more seemly,' Gil said.

The harper turned blank eyes on him, and his white beard twitched as if he smiled slightly. 'You should not be risking your hands like that again. A scholar must write, as a musician must play. And have you ended the other matter yet? Have you found the ones that you are hunting?'

'Not yet.'

'It will be soon,' said McIan. 'But you must be very certain. You will take the holy woman's advice.'

'Your pardon, sir?' said Gil, startled.

'Och, come away,' said Ealasaidh, as Gil stared open-mouthed. 'We must go offer a candle at St Mary's for the bairn's breaking his fast, and Maister Cunningham wants his dinner. Good day to you, maister.'

She bowed, gathering her plaid about her, and tugged at her brother's arm, to draw him down the High Street towards their lodging. He turned obediently, but added over his shoulder to Gil, 'It will be as the cartes fall, even if you are playing with a damaged hand.'

'What cards?' Gil asked, but the two continued down the street without seeming to hear him.

Alys was crossing the hall as he entered from the fore-stair. Her face lit up, and she came to greet him, then drew him to the nearest window-seat, saying in concern, 'Gil, you have done too much. Have they fed you at the college?'

'I'm all right,' he said, sitting down gratefully. He raised her hand to his lips, and she turned it and stroked his cheek, a little shyly.

'I will fetch food.' She slipped away, and he sat with his palm to the place she had touched, marvelling at the feel of her fingers on his skin. Musician's fingers, he thought, and found himself trying to make sense of the harper's words. And had he really seen Dorothea? And what was he thinking about before that?

'William's victims,' he said, opening his eyes.

'We must make a list,' said Alys, seated opposite. The wolfhound raised its head from his knee and beat its tail on the cushion.

'I wasn't asleep,' he said hastily. 'I was thinking.'

'Good. Drink this.'

'More willow-bark tea?' She nodded, and he drank off the little beaker and handed it back to her. 'Still not foul enough. You'll never get your 'pothecary's licence.'

She smiled, and the elusive dimple flashed. 'Now eat. What were you thinking?'

'It seems very likely,' he said, reaching for the pasty on the tray beside him, 'that William was killed by one of the people on whom he had practised or attempted his extortion.'

'It's very possible,' said Alys, as he paused to take a bite. Flakes of pastry scattered down his doublet, and the dog's nose twitched. 'How many are there? You have mentioned several already.'

'Not more than a dozen or so.'

'So many? Are you joking?'

'No,' he said ruefully. 'Alys, what's in this pasty? It's very good.'

'Cheese and roots and fresh herbs,' she said dismissively. 'But also, Gil –'

'Ah, Gilbert,' said the mason, emerging spruce and newly barbered from the stair which led to the upper floor. Alys glanced at him, and away again. 'Good, you have been fed. What did you learn from the chaplain?'

'He claims he was never in the Outer Close after he left at the end of the play.'

'He was seen there,' Alys said.

'I think he was the one who searched William's chamber,' said Gil, 'which would take him across the Outer Close. What I am not yet certain of is when or why he did so. What was he looking for?'

'Papers,' said the mason. 'Secrets. We know William collected secrets.'

'It could be.' Gil poured himself a beaker of ale from the jug on the tray. 'Father Bernard is kin to the Earl of Lennox, who was a supporter of James Third but is now in favour with the present King, so I suppose William could have learned something inconvenient to him.'

'The letter you delivered for Kittock's guest?' suggested Maistre Pierre.

'No,' said Gil doubtfully. 'That came ultimately from the boy's mother, and William seemed not to know what was in it. Although,' he added, 'after he read it he demanded a word with Father Bernard, which I do not think he got.'

'What about the spying?' said Alys. 'Could that have brought about his death?'

'I'm reluctant to put much weight on something Father Bernard suggested.'

'No, but it is true. He was dealing in information. It is clear from the letter to Lord Montgomery –'

'You have deciphered that?'

Alys, with a triumphant air, drew a little sheaf of papers from the hanging pocket at her waist and held it out. Biting off another mouthful of pasty Gil set the savoury thing down on the tray and took the bundle one-handed, tilting the papers to the light.

'Well!' he said after a moment. 'Sweet St Giles, the boy was in deep.'

'Is it all genuine, then? Who is this A he refers to? Is it the Earl of Angus?'

'It looks it.' Gil returned to the beginning of the letter with its formal salutation to William's *richt weel-belovit & respectit kinsman, the Lord Hugh, Baron Montgomery.* In Alys's elegant, accomplished hand, the dead boy's voice was still clear. *I have stablisshit*, he had written, and again, *I have maid certaine of this.* 'I think it must be Angus. He mentions a betrothal. It must mean this betrothal of Angus's daughter to my kinsman Kilmaurs.'

'It is confusing,' said Alys thoughtfully, 'that the Earl of Douglas was a Douglas, but the Earl of Angus is not an Angus but another Douglas.'

Gil nodded, half listening. Most of the document concerned the doings of the Earl of Angus, the ambitious, misguided head of the house of Douglas. *I have learned what is to be the marriage settlement*, William had written, and gave the details. From Gil's conversations with his uncle, he judged these to be accurate. *A is gathering his men at Kilmarnock*, the letter went on. And then, sending Gil's eyebrows up, the statement: *I have seen by means of M the copy of a letter of A to the king H.*

207

'Sweet St Giles!' he said again. 'Alys, you are certain of this part? That Angus is writing to English Henry?'

She twisted her head to look. 'Quite certain. I went over it several times.'

'What is it?' asked Maistre Pierre.

'There's been a rumour of this.' Gil handed the papers to his prospective father-in-law, took another bite of the pasty, and chewed thoughtfully. 'Michael mentioned it earlier. My uncle thinks it won't harm Angus with King James, who likes him, but Chancellor Argyll is a different matter.'

'And the Montgomery has his ear,' said Maistre Pierre.

'Exactly. And proof of the correspondence – I wonder if the letter he saw is genuine?'

'There is a truce with England just now, is there not?' said Maistre Pierre.

'Quite so. But Angus is neither a councillor nor an ambassador, he has no authority to be dealing with King Henry. Proof of the correspondence could damage him badly, and the Cunninghams don't want that, not just now.'

'And who is M?' said Alys. 'It can hardly be Montgomery himself.'

'It could be Michael,' said Gil thoughtfully, 'but when he spoke to me I did not get the idea he had seen such a letter, much less shown it to William.'

'How can you say the King likes Angus?' objected the mason, looking up from the letter. 'He stripped him of his Lanark honours and all his holdings in Teviotdale, only last Yule.'

'But then he gave him the lands and lordship of Kilmarnock,' Gil pointed out, 'in the hope that he would live in Ayrshire and put down Hugh Montgomery and his arrogance, which is no doubt why my kinsman is marrying his daughter. Angus goes on pilgrimage with the King, and they play cards together. Angus's countess is a Boyd, from Kilmarnock and those parts,' he added. 'She is some kind of cousins with my mother.'

'Do you think someone killed William because he knew this?'

'This or something else. It's possible.'

'Where did he get all this from?' Alys wondered. The mason cut himself a slice from the wedge of cheese on the tray and popped it in his mouth, watched intently by the wolfhound.

'Here and there?' he suggested. Alys glanced briefly at him again, expressionless.

'Very possibly,' said Gil. 'Not all of this is new. The marriage has been known in my family for some weeks, though the settlement is not common knowledge, and the matter of the old title is very cold kale. Only Angus's letter is fresh news. I do not like this.'

'So does it seem William was killed by a supporter of the Douglases?' asked Maistre Pierre. 'The boy Michael, for instance?'

'Michael has witnesses to show he was elsewhere,' said Gil, and was aware of a strong sense of relief. This would not be a good time to accuse my mother's godson of murder, he thought. But spying for the Montgomery? 'No, I think if this had been the immediate cause of William's death the letter would have been removed from his purse. We must leave this piece in play, but it doesn't check anything.'

'So what must we do now? Make a list of the pawns?'

'Precisely. All those on whom William tried his extortion.'

Alys, without comment, drew a pair of wax tablets from her pocket and opened them. Smoothing the wax with the bone stylus which fitted in the box, she said, 'Do we begin at the top? Did William approach the Dean?'

'I hardly think the Dean would like to be referred to as a pawn,' said Gil, 'but yes, write him down, though I don't know that William spoke to him privately. I know he did speak to Maister Doby, and there are the two men of law – that's Archie Crawford and David Gray.'

'But they all swear to each other,' objected the mason.

'I know.' Gil frowned, trying to recall names. 'Nick

Kennedy swore in my hearing he'd throttle the boy. Patrick Coventry. Maister Forsyth. That's all the regents I can think of. John Shaw the Steward.'

'Father Bernard,' said Alys, writing carefully.

'He denied that William approached him,' said Maistre Pierre. Alys glanced at him again, and went on writing.

'Now the scholars.' Gil took another draught of ale. 'Michael Douglas. Richie – now what is his name? Write down Richie Scholar, Alys. And I suppose Ninian Boyd.'

'Any more?'

'Agnes Dickson and one of the kitchen hands. Tam, I think his name is, like my uncle's man.'

'The boy's friends?' suggested Maistre Pierre. 'That poor Ralph and the young man Montgomery.'

'Yes, if you think Ralph has the gumption to do such a thing. As Nick said, I'd put nothing past the Montgomery, but Robert was in the kitchens with Nick Gray.'

'Laughing a vengeful laugh,' said Alys. Her father looked startled.

'Who else?' Gil wondered. 'It must all be in the book, which we must look at next.'

'That makes sixteen names,' said Alys.

'The porter?' suggested the mason. 'This elusive dog-breeder?'

'The dog man was at the door,' said Alys. 'I'm sorry, I had forgotten. He came by this afternoon asking for you by name.'

'Did he so?' Gil stared at her. 'What did he want?'

'He asked after the dog. He was supposed to take it back to his kennels yesterday morning, but he didn't get it before William died. Its keep is paid for, it seems.'

'And he is worried by this?' asked the mason. Alys flicked him another glance, and tightened her mouth.

'I thought he was concerned for the dog,' she added to Gil. 'About its food, and whether you had collar and leash for it. I assured him you were well able to rear and train a hunting dog, and he went away.'

'Collar and leash?' repeated Gil. He reached into his doublet. 'We found a collar and leash in the press in

Jaikie's chamber.' And was this the collar Dorothea meant in my dream? he wondered.

'The dog's, do you think?' said the mason. 'Certainly the boy Livingstone assumed it.'

The pup stood up to put a paw on Gil's knee, and sniffed carefully at the strips of leather.

'He recognizes it,' said Alys.

'And I recognize the badge on the leash.' Gil held it out. 'I'd say it was a piece off someone's bridle, put to good use, and look what's stamped on it. Little fish-tailed crosses, all along the leather.'

'The cross of St John,' said Alys.

'Oh!' said her father, craning to see. 'And where has that come from, do you suppose?'

'Anyone may use a second-hand bridle,' said Alys thoughtfully.

'I think they were gilded.' Gil tilted the leather so that it caught the light. 'This has been expensive work.'

'Something the dog man had by him?' said Alys.

'I had best go and speak to him,' said Gil. 'It sounds as if he feels responsible for the beast.' He glanced at the sky. 'It's still an hour or more to Compline. I can go down there after we finish making this list.'

'And what about the porter's death?' said Maistre Pierre.

'Michael Douglas again,' said Gil, 'and Robert Montgomery and his uncle Hugh.'

'I know where my money lies,' said the mason. He cut himself another slice of cheese. Gil did the same, and shared it with the dog.

Alys, writing names, said, 'So two people are on both lists.'

'My own thought is that Hugh Montgomery killed Jaikie,' said Gil, 'though I have no firm knowledge of why, but the two scholars were also at the yett without witnesses shortly before he died.'

'The Montgomerys will bear witness for each other,' observed the mason.

'My point precisely,' said Gil.

'Do all these names remain on the list?' asked Alys, surveying it. 'I am sure you said these two were under your eye, and these four, no, five remained together.'

'I am certain of Nick Kennedy and Maister Coventry,' Gil agreed. 'The group of five all swear to one another, so unless we impute conspiracy as well as secret murder to the senior members of the Faculty, we must cross them off. A pity,' he added, 'for they were the only ones who ate the spiced pork, apart from Jaikie and the kitchen hands.'

'I told you before you should question the kitchen,' Alys said.

'The scholars – Michael and Ninian can go, and Ralph. Who does that leave us with?'

'John Shaw the Steward,' Alys read, smoothing names out of the wax. 'Father Bernard. Robert Montgomery and Richie Scholar. Mistress Dickson and Tam.'

'All equally unlikely but one,' said the mason gloomily.

'I agree, there is a case against him,' said Gil. 'But the trouble is, while he denies that William approached him, I don't know what reason he would have to kill him, and in fact I suspect he might have had good reason to give the boy support and some sort of acknowledgement.'

'What?' said the mason.

'Father Bernard,' Gil pointed out, 'knew exactly how old William was.'

The shops and stalls at Glasgow Cross were being packed up, with a lot of shouting and joking about the day's trade. Apprentices cleared their masters' wares off counters which would fold upwards like shutters, journeymen stowed the stock in bags or boxes or great trays. The burgh's licensed beggars whined hopefully round the food stalls.

'And there,' said Maistre Pierre, nodding at one of the booths against the Tolbooth, 'is William's barber. I asked another of the students, before you reached the college this afternoon.'

'Ah,' said Gil. 'Is he any good?'

'I may not go back, but he is certainly popular. He has two assistants, and there were several people waiting while I was barbered, even on a Monday.'

'So what did you learn?'

His companion pulled a face. 'The Watch cleared several alehouses last night. Two of the girls at Long Mina's are planning to retire. Robert Blacader has made over land to somebody's nephew. It may be that they were guarding their tongues because I am not a regular,' he admitted. 'In general I let Daniel Dickson clip me. But it does seem to me that one must spend a lot of time there to gather much information.'

'So perhaps that wasn't William's source.'

They picked their way through the bustle, avoiding the rotting vegetables and broken crocks underfoot, and turned eastward past the Mercat Cross into the Gallowgait.

'I can walk this far on my own,' Gil said.

'I am happy to leave the house. I am in disgrace, a little.'

Gil turned his head to look at his companion. 'She was very much alarmed when Wattie came to the door asking for you.'

Maistre Pierre nodded. 'Life was a little difficult before we left Paris,' he admitted. 'It is four years since, but Alys is still concerned if she does not know where I have gone.'

Gil waited, pacing along the sandy roadway, but no more information was forthcoming.

'There was rioting on the Left Bank,' he recalled, 'when the King tried to impose his will on the Faculty of Theology again. Students on the Continent are more combative than in Scotland, I suppose because they are generally older.'

'And the universities are larger, so there are more of them,' said the mason absently.

They made their way to the East Port and out through the gate, nodding to the two keepers. The senior, a stout man who reminded Gil strongly of the late Jaikie, eyed

213

them suspiciously, but appeared to decide that they had neither goods nor profits to be taxed, and waved them idly through.

'Where does the dog-breeder stay?' Gil asked, pausing.

'It's no far,' said the younger gatekeeper, taller and more helpful than his colleague. He pointed. 'A wee bit out yonder. Ye canny miss it, maisters, the reason being, all the dogs is barking. Ye can hear it from here.'

'You can indeed,' agreed the mason.

'Just follow your ears,' said the senior keeper, and laughed raucously.

'We return before Compline,' said Maistre Pierre.

'Well, you'll no return this road after it, maisters,' said the younger man, 'for we'll shut the gate.'

Beyond the port, over the wooden bridge which crossed the Mill-burn, the condition of the roadway deteriorated sharply. Inside the burgh there were regulations about middens, about the housing of pigs, about keeping the street before one's door passable. Since most of the burgesses observed these from time to time, particularly when threatened with a fine by the burgh officers, they had some effect. Outside the gate there were no regulations, and though the road which led in from Bothwell and Cadzow was well defined, since carts and pack-trains came in this way, it appeared to go through some of the middens. On either side was the usual suburban huddle of small houses, the homes of those who could not afford to live in the burgh, with a few larger properties among them where some tradesman had become wealthy enough to ignore the by-laws about indwelling burgesses. Children, pigs and hens scuffled in the alleys, a goat browsed thoughtfully on a patch of nettles, and over all the dogs howled.

'That way, I think,' said Maistre Pierre, gesturing to their left. 'There is a vennel of sorts which goes in the right direction.' His glance fell on the crumbling chapel standing where the paths diverged, and he added, 'Ah, there is Little St Mungo's. Your uncle was saying the roof needs repair, and he is perfectly right. Those children will have the building down.'

'The vennel goes on to the Dow Hill,' said Gil. 'The dog man lives on the Gallowgait, so Robert Montgomery said.' He caught the eye of a dirty boy, one of several waiting to swing on a heavy rope knotted into the overhanging eaves of the chapel. 'Can you take us to Billy Dog's?'

'What's it worth?' demanded the child. Two or three more came jostling eagerly forward.

'I ken, maisters. I'll show ye! Dinna tak him, he'll lead ye astray. I'll show ye, maisters!'

The dog-breeder's home, down Little St Mungo's Vennel, was a low thatched cottage like its neighbours, distinguished mainly by being next to a tanner's yard. One of the boys led them confidently past the interested stares of several gossiping women and stopped in front of the open door. He gestured at a well-trodden path which emerged round the end of the house and led down the vennel to a plank bridge over yet another burn.

'That's where she walks the dogs. Mistress Doig!' he shouted. 'Here's two men wants ye!'

Gil handed over the coin they had agreed on, and the boy bit it, thrust it into some recess of his filthy clothing, and ran off, followed by the friends who had escorted them.

'There is nobody at home,' said the mason doubtfully. 'Perhaps they have been driven out by the smell.'

'I should have kept that compress on my wrist,' said Gil.

'It takes folk that way at first,' said a rasping voice, low down behind them.

Gil turned, and stared.

The dog-breeder was not much taller than an ell-stick, and consisted mainly of a big-featured head and a barrel chest. His arms were short, bare and furred with coarse black hair, and at first glance he seemed to have no legs, but a pair of well-shod feet which were just visible under the turned-up hem of a leather apron. Gil found himself recalling one of his nurse's tales.

The man moved forward, raising his blue woollen bonnet, and ducked a grotesque courtesy which made it clear that his legs were short and bowed.

'Good e'en to ye, maisters,' he said politely, though from his wry smile he knew exactly Gil's thoughts. 'And what can Billy Doig do for ye?'

Gil, recovering his own manners, introduced himself and the mason with equal politeness.

'I've got William Irvine's dog in my keeping,' he said.

'I hear he's deid, poor laddie.' Maister Doig crossed himself with a hairy paw.

'He is,' said Gil. 'I think you had some arrangement with him about the pup's keep.'

'Oh, I had,' said Billy Doig rather hastily, 'but the money's all used up, maister. If I was to get the dog back, I'd need more coin for it.'

'That's understood,' said Gil. 'What was the arrangement you had?'

Maister Doig looked at them, his eyes wary under thick greying brows.

'Come in the house,' he said. 'No need to discuss it afore half the Gallowgait.'

'May we not rather go round to the dog-pens?' asked the mason.

'Aye,' said Maister Doig after a moment, and set off with a rolling gait like a cog in a cross-wind, round the end of the house.

The barking redoubled in volume as they followed him into the yard at the back. It was lined with rows of pens, from which big dogs, little dogs, wolfhounds, deerhounds, otterhounds, spaniels, two sorts of terrier, barked and howled and leapt up and down, tails going madly, demanding attention.

'*Mon Dieu!*' said the mason.

'What a lot of dogs,' agreed Maister Doig, with irony. 'Be quiet!' he shouted, and most of the dogs fell silent, watching him intently. A pair of terriers in the nearest pen yipped impatiently. 'Quiet, youse!' he said again, and they scurried to the back of their cage, where they could be heard squabbling over something.

216

'All the dogs from Dunbar to Dunblane,' said Gil. Maister Doig had clearly heard the quotation before. 'Are these all your breeding?' Gil continued, peering into a pen of spaniels. A black-and-white speckled bitch stood up against the palings to speak to him, and he offered her the back of his hand to sniff.

'That's Bluebell. Soft as butter she is. Had five good litters off her,' confided Maister Doig, 'but she's resting the now. Aye, they're mostly mine. That one there I got off Jimmy Meikle out past Hamilton.' He pointed to another pen. 'He throws good deerhounds, but his tail's a wee thing short. The gentry likes a dog wi' a good long tail.'

'That never bothered us,' said Gil, scratching the spaniel's ears. 'How is Jimmy Meikle? He was our dog man,' he added to Maistre Pierre.

'Jimmy Meikle's deid,' said the dog-breeder curtly, 'as you'd surely ken if he was your dog man.'

'We lost the land in '88,' Gil reminded him. 'He went to the Hamiltons, like all else. I'm sorry to hear that, for he knew dogs like no other. That's another of his breeding, isn't it?'

'No, she's mine,' said Maister Doig, 'but you're right, her sire was one of Jimmy's.' There was a pause, in which the terriers could be heard snarling. 'So what did you want to discuss, maisters?'

'How did you come to meet William Irvine?'

'How did he die, maisters?' countered Doig, looking from one to the other. 'It was sudden, I take it, for he was well enough on Saturday.'

'You could say that. It was murder,' said Gil.

Maister Doig's big-featured face tightened briefly.

'How?' he said after a moment. 'Where did it happen? Jaikie never –'

'Strangled,' said Gil, 'within the college.'

'No by Jaikie?' speculated the dog-breeder. 'He threatened it often enough.'

'Probably not by Jaikie,' said Gil. 'Do you know of any other enemies William had?'

'Me,' said Maister Doig frankly, 'but I wasny by the

college till after he was found. I came up to ask for the dog as arranged and Jaikie told me William was dead and he didny ken where the pup was.'

'Why would you have killed him?' asked the mason curiously. 'What did you have against him?'

'I never said I would have killed him,' retorted Doig. 'I said I was one of his enemies.'

'You would have killed him if you had the chance?'

The light eyes under the grey brows turned to Maistre Pierre.

'Look at me, maister. How could I kill something the height of that laddie?'

'I look at you,' said Maistre Pierre. 'I see a very strong man.'

'Aye, well.' Maister Doig turned away. 'I didny. As for why I might have, maister, he was a boldin wee bystart, and no near as clever as he thought he was.'

'Was he no?' asked Gil with interest. 'His teachers were pleased with him.'

Doig grunted.

'But he was a customer,' said Maistre Pierre. 'Did he pay well?'

'Him?' said Doig witheringly. 'Aye after what he could get, and never opened his purse if he could avoid it.'

'So what arrangement did you have with him?' Gil asked.

'Arrangement?' said Doig, visibly startled. 'About the dog, you mean? I kept him here. Is he well, maister?'

'He's well. Someone broke his head for him, but it's a skin wound only, and Maister Mason's daughter physicked it –'

'What wi'? What did she put on it?'

'Comfrey,' said the mason confidently. Maister Doig pursed his wide mouth and nodded.

'He's like to eat the kitchen bare. If I can settle it with William's kin, I'd like to keep him,' said Gil casually, 'so I'll want to know about his feeding and rule. What did William name him?'

'Mauger,' said Doig.

'Despite,' Gil translated into French for the mason. 'Not a bad name for a wolfhound. So he lived here, did he? And you took him up to the college now and then?'

'Aye, to get to know his master.'

'More usual, surely,' said Maistre Pierre, 'for the boy to visit the dog?'

A seismic movement of the massive shoulders appeared to be a shrug.

'It suited. It would ha' suited better if Jaikie had been less of a glumphy scunner.'

'So the dog passed back and forth between you,' said Gil, 'with Jaikie as middle-man.'

The spaniel he was still petting dropped on to four paws and rushed to the corner of her pen where she stood whimpering and peering through the slats, her tail going.

'No always,' said Doig. 'Times William brought him back himself.'

'Times I took him up for ye,' said a harsh female voice at the house-corner. Gil turned, and saw an angular woman being towed across the yard by a leash of spaniels.

'My wife, maisters,' said Doig informally. Mistress Doig inspected her husband sharply, while the dogs pawed at their friends through the fence as if they had been parted for weeks. 'Maister Cunningham's asking about the wolf-hound, mistress.'

'I hear that, Doig,' she said, turning the acute gaze on them. 'And why would they be doing that?'

'I'm trying to find out who killed William,' said Gil, 'so I'm asking questions of everyone that knew him.'

'Well, you needny bother asking us,' she said in her harsh voice, 'for we didny kill him. Doig never saw him all day, did ye? For all he was up the town three times asking at the college yett. Did ye say about the collar?' she added to her lord. He tipped his head back and gave her a hard look, and she turned to unleash the spaniels and let them into their pen, expertly using the bedraggled hem of her heavy homespun skirts to stop the other dogs getting out of the opened gate.

'Collar?' said the mason.

'There's a dog-collar of mine,' said Doig, 'outstanding as movable property. Cost me a penny or two at the cordiner's, it did, and I'd be glad to see it back and the leash with it. What was on the pup when you had him?'

Gil opened his mouth to reply, but was forestalled by a fearsome outbreak of snarling, worrying noises from the terrier pen. Doig rolled across to bang on the gate and shout, without effect. The snarling grew more savage, and one of the dogs yelped in what sounded like pain.

'Fiend take it, stop that!' yelled Doig, fumbling at the catch to the gate. His wife hurried over to join him, and they hauled the gate open and pounced on the rolling mass of brindled fur which tumbled out. The dogs were dragged off one another, still snapping and snarling defiance, long white teeth bared. Mistress Doig bundled one into her brown woollen skirt, revealing a patched grey kirtle, and Doig thrust the other back through the gate with his foot and fell back, cursing a bitten thumb.

'*Mon Dieu*, have they run mad?' the mason exclaimed. 'You must have the bite burned.'

'Naw. All terriers fight.' Doig inspected the thumb and pushed it into his mouth. 'You were telling me about the pup's collar, maister.'

'Just an ordinary collar,' said Gil, as Mistress Doig shut the gate with her free hand. The mason leaned cautiously over the fence to look at the frantic dog, which was hurling itself against the fence raging at its kennel-mate. 'But there was another in Jaikie's chamber when we searched it, along with a great bundle of papers. Could that be the one you want?'

'Along with the papers? Where?' asked Doig round his thumb, frowning, but his wife turned with the latch-rope of the terrier pen still in her hand. The dog still bundled in her skirts squirmed convulsively.

'Searched Jaikie's chamber?' she repeated. 'Where was Jaikie? That sirkent ablach let ye search his chamber?'

'After he was dead,' explained the mason, and she stared at him.

'Jaikie's deid and all? When was this?'

'This day about noon,' said Gil, studying both Doigs.

'About noon,' repeated the dog-breeder, and gave his wife another hard look. 'That would be about when I took the hounds up the Dow Hill, wouldn't it no, mistress?'

'Aye,' she said, and licked her lips. 'Aye, Doig, it would,' she agreed earnestly.

'We should get a Mass said for him,' continued Doig. 'He put folk in our way now and then. It's aye good to get new custom,' he said to Gil with a broad smile.

'That's true,' agreed Gil, 'though I would think you had custom enough. Dogs like these are far to seek.'

'That's a true word,' agreed Doig. 'My lord Bothwell had two off me last summer, and he put more of the Hepburns and the Humes on to me. I'd even the Earl of Angus after me for one of Bluebell's last litter, but they were all spoken for already.'

'You must hear a thing or two,' said Gil. 'You get a few men leaning over a fence like this, the talk must be of some strange matters.'

'Oh, aye,' agreed Doig easily. 'Only last week, there was two young Hepburns and a gentleman from the Bishop's household – Archbishop,' he corrected himself, 'all wi' wonderful tales of some merchant in the Low Countries and what like things he'd send. Fair to split his sides one of them was,' he reminisced, 'telling of how his lord sent for cushions and got a barrel full of straw mats.'

'Clearly, they have never tried to import a wheelbarrow,' said Maistre Pierre, without looking up from the silent terrier pen.

'And what were you doing, Mistress Doig,' Gil asked politely, 'while your man was exercising the dogs on the Dow Hill? There must be plenty for two to do in a trade like this. Jimmy had two boys just to keep the pens clean, I mind.'

'The pens is no bother,' said Doig, 'the reason being, I've an arrangement wi' Sandy the Tanner next door. He sends

221

two of his laddies twice a day wi' buckets and shovels, and he gets to keep what they lift. So if you had they boots in Glasgow in the last four years, Maister Cunningham, it was my dogs provided the making of the leather.' He grinned broadly, exposing the blackened teeth again. Gil looked down and flexed one ankle in the newly waxed boot.

'They're wearing well,' he said. 'Did he make that apron to you?'

The dog-breeder looked down at himself, and up again.

'Aye. Aye, he did. That's his work, right enough.'

'I thought it might be. I can see he's a good neighbour,' said Gil. 'Is that dog suffocating, mistress? He's very quiet.'

'He's asleep.' She let the layers of damp brown cloth fall over the grey kirtle, revealing a somnolent dog tucked under her arm. As they all looked, the little beast emitted a buzzing snore. 'I'll put him in an empty pen. We'll ha' to keep them apart for a bit, Doig.'

'Aye, do that.' Doig was wrapping his thumb in the hem of his jerkin.

'So what were you doing, mistress?'

'Seeing to the dogs' feed,' she said. She suddenly turned and bent to check that the latch-rope was fitted over the peg on the gate. 'Aye, that's right,' she added, kicking the turnbutton on the bottom of the gate into place. 'I was making the dogs' dinner –'

At the word, the spaniels in the pen began to bark, leaping up and down, and every other dog in the place joined them. Gil covered his ears, laughing, and Maistre Pierre flinched.

'Quiet!' screamed Mistress Doig, and silence fell, broken only by excited whimpers from the nearest dogs. 'Doig cuts the meat up fresh every time, but the mash takes the best part of an hour to boil beforehand. And they're to be fed again, maisters, so if you'll excuse us –'

'We'll get out of your way,' agreed Gil. 'I thank you for your time. Oh, one other thing.'

They stared at him, with identical expressions of faint dismay. Behind them, the mason stooped quickly to lift something from the cobbled surface of the yard.

'William was given to extortion,' Gil continued. 'I wondered if he ever approached you, or any of your other customers.'

'He tried nothing wi' me,' said Doig confidently, 'for he'd ken fine that I would just turn round and let on to his teachers what he was up to. And if he'd spoke to the Hepburns or the Humes, maister, do you think they'd tell me?'

'True,' agreed Gil. 'What do you mean, what he was up to? What would you tell his teachers?'

'Why . . .' Doig paused, and swallowed. 'About him keeping the pup, and having it in his chamber, and coming down here, all at times he should ha' been at his studying.'

'No more than that?'

'Is that no enough? I could have tellt his sponsor and all. The Lord Montgomery wouldny care to hear how his money's being wasted,' declared Doig with fluency.

'Ah, well,' said Maistre Pierre, leaving the terrier pen. 'That expenditure is at an end now. God rest the boy's soul.'

'Amen,' said Doig, and he and his wife crossed themselves. 'I'll see ye out, maisters. And if ye gang down this vennel and cross the Poldrait Burn, the track links up with the one frae the Old Vennel and ye'll find yourselves back on the High Street.'

'That must cross the Mill-burn too,' said Gil, interpreting the stumpy gestures. 'Is that where you exercise the dogs, Maister Doig?'

'Between the two burns,' agreed the dog-breeder. 'They need to get running about. They bring me a cony now and then,' he added.

Pausing on the far bank of the Poldrait Burn, Gil looked back at the mason splashing through the shallows and beyond him, back up the track. Billy Doig still watched them, a small grotesque figure like a chess-piece standing in the middle of the way. As Gil looked, he nodded briefly and turned to shamble back into his own yard.

'That was interesting,' said Maistre Pierre, coming up out of the burn. He stamped water from his boots and went on, 'He knew more about William's doings than he would admit.'

'I agree.' Gil began to stroll up the track away from the burn. 'It was also interesting that he asked about William's death but not about Jaikie's.'

'There is more than that.' Maistre Pierre groped in his purse. 'What about this?'

He handed over a twist of wet rag. Gil shook it out to inspect it, and a waft of spirits reached his nose.

'Usquebae!' he exclaimed.

'I suspect the two little dogs were quarrelling for possession of that cloth. It fell when they came out fighting and were seized by their owners. The dogs,' said the mason portentously, 'were not mad, but drunk.'

'Jaikie's missing bottle?'

'Was in the pen. I saw it. It had been hidden under the straw, I surmise, and the dogs found it. The one that was put back into the pen had also fallen into a stupor, like his brother. I never knew that dogs would take spirits.'

'We had one liked red wine,' said Gil, 'and most will drink ale if they get the chance. These two must have liked the smell on the rag, and unstopped the bottle when they fought over it.'

'It was on its side, half-hidden. They may not have had much.'

'Enough to make them fighting drunk. Sweet St Giles, I wouldn't like to have to handle them tomorrow!'

'But you see what this means.'

'I do.' Gil paused where the track branched, on the spur between two burns. 'The laddie that led us to the Doigs' door said *That's where she walks the dogs*, but Harry Hubbleshaw yonder – Doig himself – said he had walked them today at noon.'

'I thought this was news to his wife,' commented the mason.

'So did I. You see, this goes over the Mill-burn and into the High Street as Doig said, and that goes out on to the Dow Hill and the butts.' He looked down the track to the wooden bridge that led back into the burgh, and pointed. 'Isn't that your garden?'

'It is,' agreed the mason in slight surprise. 'It looks different from here. And there is the land of Blackfriars, and beyond it the college kitchen-yard. I do not come here often.'

'I have, on my way to the butts to practise archery when I was a student, but we'd have had no reason to take the other track, I had no idea where it went. It would be easy enough for both the Doigs to come this far while the neighbours were watching, and then go separate ways.'

'You think the woman killed the porter?'

'There was no blood on her gown,' said Gil with regret, 'and she seemed startled to learn of his death.'

'Whereas the dwarf wore a leather apron which would successfully conceal any stains.'

'And which was much too long for him. I suspect it is his wife's.'

'But why should he kill the porter? And is he capable of it?'

'I wonder.' Gil looked back along the way they had just come. 'He picked up my reference to the bundle of papers as if he had seen them.'

'You mean,' said the mason after a moment, 'he was in the porter's chamber after the Montgomery men?'

'Instead of walking the dogs.' Gil handed the reeking rag back to Maistre Pierre and set off down the slope to the wooden bridge over the Mill-burn. 'I would say he has the strength to bind bears, like the dwarf in the play, and if he cuts up the dogs' meat he is used enough to wielding a knife. Whether he has the reach –'

'The wound that killed the man went straight in, I thought, between two ribs.' The mason demonstrated, levelling two fingers at the palm of the other hand. 'It must have pierced the heart or come near it, to cause blood to run from his mouth after he fell down. Doig could have

225

reached so high, I suppose, and struck level, but would such a blow have the necessary strength or accuracy?'

'Unless Jaikie had been drinking again,' said Gil thoughtfully. 'You asked me if there was a fight, and I thought not, but Jaikie could have fallen over, or out of his chair.'

'You mean he was stabbed when lying on his back?' The mason considered this. 'It would work. Or perhaps the boy Ninian had struck him down for snooping, as he did William. He was certainly very much overcome by the porter's death.'

'I don't like that,' said Gil after a moment. 'It could have happened, but it is too symmetrical. Let us suppose Jaikie was drunk as usual, and fell over. Easy enough for Doig to strike, vertical and true. There still remains the question why? And when? Why was Doig up at the college this noon?'

'Seeking the dog, surely. Then he came straight by my house and spoke to Alys.' Maistre Pierre grimaced and looked about him at the fenced gardens of the small houses on either side of the vennel. Further up the fences gave way to walls, then to the stone flanks of the grander buildings on the High Street. 'We are overheard, perhaps. We discuss this in my house. Also the question of your betrothal,' he added. 'Now your mother is here we should go ahead with signing the contract.'

'Aye.' Gil turned his head to look at the mason. 'Though she may not be present. She was very civil to Alys this morning, but she wouldn't let me mention the marriage.'

'Why? What is wrong?'

'You saw her letter. She must have a reason, but I don't know it yet.'

'Ah.'

They walked on in silence. Gil was becoming aware of his aches and bruises again, and was conscious of a feeling that his own bed, in the attic of his uncle's house in Rotten-row, would be a welcome sight. The vennel debouched on to the High Street, where a few people were still about, and as they turned down the hill towards Maistre Pierre's house the bell began to ring in Greyfriars.

'Can that be Compline already?' wondered the mason.

'I think it must be,' Gil began, and was interrupted. From above his head a harsh, familiar voice spoke.

'You! Cunningham law man! A word wi' you.'

He paused, looking up. They were passing the tall stone tower-house with the Montgomery badge over the door. The shutters of one of the windows stood open, and leaning on the sill, glaring down at him with that dark glow of rage, was the owner.

'Come up, Cunningham,' said Hugh, Lord Montgomery. 'I want to talk.'

Chapter Eleven

Gil stepped back, the better to meet the dark Montgomery gaze.

'You expect me to come under your roof? What warranty will you offer me?' he challenged.

'Feart, are you?'

'I've no wish to be the third Cunningham head at your gates.'

'Ach –' Lord Montgomery shook his head angrily. 'I'm no killing the day. Bring your good-father up wi' you if you wish. He's safe enough – I can't afford the blood money for a merchant-burgess of Glasgow before next quarter-day.' He spread his hands. 'I'm no armed, save for my eating-knife. Come on, man. I want a word.'

Gil exchanged a glance with Maistre Pierre, who shrugged, and gestured towards the wooden fore-stair of the tower.

They were admitted by a grim-faced man who looked as if he missed his armour. Across the bare hall, Hugh, Lord Montgomery stood scowling by a fireplace which would have sheltered a small encampment. A diminutive blaze perched across the fire-irons was putting out no heat whatever. Two large dogs rose and growled as Gil crossed the threshold, and their master cursed and kicked at the nearer.

'Cunningham,' he said, apparently in welcome. 'And you, Maister Mason. Thomas, we'll have some ale.'

Thomas grunted, and slouched off. The dogs lay down, still watchful.

'Right, man,' said Montgomery, turning to Gil in the

firelight. 'What have you learned? How near are you to finding who killed our William?'

Gil, who had been expecting a question like this, shook his head.

'I've struck a lot of people off the list,' he said, 'but I still have more names on it than I want.'

'All I want's one name,' said Montgomery.

'The boy was dear to you?' asked Maistre Pierre.

'Dear enough. He was close kin.'

'For his mother's sake?' Gil suggested. 'Grievous to lose the boy so soon after the mother.'

Montgomery's eyes glittered in the firelight. 'What do you know about his mother?'

'I know who she was, and her husband. She's dead, no need to fling her name about.'

Montgomery made a sound between a grunt and a snarl. The manservant reappeared with a jug, a handful of wooden beakers, and a platter of small cakes. He set these on a bench by the fire, and stumped off glowering at Gil.

'Aye,' said Montgomery. 'Well. She never let on who was the father, though I've aye had my suspicions.' He turned away from the fire to pour ale into the beakers, and thrust two out at arm's length so sharply that liquid splashed into the hearth, making the dogs jump and glare at the fire. 'Drink, maisters,' he said abruptly over the hissing of the embers.

'To a satisfactory conclusion,' said Gil.

'To the name of someone I can hunt down.'

They drank. The ale was cool and strong.

'Do you know if William had enemies?'

'He was one of ours. We have enemies. Maybe it was a Cunningham!' said Montgomery with a mirthless laugh.

'There are no Cunninghams in the college just now,' said Gil. And the saints be praised for that, he thought. 'Had he no enemies on his own account? How much do you know about what he was doing?'

'He was studying,' said William's kinsman. 'I intended him for the Church. Or maybe the Law,' he added. 'What do you mean, what he was doing? What should he have been doing?'

'We think,' said Maistre Pierre with caution, 'he was gathering information.'

'Aye?' said Montgomery after a moment. 'And what was he doing with it?'

'Selling it,' said Gil succinctly.

'Or asking payment not to sell it,' expanded Maistre Pierre.

'Then he'd ha' been a wealthy man,' said Montgomery, 'for anything William did, he did to extinction.'

'Oh, he was,' said Gil. 'He was. We found both coin and jewels in his chamber, and new boots and good clothes.' He met Montgomery's eyes in the leaping firelight, and grinned at him. 'A meld of twenty points, I should say, my lord.'

'You play Tarocco? Both of you?'

'I do,' said Gil with confidence. 'Pierre?'

'Not I,' said the mason, shaking his head.

'Then we'll play now, Maister Cunningham.'

'For what stakes?'

'Information.' Montgomery was searching inside the cupboard at the end of the hall, patting the shelves with a hard hand. A pewter dish fell with a clang and he kicked it, cursing. One of the dogs raised its head to look, then went back to sleep. 'Aye, here they are. Information, Maister Cunningham. The currency of this reign. Here, sit down. Where the devil has Thomas put the candles?'

The bench was hard, but it was against the wall. Gil leaned back gratefully while their host dragged a pricket-stand closer, lit the strong-smelling tallow candle, kicked two stools across the room and placed them where they would catch the light.

'Ye might as well be seated,' he flung at Maistre Pierre, seating himself. 'Who deals?'

'The cards are yours, my lord,' said Gil, trying to gather his thoughts. 'A short game, do you think? Twenty cards each, one point for a trick?'

230

Montgomery grinned. 'You've no patience for a long game, is that it?'

'I've no strength for a long game,' said Gil frankly. This was more like Paris. Although two of his books had been the prizes of a game, he had never played for large sums in money or jewels, but he had once defended a friend's mistress on a charge of theft, won her freedom, and learned some remarkable things about the city, all as the result of a casual stake. 'As you know well, my lord,' he added.

'Nor has Thomas,' said Montgomery with a feral grin. 'I'll shuffle if you'll cut, and then I deal. Is that agreeable?'

He was already running the cards from hand to hand. Gil nodded, and he riffled the slips of pasteboard a couple of times and set the pack down to be cut.

The dark-eyed foreign faces were the same ones current in Paris. Propping his aching wrist on his knee, Gil found enough strength in his right thumb to hold the cards, and arranged them clumsily with his left hand. The Fool and two Kings, three of the great Trumps (a meld of twenty points, indeed, he thought) and a handful of small cards. Not a good hand.

'I'll change four,' he said.

'Oh, those rules. Aye, if I can change five.'

They made the exchange, a card each in turn, and Gil propped his new cards in his hand. His opponent held his own cards close to his chest, tilting them from time to time to let the candlelight fall on them.

'Twenty points,' he said, looking up at Gil.

'And I have twenty-five.' Twenty points, he thought, could be one or two of the big melds, or several smaller ones. Five points for a run of four cards, or fifteen for the other two Kings and the World or the Magician.

'Your good-father can keep the score. You'll find a bit chalk on the cupboard yonder, Maister Mason. Just mark the tally on the wall.'

There were advantages and disadvantages to the short game. One of Gil's talents, that of knowing almost without thinking what cards were in hand and who held them, had

231

no place in a situation where barely more than half the pack of seventy-eight had been dealt out. His other gift, for reading his opponent's play, would be more help. He had already summed Hugh Montgomery up as a practised player rather than a good one.

'A question for every trick,' said Montgomery, 'and the winner gets to ask another question. Agreed?'

'Agreed,' said Gil. And what he asks could tell me as much as what he answers me, he thought.

'Your lead,' prodded Montgomery.

Gil put a card down.

'Five of Cups,' he said. Montgomery, the firelight gleaming on his teeth, laid another on top.

'Three,' he said. 'My trick.'

Maistre Pierre made a startled noise in his throat. Gil turned to nod agreement.

'Cups and Coins are reversed,' he explained. 'The ace is high, the ten is low.'

'My question,' said Montgomery. He paused a moment, frowning, and one of the dogs snored. 'What was in William's purse?' he asked, and laid a card out.

'Coin,' said Gil. 'And a letter in code. Some notes, and a draft will on a set of tablets.'

'So you did find the purse. No key?'

'That is another question,' Gil pointed out. 'No, there was no key.' He selected a card and set it down. Montgomery lifted both.

'My trick,' he said again. 'What was in his chamber, besides what you already narrated?'

'Little of interest,' said Gil.

'Very little paper,' said Maistre Pierre.

'The dog,' added Gil.

'Aye, the dog.' Montgomery scowled at Gil's response to his next card. 'The one you had with you at the college? That's mine and all. Where is the beast now?'

'In my house,' said Maistre Pierre. Montgomery, thinking deeply, took another trick.

'And the papers?' he asked. 'Where are they?'

'In my house,' said the mason again. He chalked the

232

mark against Montgomery's tally, and cast Gil an anxious look.

'In safe keeping,' said Gil, ignoring it. Montgomery's scowl grew blacker.

'And the boy's clothes, that he died in?' he said, gathering up the next two cards.

'Also in my house,' said the mason.

'I'll maybe just move in myself,' said Montgomery sardonically. 'When can I have them back?'

'That's another question,' Gil observed. Montgomery played another card. Queen of Coins, Gil thought, setting the King on top. Has he no more Coins, or is he testing the play? 'That's mine, I think. Why were you at the college yett this day noon?'

'I wanted a word with our Robert.' Montgomery tipped his head back to look at Gil down his nose, then turned his attention to his cards.

'And mine again. What about?'

'Family matters.'

'Such as?'

'William's funeral. Money. Show me the student that can live inside his allowance. Your play.'

Gil laid down the seven of Batons. Montgomery looked at it, then at his cards, and selected one.

'My trick.' He set out the King of Batons, its double ended figure entwined in tendrils of leafy growth from its wand, the crowns barely visible among the arrow-head leaves. Three court cards and three numbers, Gil thought, and I have the Knave. What's still in his hand?

As if for answer, his opponent played the two. Gil put the Knave down and swept the two slips of card to his end of the bench.

'Who did you see at the college?' he asked.

'My nephew. That snivelling boy, what's his name?' Gil recognized Ralph. 'Couple of other scholars were sent to find Robert when I wanted him. Who should I have seen?'

'That's a question?' Gil played the seven of Coins, and Montgomery slapped the three on top of it.

'Let's stop playing here,' he said, apparently not in reference to the card game. 'What do you know about how William died?'

'That's quite a question.' The Knight and Knave of Coins. 'Your trick. We know,' he said carefully, 'that William was knocked down and put in the limehouse as a joke. His hands were bound, to make it harder for him to free himself. While he was still dazed, someone else whose hands smelled of cumin came into the limehouse and strangled him with his own belt. After he was dead, he was moved into the coalhouse, where he was found.'

'By the same person? My trick.'

'I don't know,' said Gil, 'but there are already too many people running in and out of the limehouse for the story to have any credibility. It seems ludicrous to postulate another.'

'Credibility?' exploded his opponent. 'I never in all my days heard such a tale. What has the cumin to do with it? Why the devil move him into the coalhouse? What gain is that? Was he robbed? No, you said there was money on him. His chamber had been searched, but I canny tell whether they got anything of value. Why was he killed, Maister Cunningham? Tell me that? You haveny found that out, with your nonsense about cumin and coalhouses.'

'When I know why,' said Gil calmly, watching Montgomery add five pairs of cards to his pile of discards, 'I'll know who.'

Montgomery glared at him, and put down the two of Coins. Gil stared at it, thinking, Is that all he has left, or is he bluffing? It hardly mattered; there were no more Coins in his own hand. He selected the picture-card with the image of a naked woman incongruously called *L'Estoile*. 'My trick, my lord. If you're asking me why William was killed, I take it you don't know, so I'll ask you a different question. Why was Jaikie killed?'

'Who the devil's Jaikie? What's he got to do with it?'

'Jaikie was the college porter.'

'Oh, him. Glumphy impertinent bugger. Tried to buy –

tried to make out he knew all about William's affairs. Gave him the back of my hand for it.'

'Knocked him down, you mean?' asked the mason.

Montgomery threw him a glance. 'I did not. Last I saw him, after Robert went back into the college, he was snoring in that great chair of his, with half a jar of usquebae under his belt. I heard he was dead, but it wasny me that stabbed him,' said his lordship, sounding very like his nephew. 'Likely it was whoever I heard arguing with him.'

'Arguing?' Gil repeated. 'When was this?' Jaikie argued with everyone, he reflected.

'Is that another question? When I got to the yett, looking for Robert, I heard someone arguing with the porter. Your play, Cunningham.'

'A moment,' said Gil. 'Did you see this person?'

'I did not. The surly chiel never rose to let me in, and when I stepped into his chamber to tell him off for that there was no other there. And I looked behind the door and all,' he added. 'Are you going to play this game or no?'

Gil, setting aside disbelief, surveyed the four pairs of cards aligned beside him, and the row of tricks now neatly herringboned on the bench by Montgomery's knee. He had weeded out all the small stuff, and had only high-value cards left. Let's see what's in his hand, he thought.

The next trick went to his opponent. Gil, avoiding Maistre Pierre's eye, watched Montgomery arrange his cards while he considered his questions.

'Who d'ye suspect?' he demanded bluntly at last.

'I won't answer that,' said Gil with equal bluntness. 'Never mind the law of slander, my position if I name someone in error and you act on what I say, my lord, would be very precarious.'

'Lawyers,' said Montgomery in disgust. 'Tell me this, then. What else of William's have ye found?'

'There was the notebook,' said Gil.

'A notebook,' repeated his opponent. 'What like note-book?'

'Just a notebook,' said Gil. 'Red leather cover, a lot of writing in it. Mostly notes, by the look of it, and accounts. It's in Maister Mason's house,' he added. Montgomery snorted, but did not interrupt as Gil continued, with all the innocence he could muster, 'And there was some kind of medallion, or pilgrim badge, or such like. Made of brass, with a figure in the middle and the alphabet round the outside like a criss-cross row. That was in the lining of his doublet, as if it was something he valued.'

'It was, was it?' said Montgomery with equal innocence, rearranging his cards again. 'I'll send Thomas for that. He can lift the lot off your hands. He'll come by your door with ye when ye leave here.'

'As you please,' said Gil. He watched as Montgomery, tight-lipped, played the four of Coins, and after a moment set the trump called *La Lune* on top of it.

'So who did search William's chamber?' he asked.

'Not me,' said Montgomery.

'Who do you suspect it was?'

'Now why should I answer that one, after what you just said?'

Gil half-bowed over the cards in acknowledgement of the point.

'Today,' he said, picking up the next trick wrong-handed, 'there was a bundle of papers in Jaikie's brazier –'

'No idea. Your play.'

'And what was Billy Doig doing up at the college?'

'Doig?' said Montgomery sharply. 'When?'

'About midday.'

'Never saw him. Who is he, anyway? Your play.'

Gil looked at the two cards in his hand, and laid down Judgement. The woodcut figure, in angular draperies with sceptre and scales, flickered in the light. One of the dogs raised its head, then sat up, staring across the hall.

'Uncle?' said a voice in the shadows.

Gil jumped convulsively, and looked beyond the circle of brightness. He felt the hair on the back of his neck prickle, and Maistre Pierre drew breath sharply. Outlined against the half-lit door to the stair was a gangling figure in a student's belted gown, a chance beam from the distant lantern glowing redly on its springing, curling hair.

'Uncle?' said the voice again. The figure moved, and stepped into the hall. 'I'm just away back to the college,' said Robert Montgomery, coming nearer the fire.

'Aye, right,' said his uncle, twisting round to look at him. They exchanged a significant look, before the older man added, 'Can you get in without trouble?'

'There are ways,' Gil said. Robert's glance flicked to him and back to his uncle, before he raised his cap in a general courtesy to all three adults.

'Good night, sirs. I'll see you the morn, uncle.'

Hugh Montgomery waved his free hand and muttered a perfunctory blessing, and Robert left. Gil sat staring after him for a long moment.

'Your play,' said Montgomery impatiently. Gil, looking down, found Judgement neatly obscured by the Knave of Swords.

'How well do you know Bernard Stewart?' he asked, setting that trick with the others he had gained. His opponent stared at him.

'What in the Fiend's name has he to say to the matter? He was chaplain in my house for a good few years, tutored my brother Alexander and – and others, but it was better than sixteen years since. I know that, for he went to the Blackfriars' Paris house before Alexander was wedded. His mother married my grandsire's youngest brother as his third wife, but I haveny set eyes on him since, not till he came to Glasgow and they made him chaplain here, just after Robert came to the college. Are ye playing that last card, Cunningham law man, or are ye turning to stone at my hearth?'

'The card.' Gil looked down, and set the Fool on the bench beside him. '*Je m'excuse.* The last card out.'

'Your trick,' said Montgomery in disgust, throwing down the image of a woman improbably wrenching open the jaw of a complacent lion. 'Ask your question, while your good-father tots up the scores.'

'I've no more questions for now,' said Gil. 'I'll save them for tomorrow, when I'll have two, for I think I've won the game.'

'You have,' agreed Maistre Pierre, counting strokes of chalk on the wall by the hearth. 'But it was close. You have taken eight tricks, his lordship has twelve, and with the other points from the cards you held I think you win by one point.'

'Aye,' said Montgomery sourly, and looked at the windows, where the last of the sunset was faintly red beyond the rooftops of the houses opposite. 'Well. It's been an interesting evening.'

'It has,' agreed Gil, stretching his long legs. 'You're a gratifying opponent, my lord.'

For a moment he thought he had overreached his mark. Hugh Montgomery's face darkened in the candlelight, and his eyes glittered. Turning his head he roared, 'Thomas!' The dogs leapt up, barking, and he cursed at them. 'Thom-*as*! Get up here wi' your boots on, you lazy ablach.'

'I'm in the lower hall, no' in Irvine,' said Thomas on the stair. 'No need o' the shouting.'

'Then why so long to answer me? Be silent, Ajax, you stupid lump! I want ye to convoy these gentry home and bring back the things they'll gie you. Not the dog, I canny take the dog while these brutes are here, but I'll want a look at it. It's a matter of our William's graith, Thomas, it's no likely to tax your strength.'

'We may not be able to put hand on all of it at this hour,' said Gil, realizing with resignation that Montgomery had not forgotten this threat.

'Then Thomas can wait till ye do, can't he no?'

'No, he can not,' said the mason unexpectedly. 'It is after all my house, my lord, and I do not choose to entertain your man.' He rose and came forward from where he sat. 'I myself will undertake to return all your kinsman's goods before noon tomorrow. Agreed?'

'That's a fair offer,' commented Thomas.

238

'You keep out of this,' snarled his master. He glared at Maistre Pierre, showing his teeth, and finally said, 'Aye. Agreed.'

'My hand on it.'

They spat and shook hands as if it was a trading agreement.

'Now get out of here,' said Montgomery. 'I've a lot to think on, and William's funeral tomorrow.'

Maistre Pierre set the jug of ale down on his desk and wiped his mouth.

'The house was like a barn,' he commented. 'No hangings, no cushions, no comforts at all, and only that ill-conditioned servant to wait on him.'

'He planned a brief visit,' Gil surmised as the wolfhound scrambled on to his lap. 'His lady has stayed behind in Irvine. She might not wish to leave the children, and bringing them would be a lot of work for a short stay. I've no doubt there are cushions in plenty in his other houses.'

'And I did not understand the play at all.'

'It was hardly play,' said Gil.

Alys, rubbing violet-scented oil into the bruising on his wrist, nodded, but her father said, 'What do you mean? I was keeping score.'

'They were both more interested in the information than the game, father,' said Alys. She turned Gil's hand, and he winced. 'You should not have used this. You won't be able to sign your name for days.'

'You are quite right,' he said, and smiled wearily at her. 'I was certainly buying questions, and the ones Montgomery asked were even more interesting than the answers he gave me. I don't know whether he felt the same way,' he added. 'He isn't a strong player but I should hate to underestimate him.'

'So what have we learned?' asked Maistre Pierre. 'And what have we given away, apart from the cipher disc?'

'The cipher disc is small loss,' said Alys. 'It isn't a simple substitution, so we would need another the same, so that the message could be deciphered at its destination.'

'Montgomery seemed eager to get it back,' said Gil, heaving the wolfhound into a more comfortable position. 'This creature has grown again. We have promised Montgomery – you have promised,' he corrected himself, and Maistre Pierre pulled a face and nodded. 'William's clothes, the notebook, the papers, and the cipher disc. I must have a look at the notebook, but the rest can go back to his kin without harming anyone.' He scratched rhythmically behind the pup's ears, and it groaned in ecstasy. 'What have we learned? Montgomery knows or suspects who William's father was, and he knows that William was gathering information. He didn't search the boy's chamber, he doesn't know who killed him, and he probably didn't kill Jaikie, which leaves us with the dog-breeder for that. I hope he thinks we haven't read the cipher letter. He would have liked us to believe he didn't know Billy Doig, and I have brought Bernard Stewart to his attention. Oh, and I think he wants a look at the dog too.'

'Pretty well, for one game of cards,' said Alys approvingly.

'But what don't we know yet?' asked her father. 'And what have we let Montgomery know? I thought you let him win far too many questions, Gil.'

'His questions were very informative,' said Gil. 'As I let him find out, which was a mistake. What don't we know? We don't know who killed William, or why, though we know he had cumin on his hands. I think we know who killed Jaikie, and possibly why, but for William's killer we are still searching in the dark.'

'I thought that was the object of our search.'

'So did I. Pierre, I must go up the hill. I am too tired to think. Saints be praised, there is a moon tonight. Alys, where is the notebook?'

'I will fetch it.'

She slipped away, and Gil sat quietly petting the dog and staring at the painted panelling of the small room.

'I suspect we don't have all the pieces,' he said at length.

'Did you ever break a plate? One of those majolica ones with a picture?'

'Frequently.'

'Some of the pieces may have a hand and a foot, or an elbow and a head, and only when you set all together do you see they belong to different figures. I think it's like that – too many of the pieces we have refer to more than one figure.'

'I was never good at metaphor,' declared the mason, and poured himself more ale. 'We have till noon tomorrow. What will that man do if we have no answer for him?'

'I feel he will not challenge the Dean and the Faculty to Tarocco.' Gil sat up straight as Alys returned, holding the notebook.

'Kittock has just told me,' she said, 'that someone came from the college an hour or two since, to say Maister Coventry would like a word with Maister Cunningham.'

'Too late now,' said Gil, glancing at the window. He fumbled one-handed with the buckle of the dog's collar. 'I'll leave this beast with you again, and be off up the road, but first I must loosen this. He has quite definitely grown. It fitted him yesterday.' He slipped the long tongue of the collar through the keeper, and pushed the animal off his knee. 'Go with Alys. Good dog.'

The pup looked up at him, then doubtfully at Alys, and wagged its tail.

'Good dog!' she exclaimed. 'Gil, he knows my name!'

'He is an exceptional dog,' said Gil, as he had said before, and got to his feet. 'I must go. I'll talk to Patrick Coventry in the morning.'

The stone house in Rottenrow was quiet, but not dark. Picking his way by moonlight from the Girth Cross, Gil could see the glow of candles in several windows. By this hour the great door at the foot of the stair-tower would be barred, so he plodded wearily along the house-wall and in at the little yard by the kitchen door.

He paused there, hand raised to the latch. It seemed like

241

a very long time since he had left the house by this door. Could he remember what was behind it? Was there still a place for him? Would everything have changed? He was assailed by a sudden feeling that he was about to step into the unknown. It was yesterday morning, he told himself irritably, and rattled at the latch.

'Is that you, Maister Gil?'

'It's me,' he agreed. His uncle's stout, red-faced house-keeper opened the heavy plank door, closed it behind him and dropped the bar across.

Inside, all was warm and familiar. The kitchen-boy snored in the shadows, and his mother's maidservant Nan sat by the fire with a cup of spiced ale.

'Your minnie's about given you up, I jalouse,' said Maggie. She returned to the hearth and lifted her own cup of ale. 'And what have you been doing to yourself?'

'Fighting, Maggie.' Gil sat down on the bench opposite Nan. She clicked her tongue.

'Haven't I aye warned you about that? I hope you gave better than you got.'

'I think so. They seemed satisfied. Is all well in Carluke, Nan?'

'It is,' she said, beaming at him over her ale. 'And my lady Gelis is well and all,' she added, using the Scots form of Lady Egidia's name. 'Likely she'll still be up, Maister Gil.'

'She said she'd wait for me. Is the old man abed?'

'He was at his prayers, the last I saw him,' said Maggie. She sniffed. 'Is that violets?'

'To draw out the bruising,' said Gil. 'Or so Alys said.'

'Oh, if she put it on you, that's another matter. Were ye wanting anything, Maister Gil, or will ye get out of my kitchen and let Nan and me get to our beds? There's a candle there on the meal-kist.'

He rose obediently, and suddenly put his good arm round her ample waist and kissed her cheek. She bridled with pleasure.

'Huh! What's that for?'

'For being Maggie.'

'Saints preserve us, who else should I be?' she demanded, but he was quite unable to explain.

The hall was dark, and smelled of the herbs his mother liked to burn. He crossed it in the pool of light from his candle, the shadows leaping avidly round him, and made his way to the upper floor. The solar was also in darkness, but a line of light showed under his uncle's chamber door, and another under the door to the best chamber. He paused for a moment, then crossed the room towards the smell of herbs, and tapped on the painted planks.

'Come in, dear,' said his mother.

She was seated by the fire, wrapped in a furred bed-gown he remembered from before he went to France, her prayer-book on her knee. He stood just inside the door and looked at her, and she stretched out a hand to him, smiling.

'Come and sit down. Are you very tired?'

'Very,' he agreed, and obeyed, kneeling first to kiss her hand. 'Aren't you?'

'I said I would wait up for you.'

'And I said I would be late,' he countered.

'And are you late to good purpose? Have you found who killed the poor boy?'

'Not yet. Why is Nan not with you? I saw her in the kitchen just now.'

'She snores, which is why she's not on the truckle-bed here, or in the attic next to you as David suggested. I hope she won't keep Maggie awake.'

'I think nothing would stop me sleeping tonight,' he confessed. She drew the candle nearer, and surveyed him, then rose, tightening the girdle of her furred gown, and began to delve in one of the packs which were stacked beyond the great curtained bed.

'I know what you need,' she said, as she emerged with a pannikin and a waxed linen scrip.

'How are my sisters?' he asked, watching her without seeing what she was doing.

'Kate and Tibby are well, and send their love.'

'Give them mine,' responded Gil automatically.

'I will. I wrote to Dorothea a week since, but I've heard nothing, which I assume is good news.' She was measuring spices, a pinch of this and a speck of that, out of little packages in the scrip. 'And Margaret is like to make you an uncle again this autumn.'

'How many is that?'

'Only her third, as you know very well.' Lady Cunningham poured ale from the jug on the dole-cupboard on to the spices in the pannikin, and set it in the hearth, then tilted her head, sniffing. 'Do I smell violets?'

'My wrist.' Gil held up his hand. 'To draw out the bruising, so Alys said.'

'Ah.' His mother suddenly became intent on the pannikin of ale. 'The demoiselle Mason. A very giftie lassie.'

'Mother,' said Gil. She looked up, and met his eye.

'I am not blind to her virtues, my dear,' she protested. 'And her nurse is by-ordinar. I had quite a conversation with the nurse. Her father, too. That is a very civilized man. Their house might almost be in Paris. I'm glad to see you with a friend who shares your interests, I told you so this morning.'

'Alys shares more than that.'

'*What?* Gilbert, what have you done?'

'Mo*ther!*' said Gil, as he had not done since he was eighteen. 'I mean that she's clever, and learned, and she thinks more clearly than any woman I know except you and Dorothea. She was of great help in finding out who killed the woman I found dead in the building site at St Mungo's two weeks since, and she has been at least as much help as her father over this business at the college. I want to teach her philosophy,' he added irrelevantly.

'You're too late,' she said, staring at him.

'Too late? What do you mean?'

'I think she already knows some. At least, she quoted Plato today while I was washing my hands.'

Gil's jaw dropped.

'Plato?'

'She said it was Plato.' Lady Cunningham bent to the

little pan on the hearth. 'Oh, my dear. You've got it very bad, haven't you?'

'There was never a girl like her in the world,' said Gil, recovering. 'Now do you see why I want to marry her? How many women in Scotland can quote Plato?'

'Not many, since the Queen died and the old King's sister Eleanor was married abroad,' said his mother, 'but still I canny countenance it.' She swirled the contents of the pannikin, and set it down again. 'Sugar. I know I have some sugar.'

Gil watched her cross the room to the pile of baggage.

'Why in this world not? Is it only the money? The living?'

'Gilbert.' She peered at him round the neatly bagged wool brocade curtain of David Cunningham's best bed. 'We never planned this for you. I told you, we –'

'I never planned it either, mother!' he expostulated. '*An hendy hap ich hab yhent.* I met her on May Day, I met her father the next day – about cathedral business,' he added hastily, before she could comment, 'and by the Sunday, last Sunday indeed, only a week since, he had approached my uncle and then spoken to me. I admired Alys the moment I met her, but I had no thought of overturning your plans for me till the offer was put to me. It came from them, I didny seek it, but I wish it now more than I've ever wished anything in my life.'

'But my dear, you've no land, you must get a benefice or preferably two so you can live on the teinds, you must be a priest.' She made it sound like a logical progression.

'Pierre will dower her –'

She straightened up and returned to the fire with another small waxed packet.

'How can we match that? We've no land to spare, Gilbert!'

'My uncle has offered –'

'Your uncle, your uncle! Well enough for him,' said his mother desperately, 'with all his benefices. Son, I have two parcels of land, you know that. I can keep myself and your sisters on the rents of one, and run the horses on the grazing of the other, and we win a living. If I give you either property for your home, how can I –'

'Are you feart I'd make you homeless?' he said incredulously.

'What else could you be planning?'

'Mother, listen!' He leaned forward and caught her wrist left-handed. 'Listen to me. I don't want to live in Avondale or Clydesdale.'

She stared at him.

'We lost those lands. You know that,' he said, echoing her phrase deliberately. 'I don't want to live where I can see the Hamiltons hunting our game and taxing our tenants.'

'Not in Lanarkshire?' she said. 'But what will you live on? Where would you stay?'

'Oh, in Lanarkshire,' he assured her. 'I'll stay in the Lower Ward. If I marry Alys, we'll settle here, in Glasgow. She has no kin but her father in Scotland, her mother is dead. How could I take her out of the place she knows? My uncle has offered two or three properties within the burgh that bring in a good rent. Pierre will dower her well, and I've a mind to convert at least some of that to property too. And then my uncle has some salaried post in mind, that he's negotiating for. We wouldn't be rich, mother, but we'd be comfortable.'

'You'll never make a living as a clerk outside the Kirk.'

'There are more lay notaries than priested nowadays. They seem to do well enough.'

She stared at him a moment longer, then looked down at the pannikin.

'Oh, your posset,' she said. She added a pinch of sugar from the packet in her hand, and swirled the contents of the pan carefully, testing its warmth with the back of her wrist. Gil sat watching her, in a sort of daze of fatigue. The incongruity between the effort required to present an argument on such a subject and the aching familiarity of sitting at the hearth in his mother's chamber, with the smell of her remembered herbs in his nostrils, had unbalanced him slightly. She was pouring the spiced and sweetened ale into a beaker now.

'Drink this, Gibbie,' she said, holding it out to him. He took it, and drank obediently.

'And what of your sisters?' she went on, as if he had not just made a long speech. 'What's to become of them when I'm not here? Are they to *fast With water-kail, and to gnaw beans and peas*? If you haveny an income, you canny support them, much less dower them, and whatever your uncle has in his mind,' she hurried on, as he drew a weary breath to speak, 'I'll not believe it till I see the first quarter's salary in your hand.'

'Mother, my uncle approves. He likes Alys herself –'

'I told you, he's a sentimental old man.'

'– and he is greatly impressed by her accomplishments and her learning.'

'She is clearly an excellent housewife,' his mother agreed, 'and obviously widely read as well.'

'I think more clearly when I can talk to her.'

'Gil, there's my point exactly! Marriage holds a young man back – here you are already, running after her instead of working.'

'I am working!' he said indignantly. 'The Principal commissioned me to find William's murderer. And Alys has already been a great help. Listen,' he pursued as she drew breath to speak. 'Hughie's bairn died with its mother, didn't it? And Edward was no even betrothed?'

'He was six-and-twenty,' she said, with the wooden expression she still wore when someone else mentioned her dead sons. 'We were just beginning to seek – Christ succour me, Gil, it's only four years since!' she burst out, and covered her face with one hand.

'I know, mother,' he said more gently. 'But you have no Cunningham grandsons. If I marry Alys, and we –' He stopped, his throat tightening, as the full import of what he was saying struck him. His child and Alys's – his own son. Alys's son. 'Do you not wish for my father's name to go on?'

'But what will you live on?' she repeated.

247

'Mother,' he said, setting down the empty beaker, 'I've heard enough.'

'You'll abandon the marriage?'

'I will not,' he said. 'I have you deaving one ear and my uncle at the other, with argument and counter-argument.' He winced as he spread his hands. 'When my closest kin fall out, I'm free to please myself. I'll sign the contract as soon as I can hold a pen.'

She stared at him, her expression unreadable.

'But you can aye be sure, mother,' he concluded, 'of our loving duty. And I know fine I speak for Alys in that, as well as myself.'

Chapter Twelve

'I'm glad you came by, Maister Cunningham,' said Maister Coventry, waving him to a stool by the window of his chamber in the Arthurlie building. 'We were wondering what success you have achieved in the matter of William's death.'

'Call him by his first name, for God's sake, Patey,' said Maister Kennedy from the other side of the chamber. 'We're all equals here, and he's in minor orders at least.'

Maister Coventry raised his eyebrows at Gil, who nodded.

'I should be honoured,' he said. 'As to what I have achieved in William's matter, the answer is very little. The people with a reason to kill the boy had no opportunity, and the people with an opportunity had no reason that I can discern.'

'Who had a reason?' demanded Maister Kennedy.

'Most of the Faculty, I suspect,' said Maister Coventry before Gil could answer. 'It's good fortune that all were together at the critical moment.'

'What is the critical moment, anyway? When was he killed, exactly?'

'I think,' said Gil carefully, 'that he was throttled just about the time the Dean rose at the end of the play. Certainly he was dead and locked in the coalhouse by the time we all gathered in the Fore Hall again. I can't say closer than that yet, and I may never be able to.'

'Oh,' said his friend. He stared out of the window at the wet tree-tops of the Arthurlie garden, his lips moving, and finally said, 'Aye, that was it. D'ye ken, Gil, unless he spoke to whoever killed him, I must be the last to have had any converse with the boy.'

Gil, noting with interest that William was no longer *that little toad*, said, 'And what did you converse about?'

'Well, no to say converse. You mind when his tail got ripped and he marched off the stage.' Gil nodded. 'He stopped behind the curtains and got out of the dragon costume. Then he took up his gown –'

'His gown?' Gil interrupted. 'You mean he had taken it backstage with him?'

'Aye.'

'So he had planned to go snooping,' said Patrick Coventry thoughtfully.

'Very likely. Anyway after he had his gown on, and done up all the wee hooks and fastened his belt –' Maister Kennedy stopped and grimaced. 'His belt. Aye. He set off towards the door. I got a hold of him and said something about, *You're not going, are you?* He says, *Yes, I am, my part's finished.* All this in whispers, of course. I said, *Who the – who do you think you are? I decide when you're finished,* I said, and he shook me off and answered me back, looking down his nose that way he had, *For the first time in my life I know exactly who I am.* Then he went off out the door and the next time I saw him he was dead. Wasny that a strange thing to say?'

'Strange indeed,' said Maister Coventry. 'But he was in a strange mood that morning. I thought he seemed elated, out of himself in some way.'

'I wonder what was in the package from his mother,' said Gil. 'And what he did with it.'

'You think she sent word of who his father was?' asked Maister Kennedy.

'I think that might explain a great deal,' said Gil.

'Had he never known his father's name?' asked Maister Coventry curiously.

'Montgomery claims that he himself never knew, but had his suspicions,' said Gil. 'Though of course there is no saying what the boy had been told.'

'If anyone else knew it,' said Nick Kennedy, reverting to

realism, 'William would pick it out of the air. So maybe she'd sent him some kind of proof, then?'

'Was that why his chamber was searched?' speculated Maister Coventry.

Gil shrugged his shoulders. 'Who knows? I feel we are close to a solution, to finding justice for the boy, but the last links in the chain elude us. So many strange things have happened – William's chamber searched, yours searched, Nick, the pile of William's papers burning in Jaikie's brazier.'

'I have another strange thing to recount,' said Patrick Coventry. 'This is why I sent word to you, Gilbert.' He hesitated. 'I still – I don't know its significance.'

'Spit it out, man,' said Maister Kennedy bracingly, 'and let Gil judge for himself.'

'You know, I think, that I am studying for a bachelor's in Sacred Theology,' said the Second Regent, taking refuge in the Latin again. Gil nodded. 'I should have been at the lecture our chaplain gave on Sunday at two o'clock, save that I was at the feast. So I asked one of my fellow Theology students in advance if I might copy his notes.'

'We've all done it,' said Maister Kennedy.

'What with one thing and another,' said Maister Coventry, 'and the Montgomery boy having a nightmare, and the death of Jaikie our porter, it was not until yester-day before Vespers that I asked Alan Liddell for his notes in order that I might copy them. But he had no notes. I do not like the implication of what I am saying, but I must say it. Father Bernard did not teach at two o'clock on Sunday. There was no lecture.'

'None?' said Gil. 'Did he cancel it, or not turn up to deliver it?'

'He cancelled it,' said Maister Coventry, nodding approval of the question. 'Alan said he was present in the Theology Schule while they were gathering, and left the room less than a quarter-hour before he was due to start. He was gone for a little time, and returned just after the ringing of the two o'clock bell in order to dismiss the class,

251

saying he was unwell and would give the lecture on another day.'

'*Class* is ambitious,' said Maister Kennedy. 'There are five of you when you're all there.'

'Unwell in what way? Did he specify? Did he seem as normal?'

'Alan did not tell me that, though he did say that Father Bernard seemed quite distressed, as if ill in truth. I think he said he was trembling. He said that two of the students offered to fetch help, or assist their teacher round to the House, but these offers were spurned.'

'Well!' said Gil. 'Father Bernard went to some trouble to make me think he had taught as usual, although,' he qualified, reviewing the conversation, 'I don't think he lied outright. What did his class do? Did he leave first, or did they?'

'Alan did not say. It seems the class went up to the Laigh Hall, since it was raining, and held an informal disputation which lasted till the college dinner.'

'So they would not have seen where their teacher went next.'

'Probably not,' agreed Maister Coventry.

'So Bernard Stewart skipped a lecture,' said Maister Kennedy. 'So what? Is it important, Gil?'

'It might be of great value,' said Gil cautiously. 'It confirms something I had suspected. I heard Wycliff mentioned in the Laigh Hall that afternoon. *The ship of faith tempestuous wind and rain Drives in the sea of Lollardy that blaws.* How close to the wind of reform does Father Bernard sail, Patrick? Is he at risk from a charge of heresy?'

'Such a charge as William was hinting at on Sunday? It's hard to teach theology without mentioning ideas which have been thought heretical at one time or another. Wycliff in particular appears from time to time.' The Second Regent peered out at the much-trampled grass under his window. 'I should have said Bernard was not at risk. As Dominicans go he is hardly a radical, so if any charge were to be laid his Order would support him without hesitation.'

'Then William's hints were an empty threat?'

'Not completely,' said Maister Kennedy unexpectedly. 'There would be questions asked, his teaching suspended, delays to his students, confiscation of his books till somebody got here from Cologne to read them. Bloody inconvenient. And he'd lose the income from the chaplaincy.'

'That goes to the Order,' said the Second Regent.

'Oh, aye, so it does,' said Maister Kennedy without inflection.

'It would be an extreme response nevertheless,' said his colleague, 'to kill in such a calculating way merely to avert a great inconvenience.'

'We keep coming back to this,' said Gil. 'Those with a reason had no opportunity, those with opportunity had no reason that I can uncover. And yet the boy is dead.'

'And his funeral is this morning,' said Patrick Coventry.

'Christ save us, it is,' said Maister Kennedy. 'I'd best be away. I've to rehearse the order of the procession with John Shaw. *What a day, what a day,*' he mimicked.

'And I have a lecture to deliver.' Maister Coventry began searching his desk. 'More Euclid for the bachelors, though I do not think they will listen. Perhaps Michael will have conned his answer by now.' He lifted a sheaf of notes. 'Gilbert, will you attend the funeral?'

'After Sext, isn't it? Yes, I'll try to be there. And after it I have to present some kind of case concerning who killed the boy.'

'The Dean will speak for most of the morning,' Maister Kennedy warned him. 'I've seen the notes.'

Gil left by the main door of the college, nodding to the Dominican lay-brother he found on duty there, and turned down the hill and in at the pend of the Masons' house. Crossing the courtyard, he heard a succession of anguished barks from inside the main block. They continued until the door opened, and the wolfhound hurled itself out and down the steps, to rear up and paw at his jerkin, pushing urgently at his hand with its long muzzle.

253

'I always thought wolfhounds were dignified creatures,' said Alys in the doorway. She was wearing the blue linen gown again, its colour turning her honey-coloured hair to tawny and emphasizing the warm creamy tones of her skin. Impeded by the dog, he hurried up the steps to embrace her, and she returned his kiss, then held him off with a hand on his chest, looking up into his face. 'What is it, Gil?'

He made a wry face.

'I had matters out with my mother last night. She would not be persuaded, and in the end I told her I would be married in spite of her views.'

'And what did she say to that?' asked Alys, looking troubled.

'Nothing, at first. Then she compared me to my grand-father Muirhead.'

'Is that good or bad?'

'It wasn't a compliment, if that's what you mean. I assured her that she could be certain of our loving duty, and that I spoke for you as well.'

'But of course.' She looked up at him, then hugged him tightly. He clasped her close, relishing the warm slender armful she made. The pup, seated at his feet, pawed at his hose again. He looked down at it, and Alys drew away a little as her father crossed the hall.

'Father, come and hear this.'

'My mother will not be persuaded,' Gil explained, 'and I have told her I'll bide by my uncle's advice.'

'Well, well, you must take one or the other,' said the mason robustly. 'There is no middle way in this case. Are you hungry, Gilbert? Come up and be seated.'

'I'm not hungry. I called by the college, to speak to Maister Coventry, and he offered me bannocks and cheese too, but I'd not long broken my fast,' said Gil, following Alys into the little panelled closet. 'To be fair, my mother did say some very gratifying things about Alys. She dis-likes my marrying at all, not the choice I have made.'

'I call on her, perhaps,' said Maistre Pierre. 'We do the thing with all formality.'

Gil sat down, and the pup clambered on to his knee.

'That would likely be well received. I had a long word with my uncle this morning, and he asked me to say the contract is nearly ready.' He looked at the dog, which was licking industriously at his right wrist. 'What has this fellow done with his collar?'

'Oh, he must have got it off!' Alys exclaimed. 'Jennet said he was kicking at it half the night. It seemed to be irritating him after you made it looser.'

'It will be in the kitchen,' said her father.

'Yes, very likely. I will look for it shortly. What did you learn at the college?' Alys asked.

'That Father Bernard didn't give the lecture he claimed to have at two o'clock.'

'Ah,' she said.

'So where was he?' wondered her father.

'Searching William's chamber, I should say,' said Gil.

'And for what?'

'For whatever was in the package I gave William. The more I look at this,' said Gil, 'the more I think that package was the base from which the whole action sprang. As soon as the boy opened it, he began a course of actions which caused someone to kill him.'

'You think it contained money? Some instruction, perhaps? Some vital piece of information he could sell to English Henry?'

'What, a deed of purchase for the realm of Scotland, made out in Edward Longshanks' name? No, I don't think that. Consider – William's first act was to attempt to speak to Father Bernard, though Bernard claims he didn't have time for him. Then he spent the next two hours accosting various people in public. I watched him doing it. None of the people he spoke to seemed to be glad of the conversation.' Gil paused, counting them off in his mind. 'Aye. Father Bernard, David Gray, the Principal, the Steward. Some of his fellow students. I think I have got an account of all those.'

'Extortion,' said the mason. 'We knew that.'

'Yes, but several of the people who mentioned his extortion methods said in so many words that he would gather secrets and then come *privately* and ask for money. Not in front of the entire Faculty of Arts, not in a manner so obvious that it caught my eye. He asked awkward questions, very publicly, at the Faculty meeting. He nearly spoiled the play, and when his costume was damaged he went off without waiting for the end, as if it was all beneath his dignity.'

'He was practising making a will,' said Maistre Pierre.

'Yes. I thought he was pretending to be legitimate. What if I was wrong – what if he had just discovered he was entitled to the name he used in the will?'

'An attested birth record, you mean? Or some sort of authenticated statement of his parentage?'

'Exactly.'

'And it went to his head,' said the mason slowly, 'so that he no longer behaved with secrecy. Ye-es.'

'He does seem to have been naturally arrogant,' Gil said. 'He would certainly feel that a Montgomery had no need to act in secret.'

'Then what was his parentage?' asked Alys. 'And why should it cause someone to kill him? I thought you thought Father Bernard might be his father.'

'Only because he knew exactly how old the boy was,' said Gil fairly. 'That's the problem. Two problems. There are a lot of Montgomery men old enough to be his father, and he didn't mention his parentage in the will, so we don't know his father's forename. And even if he is a Montgomery, why that should provoke someone in the college to kill him I can't see at all.'

'Was not his mother a Montgomery?' asked Alys. 'He was entitled to the name anyway.'

'He has never used it,' said Gil.

'Better one's foster-mother's name, I suppose,' said Maistre Pierre, 'than use one's mother's name like any unacknowledged bastard.'

'Indeed,' agreed Gil. 'But if he is doubly entitled to the name, he has double reason to use it now. And yet we come back to this: why should that get him killed?'

'As you said, there are no Cunninghams in the college just now.'

'Our Lady be praised, you had someone with you all the time we need to worry about,' said Alys. 'But isn't the boy Ninian a Boyd? I thought the Boyds were also enemies of the Montgomery.'

'He is,' said Gil. 'If Ninian did it, he and his friends are all three of them in it together, for their story hangs together. I don't think it was Ninian, though I'm keeping an eye on him.' He freed one hand, patted the breast of his doublet, causing the now somnolent dog to raise its head and look at him, and drew out the red notebook. 'We must deal with this before Hugh Montgomery sends for William's gear. If we can destroy the pages, by accident, and return the binding to the family, then honour is satisfied all round and nobody is in danger.'

'The kitchen fire, I think,' said Alys, taking it. 'What did you learn from it?'

He grimaced. 'He was an unpleasant boy. Parts of it are a record of student misdemeanours, rules broken and goods expropriated, and the small sums and favours he extorted in return for silence. They add up well, but they are mostly in placks and pence. Other parts are lists of word or deed of his seniors. That list of chance remarks Maister Forsyth mentioned is in there. And finally there is a long section headed with a large D which I take to be material from Doig the dog-breeder, with some very rare and curious facts in it. A lot is in William's private code,' he admitted, 'which I may not have read correctly, but I think I have the key to most of it.'

'And you simply destroy that?' said the mason.

'My uncle agrees with me,' said Gil airily. 'The material is not for dissemination.'

'Ah.'

'I shall go and burn it,' said Alys.

She slipped out, and her father said, 'I am still at a loss about last night's game of cards. What were you doing, losing all those tricks, giving away so much information? Information again,' he added in disgust.

257

'As Montgomery said, it's the currency of this reign. I suppose,' said Gil slowly, 'I was using him. He's no fool, and he may be more subtle than I allow, but I have given him such facts and suspicions as I pleased to give him, and I hope he will make good use of them even if he suspects he was fed them for that purpose.'

'What, the list of the boy's possessions?'

'And the possession of them,' Gil reminded him. 'Has he sent for them yet?'

'Not yet. What else?'

'Well, I hope I've convinced him that we don't understand the cipher disc, though I don't rely on that. And I've drawn his attention to Jaikie's death, and flown him at Billy Doig, and Bernard Stewart. Whether he'll stoop on either we'll just have to wait and see.'

'More metaphor,' said Maistre Pierre. 'And what –'

He was interrupted by a voice on the stairs, exclaiming in gruff French, 'Where is that dog? Where is the bad dog?'

'Catherine? He is here,' the mason called, raising his eyebrows at Gil. 'What is the matter?'

'This wicked dog!' Catherine stumped into the little room, brandishing the missing collar. 'Look what he has done to his handsome collar. We found it in his corner just now. It is quite destroyed!' She thrust the object at Gil, who took it. The pup, wakened by the commotion, raised its head to seize one end of the leather and tried to start a game with it.

'No,' said Gil firmly, pinching the animal's jaw to make it let go. He pushed the pup off his knee and fended it off with one foot while he inspected the damage to the collar. The padded centre-section had been well gnawed. The leather was torn and wet and the straw packing was escaping, but something white also showed in the gap. Gil drew it out carefully.

'The lining is coming out. He has chewed up the stitching. You must beat him for such destructive behaviour, *maistre!*' declaimed Catherine.

'He's only a baby,' said Gil absently, unfolding a curving

spill of paper. 'All young animals chew things. I dare say he is cutting teeth, they always are at this age. Would you beat John, *madame*, for chewing –' He stopped speaking to stare.

'What is it?' asked Catherine. 'Is it something important, *maistre*? The dog man was here again this morning asking for the collar. Is that why he sets such value on it?'

'I don't know if this is what Billy Doig wants,' said Gil, 'but it is certainly something I want.' He passed it to the mason, and continued, 'You know the dog man, *madame*?'

'Not to say know him.' She sniffed. 'I know his wife by sight, for I see her every day exercising the dogs out there.' She gestured to the window, with its view down the long garden and across the Mill-burn.

'On the Dow Hill? Did you see her yesterday?'

'I did. My sight is good at a distance, *maistre*, and I saw her clearly from the demoiselle's chamber where I was attending your lady mother as she washed the dirt of the roads from her person.' She stared across the burn. 'As clearly as I see her now, indeed.'

'What?' Gil twisted round to look. 'Sweet St Giles! Pierre, see this.'

The mason rose to join them at the window and watch the cart jolting up across the Dow Hill. On it were piled a precarious heap of household goods, and what seemed, from this distance, to be the kind of basket in which puppies were transported if necessary. Beside it and leading the fat pony trudged the small chess-piece figure of Maister Doig, and behind it his wife was attempting to control the largest mixed leash of dogs Gil had ever seen.

'Pray God they do not start a rabbit,' said Maistre Pierre after a moment. 'What do we do about that?'

'Little we can do,' said Gil, still watching.

'But he is escaping.'

'We have no proof he killed Jaikie,' said Gil slowly, 'only a strong supposition. Short of a witness in the street yesterday or a signed confession, there is no case worth bringing against him. Even if we did bring a case, he could always claim it was a fair fight, or an accident. There might be blood-money for the man's kin, but I hardly think Doig would hang.'

'A fair fight? A man that height, against one like Jaikie?'

'Precisely,' said Gil.

'So it does not matter,' said Catherine, 'that the dog has destroyed his collar? Is he not to be scolded for his misdeed?'

'I'll scold him,' Gil promised her. She grunted at him, and stumped out muttering darkly, passing Alys in the doorway.

'So is this paper what I think it is?' asked Maistre Pierre. 'Alys, look at this. It was in the dog's collar.'

'I'm sorry I was so long,' she said, handing Gil the singed covers of the notebook. 'Nancy was feeding John by the fireside, and he spilled his sops on my gown.' She looked over her father's arm at the paper he was holding, and read, '*Hodie in matrimonio* – This day, the morrow of the feast of All Souls, 1475, were joined by me in holy matrimony Isobel Montgomery and – and who? The paper is torn. Oh, how tantalizing! What can the missing name be? Is there nothing to tell us?'

'Say rather, it's chewed.' Gil took the page, piecing together the damp flaps of the ragged lower margin. 'That's an A.'

'A-L,' said Alys, pointing with a slender finger.

'E,' contributed her father.

'Then there is a piece missing completely. But that is definitely an N, and a D.'

'Alexander?' wondered Alys.

'I think it must be. And we know the surname. We have the name of William's father.'

'Alexander Montgomery,' said Maistre Pierre. 'But is this a reason to kill the boy?'

'There is another name missing,' said Gil thoughtfully. 'The officiating priest usually signs this kind of document. It says *This day were joined by me* – I think he did put his name to it.'

'You think that was why William wanted to speak to Father Bernard?' said Alys.

'You mean it was his name? He married them?' The mason craned his neck to see the ragged edge of the paper. 'No, there is no more writing. The dog must have eaten it. May I assure you now, I shall not follow him round the yard waiting for the facts to emerge.'

'Nor I.' Gil sat down again, looking at the fragile document. 'If Bernard Stewart did marry these two, he would be in some trouble, even sixteen years later, both from the Montgomery for going against his wishes, and from his Order for marrying two people who were within the forbidden degrees of relationship.'

'Surely he could brazen it out?' suggested the mason.

'One of the pages in the notebook was headed *B.S.* and contained a number of reformist quotations which I would not like to have imputed to me,' said Gil. 'What if William did have speech with Father Bernard on Sunday morning? He – Father Bernard told me he had to arrange for the music to be carried to St Thomas's, and therefore had no time for the boy, but John Shaw itemized the music in the list of things he had had to see to.'

'So he did,' said Maistre Pierre. 'I remember.'

'If William showed Father Bernard this document,' said Gil, 'or at least told him he now had possession of it, and threatened to report him for heresy if he would not support a claim of legitimacy –'

'I should think Father Bernard would be desperate,' said Alys.

'He would lose either way,' said Maistre Pierre.

'But is it sufficient reason?' Gil looked up as the Blackfriars bell began to ring. 'Plague take it, that must be for the boy's funeral! I meant to borrow a Master's gown and hood and join the procession, but it's too late now. I must go as I am and slip in at the back. Pierre, are you coming? Does Mistress Irvine go?' He folded the paper with care and tucked it into his purse.

'Brother Andrew forbade it,' said Alys. 'She is still sore stricken with grief. Gil, I know you have no gown, your

261

own won't come back for several days. That kind of mending is specialized work. But at least let me find the funeral favours, so Lord Montgomery won't be offended.'

'It was Montgomery's men who ruined my gown,' Gil pointed out, but she had hurried off up the stairs.

Blackfriars kirk was half-full. Gil made his way in by the west door just as the first singers of the University procession reached the north porch, and was surprised by the numbers already present, and the buzz of conversation in the nave.

'I suppose half the town is here out of interest,' said his friend behind him.

'You could be right,' Gil answered him, staring over the heads. Seats had been placed nearest the nave altar for the Dean and Principal and other senior members of the college, and the small stout Dominican who had laid Jaikie out was keeping space behind these for the ranks of scholars, not without some difficulty. On trestles before the altar, with candles at head and foot, lay a solid elm coffin. Hugh Montgomery had evidently decided to do the thing properly. He and his henchmen were standing on the south side of the church, their predatory stares directed at Father Bernard who was fidgeting about on the altar steps.

The procession sang its way into the nave and filed into its places. Dean Elphinstone, in his silk gown and hood with the red chaperon pinned to his shoulder, glared along the length of the coffin at Lord Montgomery while the scholars, behind him, worked their way through an elaborate setting of the funerary sentences. *Man that is born of woman hath but a short time to live* . . . But some of the singers were younger than the dead boy, Gil reflected. It seemed unkind to put these words into their mouths. And what Patrick Paniter, chanter at St Mungo's, would make of their rendering of his setting did not bear thinking about.

The last of the sentences wound to a close, and Father

Bernard lifted up his powerful, musical voice in the opening words of the funeral Mass. Gil, half attending, surveyed the congregation and turned over in his mind what he must say to the Faculty afterwards.

As Maistre Pierre suggested, a number of those present were probably moved by curiosity. A burial following a murder that touched the college and also the landed class would be a great draw. But the Provost's steward was here as a courtesy to the college, and there was also a scattering of journeymen from within the burgh. Gil recognized James Sproat's junior man, come straight from the cordiner's shop with his leather apron bundled under his arm. William must have been a good customer, he reflected.

The Dean was speaking. The Latin phrases flowed elegantly over the heads of most of his hearers, who took the opportunity to continue their various conversations. Two men near Gil appeared to be compounding some transaction concerning their masters' goods, to be ratified by their principals later in the week. Behind the Dean the scholars stood in obedient silence with the younger regents watching them. Gil saw Maister Kennedy glare at Walter. At the other end of the same row Ralph Gibson was weeping openly, and Patrick Coventry put his arm about the boy's shoulders.

In the middle of the ranks of bachelors, both junior and senior, Robert Montgomery stood, head tipped back, glaring down his nose at the Dean's back. Gil glanced at the other side of the church, and found Hugh, Lord Montgomery, in identical pose, glaring at the Dean's face.

'They breed true, these Montgomery men,' said the mason, who had evidently seen where he was looking.

'They do,' said Gil, adding absently, '*Lyk as a strand of water of a spring Haldis the sapour of the fontell well.*'

He was very close to the solution, he was certain. He could feel the shape of the argument. But there was still something missing, something which did not quite support his proof.

The Dean's address wore on, but from the back of the

church, what with the surrounding noise, Gil could hear only the occasional word. Those phrases he did catch seemed to convey the wish, rather than the hope, that William's time in Purgatory would be shortened by his academic achievements and the respect he had borne his teachers. Maister Kennedy's face as he heard this was studiously blank, and Gil recalled that his friend had seen the Dean's notes.

The Dean reached a benediction, and seated himself. One of the Theology students leaned forward and gave out a note, marking the beat with his hand raised above his head, and the scholars launched into another funerary setting.

'I must go outside,' Gil said to Maistre Pierre, and got a nod in reply. He slipped out of the open west door into the yard, and stood for a moment in the brighter light, looking about him. To his right, at the corner of the church, was the bell-tower whose base served as mortuary chapel. It seemed likely that Jaikie was still laid out there. To his left the cloister wall extended south of the church, with the small guarded gate by which guests entered or the friars went out into the burgh to preach. In front of him, stretching to the back walls of the small properties on the High Street, the lumpy grass of the public graveyard was broken by a few bushes and the occasional marker of wood or stone. A mound of fresh earth near the bell-tower indicated William's immediate destination. Trying not to think about that, or about the clump of bigger bushes in the far corner where a girl had been stabbed ten days since, Gil wandered along the cloister wall. One of Montgomery's men emerged from the church and strode to the gate, where he leaned against the pillar watching Gil and stropping his dagger on his leather sleeve.

There was an elder-tree by the gatehouse, covered in creamy platters of blossom. Gil stopped beside it, breathing the mixture of the rank odour of the leaves and the sweet, heavy scent of the flowers, and the porter put his head out of his lodge, hand raised to deliver the customary blessing.

'The funeral's in the kirk, my son,' he said. 'Oh, it's yourself, Maister Cunningham. Not seeking any more bodies in the kirkyard, are you? We've enough for the moment.'

'I think Dean Elphinstone feels the same way,' Gil said. 'No, I was admiring the bour-tree.'

'We'll have a good crop of berries off that in the autumn,' said the wiry Dominican. 'The cellarer makes a good wine with them.' He smacked his lips appreciatively. 'Good for coughs and colds, that is.'

'Better a linctus with cherries,' said a familiar voice behind Gil. He turned, to see both the harper and his sister approaching. The watcher at the gate glowered after them.

'And upon you, brother,' said McIan in reply to the porter's blessing. 'Good day, Maister Cunningham. We came for the burial, but I think we are late.'

'The boy's no yirdit yet,' said the porter. 'They'll come out in procession shortly. Wait up yonder by the college wall if you want to be nearer.' He surveyed them with a bright eye, assessing the need for his professional services. 'It gars any man look over his shoulder for his own fate, to see so young a laddie put in the ground.'

'I have much to be thankful for,' said McIan, and his sister nodded. 'With God's help, my own son is brought back from the brink of death. I came to offer prayers for the kin of this boy, since they have lost what I have regained.'

'We were by the house the now,' said Ealasaidh to Gil. Her severe expression cracked into a fond smile. 'It seems the bairn will feed himself, so Nancy says, and shouts with wrath because his sops go everywhere but into his mouth.'

'I mind that stage,' said Brother Porter unexpectedly. 'My sister's eldest ate porridge with his fingers till he was two. Mind you, he canny count beyond ten with his boots on,' he added. 'How old is your boy?'

'Not eight months,' said Ealasaidh proudly. Brother Porter looked properly impressed. Behind them the west door of the church was opened wide, and the processional cross was borne out, followed by the singers. Gil ignored them. He found himself thinking of his nephew, who as an infant had borne a strong resemblance to Maister Forsyth. But then, he reflected, most babies looked like Maister Forsyth.

The last fragment of the picture fell into place.

Chapter Thirteen

The scholars, filing past, each stooped to lift a handful of earth from the mound and throw it into William's grave. As the clayey lumps thudded on to the elm coffin-lid, Gil found Maister Kennedy at his elbow.

'They're comporting themselves well, Nick, but is this wise?' he commented. 'It sounds like the drums for the Dance of Death. You'll have nightmares again tonight, surely.'

'A touch of the *Ut sum, cras tibi*? No, I think it means they can be the more certain William's dead,' said his friend, and then with more formality, 'Maister Gilbert, the Dean commands me to say that he and the Faculty will hear your findings on this matter in the Principal's chamber after this. Lord Montgomery will also be present. '

'I am ready to make a report,' replied Gil with equal state. He looked across the scene of the burial, and encountered three stares: the Dean's blue and acute, Maister Doby's anxious, and off to one side Hugh Montgomery's hotly alert. He raised his hat and flourished it in a general bow, and the two academics nodded and turned away to take their places in the procession as it formed.

'I'll see you there,' said Maister Kennedy, and slipped away to round up the last few scholars before Gil could comment.

'An interesting ceremony,' said Maistre Pierre behind Gil, as the Steward began to circulate among the mourners, issuing select invitations to the cold meats and ale waiting in the dining-hall of the University.

'The college looks after its sons,' Gil returned. 'There

wasn't much smoke, because incense costs money, but we
have a ready-made choir which doesn't have to be paid,
and plenty of breath for speech and singing. Ceremony
comes naturally.'

'Now what happens?'

'I'll tell ye what happens,' said Hugh, Lord Montgomery. The tail of the procession vanished singing into the
church, and as the remainder of the congregation drifted
towards the gates he left the church wall and came closer.
'You, Cunningham lawyer, are about to tell me whose
work that is –' He jerked a thumb at the open grave behind
him. 'I warned you, and I warned the clerks in the college.
I'm quite prepared to put them to the question one by one,
starting with the youngest.'

'I've no doubt of that,' said Gil politely. 'Shall we go?
Maister Doby and the Dean are expecting us.' He saw the
slight widening of the eyes, and pressed the advantage.
'Oh, aye, you mind I was asking you about William Doig
the dog-breeder, my lord? Here's a strange thing. Maister
Mason and I saw the same man this morning, leading a
cart over the Dow Hill, and his wife and all the dogs with
him.'

'The Dow Hill?' repeated Montgomery in amazement.
'Why should – why should the man's deeds be any concern of mine? I told you before, I've no knowledge of
him.'

'So you did,' said Gil, pausing at the foot of the grave.
Montgomery bent and angrily threw in a yellow clod.

'So it's your problem, no mine, if the wee mimmerkin's
run,' he added, wiping his hand on his jerkin. 'Get a move
on, man, I want to get a hold of Bernard Stewart before he
takes refuge the wrong side of that wall. And we'll have
my nephew Robert present, since none of my sons is here
at the college. He's full old enough to be involved.'

'How old is he?' Gil asked casually.

'Sixteen on St Lucy's eve next. A man grown.' Montgomery grinned evilly, and seizing Gil's elbow hustled him into
the church, just in time to see Father Bernard and the
colleague who had deaconed for him, about to retreat into

the enclosed portion of the church with the newly washed Communion vessels.

'Bernard!' roared Montgomery, in much the same tone as he had used to the dogs at his fireside.

Father Bernard jumped convulsively, and dropped the paten from the top of his chalice. It bowled away across the paved floor, pursued by the other friar and by Maistre Pierre.

'My lord?'

'To the college. Now.'

'I have a disputation to prepare –'

'You'll do as I bid you, or you'll have more disputation that you've stomach for, priest.'

'My lord,' said Father Bernard with a spurt of courage, 'I'm not your chaplain any longer –'

'For which we may both thank God and St Dominic. Are you coming or do I make you?'

'You offer violence to a priest, my lord, in the sanctuary?' exclaimed the other Dominican, returning with the paten.

'No,' said Lord Montgomery softly, 'I'm no offering it. I'm promising it, if he doesny *do as I say*!' he bawled.

Both men flinched, and Gil interposed in Latin, 'Father Bernard, I am about to report to the Dean and Principal on what I have learned about the death of the scholar William Irvine. I think it might be proper for you to be present.'

'I? For what reason?'

'You are the college chaplain.'

'Oh.' Father Bernard closed his mouth over the large teeth and looked down at the chalice and paten in his hands. 'Very well. Edward, could I ask you –?'

'I got the Steward to set aside a platter for us,' said Maister Doby doubtfully, surveying the single wooden dish on the linen-draped trestle table in the great chamber of his house, 'but there's more folk here than I looked for.'

'I could go ask him for more,' suggested Maistre Pierre.

'And wine also, I think. Where are they served? In the Laigh Hall?'

He bustled off. Gil, mentally dividing the food into portions, could not blame his friend. Like the Principal, he had not expected so many to be present, though it was hard to see who could be dispensed with. The five senior members of the Faculty, whom he had encountered here in this room less than two days since, had every right to be present. So had the Second Regent and Maister Kennedy. Hugh Montgomery, unfortunately, had even more right, and Gil did not feel like voicing any objection to either of the supporters the man had summoned.

At least we made him leave his retinue outside, he thought.

'Well,' said Montgomery, as if on cue, 'are we to keep my men kicking their heels in the yard the rest of the day, or are we to hear this report?'

'I feel,' said the Dean more civilly, 'that we should begin, the sooner to put an end to the matter, if this should be possible.'

'And anyway there's no enough food,' said Maister Doby. 'We can hear Gilbert and get a bite after.'

'I am ready,' said Gil. He watched as his audience settled itself before the painted hangings, the Dean and the Principal in two great chairs, the two lawyers with their heads together on stools next to them, Maister Forsyth on the padded bench near the window. The younger regents and the chaplain were seated off to his right, and in the corner near the door, in another chair hastily borne in from the Dean's own lodging, glowered Lord Montgomery with his nephew standing behind him like a body-servant. On the hangings the philosophers, impassive, stared into the distance.

Tucking his thumbs in the armholes of his gown, speaking in Scots out of courtesy to Hugh Montgomery, Gil began.

'I first set eyes on William Irvine when he greeted me at the college yett on Sunday morning. He was very civil to me, until he discovered I was a Cunningham.'

'So?' said Montgomery. Gil glanced at him, and beyond him at his nephew's superior smile.

'His nurse Nan Irvine had asked me to deliver a package to him, one which had come from the boy's late mother. I handed it to him, and what with that and his height and the colour of his hair, he caught my attention a few times during the rest of the morning, in the procession and at the Mass and the feast. He seemed excited about something, out of himself in some way. Generally he was speaking to someone, but none of the people he spoke to seemed to be glad of it.'

David Gray was staring at Gil with that haunted look on his face again.

'After the feast there was the play. William left the hall before it was finished, though he had several large parts.' Maister Kennedy grunted, and stuck out his legs to cross them at the ankles. 'None of his teachers saw him alive again, although he was not missed until an hour or so later.'

'None of his teachers?' Montgomery broke in. Gil nodded. 'Then who –?'

'I hope it will become clear before long,' Gil said. Montgomery glowered at him for a moment longer, then snarled, and gestured angrily for him to continue.

'I was among those who searched. We found him lying in the college coalhouse. He had been strangled with one belt, and his hands were bound with another. His purse was missing, which might have meant robbery, but the coalhouse was locked and the key was not in the door. His death was certainly secret murder. I was commissioned and required to investigate,' said Gil, bowing to Maister Doby as generally representing the college, 'so Maister Mason and I inspected the corpse and began asking questions.

'William had been dead about an hour when he was found, perhaps two or more by the time we examined him. He had been knocked down before he was killed, and there were fresh quicklime burns on his gown and scuff-marks on the toes of his boots, which were otherwise well

271

cared for. There was nothing else on him or in his clothes to tell us more. The belt round his neck was his own, and had recently been handled by someone whose hands smelled of cumin. And other spices,' he added scrupulously.

'You mentioned the cumin before,' said Montgomery with impatience. 'I canny see that it has anything to say in the business.'

Behind him his nephew eased imperceptibly backwards, to lean against the wall.

'We next spoke to many of William's teachers and fellow scholars and the servants of the University, and learned a number of valuable things. In the first place, the people who knocked him down and tied his wrists had left him, alive but dazed, in the limehouse. As a sort of student joke. Their story fits the facts I had observed, and I do not think they killed him.'

'Their reasons were very unworthy,' commented Maister Doby in grieved tones, 'but I have no cause to doubt what they told me either.'

Montgomery grunted sceptically, but Maister Crawford rose to address the air between the Dean and the Principal.

'What my colleague has described was common assault,' he objected in Latin. 'Are we to permit our scholars to attack one another without penalty? This will resound most grievously to the discredit of our University.'

'It was not without penalty –' began the Principal.

'Students will aye be students,' said Maister Forsyth in Scots. 'Sit down, Archie, and hold your peace. Gilbert has a lot to tell us.'

Montgomery grunted again in what sounded like agreement.

'Therefore,' Gil continued, as Maister Crawford sat down with a dissatisfied expression on his face, 'someone else had killed him and put him in the coalhouse, for a reason which was not apparent.

'In the second place, we found William's purse. It contained a great sum in coin, a letter in code, and a draft will, in which he would have left his property to be divided between his friend Ralph Gibson and his nurse Ann Irvine.'

'He was capable of the generous impulse,' said Maister Forsyth approvingly.

'There was no key, not even his own key to his chamber, which was locked. Using another of the college keys, we opened his chamber and found it had been searched and stripped of all the paper it contained, leaving behind a ransom in jewels and other valuables. William's wolf-hound pup, which shouldn't have been in the room, had tried to defend its master's property and been struck a blow on the head.

'In the third place, we discovered that William had been in the habit of getting information and making it work for him.'

'No harm in that,' said Hugh Montgomery suspiciously.

'Nobody was free of his attentions, though their responses varied. He extorted money or favours from fellow students, teachers, the kitchen staff, the college porter, on the basis of what he knew, and recorded it all in a note-book.'

'Notebook?' said David Gray, startled. 'What notebook is this? Are you saying the boy wrote down all his misdeeds in a book?'

'He did,' said Gil, and looked round the room in a short silence. Most of the Faculty was frowning in what appeared to be disapproval. Hugh Montgomery was watching him with a deepening scowl, and behind him his nephew stood, rather pale, glaring down his nose in that Montgomery way. Father Bernard, as Gil's eye fell on him, crossed himself and bent his head, his lips moving as if in prayer for William's soul.

'Now we go back in time a little. William left the hall where the acting was just before the play ended. Shortly after it ended there was a great clap of thunder and a very heavy shower, and the scholars all ran out to shut windows and rescue books. This was when William was discovered poking in someone else's property, knocked down and tied up, and put in the limehouse. Shortly after that, the senior members of the feast dispersed in a more orderly fashion, so that many people were moving about the college for a quarter-hour or more. Unfortunately, I think it was during that time when William was killed.'

'What makes you think that?' asked the Dean, frowning. 'On what do you base the statement?'

'On several things. The extent to which the body had cooled when it was found, the fact that when my good-father and I inspected it later it was only just beginning to stiffen, and the supposition that if William had roused while he was in the limehouse he would have shouted, kicked on the door, and made other attempts to get the attention of the kitchen hands. Therefore I think he was killed before he had a chance to recover his senses.'

'I see,' said the Dean, though he sounded doubtful.

'Thanks to some patient questioning,' Gil bowed to the two regents, 'and clever casting-up of the results, we managed to establish that nearly everyone whose initials were later found in the notebook, or whom I saw in speech with the boy that morning, had been in sight of one or more others for most of the break.'

'Do you mean you have the notebook?' asked Maister Crawford.

'It fell into my hands yesterday,' said Gil. 'It has since met with a sorry accident and the pages cannot be read.' He looked round his audience. Both the lawyers appeared to have relaxed a little. Montgomery's jaw had tightened, and behind him Robert was watching with a glazed stare. The remaining members of the Faculty were stolidly unmoved. He drew breath to continue, and the door opened.

'You pardon, maisters,' said Maistre Pierre. 'Here is more food, but these good fellows are needed back at the hall, so we must serve ourselves.'

He stood aside for two of the velvet-gowned college servitors, each with jug and heavy platter.

'Robert can serve us,' said Montgomery. 'Make yourself useful, boy.' He watched grimly as the trays of food were

274

set on the trestle table, the servants left, and Robert with some reluctance stood away from the wall and approached the table. 'Come on, you can serve out wine without a towel for once. As for you, Maister Cunningham. You've spent a while proving that nobody could have killed our William. When are you going to get to the name I want? The boy's dead, and somebody's to suffer for it.'

'I'm in no doubt of that,' said Gil. 'I'm making a report, my lord. The Faculty will wish to be certain we have looked at everything that might have a bearing on the matter.'

'Oh, get on with it!' said Montgomery savagely. He took a wedge of cold pie from the tray Robert was presenting to him and nodded to the boy to proceed round the company.

'On Sunday evening,' Gil continued, 'the dog-breeder called at the college yett asking for the wolfhound. Two more chambers were searched, by different hands, and I was robbed in the street of a bundle of papers. From all this I concluded that at least one party was still looking for something on paper.

'On Monday, the bundle of papers was returned, for which I was grateful, and it became clear from the admission of one of his victims that William was gathering information not just round the college but more widely. He had that knack of fitting stray words and scraps of news together to make a story that would interest the King's advisers.

'Then Jaikie the porter was found stabbed at the college yett. There was another bundle of papers smouldering in his brazier which turned out to be William's lecture-notes and other papers. Likely they had been lifted from the boy's chamber when it was searched. Also in Jaikie's chamber I found a dog-collar, hidden in a press.'

'What has that to do with anything?' asked Maister Crawford.

Maister Forsyth stirred irritably on his bench, but Gil answered, 'It was a thing out of place. Why should the porter have a dog-collar in his chamber? And there is a dog in the matter, and the dog-breeder had been at the yett a number of times asking for the dog and therefore speaking to Jaikie.'

Maister Crawford grunted.

This was not going well. Lord Montgomery's scowl was intent, but the other members of the Faculty wore assorted expressions of puzzlement, except for David Gray, who appeared to have settled into a blank exhaustion. Gil accepted a cup from the mason and sipped it. Wine, he thought, and well-watered. Bless the man. He drank deeper, and groped for the thread of his argument again.

'It seemed likely that Jaikie's death was connected with William's –'

'I don't see that,' said Montgomery in argumentative tones.

'I can well believe, my lord,' said Gil with a slight bow, 'that you would accept the existence of two separate enemies of the college at one time, but I find it more economical to think they are connected.'

Montgomery grinned at him, and gestured for him to continue. Robert reached the Dean and knelt before him with the depleted tray.

'We therefore began to ask questions about both. Jaikie was a disobliging and ill-mannered employee, and quite capable of learning from William's example, but none of William's victims inside the college had been near him about noon. I think he might have tried to get money from someone who came to the yett from outside, someone else involved in William's schemes, and been knifed for it.'

Robert had paused before him with the food. Gil looked down as the last slice of pie on the tray fell on its side.

'No,' he said with regret, 'I'll eat after I've done talking, Robert.'

'Are you saying Jaikie was killed by one of William's accomplices?' asked the Dean. 'Does this mean William was killed by someone from outside after all?'

'Gilbert, I must remind you,' said Father Bernard, 'I have a disputation to organize this afternoon. Will this take much longer?'

'You'll sit here for as long as it takes, priest,' said Montgomery, 'and so will the rest of you. Get on with it, Cunningham.'

There was a knocking away through the house. Maister Doby looked up, startled.

'The street door,' he said. 'There's nobody to answer it – they're all at the Laigh Hall to serve the food.'

'Robert,' said Montgomery curtly. The boy set the empty platter on the table and left the room with an expression of something like relief. His uncle nodded sharply at Gil, who took another draught of the watered wine and continued.

'We asked questions of a number of people concerning Jaikie's death. The last to see him alive seemed at first to have been Lord Montgomery and his nephew –' He met Montgomery's wary scowl and continued smoothly, 'who were each, separately, at pains to convince me that the other had left him first and that the man was alive when they last saw him.'

'There is a contradiction there, Gilbert,' said Maister Forsyth. 'Almost an oxymoron, eh?'

'I think rather a paradox, sir,' said Gil. Montgomery was staring through the open door of the chamber, frowning. 'Montgomery men will back each other to the death. I took it to mean that neither of them had killed Jaikie, but each feared the other might have.'

Maister Forsyth nodded approval of this, but Montgomery turned his head to look at Gil, his eyes narrowed.

'We also questioned the dog-breeder. His answers were not in concordance with the observed facts, and though he claimed to have been exercising the dogs at noon yesterday someone else had seen his wife walking them as usual.'

'Out on the Dow Hill,' said Maister Crawford unexpectedly. 'I saw her myself. There's a black-and-white spaniel –' He found the Dean's eye on him and stopped.

'A useful contribution, Archie,' said the Dean ambiguously. 'Go on, Gilbert.'

'We know Doig had been at the yett a number of times

277

asking about the wolfhound. I think he was passing information to William, and possibly getting more information back and passing it on elsewhere as well. I know Jaikie was doing the same. I think Jaikie tried to get money or favours from Doig and was knifed for it.'

'By Doig?' said Montgomery incredulously. 'He was twice the size. How could –'

'Jaikie was drunk,' Gil said.

'As usual,' muttered Maister Kennedy. The Dean turned his blue stare on him.

'You said yourself, my lord,' Gil continued, 'that he was sprawled in his great chair when you last saw him. A strong man, even one of Doig's stature, could have knifed him easily enough in that posture.'

'But have you no other evidence?' asked Maister Doby. 'We couldny make an accusation like that about a Glasgow burgess, just because it could have happened.'

'Was his clothing marked? Had he stolen anything of the porter's?' asked Maister Forsyth.

'I do not think Doig is a burgess, but whatever his status the accusation would not be well founded,' said Gil punctiliously. 'He was wearing a leather apron when we saw him. It was much too big for him, very apt for hiding marks of any kind between chin and ankle.' Several of the Faculty members nodded their understanding of this point. 'And hidden in one of the dog-pens there was a bottle of usquebae. It had been stopped with a rag, precisely the way Jaikie used to stop his current jar. The evidence is circumstantial, no more.'

'Perhaps he aye keeps his supply there,' suggested Maister Kennedy.

'The dogs had got at it,' said the mason, grinning reminiscently. 'I do not think they were used to having it in their pen.'

'This isny getting any nearer to the name I want,' said Montgomery abruptly. Robert, slipping in through the open door, flinched as he spoke.

'So where is this man now?' asked Maister Crawford,

ignoring this. 'Are we to send some of the college servants to fetch him in for trial?'

'Ye willny do that, clerk,' said Montgomery, 'for Doig's run, so I hear. Now can we get on to the matter of who killed William?'

'Run?' repeated the Dean. 'What do you mean, run?'

'Maister Mason and I saw him leaving this morning,' said Gil, 'over the Dow Hill with a cart and his wife with all the tykes of Tervey on one leash.' He met the Dean's icy blue stare. 'I had no authority to stop him. It was hardly secret murder, since the body was left in plain sight in the porter's chamber, and he could have claimed easily enough that it was a matter of self-defence. There's the matter of blood-money to Jaikie's kin –'

'He had no kin,' said Maister Doby.

'Can we get on?' demanded Lord Montgomery.

'Very well,' said the Dean in dissatisfied tones. 'We must leave the matter of Jaikie's death there, but I do not feel you have acted well in this, Gilbert.'

'I do,' said Maister Forsyth unexpectedly. 'We must deplore the death of our porter, but the college has neither lost nor gained by it, which is better than might have been expected.'

Maister Crawford opened his mouth to speak, caught the Dean's eye, and subsided.

'To return to the question of William's murder,' said Gil. Montgomery muttered something. 'When we set out all the information we had gathered and looked at it, we found inconsistencies. One or two people had lied about one or two matters. In particular, one man had lied about where he was during the time when I think William was killed, the time which began with the great clap of thunder and ended when the feast reconvened.'

The members of the Faculty were watching him intently. Beyond Maister Kennedy the chaplain sat upright and tense. Between him and the door, Montgomery's narrow-eyed glare was backed by his nephew's, though the boy appeared to be leaning surreptitiously against the wall again.

'Someone in this chamber?' asked Maister Forsyth. Gil flicked him a glance, and nodded.

'Bernard,' said Hugh Montgomery, low and dangerous. 'Bernard, what have you done?'

Father Bernard unclasped his hands to cross himself.

'Christ and all his saints be my witness,' he said with great dignity, 'I did not kill William.'

'Then where were you at the time you should have been giving a lecture in the Theology Schule?' Gil asked.

'I was taken ill. The spiced pork –' began the chaplain, casting a look of loathing at Maister Coventry.

'Yesterday you blamed the rabbit stew,' said Gil.

'And on Sunday,' said Maister Forsyth, 'you complained that you had got nothing at the feast beyond some of Agnes's onion tart. Bernard, you must tell us the truth. You understand that.'

'I will speak before my superior.'

'You'll speak now,' said Montgomery quietly, 'and you'll speak truth. What have you done, Bernard? What have you done to Isobel's boy?'

Nobody had moved, not even Montgomery, but suddenly the scene was a trial rather than a hearing. Gil caught Maister Crawford's eye, and the other man of law nodded briefly and rose.

'We must assume,' he said, again addressing the gap between the Dean and the Principal, 'that my colleague has good reasons for his implied accusation. Should not these reasons be heard before the accusation is consolidated? Then my cli– our chaplain may defend himself against them, refuting them one by one if he is able.'

'Aye, if he's able,' said Montgomery, apparently following the Latin without difficulty.

'Expound your reasons, Gilbert,' said the Dean, and the Principal nodded, without removing his shocked gaze from Father Bernard.

'I do not have to defend myself –'

'You do, Bernard. You do. Or I'll make you,' declared Montgomery, still in that quiet dangerous voice.

Gil, looking round the room, marshalled his thoughts and continued.

'In the first place, Father Bernard claimed he had not had time to speak to William, early in the day before the procession, because he had to get the music-books to St Thomas's. But the Steward remarked later that he had seen to flitting the music.'

'He has just confirmed that he did so,' said Maistre Pierre. 'I asked him, over in the Laigh Hall.'

'I think they did speak. William showed you whatever it was in the package I had just delivered to him, didn't he?'

Father Bernard stared at Gil, dark eyes impassive. After a moment, Gil went on, 'Just before the end of the play, Father Bernard said he returned to the Dominicans' house.'

'My colleague will swear to it,' the chaplain said, breaking his silence. 'We discussed the subject of my lecture.'

'I have no doubt of that,' said Gil. 'Then he returned to the college. By the time he did so, William was hidden in the limehouse. The scholars who hid him noticed their chaplain crossing the Inner Close behind them towards the Theology Schule, where his students were waiting for him. Something caused him to leave the lecture-room again, almost immediately –'

'I told you, I was taken ill –'

'It was the package, wasn't it?' said Montgomery harshly. 'What was in it, Bernard?'

'I saw no package!'

'The boy showed you a piece of paper,' said Gil. 'I witnessed that.'

'Only your word for it, Cunningham!' said Father Bernard, showing the yellow teeth.

'True,' agreed Gil, 'but why should I invent such a thing?'

'He has mentioned it to me more than once,' said Maistre Pierre, 'from the beginning of the investigation.'

'We have witnesses who confirm these movements. They saw Father Bernard,' Gil continued, nodding his thanks for

281

this comment, 'crossing the Inner Close after the end of the play, before the two o'clock bell rang. However we have two further witnesses who saw him in the Outer Close, just after the two o'clock bell, when he led me to believe he was giving a lecture. A lecture which did not in fact take place.'

'Who –' began Father Bernard, and closed his mouth.

'You may not realize,' Gil said to Hugh Montgomery, who was staring intently at him, 'that the door to the Theology Schule is in the Inner Close. Nobody lecturing there would need to be in the Outer Close.'

'Aye,' said Montgomery, and nodded. 'But William's chamber was in the Outer Close. I mind I asked him how come he was out here with the great ones and he tellt me he was valued in this place.' Robert muttered something, and he turned his head to look. 'What was that?'

'Kind of thing he would say,' repeated Robert with reluctance.

'William's chamber was in the Outer Close,' agreed Gil. 'Do you have your college key on you?' he asked the chaplain, holding his hand out. Father Bernard stared at him, then slowly drew the cord over his head and dragged the key out from the breast of his habit. Gil turned it over. 'When you showed me this yesterday there was a patch of rust on it, which is gone now.'

'Anyone may clean a key,' said Maister Crawford, suddenly remembering his role.

'Not many does,' said Montgomery. 'What's this to say, Cunningham?'

'The dog,' said Gil. 'Someone struck the dog over the head.'

'It was a patch of rust,' said Father Bernard rather shrilly. 'You're reading too much –'

'I've cleaned too many hunting knives,' said Gil. 'That was blood on the key. The dog went for you, as he would have gone for you again next time he saw you. You struck him down.'

'An ill-schooled puppy –'

282

'He is a remarkably intelligent and well-taught animal,' said Maistre Pierre.

Gil put the key into Montgomery's waiting grasp and said, 'What were you searching for? You took all the paper in William's chamber, and left the money and jewels. You were searching for something in writing. The piece of paper William showed you in the morning?'

'I admit nothing,' said Father Bernard steadfastly.

'And during your first absence from the Theology Schule?'

'Why should our chaplain so far forget himself as to strangle one of our scholars?' asked Maister Crawford. 'And not even one of his own students?'

'This is ridiculous,' said the Dean. 'We are going round in circles here. Gilbert, where does your argument lead?'

'It leads to the thumbscrews in my lower hall,' said Montgomery. 'And I've a couple more devices I've a notion to try.'

Father Bernard shuddered, but said nothing. Maister Crawford bobbed up from his stool again, his round legal bonnet slipping sideways.

'Has my colleague quite finished his accusation? May we discuss our chaplain's defence?'

'I do not have to defend myself –'

'There is more,' said Gil. 'The explanation Father Bernard offered when the dog would have gone for him, yesterday in Maister Mason's house, was that dogs often dislike him because of his habit.'

'You've hunted with dogs for years!' said Montgomery explosively.

'So I hear,' agreed Gil. 'Further, this man who claimed he scarcely knew William was the only person I spoke to, save his foster-mother, who knew that the boy had turned sixteen.'

'That could be chance,' said Maister Doby. 'I would say half the junior bachelors are turned sixteen by now.'

'Perhaps,' said Gil. 'But he was also heard giving something in writing to another to be destroyed, very shortly before William's lecture-notes turned up smouldering in Jaikie's brazier.'

Maister Crawford popped up again, like the figure on a toy Gil had once had.

'Dean, I must object!' he began. 'Is this the sum total of the case against our chaplain? It is a farrago of invention and nonsense. *He was heard*, indeed!'

'Gilbert,' said Maister Forsyth before the Dean could speak. 'You have given us a number of circumstantial instances which may add up to an accusation. What you have not given us is any reason why Father Bernard, who is after all *clericus*, and the chaplain or pastor of this college, should do such harm to one of his flock.'

Father Bernard's deep-set eyes turned towards him, glittering in the light.

'That's what I want to know too,' said Montgomery. 'Why, Bernard? Did you not ken he was Isobel's boy?'

'Oh, I recognized his parentage,' said Father Bernard. 'You had only to look at him. But I repeat, I did not kill William.'

'Then where were you before the two o'clock lecture? Why did you cancel it? Why did you search William's chamber?'

'I admit nothing!'

There was a movement beyond the door, a footstep and another and a rustle of taffeta.

'Perhaps I can shed some light,' said a voice.

Chapter Fourteen

Everyone turned to stare at the door, frozen in mid-argument. They could have posed, Gil thought irrelevantly, for a tableau on a cart in one of the big festival processions, though what the subject could be was past speculating. Some obscure martyrdom, perhaps.

'Forgive this intrusion, Principal, Dean, learned maisters,' said Egidia, Lady Cunningham. She made a general, formal curtsy and moved into the room, assuming the position which nobody had realized was waiting for her. 'We would have waited till you were finished, but that might be too late.'

Robert, kicked on the ankle by his uncle, dragged a stool forward and seated her. Straight-backed, her crimson taffeta skirts crackling round her, her head dressed in a complex arrangement of cap, coronet and jewelled caul, she folded her hands in her lap and smiled round the company. Gil recognized the last of her court clothes, and suddenly also recalled the gold-painted headdress on the lady on his father's tomb. Alys had entered behind his mother and was now standing at her shoulder, elegant in the gown of black Lyons silk brocade which he had seen once before, her hair hidden under the fashionable French hood. She had cast one quick, glinting look at him and another at her astonished father, and was now preoccupied with the twist of black gauze which reached to the nape of Lady Cunningham's neck. Behind them both, Catherine scowled disapprovingly at all present.

'Gelis,' stated the Dean. 'This isn't –'

'I have been listening, Patrick,' she said. 'I am here, with my daughter-in-law and her governess –'

What? thought Gil.

'– because I feel this is the moment to point out that although Bernard was deeply attached to Isobel Montgomery –'

'I knew that,' said Lord Montgomery, glaring sideways at the chaplain. 'Like the rest of us.'

'There was,' she continued, 'someone he was even more attached to.'

'Oh, aye. You knew his mother,' said Montgomery in an odd voice.

'Is this relevant?' asked Maister Crawford.

'I knew Bernard's mother,' agreed Lady Cunningham. 'She married into the family, so she was hardly impartial, but she told me often, to the point of boredom, that Bernard would do anything in the world for one person.'

'Not quite,' said Gil. 'Not quite anything.'

'He wouldny conduct Alexander's marriage to Maidie Stewart,' said Montgomery with harsh contempt. 'Gave me some nonsense about his conscience, didn't you no, Bernard? I saw what was behind it, and I got him moved before he could contaminate Isobel –'

'*No!*' said Father Bernard, almost howling. 'I knew what you thought, my lord, and I never, ever – it was the fondness of a teacher for his pupil. You know, don't you?' he appealed to his colleagues. 'How one pupil, and not necessarily the most brilliant – one particular pupil can make a life's teaching worthwhile.'

'Aye, very possibly,' grunted Montgomery, 'but what's that to stop you conducting his marriage?'

Father Bernard bent his head, and gave no answer. Gil cast a quick look round the room. Maister Forsyth, his round face very serious, his lower lip stuck out as he considered this new development. The Dean distasteful, Maister Doby perplexed and disbelieving. Maister Crawford frowning intently, David Gray blankly puzzled, Maister Kennedy critical. Patrick Coventry might have reached the answer already: he had shut his eyes and

286

seemed to be praying. The three women were staring solemnly at the chaplain, though Alys threw him a quick glance and her smile flickered. Montgomery still waited, and behind him his nephew was leaning against the wall, pale and sweating.

Gil looked at Maistre Pierre's worried frown and reached into his purse.

'He had already conducted a marriage for Alexander Montgomery,' he said. 'This is what was in the package I handed to William on Sunday morning.'

'What?'

Montgomery took two strides forward, but Gil turned and handed the ragged document to the Dean.

'Read it out, would you, Dean?' he requested.

Father Bernard had closed his eyes. Against the wall, Robert covered his face with one hand.

'It is the document of a marriage,' pronounced the Dean. 'It is dated – third of November, 14 . . . yes, 1475.' Gil, recalling Alys's fluent deciphering of the Roman numerals, smiled to himself. 'It records the marriage of Isobel Montgomery to some man whose name is now missing, and I regret to say the writing appears to be our chaplain's.'

'Missing? I thought you said –' Montgomery turned savagely on Gil.

Maistre Pierre moved forward watchfully, but Gil retreated a step and said, 'The name can be made out. Not the surname, I grant you, but we can guess that. William's draft will was made out in the name of *William Montgomery, sometime called William Irvine,* so we can assume he had just learned his father, as well as his mother, was a Montgomery. As to the given name – would you look closely at the torn portion, Dean?'

'It begins with A,' said the Dean after a moment. 'Then there is an L. There is a portion missing, but here is N-D.'

'Where was this?' asked Montgomery, facing Gil with that soft dangerous manner. 'Where had ye hidden it, Cunningham law man? Where has it been?'

'You knew of it, my lord?'

'I did not.'

'Tell us where you found it, Gilbert,' urged Maister Forsyth.

'It was in a pocket inside the dog's collar,' said Gil. 'William must have hidden it there on Sunday morning after he showed it to Father Bernard.'

Montgomery looked over his shoulder at the chaplain, then suddenly pounced on him, hauling him bodily to his feet.

'I've a good mind to slit your throat now,' he said. 'Was that it? Third of November. Not eight weeks before he wed your kinsman's daughter. Was that why you wouldny conduct his marriage? Was that why Isobel grat that entire winter?'

'My lord,' said Father Bernard, stammering slightly but with a dignity and a courage Gil would not have credited to him, 'as well slit your own throat. They were feart to tell you she went with child by him, and whose doing was that?'

They stared at one another for a long moment, until Montgomery snarled something and thrust the Dominican away from him. Father Bernard went sprawling backwards over the stool, and landed at the painted feet of Socrates and his companion Philosophia. Maister Kennedy came to help him up.

'This does not,' said Maister Crawford, valiantly harrying the pursuit, 'prove that our chaplain is guilty of the crime imputed to him by my colleague. It is all supposition and circumstance, not fit to hang a flea.'

'But why kill the boy?' asked Montgomery, his back to the chaplain. 'Why kill him, Bernard?'

'I did not kill William,' repeated Father Bernard steadfastly. Lady Cunningham looked up at Hugh Montgomery with an expression of some sympathy.

'Then who did?' demanded Montgomery. 'This Cunningham's just spent most of the day proving you did. If it wasny you, who was it, Bernard? Who are you hiding?'

Gil opened his mouth to speak, but was forestalled.

'Ask yourself, my lord,' said Maister Forsyth very

gravely, 'who else had much to lose by William's legitimation. If your brother's first marriage stood, his second
became invalid.'

Hugh Montgomery stared at him for a moment. Then,
dawning horror in his eyes, he swivelled to look at his
nephew standing against the wall.

'Robert?' he said hoarsely.

There was a pause, in which they all followed Montgomery's gaze. Then Robert nodded, gulping, and Gil
realized the boy had been weeping silently for some
time.

'I – I –' he began, and then, gaining control, 'He was
boasting of it! He was crowing at me, uncle, how he would
be my father's heir and Hughie and I and my sisters
would be bastards and my mother in mortal sin.' He
scrubbed at his eyes with his sleeve. 'It was more than
anybody could bear.'

'So when you saw the chance to kill him secretly, you
took it,' said Gil.

Robert nodded again, and suddenly stumbled forward
and dropped to his knees at Hugh Montgomery's feet.

'Will I hang for it, uncle?' he whispered.

'Will he?' said Alys.

'Probably not,' said Gil. 'I think Montgomery will win.
Besides, the boy knows his neck-verse.'

They were seated close together in the hall of the house
in Rottenrow, their elder kin about them and the wolfhound asleep on the bench beside Gil. The evening sun
was sliding in at the open windows, raising gold lights in
the tawny new-honey shades of Alys's hair and shining on
the silk braid which trimmed Egidia Muirhead's everyday
headdress of black velvet and fine black linen.

'The Dean was very angry,' said Maistre Pierre.

'Montgomery was angrier still,' Gil observed. 'All his
promises of vengeance have been set at naught.'

'It will do Hugh Montgomery great good,' pronounced

Lady Egidia in her fluent French, 'to recognize that he may be at fault in something that touches him so closely.'

'Pour us some wine, Gilbert,' commanded the Official, 'and tell us all about it. I wish to hear the whole story.'

'And I, indeed,' said the mason as Gil moved obediently to the jug and glasses set on the carved cupboard by the hearth. The dog woke and scrambled down to follow him. 'I thought we were trying to get a confession from the priest. I was as startled as Montgomery when the boy came forward.'

Gil handed his mother wine. She accepted it, then reached up and gripped his good hand tightly, smiling, but did not meet his eye.

'But what will happen to the boy?' pursued Maistre Pierre.

'His uncle will deal with him,' said Gil, handing more glasses, the dog at his knee.

'Can he do that?'

'Montgomery is justice on his own lands,' said Canon Cunningham. 'This touches him very close, as you say, Gelis – victim and evil-doer are both his kin, both recently under his tutelage. Properly it should go to be tried at Edinburgh but I have no doubt he will find a pretext for settling the matter privately in his own courts.'

'He certainly wasn't going to let anyone else settle it, least of all the University,' agreed Gil, thinking of the long and painful scene in the Principal's great chamber after Robert had confessed, 'and though I suspect the Dean was prepared to argue the point, I'd put my money on Montgomery on this one.'

'He could of course turn Robert over to the Church rather than the State,' Canon Cunningham said thoughtfully. 'The penance for what he did should be heavy enough to satisfy anyone.'

'And Father Bernard?' asked Maistre Pierre.

'No doubt the Order will pass its own sentence on him,' said Gil, sitting down again beside Alys. She tucked her free hand under his and smiled at him. The wolfhound jumped up, and settled firmly with its head on his knee.

'If that creature thinks it's a lap-dog,' Gil's mother commented, 'you'll be in trouble in two or three months.'

'When did you know it was Robert?' Alys asked. 'When were you certain?'

He looked down at her.

'When McIan was talking about his son, and I realized we had proof,' he said. 'It was obvious from early on that Father Bernard had some hand in the matter. The way he was lying made that clear. But it also seemed possible Robert was involved. He was one of the people William approached on Sunday morning. I couldn't see that he had more reason to kill his kinsman than anyone else, until we found the marriage document this morning. And then, when I stepped out from the funeral, I met McIan and his sister in the Blackfriars yard. They were talking about the baby, and Ealasaidh remarked on him throwing his food everywhere, and I remembered how some of it got on your gown.'

'The belt that smelled of cumin!' said the mason.

'Exactly. Robert was serving at the high table after William spoke to him. I saw him. His hands must have been shaking, for he nearly spilled the spiced pork on Maister Forsyth, and some of it must have got on his skin or his cuffs, then or later.'

'And then he heard that his enemy was shut helpless in the limehouse,' said Maistre Pierre.

'He did insist to his uncle that he went down to bargain with the other boy,' said Lady Egidia, 'and only thought of killing him when he saw he was still dazed.'

'That makes a difference,' said the Official. 'Though perhaps only in canon law.'

'So Father Bernard,' said Alys slowly, 'must have looked out of the lecture-hall and seen Robert coming from the limehouse. But why should he think anything was wrong?'

'Something about Robert's bearing may have alerted him. After all, he knew William was shut in there.'

'Ah!' said the mason. 'He had overheard those who put him there.'

'Exactly. So he left the lecture-room, as if heading for the kitchen-yard and the privy, and went into the limehouse, and found William newly dead. He must have taken time to check the purse, missed the papers it held under the coin or simply found the document he had already seen was not in it, and threw it behind the lime-sacks. Then he dragged the body into the coalhouse and locked the door, using his own key, to gain a little time. He went back and cancelled his lecture, and then went to search William's chamber.'

'Looking for the document?' suggested Lady Cunningham. 'But Gil, I thought Alys said all the papers had been removed from William's chamber. Surely Father Bernard would know his own writing? Why take all the papers away?'

'I know!' said Alys. 'He was pressed for time. Someone else might come at any moment. So he gathered up all the papers to go through them at leisure.'

'Exactly,' said Gil, smiling at her. 'Then he gave them to Robert to put back, as your father overheard, and instead of doing so Robert put them in Jaikie's brazier. I think from Father Bernard's demeanour today that Robert may have made confession to him. He was determined to keep the boy's actions secret.'

'Did the priest then search the other two chambers?' asked Maistre Pierre.

'I think not. Those were turned over by two different hands. It was likely Robert who went through Michael Douglas's things, and his friends', and I would say Nick's chamber was searched by Montgomery's men, looking either for William's notebook or for the coded letter, which Robert had discarded with the purse when he removed William's belt to – to make use of it. Montgomery plays his cards close – he's known more than he let on, right from the start.'

'Though not who killed William,' said the mason.

'I have never seen Hugh Montgomery so chastened,' said Lady Cunningham.

'And then what?' said Alys. 'Was it Montgomery who

attacked you? Why did Father Bernard go on lying? What did the porter's death have to do with it?'

'Jaikie's death was a crossed scent,' Gil admitted. 'I think it was the result of a quarrel between Jaikie and Doig, who were both involved in the information-gathering. Montgomery said he had heard an argument when he came to the college at noon.'

'But he saw nobody,' objected Maistre Pierre.

'Montgomery was talking to Jaikie, not searching the place, and the room is poorly lit. I surmise that Doig had hidden under the bed. He would fit in there quite well.'

'The marks in the dust!'

'Precisely. And the dog-kennel smell that Michael noticed. Then when both Montgomery men had left, Doig emerged and killed Jaikie. Possibly the fellow had threatened him in some way. We may never know – Doig has run and the University has no serjeant or armed men to send to bring him back.'

'No doubt they will make a note at the next meeting,' said Maistre Pierre, 'that if he comes back he is to be charged with the porter's death.'

'He will probably turn up on one of Montgomery's holdings,' said Lady Cunningham.

'And Montgomery and his nephew, though they didn't lie outright, were each stretching the truth for fear the other had knifed the porter, which led me to assume that neither had done so.'

'That will also stand in Robert's favour,' said the Official.

'And Father Bernard was protecting his favourite pupil's son?' prompted the mason.

'One of his sons. I wonder which way he would have jumped if William had survived, with his threats?' Gil cast his mind back over the several interviews he had had with the chaplain. 'He was protecting the other boy, but he was also trying to cover his own back. The Church will not be pleased to learn of Alexander's marriage to his cousin. How close were they, mother?'

'First cousins, if I recall. Much too close to marry without dispensation. And Robert's mother, poor woman, is a

Stewart, no closer than fourth cousin, and brought the family some useful land in – in –'

'The Lennox,' supplied the Official.

'The one I feel sorry for,' said the mason heavily, 'is that wretched creature Ralph.'

'Patey Coventry was to break it to him,' said Gil. 'And I think Nick was going to organize an unofficial game of football, since the quodlibet disputation had to be cancelled.'

'What is a quodlibet disputation anyway?' asked Alys.

'It starts with a serious question – I think Patey was to propound it, and Father Bernard was to answer – but after that has been dealt with the scholars are allowed to ask more frivolous questions of the regents, provided they aren't obscene or defamatory. It's always unexpected and sometimes it's good entertainment.'

'I recall one,' said Canon Cunningham, straight-faced, 'in which John Ireland – yes, I am sure it was John Ireland – was asked what he would do if he found himself standing on the moon. Mind you,' he added, 'he spoke for near half an hour by way of answer, and I think he brought in the duties of sovereignty and the Doctrine of Atonement. The bachelor who asked it regretted it. But it seems, Gilbert, as if the young man's death was a family matter rather than being related to his spying and extortion.'

'The spying was not connected,' Gil agreed. 'So I kept it out of the argument so far as I could. No sense in angering the Montgomery more than was necessary. As for the extortion – well, if William had been a different person, he would have responded differently to the news of his legitimacy, and Robert might not have felt the need to act to protect his mother and siblings.'

'Montgomery as good as admitted he had attacked you,' recalled the mason, 'while you were losing to him at cards.'

'Losing? Gilbert!' said his mother, in some amusement.

'It was deliberate,' he said. 'We were exchanging information, a question for every trick, and I don't think he realized how much his questions gave away.'

'You never asked him your last two questions,' said Maistre Pierre.

'I did,' said Gil, 'this afternoon, while Robert was packing his goods.'

He hauled the wolfhound further on to his knee, and it turned to lick his hand. He scratched the corner of its jaw, recalling the awkward conversation. Strangely diminished, the angry fire in his eyes banked down to a dark glow, Montgomery had stared hard at Gil, then had suddenly come out with, 'I canny thank ye for this day's work, Cunningham.'

'I'd not expect it,' Gil had answered him. 'I'm aware I've done you no favour, my lord.'

'Did ye ken, yesternight? When we played at the cards? Was this where all your questions were leading?'

'No at the time,' said Gil. 'I only pieced it together this morning.'

Montgomery grunted, ignoring the Dean, who was attempting to catch his eye.

'I owe ye yir two last questions,' he said at length. 'I pay my gaming debts. Is there still aught to ask?'

'Do you pay your legal debts?' Gil asked hardily. 'Do I get a fee for this?' Montgomery's right arm moved involuntarily, and Gil prepared to dodge a blow. 'And what of the pup? What will happen to him?'

'The pup?' The other man grinned mirthlessly. 'You can take the brute for your fee, then, Cunningham, and I wish you joy of it.'

'Will you say that again before witnesses, my lord?' asked Gil formally. Montgomery nodded impatiently, and gave Gil another diminished stare.

'I'll tell ye something else,' he said abruptly. 'For another fee, if ye like. I saw your father fall, on Sauchie Muir in '88.'

'My lord?' Gil had said, shocked.

'I didny strike him down,' Montgomery continued, 'never fear, but you may be proud of him. He dee'd well. You minded me of him this afternoon.'

295

'Thank you, sir,' Gil had answered, swallowing hard. 'Thank you indeed.'

'No trouble,' said Montgomery ironically, and swung away across the room as his nephew, escorted by Maister Forsyth and Maister Coventry, returned with his bulging scrip and an armful of books. 'Aye, Robert, bring your books. You'll have plenty leisure for them.'

Behind Montgomery, Lady Cunningham had risen in her crackling silk to come forward, seizing Gil's elbow as she passed.

'Your uncle has the right of it,' she said quietly. 'That lassie thinks just as she ought. There are great advantages for you in this marriage, Gil, I see that now.' Before he could speak she had let go of him and moved on to corner the Dean, saying, 'Patrick, I want to talk to you.'

'And I had a long word with Patrick Elphinstone,' she said now, with the expression of a cat over a dish of cream. 'He'll mention your name when he reports to the Archbishop, Gil. He feels you dealt with the whole affair very discreetly and quickly, and I hope he'll make sure Robert Blacader shows his gratitude properly.'

Did Patrick Elphinstone know he felt that before she had a word with him? Gil wondered, and smiled across his uncle's hall at her, in affectionate admiration. The Dean had flinched from her a little as she crossed the room, in just the way his father used to. I'll pass on to her that encomium on my father, he thought, but not here, not now.

Instead he said, 'Montgomery has given me the dog. A valuable fee.'

'You must name him then,' said his mother, 'if only so you can order him off the furniture.'

'What will you call a wolfhound?' asked his uncle. 'Birsie? Bawtie? Lyart, like the one your father kept?'

'There was only one Lyart,' said Gil firmly. 'William called him Mauger . . .' The dog looked up at this, and his stringy tail twitched. 'But I don't like that so much. No, I know exactly what to call him, with his long nose and his solemn face.'

'I know too,' said Alys, laughing.'Socrates!'

'You saw the likeness too?' he said, turning his head to look at her.

'Yes – the figure on the hangings behind Father Bernard. And William gave him a scroll to carry, as well! Though I don't think William would have been convincing as Philosophy,' she added.

'No, the metaphor doesn't stretch that far,' agreed Gil.

'Oh – metaphor!' said the mason. 'So the dog is yours, and his name is Socrates. Well, I have heard worse things to shout across the Dow Hill. And now tell me, *madame*. How did you and my daughter and her governess manage to arrive, like the Muses or the Sibyls or three goddesses in a cart of clouds, at precisely the moment it needed to break the *impasse*? I truly think, if you had not appeared, we could have been there yet with the priest denying everything and telling nothing.'

Lady Cunningham exchanged a look with Alys across the room. They smiled.

'I must say,' Gil agreed, 'Pierre is right, mother. I was beginning to doubt whether either Father Bernard or the boy would ever break.'

'I was surprised to recognize the laddie himself admitting us,' she said. 'I thought you would have kept him under your eye.'

'His uncle wanted him present,' said Gil, 'so I had no need to insist. Your timing was superb, and your contribution was wonderfully apt. Had you been waiting in the outer room all that time?'

'Lord Montgomery knew we were there,' said Alys. 'I could see him wondering what our business might be.'

'It was obvious that we could assist, so we assisted,' said Lady Cunningham simply.

'Speaking of Robert our Archbishop,' said Canon Cunningham, drawing a paper from the breast of his long gown, 'as you were this moment, Gelis, I had a letter from him this morning in the bag that came to St Mungo's.' He unfolded it, and settled his spectacles further up the bridge of his nose. 'A scrape in his own hand, what's more, none of your secretary copies. He sends that he's minded to do something for you, Gilbert, after the other matter you sorted out, about the bairn's mother, and that he has two suitable posts in mind, each with a living attached, and he'll tell us more when he knows which is free.'

'Let us hope his gratitude is cumulative,' said Maistre Pierre.

'It sounds promising,' said Gil. He looked down along his shoulder at Alys, and she smiled quickly at him, then looked away in sudden shyness. 'We won't starve, then.'

'Well, if all else fails,' said the mason, 'you may set up a pavilion in my courtyard, and Alys may continue to oversee the household. Then I can send you the broken meats from the dinners Alys cooks for me.'

'That might not be such a bad idea,' Gil said, struck by it. 'Perhaps not a pavilion, in a Glasgow winter, but we could live somewhere about the place, if you had space for us.'

'You'd be in the midst of the burgh,' said Alys, 'and you could hang out your sign as a notary and get the passing trade.'

They looked at each other. There was what seemed to Gil a long pause, as if time was standing still; then Canon Cunningham said in resigned tones, 'We'll have little sense out of either of them the rest of the evening. Take that dog into the garden, Gilbert,' he ordered, raising his voice slightly, 'and we'll get a look at the last few points of that contract while you're gone. If we can all agree on the wording, it should be ready for signing by the time you can hold a pen.'

The garden was warm in the evening light, full of scents of green stuff and damp soil. A blackbird was singing from the top of the roof, and the occasional sweet, heady waft from the bean patch further down the slope reached them as they walked slowly along the gravel path, Socrates ranging round them.

'I want to invite Dorothea,' said Gil, and paused at the gap in the hedge to look out over the burgh. Another blackbird shot across the view, calling in alarm, and the dog turned his head to watch it, ears pricked.

'To the marriage, you mean?' He nodded. 'That's your sister who is a nun,' she recalled.

'That's the one. And my other sisters as well, I suppose,' he added.

'We have no kin in Scotland,' she observed, 'but we have friends in plenty in the burgh. It may be a very great feast.'

'Soon?' Gil said hopefully. He drew her to a stone bench by the hedge, and Socrates came and sat at her feet.

'Soon,' she said. 'As soon as we can arrange all.'

'And as soon as we're certain we have enough to live on,' he said ruefully. He took her in his arms. 'But Alys, what did you say to my mother, to make her change her mind?'

She turned within his clasp to look at him.

'I don't know,' she admitted. 'I wanted to speak to her. I thought I would assure her of my duty too, just as you said.' He nodded. 'So I dressed in my best, and took Catherine, and we had the horses brought and rode up here.'

'That took courage,' he said.

'No, no, for she was perfectly civil to me yesterday, Gil. And so she was today. Maggie served wine and cakes, and I said what I had come for, and then I said I hoped Our Lady would send that we would give her grandchildren, and that we would both wish her to have an eye to their upbringing.' Gil tightened his arms about her, and she looked down, then shyly up at him again. He bent his head to kiss her. After a while she went on.

'Catherine talked genealogy with her for a long time. Perhaps it was that,' she added thoughtfully. 'I think they found a connection somewhere, though it involved three marriages.'

'What, between your family and mine?' he said,

alarmed. The wolfhound looked at him anxiously, then put his nose down on his paws again.

'Between Catherine's and your mother's,' she reassured him, her elusive smile flickering. 'Don't worry, we won't need a dispensation.'

'Praise Heaven for that!'

'Amen, indeed. And then your mother asked me about this matter – William's death, and the messages, and the spying. I told her what we knew, and she saw that what she knew about Father Bernard could be of use to you. So she also put on her best gown, and we went down to the college. But that was all we discussed. I don't know what made her change her mind.'

'*Garneist with governance so gude Nae deeming suld her deir.* She had brought that court dress with her?' said Gil. Alys nodded. 'She keeps it for great occasions. I wonder if she came prepared to be talked round?'

'She certainly seems to favour the marriage now.' She giggled. 'And I haven't heard my father making flowery compliments like that since we left Paris.'

Gil grinned. He had not yet had time for a private conversation with either Maistre Pierre or his mother. By the time he had extracted himself from the University she and Alys had already returned to Rottenrow, and when he and the mason arrived at the house in mid-afternoon she had come down in her everyday clothes to greet them, closely followed by his uncle. The compliments Alys referred to had gone in all directions, even Canon Cunningham making stately puns which not everyone noticed.

'So we can be married soon,' he said again.

They sat close in silence for a while. Gil found his mind ranging back over the day again, and further back, to the feast and all its consequences. Some of those young men at the University would be worth keeping an eye on. Ninian Boyd was probably destined to be a small laird and a good master, but the Douglas boy was promising, and Lowrie Livingstone was a very interesting character. Was I like that at seventeen? he wondered. Did our teachers look at

Nick and me with that resigned expression? He thought of the Dean, glowering at Alys across the room, and then of Maister Forsyth, who had intercepted him just before he left the college.

'That was a very impressive discourse just now,' the old man had said, in the same tone in which he had commended Gil's last disputation outside the crumbling chapel of St Thomas. 'You made all clear to us, grounded it in the truth and showed us the inevitable conclusions without fear of an armed adversary. The outcome is grievous for all of us,' he admitted, 'but Justice is a harsh mistress, and you have served her well.' He smiled at Gil's stammering response. 'It's a great pleasure to a teacher, Gilbert, when a student continues so far beyond what one has taught him. And that is your bride,' he continued, without waiting for a reply.

Gil nodded, bracing himself for a gentler response to the old man's adverse comments than the remote politeness he had used on Sunday against the Dean.

'A very good choice,' said Maister Forsyth, nodding. 'Clever, discreet and modest. A very good choice for you, Gilbert, and I wish you happy with her.'

'Thank you, sir,' Gil had said ineptly, and bowed. His former teacher had acknowledged the bow and moved off, leaving Gil staring after him.

The clever, discreet and modest girl in his arms, her thoughts clearly mirroring his, turned to look up at him, putting up one hand to cup his jaw, brown eyes glowing in the last of the sunlight, and said, 'You know, Gil, that was quite magnificent. In the Principal's lodging, I mean,' she expanded. 'All those learned old men, and you telling them what happened and making all clear to them. And Lord Montgomery was so threatening, and you never flinched from him. I'm glad I was present.'

He turned his head to kiss her palm.

'I'm glad you were present too,' he admitted, 'for I'd never have got so far without you. You deserved to be there.'

'We make a good team, I think,' she said diffidently.

301

'None better.' He kissed her palm again, then ran one finger lightly round the scooped neckline of her gown, over the fine linen of her shift, and she shivered. At their feet, the wolfhound turned his head to look at them, then ostentatiously rose and lay down again with his back to them, sighed, and laid his nose on his paws. In a small corner of his mind Gil was aware of his dog's actions, commended the animal's patience and admired his discretion.

'Sweet St Giles, Alys, I must be the luckiest man in Scotland.' She made a small enquiring noise. *'An hendy hap ich hab yhent,'* he quoted, as he had done to his mother, and continued the verse, *'From alle wommen my love is lent, And light on Alisoun.'*

'And mine on you,' she said. He drew her closer, very conscious of the warmth of her flesh and the movement of her ribcage under the blue gown, and bent his head to kiss her. She put her arms round him, a little shyly, reaching under his jerkin, and leaned into his embrace.

On the ridge tiles the blackbird sang on, the golden notes dropping through the still air as the shadows lengthened in the garden and the first lights pricked in the houses round them.

Socrates sighed again, rolled on to his side and shut his eyes.